Chinese Literature

中国文学

English-Chinese Bilingual Edition 中英双语版

2012 Volume 1 第一辑

作家出版社
THE WRITERS PUBLISHING HOUSE
新世界出版社
NEW WORLD PRESS

图书在版编目（CIP）数据

中国文学：中英双语版. 2012 年. 第 1 辑：汉英对照/《中国文学》编委会编. －北京：作家出版社，2012.3

ISBN 978－7－5063－6342－6

Ⅰ.①中… Ⅱ.①中… Ⅲ.①中篇小说－小说集－中国－当代－汉、英②短篇小说－小说集－中国－当代－汉、英 Ⅳ.①I247.7

中国版本图书馆 CIP 数据核字（2012）第 046984 号

中国文学：中英双语版. 2012 年. 第一辑

编　　者：《中国文学》编委会
责任编辑： 赵　莹
英文审定： May F.Yee　　Krisantha Sri Bhaggiyadatta
装帧设计： 大象设计
出版发行： 作家出版社
社址： 北京农展馆南里 10 号　　　　**邮编：** 100125
电话传真： 86－10－65930756（出版发行部）
86－10－65004079（总编室）
86－10－65015116（邮购部）
E－mail：zuojia@ zuojia. net. cn
http://www. haozuojia. com（作家在线）
印刷： 三河市紫恒印装有限公司
成品尺寸： 170×240
字数： 300 千
印张： 19.5　　　　**插页：** 7
版次： 2012 年 3 月第 1 版
印次： 2012 年 3 月第 1 次印刷
ISBN 978－7－5063－6342－6
定价： 35.00 元

Letter of Congratulations

I am happy to learn that a strategic cooperation framework agreement has been signed between China International Publishing Group and China Writers Publishing Group. I would like to extend my warm congratulations on this cooperation!

As a large group specialized in literary works, China Writers Publishing Group is a book and periodical publishing brand name renowned in China's literary circles for pooling substantial resources from eminent writers and publishing a large number of excellent Chinese literary works. As China's oldest and largest organization specializing in international publicity and communication, China International Publishing Group has rich experience in this regard, has established a sophisticated network of overseas marketing channels and has a solid contingent of outstanding translators in various languages. The high-level and wide-ranging strategic cooperation between the two groups, backed by their respective advantages, will be of great significance for the introduction of top–notch Chinese cultural works to the rest of the world and China's extensive participation in world cultural dialogues.

The introduction of China's best literary works to the rest of the world plays an irreplaceable role in facilitating the communication between people of different countries, promoting mutual understanding and friendship, and building a cultural homeland to be shared by all mankind. It is hoped that in carrying out the spirit of the 6th Plenary Session of the 17th National Congress of the Communist Party of China, and in line with the requirements of the Outline for the 12th Five–Year Program (2011–2015) for Cultural Reform and Development, you will go on to publish and distribute worldwide still more excellent literary works representative of Chinese characteristics, styles and charm. Your mission is to disseminate Chinese culture in an innovative manner, with determination to make progress and through close cooperation, so that you can make new and still greater contributions to inheriting Chinese culture, carrying forward the spirit of our time, making Chinese culture better understood and recognized worldwide, and promoting the great development and prosperity of socialist culture.

Member of the Political Bureau of the CPC Central Committee

Member of the State Council

March 22, 2012

中共中央政治局委员、国务委员刘延东

贺　信

欣悉中国外文局（中国国际出版集团）与中国作家出版集团签署战略合作框架协议，谨致热烈祝贺！

中国作家出版集团作为我国大型专业性文学出版集团，汇聚了大量高水平作家资源，推出了众多中国优秀文学作品，形成了享誉中国文坛的书刊出版品牌；中国外文局作为我国历史最悠久、规模最大的专业对外传播机构，拥有丰富的对外传播经验、成熟的海外营销渠道和多语种高端翻译人才队伍。两家机构依托各自优势，开展多层次、宽领域的战略合作，对促进中国优秀文化精品对外传播、广泛参与世界文明对话具有重要意义。

文学作品的对外传播，在沟通各国人民情感、增进相互了解与友谊、建设人类共有的精神家园中发挥着不可替代的作用。希望你们深入贯彻落实党的十七届六中全会精神，按照国家“十二五”文化改革发展规划纲要要求，以推动中华文化走向世界为己任，开拓创新，锐意进取，密切合作，对外出版发行更多代表中国特色、中国风格、中国气派的优秀作品，传承中华文化、弘扬时代精神，为增强中华文化在世界上的感召力和影响力、推动社会主义文化大发展大繁荣做出新的更大贡献！

刘延东

二〇一二年三月廿二日

CONTENTS

目 录

Preface

Walking Tall with Hearts Open to the World

China's ancient civilization of over five thousand years, alongside today's advances, gives the finest affirmation for Chinese people to be able to walk tall with hearts open to the world. Yet for almost the entire last century, the Chinese people had seldom been able to show their true face to the world—which in a certain sense was unjust and not in keeping with the common values shared by all human beings. This omission becomes even more poignant in considering how this remarkable and marvelous culture, belonging to both the Chinese nation and to all of humanity, should have been shared by all the world's peoples. Perhaps due to ideological differences, or perchance even to technical challenges in translating Chinese characters, this failure to attain its place among the exquisite and living literatures of other nations is indeed regrettable.

The english–chinese bilingual edition of *Chinese Literature* has been launched with the mission to bridge this chasm. We will do our best in endeavoring to enable people across the world to glean a fuller picture of today's China and her people by fostering understanding through present-day Chinese literature. Alongside, *Chinese Literature*, the Chinese people can thus walk tall with hearts open to the world, enabling exchange of ideas with other peoples living on this planet, suffusing warmth to shared spiritual and emotional worlds. This is the dream of founders of *Chinese Literature* which we hope will be realized one day soon.

Vice-president of the China Writers Association

Director on the Management Board of China Writers Publishing Group

序

在世界自由地阔步行走

中国是个古老的国度，五千多年的文明史和已经崛起的今天，证明我们是可以在世界上任何一个角落自由地阔步行走的。然而，近一个多世纪里，中国人很少以真实的形象在世人面前出现，这有些不太公平和不太符合人类共同的价值理念。特别是中国的文化，辉煌而灿烂，它既是中华民族的，同时又是全人类的，世界上每个民族都可以享受它；但也许是因为传统意识形态的不同，或者更多的是汉文字翻译的技术问题，使中国的文化尤其是同世界其他国家一样美妙和生动的文学不能被介绍到中国以外的地方，这是一件很遗憾的事。

中英双语版的《中国文学》今天问世了，它所要做的事就是期望弥补这样一个遗憾。因此我们倾力想把这件事做好，为的是让世界各国的朋友们能够通过了解当代的中国文学，更亲近和真实地认识今天的中国和中国人。同样，它还可以让中国人伴随着这本《中国文学》更阔步地在世界上自由地行走，同所有生活在这个星球上的人们交流，温暖共同的精神与心灵世界。这是创办这本《中国文学》者的一点愿望，但愿这份愿望获得成功！

何建明

中国作家协会副主席

中国作家出版集团管委会主任

TIE Ning, born in 1957 in Beijing, is president of the China Writers Association. She has published such major works as her novels *Rose Door*, *The Bathing Women*, and *Ben Hua*, plus more than one hundred novellas and short stories including *Ah, Xiangxue*, *How Long is Forever*, alongside other works of prose and delightful sketches, publishing over four million Chinese characters in total. She has won six state-level literary prizes including the Lu Xun Literary Prize. The movie adaptation *Ah, Xiangxue*, for which she wrote the screenplay, won a major 41st Berlin International Film Festival award, a Gold Rooster Award. Some of her works have been translated into foreign languages.

铁凝，1957年生于北京，作家。现为中国作家协会主席。主要著作有长篇小说《玫瑰门》《大浴女》《笨花》等4部，中、短篇小说《哦，香雪》《永远有多远》等100余篇、部，以及散文、随笔等共400余万字。作品曾6次获“鲁迅文学奖”等国家级文学奖；其编剧的电影《哦，香雪》获第41届柏林国际电影节大奖。部分作品亦有外文译本。

Runaway

TIE Ning

Over twenty years ago Mr. Song arrived from a mountainous corner of northern China into this city, and into this opera troupe.

At that time, urban residents had begun to store Chinese cabbages for the purpose of their daily needs, but also in response to the government's call. People therefore also called the trade in Chinese cabbage as buying "patriotic vegetables." When Chinese cabbage was launched on the market in the winter, all households bought enough to feed themselves until the early spring of the new year. This relation ship between the vegetable market and residents at that time could be seen through scenes of vegetable growers distributing these "patriotic vegetable" in vehicles of all sizes to every household.

One day at dusk, a relative took Mr. Song to meet the head of the troupe. A cart with rubber tires had stopped at the door, as the head of the troupe was unloading Chinese cabbages, which were weighed and stacked against a wall up to waist height, weighing at least three to four hundred kilos in total.

After the head of the troupe had paid the vegetable farmer and asked him to leave, the relative said to Mr. Song, "This is head of the troupe," and then to the head, "This is Mr. Song." The head of the troupe responded absentmindedly while devoting his attention to taking care of his "patriotic cabbages," pondering over how to move them upstairs as quickly as possible.

Mr. Song quickly figured out what the head of the troupe had to do, and asked, "Which floor"?

"The fourth," replied the relative.

"Let me do it," said Mr. Song in the dialect of many people of the mountain–ous areas of northern China. With these words, Mr. Song clutched four Chinese cabbages under his two arms and climbed up the stairs. The relative and the head of the troupe were chatting in front of the stairs, oblivious to Mr. Song moving the cabbages, and thus were surprised to find he had already moved all the cabbages by the time they took notice of Mr. Song once again. It was at that moment that the head of the troupe invited the relative and Mr. Song to come upstairs and sit down. After reaching the fourth floor, the relative and the head of the troupe noted that the Chinese cabbages were stacked at the right place as required by the troupe head—at the side of the stairs and on either side of the door.

The head of the troupe led the relative upstairs and entered through the door, against one side of which were the Chinese cabbages, and ushered Mr. Song into the drawing room and turned on the light. The relative sat down, but Mr. Song re–mained standing. At this moment, the head of the troupe looked Mr. Song up and down. Mr. Song looked fifty years old or thereabouts, and displayed an honest and tolerant demeanor characterized by a tall body, wide mouth, big face, ample forehead and a round lower jaw. He did not stand shivering and cowering like some mountain villagers, but his body leaned slightly forward with hands hanging down, rather like an old grocery's shop assistant who seemed always at the ready to lean against the counter to serve customers humbly and warmly. The head of the troupe thought, " Mr. Song seems genuine, an agreeable, quick and efficient worker." This was how Mr. Song was introduced by that relative to work at the opera troupe as a watchman for the front office.

Later, the head of the troupe began telling the relative a story about him being invited to perform in Italy. The opera troupe frequently sent performers to foreign countries, usually as extras to present acrobatic martial arts, instead of any leading roles. The performers in the opera troupe were proud of their martial arts, and were good at fighting while performing somersaults. So, the troupe head had been invited to Italy mainly for the purpose of turning somersaults. Mr. Song, who had kept silent for a long time, suddenly interrupted when Italy was mentioned: "Italy is in Southern Europe. It looks like a boot on the map, a high–hee boot." He mispronounced "high–heeled" due to his accent. The head of the troupe laughed, not laughing at Mr. Song's accent, but in surprise over Mr. Song's cleverness and cultural knowledge. It was doubtful among the troupe if the head, or even the most cultured playwright, would have known about Italy resembling a high–heeled boot. The head's laughter increased the confidence of both the relative and Mr. Song. The relative exaggerated the advantages and merits of Mr. Song, such as his simple family background, his late wife, married daughter, total devotion to his work, etcetera, as a result of which, Mr. Song's job was assured, and he became a long–term casual worker in the front office.

It was at the stated–owned Lingqiang Opera Troupe that Mr. Song worked as the watchman. The Lingqiang Opera might not measure up to Peking Opera, Ping Opera, Hebei Opera or Henan Opera in northern China, but it was still typical of the local region spanning half a province. Among the older generation of performers, its famous actors included Liusuihong, Basuihong and Jiusuihong, and such actresses as Da Luju (Green Chrysanthemum), Bai Moli (White Jasmine) and Wan Xiangyu (Tuberose). The Lingqiang Opera Troupe had been transferred to perform in Beijing over the past decade, with the "Plum Blossom Award" almost in the grasp of several young performers in the troupe. In addition, the Lingqiang Opera Troupe several times also competed for status as a provincial opera, winning glory for the genre of Lingqiang Opera despite its lack of success. The Lingqiang Opera Troupe survived amidst the twists and turns against a backdrop of a sluggish down–turn in the theater arts. Of course, four hundred open–air plays and performances each year constituted the main means for the survival of the troupe.

What Mr. Song did at the opera troupe was, conveying messages, mail pickup and delivery, and looking after one boiler for drinking water. Chinese people have a special preference for boiled water, which is considered particularly important for artists. Performers invariably pour boiled water into their bottles of tea leaves before they enter a rehearsal venue, and then keep drinking the tea, refilling it all day. In addition to the performers, their families also want to get their boiled water at fixed times and places, entering Mr. Song's boiler room in succession hauling thermos flasks or pails. Access to boiled water is a practical and unspoken benefit for an opera troupe and even to all people in a Chinese work unit: boiled water, get it for free! Mr. Song knew this full well, so he attached great importance to people's expectations of boiled water. He boiled water at fixed times, in the morning, after noon and evening, and at fixed locations each day, at the absolutely proper and exact temperature. When ready, Mr. Song would shout several times in the court–yard: "The water's boiling!" The courtyard where Mr. Song would stand was a central area surrounded by the office building, dormitory building and rehearsal venue in three different directions. Mr. Song's shouts alerted people to their need for boiled water, even if their thermoses may already be full. They were lured by Mr.

Song's shouts to get more boiled water, perhaps to wash clean a dirty drain or some greasy stains. More importantly, Mr. Song shouted out a designation, which seemed to stir their enthusiasm for boiled water. Mr. Song thought hard for the right designation at the very beginning: What should I call them? How about "Troupe head, your water's boiling"?—but Mr. Song could not just call out to the family of the troupe head because he could not violate his duty to serve not only leaders. Or shouting "Performers, your water's boiling," but there were other employees who were not performers. "Comrades, your water's boiling"—that could improperly imply that Mr. Song was giving orders like a leader. Or without any form of address, just saying, "Water's boiling, water's boiling," would be impolite to everyone. Worried, Mr. Song pondered over these designations for a long time, and finally he came up with the title: "Teacher." Those who Mr. Song respected the most were teachers. Mr. Song had got his limited knowledge of geography from a teacher when he was a junior high student in the village. At that time, what he had liked most was geography class, but he dropped out of school in his second year due to his family's poor finances. Now, Mr. Song decided to refer to all the family members of cadre, plus performers and employees of the opera troupe as "Teachers." Nobody would feel antipathy to the designation "Teacher." Performers and family members of leaders and employees would be satisfied with the title, which implied no adulation or differential treatment. Therefore, Mr. Song began to shout from the center of the courtyard: "Teachers, the water is boiling."

After a while, the leaders of the opera troupe decided Mr. Song's usual holler would be the best way to convene all the members of the troupe for work. For example, in situations such as a meeting, before loading a truck prior to departure for a performance, or for distributing rice for festivals or before a senior artist's funeral ceremony, Mr. Song would always shout loudly in the courtyard: "Teachers, it's time for the meeting!" "Teachers, it's time to load the truck!" "Teachers, it's time for rice distribution!" or "Teachers, it's time to say farewell to Teacher Jiusuihong!" That time, an offspring of Jiusuihong grew uncomfortable with Mr. Song's wail, and thought she should go to see the leaders and complain about it. Mr. Xia, an actor who played youthful roles, replied: "Thanks to Mr. Song's shouting, today's funeral was so successful. But if you got the leader to make the announcement, most people might not attend the ceremony. Which result do you prefer?"

However, this is not at all to say Mr. Song was a noisemaker, since he was usually quiet most of the time. His words thus seemed very precious, in a way different from the constant diligence of his two legs. Mr. Song distributed newspapers, magazines, correspondence and mail to all the offices and rehearsal venues on time every day. He walked gently and silently to distribute the newspapers and magazines to the people whom they were addressed to, with no mistakes. He even personally delivered those newspapers and magazines with peculiar names, and glossy pictures and words, subscribed to by the second and even third generations of family members, all without any complaint, only saying the two words: "For you." Mr. Song also did many other things in addition to his duties. Who would not ask Mr. Song for help while moving Chinese cabbages? No one. Later, even after the era of Chinese cabbage storage had ended, family members of the opera troupe would still ask Mr. Song for favors. People living on the fifth floor would say, "Mr. Song, would you please help me carry this gas cylinder upstairs," while people living on the third floor would ask, "Mr. Song, I've bought a new sofa, would you please give me a hand?"

People living on the first floor hardly asked Mr. Song to lend a hand to carry things, but there were these several women who liked knitting sweaters. They would sit under the tree by the front office in the courtyard and request, "Come here, Mr. Song, help me wind this woolen yarn," whenever they found Mr. Song available. As a result, Mr. Song would sit on a small stool, winding woolen yarn while facing the women and silently listening to their chatter. The women sometimes joked with Mr. Song, saying: "Mr. Song, who among us do you fancy? We could look out for someone with the same personality for you." At such banter, Mr. Song would simply smile silently and spread his palms more widely to hold the yarn, just as if embracing someone in front of him. Everyone could view this scene, yet no one gossiped about it, because it was Mr. Song sitting there, whose character was known to all the people in the troupe.

Mr. Song was responsible for conveying messages, getting and sending out mail, for calling "Teachers" to get their boiled water, handling both light and heavy mundane things for all the households, and at times also serving as the cook for the opera troupe. Mr. Song would invariably stand out in offering assistance when the opera troupe was busy with performances and the kitchen personnel were away due to urgent matters. Mr. Song would cook the noodles nicely, so they would not be pasty, using about seven and a half kilos of sliced cucumber for about sixty people. When the performers, without removing their makeup, would hold out big bowls to get their noodles, Mr. Song would always give them each nearly the same amount of sliced cucumber, and all would praise Mr. Song for his fairness in the sharing of the cucumber.

Mr. Song naturally enjoyed popularity among the opera troupe, although he was not always gentle with everyone, yet he would never waver in his principles regardless of the urgency. He could sternly say to an actor playing the female lead holding out a bowl to get his share: "Hey, wait a few seconds. You haven't correctly attached those small curls on your forehead. You should paste the fourth and fifth small curls close to the tip of your brow." Moreover, he could say to an actor stripping down to the waist: "You can't refuse to wear the thick robe due to the heat when you're performing onstage."

Mr. Xia, playing the young man's role, was Mr. Song's good friend, but he was still sometimes put into embarrassing situations by Mr. Song. One time, Mr. Song suddenly asked Mr. Xia: "Teacher Xia, have you performed in Lu Mengzheng?"

Mr. Xia replied, "Yes I have."

"Would you sing the four lines at the very beginning for me?" asked Mr. Song.

"You're testing me. Let me read them to you," said Mr. Xia. Lu Mengzheng was a very poor man. Then Mr. Xia read to Mr. Song these four lines which translate as:

"If the heavens lose force, stars fall into disorder,
If the earth loses force, grasses grow rootless,
If a gentleman loses force, he idles in the streets,
If a phoenix loses force, she falls among hens."

Mr. Xia asked Mr. Song whether he had made any mistakes reading the lines. "I hear no mistake in terms of pronunciation, but what does the character pronounced 'shi' refer to in terms of meaning?" asked Mr. Song.

"Of course the character means 'thing'."

"You're wrong. It should be the character meaning 'situation' or 'power.' These four lines claim that all things would entirely change if the heavens, the earth, human beings and phoenixes lost their force." Mr. Xia could not agree with Mr. Song and stuck to his own interpretation. He asked Mr. Song to turn to the head of the troupe (who used to buy "patriotic Chinese cabbages" and was now retired) for the correct answer. The head said that he was uncertain as to the meaning because the pronunciation came down from the masters.

After leaving the home of the troupe head, Mr. Song said: "You can ask the head of the troupe anything about somersaults, but you should believe me in this matter."

Mr. Xia believed Mr. Song was right, and then said: "Okay, I'll treat you to a drink."

"I must return to the front office to have some *geda* soup," replied Mr. Song.

Later, Mr. Xia still went to the office to invite Mr. Song to have a drink at his place. Mr. Xia pushed the door open and found Mr. Song squatting on the ground, scooping *geda* (dough-drop and vegetable) soup from an iron pan. Previously, no one in the opera troupe had taken notice of what or how Mr. Song ate during his meals. Actually, Mr. Song had always taken his meals like this, squatting near the pan, just as he had done in his hometown, in the mountains, on the steps under the eave, and in the courtyard. In the past he had a family and wife. But now, being alone, how he ate mattered even less, so he made do in this manner. Sometimes he even directly scooped up the food from the pan instead of using a bowl, thus not having to wash any dishes. Mr. Song was meticulous in cooking noodles and distributing vegetables for the opera troupe, but he cared less about his own meals. Mr. Xia felt very bad at this moment. He looked at Mr. Song and his complexion, wan as a stem of cabbage, and warned Mr. Song: "Mr. Song, you should pay attention to your nutrition. Look at the pallor of your face. It looks like a cabbage stem. You should eat more meat."

Mr. Song had always been cautious about Mr. Xia's friendship, not because he did not want to accept the friendship but because he believed they lived in two entirely different worlds. Friendship could only be developed on an equal basis.

Just from the perspective of his views and thoughts on this, Mr. Song could not be said to be superficial. Mr. Song absentmindedly listened to Mr. Xia's words and told himself: "How could I not know about nutrition? The human body needs at least two thousand kilocalories, which I am far from meeting. Yet if I fussed about nutrition, what would happen to my daughter and her son living in the countryside?" Slowly, Mr. Song talked only about some of his family matters with Mr. Xia. His daughter had married an idler from a poorer region. Several years ago, the idler had left Mr. Song's daughter and her one-month-old son, and no one knew where he had gone. The daughter was leading a miserable life, relying on financial assistance from Mr. Song. Mr. Xia then understood Mr. Song's situation and realized he could not blame Mr. Song. Sometime later, this daughter brought her son to visit Mr. Song at the troupe, and Mr. Xia thought that they had come to squeeze more of Mr. Song's *geda* soup.

Mr. Song's daughter appeared to be a bit of a blockhead, wearing a fake police uniform in greenish black bought at a country fair. At that time, both male and female villagers preferred wearing fake police uniforms sewn with shoulder straps. They would only wear one police uniform in the spring and autumn, and then add a cotton-padded undercoat covered by the uniform in the winter. Mr. Song's daughter wore a red cotton-padded undercoat covered by the fake police uniform. The cotton-padded undercoat was thick while the police uniform was thin. So the police uniform squeezed the cotton-padded undercoat, exposing its lower hem. Mr. Song's grandson was of school age, and also wore a fake police uniform in his size, just like his mother, as he stood alertly in the courtyard, trying to appear somehow imposing. As for Mr. Song, he could enjoy family happiness despite their difficult life. Sometimes the daughter made dumplings stuffed with chopped Chinese cabbage and small dried shrimp, but never meat. The daughter's skills at cooking were not good and she produced shriveled, shrunken dumplings. Anyway, at least they were dumplings! The daughter was making dumplings in the house, while the grandson ran about, jumping in the courtyard. Mr. Song took a look at his daughter inside the house and then at his grandson in the courtyard, and felt satisfied. When his grandson picked up and kicked around a broken soccer ball left in the courtyard, based on observation skills honed in the city over the years Mr. Song noted his grandson's village style in his kicking, running, jumping, and other gestures and actions. Mr. Song realized his grandson was not moving his shoulders on both sides of his chest, but stiffly held his neck straight up, leaning his upper body backward and stretching his belly forward, as if running with his belly instead of his legs. When lifting his leg to kick the ball, he shrank his neck and gritted his teeth, looking like he was about to kick a stone.

Mr. Song told his grandson: "You still have a lot to learn about playing soccer."

"What am I supposed to do?" asked the grandson. Mr. Song knew that he could not clearly explain such techniques in a few words; nor could he demonstrate them, so he told his grandson to keep playing soccer in his own style. The grandson insistently asked his grandfather to buy him a soccer ball before leaving, but Mr. Song refused the request. In Mr. Song's opinion, one soccer ball cost as much money as for one month of food, and it was urgent now for his whole family to supplement their calories.

How time did fly...

Mr. Xia was about to retire and Mr. Song grew older day by day. Mr. Song now shuffled about instead of striding. You would hear the grating of his soles against the ground before he appeared before you. As the times evolved, the opera troupe would also continually change some of its old habits. For example, the opera troupe had got rid of the old drinking-water boiler to follow the municipal department's call "to make the sky blue and the water green." As a result, Mr. Song was now much more relaxed, no longer always having to remind the "Teachers" to come get their boiled water in the courtyard. But he began to make other mistakes and his memory kept slipping. Sometimes he would deliver a letter to the wrong office by mistake, and sometimes he forgot to announce a meeting as required by the head of the troupe. However, Mr. Song could not be dismissed, thanks to his character and his being on his own. People were tolerant about his mistakes and errors, because they believed, to err is human. What was more, people pretended not to take account of his errors. Then one day, unfortunately, a serious disease in his leg struck him hard.

Mr. Song had never fallen sick over the past twenty years, and more particularly, would be unwilling to lie down in bed during the day. However, he had lain down for the first time that day. He also sent for Mr. Xia, and told Mr. Xia that he had to go to the hospital.

Mr. Xia had known about Mr. Song's leg disease for some time: it was peripheral vascular syndrome in the lower left limb, commonly known as "rotting leg." Mr. Xia also knew that Mr. Song would be risking amputation if his rotting leg did not receive radical surgery in time. Mr. Xia had not mentioned the leg disease to Mr. Song in the past, but now he could not conceal this anymore because Mr. Song's left leg was swollen like a tree trunk, oozing with bloody pus. Mr. Xia took Mr. Song to the hospital by bicycle.

After examining Mr. Song's leg, the doctor said: "You must have surgery as soon as possible, so you can save your leg."

"How much is the operation?" asked Mr. Song.

"About fifteen thousand yuan, but it depends on any complications with surgery and the number of days in the hospital," replied the doctor.

"Why is it so expensive?" asked Mr. Song.

"It's peripheral vascular syndrome. We have to treat every blood vessel and reconnect all the nerves one by one. Doing each nerve costs tens of yuan," said the doctor.

"Let's go home," said Mr. Song to Mr. Xia.

Fifteen thousand yuan was an enormous figure to Mr. Song—his total savings were less than one hundred and fifty yuan. After returning to the front office, Mr. Song sat on the chair in a daze, instead of lying down on the bed. After a long pause, he said to Mr. Xia: "Let it be. Anyway, I'm old. I'm ready to die and return to my native land."

"Don't worry. There is no river that cannot be crossed," said Mr. Xia.

Mr. Xia was trying to comfort Mr. Song, but to cross this river was by no means easy. He wanted to turn to the leadership for help, and then thought it was not something as simple as some money being given by the accountant subject to the leader's permission. The revenues of the opera troupe were just enough to pay everyone, and Mr. Xia always had many unpaid medical bills in his pocket, let alone Mr. Song—a casual worker. Consequently, he stopped in the front of the office building, where Mr. Song used to shout "Teachers, the water is boiling," or "Teachers, it's time for rice distribution"... An ineffable earnest hope arose in Mr. Xia when he stood there, and an idea occurred to him: why not tell everyone about Mr. Song's condition using old Song's own method?

On the following day, a notice was put up at the door to the office building, reading: "Respected Teachers, Mr. Song is facing great misfortune. Please show your love and make a contribution for Mr. Song!" Next, his condition and the required hospital expenses were clearly added to the notice, with the signature of Mr.

Xia at the bottom. The notice to all "Teachers" by Mr. Xia worked as hoped: all the personnel at the opera troupe, ranging from the head of the troupe to performers, employees and family members, donated money for Mr. Song.

Mr. Xia collected donations door to door, but after several days of hard work he only collected half of the required target, seven thousand five hundred yuan. Then, he made a list of people who had once worked in the opera troupe and had been transferred, and by bicycle he called on these people living in different parts of the city. On meeting them, Mr. Xia would eloquently describe the misfortune of Mr. Song, so as to arouse their greater sympathy. A young man, who had once served as a lighting engineer for the opera troupe and then resigned to set up an a-coustic equipment business, generously promised to contribute the remaining amount to make up the difference. The young man told his story to Mr. Xia: He had fallen in love while working for the troupe, daily returning at two or three o'clock in the morning. When he knocked at the door the sleeping Mr. Song would always get up promptly to open it for him, asking for nothing and without complaint. Mr. Song was once asked to give evidence when the opera troupe was about to take disci-plinary action against this young man, and he said he never saw the young man go out at night. "I'll never forget that, and my wife would kowtow to Mr. Song if she knew about this," said the young man to Mr. Xia.

Mr. Xia had finally made it! In one week he raised fifteen thousand, eight hundred and sixty-two yuan for Mr. Song. Then, he paid a special visit to the cur-rent head of the troupe and invited him to come and together give the money to Mr. Song, for the sake of formality and collaborating evidence, because the new head could then vouch that Mr. Xia had given all the donations to Mr. Song. They went to the front office one evening and solemnly handed over all the donations to Mr. Song.

Mr. Song was too excited to speak. His ears began to buzz and his body felt as if it were flying through the sky. The two faces in front of his eyes became vague and indistinct, and their voices grew distant. Only the thick stack of money overwhelmingly took over the scene before his eyes. It was nothing else but real money. Mr. Song had never seen so much money in his life, so much at one time.

Mr. Song counted the money through one whole night, instead of sleeping. He classified and rearranged the paper bills, stroked them one by one, observed them in the lamplight one after the other, and smelled them one by one. Some of the new paper sounded so clear, making a loud noise in the quiet night, while other older bills gave off an oily fragrance or a sticky mustiness and dampness. Even one old two–yuan bill became heavy on being pressed into his palm, as if sinking into the heart of his palm. After counting the money, Mr. Song began to deliberate: is my leg really diseased? Should I really give all this money I just counted right now to the hospital? He kept thinking about this, and suddenly stood up. He stretched out his left leg and looked at it, pondering it. He decided to no longer believe that this trunk–like swollen leg was diseased. To prove his self–diagnosis, Mr. Song went into a very strange pose: he lifted his right leg and stood on his swollen and diseased left leg, using it to support his body. He could suddenly do it! Then, Mr. Song unexpectedly managed to perform many other actions, such as shuttlecock kicking and jumping hopscotch like a child. Next, he thought of highly complex leg movements executed by performers during their exercises such as major leg lift, flying kick and butterfly jump, imitating them one by one, producing bizarre but vigorous gestures. Mr. Song grew very excited doing these moves, and a precise and vivid image appeared before him—until he fell heavily to the ground. Then with both hands he grabbed his diseased leg, and realized that it was not a leg but a rotten white gourd. The front office had had its lights on the whole night.

The next morning, after having his breakfast, Mr. Xia came to the front office to get Mr. Song to go to the hospital. Mr. Song, eyes bloodshot, replied he wanted to wait one more day for his daughter to come. Mr. Xia thought this made good enough sense: surgery requires signed approval by a family member, and Mr. Xia was not family after all.

That night, the front office was unusually quiet, as Mr. Song turned off the light at eight o'clock. The next morning, Mr. Xia came to the office to urge Mr. Song to go to the hospital early, only to find the room empty. He rushed to the hospital on his bike, but failed to locate Mr. Song. The doctor who had examined Mr. Song told Mr. Xia that Mr. Song had come and then left.

"Didn't he come here for the operation?" asked Mr. Xia.

"No, he only asked which one is cheaper: the vascular restoration surgery or amputation," replied the doctor. The doctor also told Mr. Xia that Mr. Song had left after hearing that amputation was of course cheaper, and would cost only two to three thousand yuan. Mr. Xia returned to the troupe's front office, and found a chain of keys at the center of the table by the windowsill. Mr. Xia figured out they were the keys for all the households under Mr. Song. Then, he looked about the office very carefully, and discovered that the quilts on Mr. Song's bed, one small white wooden box containing his clothes, and the iron pan on the ground had all disappeared. Mr. Xia decided that Mr. Song had left. Mr. Xia did not have the heart to use the word 'ran off' for Mr. Song.

From then on, Mr. Song never showed his face again to the Lingqiang Opera Troupe or that city.

Mr. Xia in due course became angry, as did all "Teachers" of the troupe, because they felt they had been obviously tricked by Mr. Song taking his great escape. How about their loving hearts? They had given three performances each day in the cold of winter and the heat of summer to make that hard-earned money. What Mr.

Xia could not deal with was all the people complaining to him. Some people said, "I didn't expect that"; while others said, "As the old saying goes, cats hide their claws" or "You are the one who put up the notice"—just as if it were Mr. Xia who had defrauded everyone, and even assisted Mr. Song to abscond. Mr. Xia turned to the head of the troupe, asking that the troupe send someone to bring Mr. Song back to clear things up. The head of the troupe said to Mr. Xia: Mr. Song was a casual worker, how could we force him to come back? He had not signed any written agreement with the troupe, and was thus free to come and go.

Mr. Xia remembered Mr. Song had been introduced to the troupe by a relative who lived in the city, and after much effort he found this man, and told him the whole story. After talking in a loud voice, sometimes becoming so excited that he sounded like he was about to pick a fight, finally Mr. Xia declared to the relative in a clear-cut manner: Mr. Song had been irresponsible about his own health, and had hurt and offended all the comrades of their troupe.

The relative thought nothing of Mr. Xia's eloquence and passion, and said: "I'd like to extend my many thanks to all the comrades who made donations on behalf of Mr. Song. Yet you make no sense in saying Mr. Song hurt you. You voluntarily donated the money, and were in no way forced by Mr. Song, and you offered the money to him. So, the money of course belongs to Mr. Song..."

"But we donated money to help him cure his leg," interrupted Mr. Xia.

"He's already cured that leg," replied the relative.

"How did he cure it?"

"To tell you the truth, Mr. Song had his leg amputated on the day after he returned to his hometown. The amputation at home was cheaper and cost him less than two thousand yuan, without a hospital stay," replied the relative.

"Oh, my goodness!" exclaimed Mr. Xia.

"The leg is his, so he naturally has the right to decide how to dispose of it. There's nothing wrong with Mr. Song doing that. This is much better, because he saved more than ten thousand yuan. He's a villager, and has to support a poor daughter and grandson," said the relative.

Mr. Xia stopped arguing with Mr. Song's relative, but neither was he convinced by the relative's logic. He was just unable to soothe his own anger and confusion. It was difficult for him to believe what the relative had said—amputating one human leg is not as simple and as easy as sawing off one leg of a stool. Shortly afterwards, a man who returned after performing in the northern mountains told Mr. Xia that he had seen Mr. Song at a newly developed tourist attraction, and that Mr. Song was selling film seated in a small zinc-sheet shed.

"Did you see his legs?" asked Mr. Xia hurriedly, "Did he have one or two legs?"

"I couldn't see them. He was sitting by a window, so I could only see his upper body," replied the man.

Mr. Xia decided to take a trip to the northern mountains. He wanted to personally see the current circumstances of the runaway Mr. Song, so as to arouse the man's sense of shame, embarrassment and guilt, and would directly accept this contrition. He wanted to play the secret agent specializing in invading people's privacy, or a policeman tracking down a criminal. Mr. Xia's agonizing thoughts were by no means kindly, but not unjustifiable at all, considering he had made the utmost efforts to save Mr. Song's leg. Mr. Xia climbed onto a long-distance coach, arrived in Mr. Song's hometown and then got to the newly developed tourist attraction, a more than six-hour journey. When he got off the coach he directly rushed to the small booths selling tourist souvenirs near the bus station. He quickly and easily found Mr. Song standing near a small zinc sheet she. Mr. Song was standing with crutches, directing a robust young man to unload goods into the house. Mr. Xia gazed at the lower body of Mr. Song and saw his left leg was gone, with the empty trouser leg rolled up to the upper thigh, looking like a clump of crumpled dishcloth. At this moment, Mr. Xia felt both distress and grief in his heart and was not sure whether to greet Mr. Song or not.

Mr. Song, leaning on his crutches, also saw Mr. Xia standing not far away and suddenly stopped directing the young man, becoming frozen, transfixed. Mr. Xia now found the expressions he had desired on Mr. Song's face: embarrassment, shame and guilt, as well as fright due to the unexpected shock. It occurred to Mr. Xia that Mr. Song was somehow a learned man, deeply conscious of his own self-esteem. However, Mr. Xia still did not know how to step forward to greet Mr. Song. Suddenly Mr. Song took off all at once: he exerted all his energy to hop forward, dragging his body and the two crutches with his healthy and sound right leg. He was forced to stoop and bump against the tourists, like an injured wild beast. Mr. Xia was entranced by Mr. Song's gallop, and in his trance vaguely saw him somersault, then execute a butterfly kick and flying kick. Mr. Song jumped down a mountain pathway and vanished from sight, in the twinkling of an eye.

The young man unloading goods did not know what was happening. He looked at Mr. Xia standing in front of him and said: "Do you know my grandpa?"

"Yes, we're old, old friends," replied Mr. Xia.

"It seems you scared my grandpa," said the young man.

"You're Mr. Song's grandson, right? I saw you at our troupe more than ten years ago. At that time, you were very small and were playing soccer in the courtyard," Mr. Xia responded irrelevantly.

"Oh, I see. Then why did my grandpa run away when he saw you?" asked the grandson.

Mr. Xia thought for a while and replied: "Maybe your grandpa ran to buy some meat to make a meal for me."

"You look very thirsty. Have a bottle of Master Kong iced tea. You're grand–pa's friend, so it's no charge," said the grandson.

"No, thanks. Your life must be very hard."

"It's much better now. My grandpa set up this shop after returning from the city. Back then, I'd asked grandpa to buy me a soccer ball, but he said he had no money. Actually, he had saved more than ten thousand yuan," said the grandson.

"How much money do you earn every day?" asked Mr. Xia.

"About sixty to seventy yuan," replied the grandson. Mr. Song earns in five days with this shop what he got as one month's salary working at the front office, Mr. Xia thought. The grandson gave the iced tea to Mr. Xia, but Mr. Xia firmly re–fused it. "Okay. Then, please take a tourist map so you won't get lost. The land–scapes here are very beautiful," added the grandson.

Mr. Xia accepted the tourist map as a gift. He opened the map, and the grand–son enthusiastically pointed out several attractions on it and mentioned again: "The landscapes here are very beautiful." Mr. Xia absentmindedly looked at the map but it appeared as if he saw nothing. The grandson pointed at the map once again and asked: "What do you think our hometown looks like?"

"I don't know."

"It looks like a boot, a high–heeled boot. My grandpa told me so," said the grandson. Mr. Xia looked at the map carefully and saw that Mr. Song's hometown did have the shape of a boot, just as Mr. Song had described Italy many years ago. Mr. Xia thought: Nobody would have drawn up a map for this town if it had not been worth developing; then Mr. Song, who so loved geography, might have lived all his life not knowing that his hometown on the map also looked like a boot.

This was originally a delightful topic, but it was just that now, Mr. Xia seemed to no longer have the opportunity to discuss this matter with Mr. Song.

(*Translated by Li Huayu*)

逃 跑

铁 凝

二十多年前，老宋从北部山区来到这个城市，这个剧团。

那正是城市居民储存大白菜的时代，储存大白菜半是生活需要半是政府号召，因此买大白菜还有一种买“爱国菜”的名义。冬天，大白菜下来了，各户都要买回足够全家吃到来年开春的大白菜。那时的蔬菜市场和居民的关系，就是菜农用大小车辆把“爱国菜”送至各家各户的关系。

一个黄昏，老宋被亲戚领到团长面前。团长正在卸大白菜，一辆胶轮大车正停在单元门口。白菜刚被过完秤，码成齐腰高的一堵墙，少说也有七八百斤。待团长给菜农数完钱，打发他离去，亲戚才对老宋说，这就是团长；又对团长说，这就是老宋。团长不在意地答应一声，只一个劲儿地打捋他的“爱国菜”，显然他是在琢磨怎样尽快把它们运上楼去。老宋看出了团长的意思，问了声：几楼？亲戚替团长回答说四楼。老宋便说：叫我吧。像很多北部山区的人一样，老宋把“我”说成“饿”。说完，他左右开弓地夹起四棵菜就往楼上走。亲戚和团长站在楼前聊起天，谁也不去理会老宋的搬菜运动。当他们再次注意到老宋时，白菜已被搬运一空。这时团长才想到请亲戚和老宋上楼坐坐。他们上得楼来，见白菜正好被码放在团长想要码放的地方——

无非是楼梯一侧，门的两旁。

团长领亲戚蹭着白菜侧身上楼侧身进门，把老宋让进客厅，拉开灯。亲戚坐下了，老宋却坚持站着。团长这才有机会仔细打量眼前的老宋。老宋五十岁左右，个子偏矮，阔嘴、大脸，属于那种天庭饱满、地阁方圆的忠厚长相。他的站相儿不是有些山民的瑟缩，他身子稍稍前倾，垂手侍立，像个老杂货店的伙计，仿佛随时都准备从柜台里探出身子，谦逊、热情地侍候来客。团长暗想，这分明是一个干活麻利、不招人讨厌的人——老宋是被亲戚介绍来这团看守传达室的。后来团长便和亲戚讲起他被借调出国赴意大利演出的事。这团常有人被借调出国，但他们并非担任主演，而是去做“武行”，这团的演员武功好，擅翻打，跟头翻得漂亮。团长此行便是去意大利翻跟头的。提起意大利，一直不曾开口的老宋突然插了句嘴，说，意大利属南欧，从地图上看像只靴子，高跟的。他把“高跟”说成“高更”。团长笑了，不是笑他的口音，是惊奇老宋的出其不意，聪慧和文化兼而有之的出其不意。不用说团长本人，就是这团文化水平最高的编剧，也未必想到意大利像只高跟靴子。团长的笑给亲戚和老宋都增加了信心，亲戚再添油加醋对老宋的优势做些讲解，诸如家庭情况简单，老伴已去世，一个闺女也嫁了人，他工作起来定会专心等等。老宋的事就这样定了，他成了这团传达室的长期临时工。

老宋任传达的这团叫灵腔剧团，国营。这灵腔在北方虽然不能和京、评、梆、豫相比，但在这一方，这半个省吧，还有着相当的代表性。老一代的名伶，男角就有六岁红、八岁红、九岁红；坤角也出过大绿菊、白茉莉、晚香玉。近几十年有过几次进京调演，几位年轻艺人和“梅花奖”也曾经擦肩而过。灵腔还参加过数次省剧地位的竞争，虽未成功，但毕竟又给这剧种增添了一些光彩。在剧场艺术不景气的大形势下，灵腔团却磕磕绊绊地生存了下来——当然，每年的四百场“野台子”，是维系他们生存的主要方式。

老宋在团里的任务是传达、收发，兼烧一个开水锅炉。中国人对开水本来就情有独钟，开水对艺人则更显重要。演员进排练场之前，水瓶子里的茶叶必得先用开水沏上，之后随喝随续，一续一天。不光演员，家属们也需要定时定点打开水，届时或拎壶或提桶，鱼贯来到老宋的锅炉房。打开水，对于一个剧团，乃至对于每一个有单位的中国人，真是一件实实在在、心照不宣的便宜事：开水，白打!老宋也深知这点，所以他对人们的开水观就格外重视。每天早、中、晚，锅炉不仅定时定点烧开，温度也绝对可靠。那时，老宋还必得站在当院，亮起大嗓喊几声："水开了!"老宋所站的当院，正是这团一面为办公楼、一面为宿舍楼、一面为排练场的三面合围的中心地带。老宋一喊，果然人们都坐不住了，即使有的人家暖瓶正满着，老宋的喊也会让他们心动地再去打上一锅——端回家可以把脏污的下水道冲冲，开水冲油污，有劲儿。再说，老宋的喊里是有称谓的，这称谓似更能激起人们对开水的热情。为了这称谓，当初老宋还颇费了一些心思：他当怎样称呼他们呢？喊团长水开了？他却不能只招呼团长一家，那岂不是眼里只有领导吗——这不符合老宋的做人准则。喊演员们水开了吧，这楼里还有不是演员的职工。喊同志们，同志们水开了，又仿佛把自己摆错了位置，仿佛是一个领导在向大伙儿发命令。什么也不说呢，就喊水开了水开了，可那是一种对所有人的失礼。发愁的老宋沉思良久，最后想起了一个称呼：老师。老宋最尊敬的人莫过于老师了，自己那点有限的地理知识，就来源于他在乡村初中时的老师。那时，他最喜欢的课就是地理课。后来因为家境不好，他只念到初二。现在老宋决定将全团干部演员职工家属统称为老师。老师这个称谓毕竟谁都不反感，演员听了高兴，领导和职工家属也不会挑礼，无亲疏远近之嫌，无厚此薄彼之意。于是，老宋就站在院子当中开始了他的呼喊：老师们水开了!老师们水开了!

时间久了，团领导竟把老宋的呼喊固定成最好的因事昭示全团的形式。比如开大会，比如演出出发前的装车，比如年节时分大米，比如和哪位老艺人的遗体告别，都是老宋站在院中呼喊：老师们开会了!老师们装车了!老师们分大米了!老师们和九岁红老师告别了!九岁红的后代听出了别扭，想去找领导反映，一位唱小生的老夏说，今天的追悼会就靠了老宋这一嗓子，开得多热闹。你要靠领导通知，人们十有八九不到，你说哪个划算？

不过，这并不是说老宋是一个喜爱喧闹的人，相反，他沉默寡言的时候居多。他的语言似是很金贵的，不像他的两条腿那样勤快。每天，他按时出入各个办公室和排练场分发报纸、杂志、信件。他步履轻捷，悄无声息，就会把报纸、杂志分送给该送的人，且从未出过差错。就连家属中第二代乃至第三代所订的名目古怪、图文花哨的报刊，他也会毫无怨言地亲自送至他们手中。那时他只有两个字：你哩。他把“你的”说成“你哩”。除了分内的事，分外的事老宋也没少做。二十多年，光是搬白菜，这团里有谁家没让老宋帮过忙呢？没有。后来，储存大白菜的时代终于过去了，但这团里的家属们需要老宋帮忙的事情却没有过去。五楼的人们说，老宋，帮我把这罐煤气扛上去吧。三楼的人们说，老宋，我买的沙发来了，你给搭把手吧。一楼的人们基本不用老宋帮忙抬东西，但有几位妇女喜欢织毛衣。天气热的时候她们坐在院子里，坐在传达室门前的树阴下忙手里的活计，见老宋有空，就喊，老宋过来，给我架着毛线。老宋坐在小板凳上一边和女性家属面对着面缠毛线，一边静静地听她们聊天。有时她们也打趣他，说，老宋，你看上我们当中的谁啦，我们就照着模样给你“踅摸”一个。老宋落寞地笑笑，撑着毛线的双手撑得更开，猛看去，好像要抱住眼前的谁。这场景就在众目睽睽之下，却从来没人说闲话，就因为坐在对面的是老宋，老宋的人品这团里的人是心中有数的。

老宋管传达，管收发，管喊老师们打开水，管各家轻轻重重的琐事，有时还兼任团里的炊事员。逢团里赶台子演出时，炊事员临时有事走了，老宋就来了。老宋一锅煮五六十号人的面条，不夹生，不煳锅；捞出面条，再切十五斤黄瓜的菜码儿，面条都不见“坨”。当演员们脸上带着妆拿着大碗打面条时，老宋每一把抓起的菜码儿黄瓜丝不会差出三五根。演员们都夸老宋分菜码儿没偏向。

老宋在这团里自然是被人喜欢的，但他并非同谁都一团和气。遇到真正较真儿的事，老宋从不丧失原则。他会毫不客气地对一位端碗打饭的旦角儿说，哎，你等等，今天你脑门上的小弯儿可没贴正，第四个、第五个小弯儿应该紧贴眉梢儿。他也会突然对一位光着膀子的男演员说，要是在台上，你可不能嫌热就不穿"胖袄"。唱小生的老夏在这团里算是老宋的好友了，老宋照样会在某些时刻叫老夏下不来台。有一回，他突如其来地问老夏，夏老师，你演过《吕蒙正》没有？老夏说演过。老宋说，你把出场那四句唱，给我唱一遍听听。老夏说，你这是考我，我给你念念吧。吕蒙正是个穷生，上场四句唱是这样的：天无事星斗浑，地无事草无根，君子无事大街上混，凤凰无事落鸡群。老夏念完问老宋有什么破绽，老宋说，从字音上听没什么破绽，我是问你天无事是哪个事？老夏说事情的事呗，还能是哪个事。老宋道：错了，应该是形势的势，势力的势。这四句唱是说天、地、人，也包括凤凰，失去了势力一切就变样了。老夏不服老宋，坚持他的"无事"说，并要求老宋和他一块儿去问团长（那位当年买"爱国菜"、现已退下来的老团长）。两人找到团长，团长说，都是跟师傅模仿的音儿，说不准。出了团长的家，老宋说，翻跟头的事儿你问团长行，这件事终归你得问我。老夏琢磨出老宋有道理，就说我请你喝酒吧。老宋说，我得回传达室喝疙瘩汤。

后来老夏还是追到传达室邀请老宋去他家喝酒，推开门，见老宋正蹲在地上，直接就着一口铁锅呼呼地喝疙瘩汤。在从前，这团里的人们好像谁也不曾留意老宋怎么吃饭又吃些什么饭。其实老宋一直就这样吃饭，蹲着，就着一口锅。就像从前在老家，在山上，在屋檐下的台阶上，在场院里。那时他有家，有女人。现在他只有一个自己，怎么吃不是个吃呢。必要时他甚至可以连碗都节约掉，直接从锅里舀着吃，也省得刷碗了。老宋给团里煮面条、分菜码儿一丝不苟，自己吃饭可就潦草多了。这使老夏心里挺不是滋味儿，他看着老宋的吃相儿，看着他那白菜帮子似的脸色，提醒老宋说，老宋，咱们得讲点营养，看看你的脸什么色儿？白菜帮子色儿。你得吃肉。

对老夏表现出的友情，老宋却持比较谨慎的态度。不是不想领受，是觉得自己和他们毕竟不是一种人。友谊这东西，须建立在平等基础上。就对这个问题的思考而言，不能说老宋浅薄。老宋对老夏的提醒，只有一搭无一搭地听着，心想我还不懂营养？人体每天所需热量至少是两千大卡，我离这还差得远哩。我讲营养，我那乡下的闺女呢，我那外孙子呢。慢慢地，他只向老夏诉说了一些家事。他那嫁了人的闺女，嫁的是一个更穷的地方的懒人。前几年那人忽然扔下老宋的闺女和一个刚满月的孩子走了，不知去了哪里。闺女的日子很难，处处得老宋接济。老夏明白了：怨不得。又过了些时候，老宋的闺女领着他的外孙子到这团里来看老宋，老夏想，唔，这是挤老宋的疙瘩汤来了。

老宋的闺女，看上去有点闷头闷脑，穿一身乡村集市上买来的墨绿色假警服——那些年乡村中的男女很喜欢穿假警服，肩上钉着似是而非的肩襻儿；春秋单穿，冬天就罩上棉袄。老宋闺女的假警服里就套着红花棉袄。棉袄肥，警服瘦，警服把棉袄勒得下摆都冒出来。老宋的外孙当时刚及上学年龄，和母亲一样，穿一身儿童号码的假警服，自觉站在这院里就有了威风。在老宋看来，日子虽难，可也算天伦之乐。有时闺女也给老宋包饺子，馅儿里没肉，只放些白菜和虾皮。闺女的手艺也不济，饺子包得“坐”不住，都瘪瘪地仰在盖帘上，俗称“仰巴饺子”。可那毕竟是饺子。那时闺女在屋里包着饺子，外孙在院里跑跳。老宋看看屋里，又看看院里，他是满足的。当外孙捡起一个扔在院里的破足球就踢时，老宋以进城多年的观察力，看出了外孙踢球姿势和跑跳姿势的村气。他发现外孙跑时胳膊端在两肋边不摆动，脖子生硬地僵直着，上身向后捎，肚子朝前挺，仿佛他不是用腿在跑，而是用肚子在跑。当他起脚踢球时，便缩起脖子，咬紧牙关，好似蹬踹一块石头。老宋告诉外孙，踢足球学问可大哩，可不是你这样。外孙就问那是啥样？老宋知道一句话讲不清，自己又不会示范，便说，先照着你的样式踢着玩儿吧。临走，外孙非让老宋给他买个足球不可。老宋没给外孙买足球，他想，一个球就是一个月的粮食钱，目前全家人急需补充的是卡路里——热量。

光阴像箭一样。

老夏要退了，老宋也更老了。他走路不再是快步，有点拖着腿的样子。当他走过来，人还没到眼前，你就能听见鞋底蹭着地面的嚓嚓声。时代在变，这个团也不断改变着一些旧习惯。比方遵照市政部门“天要蓝，水要绿”的要求，取消了开水锅炉。这使老宋轻松多了，他再也不必老是惦记着站在院里喊老师们打开水了。他开始在别的方面出错儿，他的记性差了，有时候会把张三的信送到李四的办公室去。有时候团长让他喊开会，他也忘了喊。但是这团的人们念着老宋的为人和他的孤单，他们没有辞退他，他们对他的出错儿持宽容的态度。是人哪有不出错儿的？而且他们假装没看见他的出错儿。直到有一天，老宋的腿不争气地真出了大毛病。

二十多年老宋没有病过，白天尤其不愿意躺在床上。那个白天他躺下了，还叫来了老夏。他对老夏说，我得上医院。

老宋的腿病老夏早就知道，他患的是左下肢周围血管综合征，俗称老烂腿。老夏也知道，老烂腿不及时根治，还有截肢的危险。从前老夏替老宋瞒着，现在是瞒不过去了，老宋的腿肿得像檩条，淌着脓血。老夏用自行车驮着老宋去了医院，医生为老宋检查之后说尽快手术吧，保腿要紧。老宋问手术得多少钱，医生说，一万五左右，要看手术难度和住院时间长短。老宋说怎么这样贵，医生说，这种周围血管病，血管要一根一根地收拾，神经要一根一根地接上，接哪根神经不得几十块钱？老宋对老夏说，咱们回去吧。

一万五千块，对老宋来说这是个天文数字，他全部的积蓄连一百五十块钱也不到。回到传达室，他不再往床上躺，只是坐在椅子上发呆。半天，老宋对老夏说，由它去吧，反正我也老了。哪里黄土不埋人，我也该叶落归根了。老夏说，你说到哪儿去了，哪有过不去的河？

老夏安慰了老宋，但要过河谈何容易。他想去找领导，转念又想，这可不是领导一拍板会计就点钱的事。一个刚够发工资的剧团，不用说临时工老宋，老夏自己口袋里就经常装着报不了销的药费单。这样，他走到办公楼前就站住了。当年老宋呼喊“老师们水开了”、“老师们分大米了”……的时候就站在这里。老夏站在这里，心中涌起一股子说不出的热望，他想，何不把老宋的事用老宋的办法昭示一下全团呢？第二天，办公楼门前贴出了一张告示，上写：尊敬的老师们，目前老宋遭了大难，请大家都献出些爱心吧!接下来，告示写明了老宋的病情及所需费用的数目，请大家量力而行。末尾的署名是老夏本人。老夏写给全体老师的告示果然在这团里发生了效应，全团上至团长，下至演职员工及家属都献了爱心。

老夏走家串户，挨门敛钱，折腾了几天，却只敛够了那个数目的一半。于是他又把从前在这团里工作过，后来调走的人列了个名单，骑上自行车，到这城市的四面八方去找这些人。老夏见到他们，口沫四溅地叙述着老宋的不幸，以唤起他们更大的同情。其中一位从前在团里搞灯光，后来自己辞职出去卖音响的青年慷慨解囊，答应其余的钱全部由他出。他说，从前在团里工作的时候，他正在搞对象，每天夜里两三点才回来。每次敲大门，睡梦中的老宋都会及时从床上爬起来给他开门，而且既不打听，也不抱怨。团里要给这青年处分，找老宋作证，老宋说没见这青年晚上出去过。这青年对老夏说，就这一条，我终生不忘，我太太知道也得找老宋去磕头。

老夏成功了，他用一个星期的时间，为老宋筹集到一万五千八百六十二元人民币。为此，他专门找到现任团长，邀团长同他一道去给老宋送钱。一来显得郑重，二来也算有个旁证，团长可以证明他把捐来的钱一分不差地奉献给了老宋。两人于当晚来到传达室，将这笔钱郑重地交给老宋。

老宋激动得说不出话来，耳朵嗡嗡作响，身子像坠入云中。眼前的两张脸影影绰绰似有似无，声音也远得不行。惟有那厚厚的一摞钱铺天盖地堵在眼前，那不是别的，是真钱啊，那是老宋一辈子也没有见过的钱，一次，这么多。

老宋一夜没睡，他数了一夜钱。他把它们分门别类再排列组合；他一张一张地抚摩它们，一张一张地在灯下照它们，一张一张地把鼻子凑上去闻它们。一些新钱嘎巴嘎巴响得很脆，在沉静的黑夜里惊天动地；一些旧钱散发着微微辛辣的油腻味儿，或者黏黏的霉潮气。即便一张两块钱的旧票，压在掌上也是沉甸甸的，直压得他掌心下坠。老宋数完钱就开始想心事，他想，难道他的腿真有病吗？难道他真的要把刚刚数过的这些东西都扔给医院吗？想着想着，他忽地站了起来，伸出左腿上下打量着它，或者叫做掂量着它。他决心不再相信这条肿得檩梁似的腿是条病腿。为了证实自己的见解，他给自己摆了一个很奇怪的姿势：他右脚离地，单用那病肿的左腿撑起全身的重量，他竟然金鸡独立般地站住了。他又做了几下类似儿童踢毽子、跳房子之类的动作，居然也做出了。接着他想起演员练功时的大骗腿、打飞脚、旋子这些用腿做出的高难动作，他依次模仿起来，形态虽然怪诞，却是悲壮。这些动作将老宋折腾得激动不已，直到他稀里哗啦摔在地上，一个形象才确凿地来到他的脑海中，他双手掐住他的病腿想，这哪儿还是一条腿啊，分明是一条烂冬瓜。传达室的灯亮了一夜。

早晨，老夏吃过饭，就来叫老宋去医院。双眼布满血丝的老宋说，我想等一天，等我闺女来了也不迟。老夏觉得有道理，动手术是要家属签字的，老夏终归不是老宋的家属。

这天晚上传达室分外安静，老宋八点钟就熄了灯。第二天，当老夏又来传达室催促老宋赶快去医院时，发现传达室已空无一人。老夏骑车赶往医院，医院并没有老宋。为老宋做过检查的医生说，那个病人来是来过，又走了。老夏说，他不是来住院做手术的吗？医生说不是，只是问做静脉修复术便宜还是锯腿便宜。医生告诉他当然是截肢手术便宜，两三千就够了，他听完就走了。老夏回到团里，又来到传达室，先发现窗台下的桌子正中摆着一串钥匙。老夏认出，这是老宋掌管所有门户的钥匙。再细看，见老宋的床上被褥没了，一只放衣服的白色小木箱没了，地上的铁锅也不见了。老夏想，这是走了。他不忍心用逃跑来形容老宋。

自此老宋就从这个灵腔剧团和这个城市消失了。

老夏终于气愤起来，团里的老师们也气愤起来，老宋的不辞而别显然是愚弄了他们。他们那一片爱心呢？他们的钱是血汗钱，冬演三九，夏演三伏，一天三开箱。尤其让老夏不能容忍的是，人们纷纷在他面前发些抱怨。人们对他说，没想到，真是没想到。人们对他说，真是知人知面不知心。告示可是你贴的。说得老夏一激灵一激灵的，好像是老夏骗了大伙儿的钱，并且协助了老宋的逃跑。老夏去找团长，要求团里派人把老宋弄回来，把事说清楚。团长说，一个临时工，怎么去弄？他和团里连个书面协议都没有，人家本是来去自由的。老夏想起当年老宋的到来是靠了一个亲戚的介绍，那亲戚当是住在本市的。于是老夏七拐八拐又找到了老宋的那位亲戚，向那亲戚述说了事情的来龙去脉，情急之中嗓门就有些高亢，像要吵架。最后他态度鲜明地向亲戚宣布说，老宋的这种做法不仅是对自己的身体不负责任，而且伤害了团里所有同志的感情。

老宋的这位亲戚对老夏的慷慨激昂并不买账，说，同志们为老宋捐款，我在这儿替老宋谢谢大伙儿了。你说伤害感情，话就扯得有点远。钱不是老宋逼你们出的，是你们的自愿。自愿把钱给了老宋，钱就当属于老宋。老夏打断亲戚说，可那钱是捐来专为给他治腿的。亲戚说，他不是已经治了嘛。老夏说，他是怎么治的？亲戚说，不瞒你说，他回老家第二天就去县医院把腿锯了，那儿更便宜，两千不到，无须住院，随锯随走。老夏惊呼道，我娘哟!亲戚说，腿在他自己身上长着，怎样处置自然是他自己说了算。他这么盘算又有什么过失？剩下一万多又有什么不好？一个乡下人，又是穷闺女，又是穷外孙子。

老夏没有再和老宋的亲戚矫情，却也没有被这位亲戚说服。他只是，只是久久地愤怒难平，疑惑难平。他难以相信那亲戚的话是真的——锯条人腿怎么也不能像锯条板凳腿那么简单。不久，团里有人从北部山区演出回来，告诉老夏说在新开发的一个旅游景点看见老宋了，老宋坐在一个小铁皮房子里卖胶卷。老夏忙问：腿呢？他是一条腿还是两条腿？演出的人说没看见，他坐在窗口，只能看见上半身。

老夏决心去做一次北部山区的旅游，他很想亲眼目睹那逃逸的老宋之现状，很想用这亲眼目睹来刺激起对方的尴尬、难堪和愧疚，他并且要直接领受对方这尴尬、难堪和愧疚。好比一个专刺人隐私的暗探，又如同一个追踪犯人的警察。不能说老夏这按捺不住的想法有多么厚道，可也不能说他这想法完全不合情理，毕竟他为保全老宋的腿出过大力。他坐上长途大巴，经过了六个多小时的旅途，到达了老宋的家乡，到达了那个新开发的旅游景点。他下得车来，直奔车站周围那一片出售旅游纪念品的小商亭，几乎没太费劲，他很快就发现在一个小铁皮屋子旁边站着老宋。老宋拄着双拐，正指挥一个健壮的年轻人往小屋里卸货。老夏的目光停在老宋的下半身，左腿那儿空着，挽至腿根部的空裤筒好像一团揉皱的搌布。这使老夏心中涌上一股酸涩，一时竟想不好到底该不该去和老宋打招呼。

拄着拐的老宋也看见了站在不远处的老夏，顿时停下对那年轻人的指挥，木呆呆地愣在那里。接着，老夏在老宋脸上找到了他想要找的表情：尴尬、难堪、愧疚，还有受了意外惊吓的恐惧。这使老夏想到，老宋到底是个有文化的人，深深懂得自尊。可他还是不知如何上前去同老宋打招呼。突然间，老宋撒腿便跑，他那尚是健康的右腿拖动着全身，拖动着双拐奋力向前；他佝偻着身子在游人当中冲撞，如一只受了伤的野兽；他的奔跑使老夏眼花缭乱，恍惚之中也许跟头、旋子、飞脚全有，他跳跃着直奔一条山间小路而去，眨眼之间就没了踪影。

正在卸货的年轻人不知出了什么事，看着近前的老夏说，你是不是认识我姥爷？老夏说是，我们是老……朋友。年轻人说，你好像把我姥爷给吓着了。老夏答非所问地说，你是老宋的外孙子吧，十几年前我在我们团里见过你。那会儿你还小呢，在院子里踢球。外孙子说，原来是这样。那我姥爷为什么一看见你就跑呢？老夏想了想，说，也没准儿你姥爷是给我买肉吃去了。

外孙子说，看着你怪渴的，喝一瓶康师傅冰茶吧，你是我姥爷的朋友，不要钱。

老夏说不不，你们不容易。外孙子说，现在好多了，我姥爷从城里回来才开了这个小卖店。那会儿我让姥爷给买个足球他光说没钱，敢情攒了一万多呢。老夏问这个店一天能赚多少，外孙子说赚个六七十块吧。老夏想，五天就能赚出看传达室一个月的钱了。外孙子把冰茶递到老夏手里，老夏坚决不要。外孙子又说，那你拿上一张旅游图吧，看图旅游省得迷路。这里的山水很好看。

老夏接受了外孙子赠送的旅游图，他把它打开，外孙子热心地指着图上的几处，再次介绍说，这里的山水很好看。老夏似是而非地看着地图，他似乎什么也没有看见。外孙子指着地图又说，你看我们这块地方像什么物件？老夏说看不出来。外孙子说，像只靴子，高更（跟）的。我姥爷告诉我的。老夏细看地图，这才看出老宋家乡的形状正好比一只靴子，如同当年老宋对意大利的形容一样。他想，这地方如果没有开发，就不会有人为它绘制地图，热爱地理的老宋便终生也不会知道，他的故乡在地图上也是一只靴子。

这本是一个让人愉悦的话题，只是，老夏似乎再也没有机会同老宋讨论这个话题了。

HAN Shaogong, is a professional writer and the 8th presidium member of the China Writers Association. His major works include the short stories *Thatched Land, Leaving and Returning Home*, the novellas *Bababa, Shoe Fetishism*, his prose *World, Perfect Presumption*, and novels *A Dictionary of Maqiao, Hint*. He has translated such classics as *The Unbearable Lightness of Being, The Book of Disquiet*, among others. Widely published abroad, his writings have been translated into English, French, Dutch, Korean and Spanish. In 2002, he was awarded the *Ordre des Arts et des Lettres* by the French Ministry of Culture. *A Dictionary of Maqiao* won the 2nd Newman Prize for Chinese Literature in 2010.

韩少功，作家，中国作家协会第八届主席团成员。主要作品有短篇小说《西望茅草地》《归去来》等，中篇小说《爸爸爸》《鞋癖》等，散文《世界》《完美的假定》等，长篇小说《马桥词典》《暗示》等。另有译作《生命中不能承受之轻》《惶然录》等。作品有英、法、荷、意、韩、西等多种外文译本在境外出版。2002年，韩少功获得法国文化部颁发的法兰西文艺骑士奖章。2010年，《马桥词典》获得美国第2届纽曼华语文学奖。

Page Forty-three

HAN Shaogong

At this point in our story I find our hero is feeling homesick, so I dispatch him on a train.

It was deep into the night, totally freezing, and there were only a few people on the vast platform, with the sound of water flowing out of the railway station's pipes.

Our hero is nicknamed Beck. His teammates call him this for he is a genuine hero on the field, like Beckham, and enjoys his European soccer star label so much that he walks with his shoulders drooping down and his back cocked up like a reticent ape.

To his slight surprise, a woman in the opposite seat opened her eyes and mouth wide with a decidedly fearful look, though he had seated himself down very quietly and politely. A fatty, sleeping with his head hung down, was awakened by the train starting off, and he too got alarmed by the first sight of Beck, then very hastily lifted up his heavy butt, grabbed his travel bag from the seat and moved to the row diagonally opposite. After a while a vacuum had formed around Beck, with several passengers in the distance craning their necks to stare or glance at him.

"What are they looking at?"

But before he had time to ask, those craning necks vanished at once behind the backs of the seats.

Is long hair that abnormal? Was he blood-stained? Or did he resemble some killer?

"Are they crazy?" After he took off his coat soaked by the autumnal rain and continued listening to his wired MP3 player, he discovered something unusual going on in the compartment. Chinese tunic suits adorned most of these passengers, and two pigtails were the universal hairstyle of the women. As well, several women kept their hair short and brush-like. In this modern age, some were still wearing big baggy pants that smelt of sweet potatoes. Would there be an old village chief, head wrapped in a white towel, holding a book by Chairman Mao Zedong? But in a flash the image of the village chief vanished from his vision, suggesting that everything was an illusion.

His nose was not feeling very good because it had detected a whiff of pig manure. Had he spoken aloud? If not, why was the attendant, who was sweeping the floor, giving him an accusatory stare and saying, "Shut up!"?

"It's freezing in here. Why not turn on the radiator?"

"You feel cold? Why don't you run to your mama?"

"What are you talking about?" He was furious.

Instead of replying him, she hit his feet with her broom to remind him to move them. She nearly got stuck on his Nike sneakers, which he found extremely rude and irritating.

Unexpectedly, after a pile of rubbish had been swept away, she drew back the thick cloth curtain for him and threw a cotton blanket at him, as if to say, "Cover yourself if you're cold."

He wrapped himself in the blanket and the warmth seeped through him. Being a star, he is not supposed to bully young women, so he picked up a magazine to kill time. It was a very old and dog-eared *New Times*, probably discarded by some passenger. Fascinated as he read, Beck became so lost in the old magazine that he heard nothing when the attendant took his wet clothes to the boiler room to dry them, and the captain came to take a passenger's temperature, and ask if anybody had lost a wallet.

Here was why he was absorbed. There was a strange story in the magazine: Midnight, rain, platform, train, and so on. Riding the train were many passengers wearing Chinese tunic suits or short pigtails. A young passenger got on the train halfway and his nose did not feel good. An attendant hit his feet with a broom and almost got it stuck on his Nike sneakers. The only difference between the story and reality was that the hero of the magazine story was not that much like Beck. He was a wandering performer, while Beck was a soccer star on his way back from a tour purchasing antiques as an amateur.

He suddenly bit a fingertip and could not help screaming out.

The attendant came over in a hurry. Pressing on her own chest she chastised him, "No screaming! The others are sleeping. You sound like a scary monster."

Not until then did Beck take a careful look at her. Yes, she had arresting eyes, just like the young woman in the story. The pair of cloth sleeve covers on her arms was also described in the story. But there was a noticeable floral collar on her stiff uniform and her short pigtails were curly at the ends, careless omissions on the part of the storywriter.

"Am I sick? Or is this a dream?" He pinched his own arm.

"Anything wrong with you?" She was staring closely into his eyes.

"Are you Mo Xiaoting?"

"How do you know my name?"

"It's in the magazine."

"That's ridiculous."

"You don't believe me? Are you nineteen? Do you have a soldier boyfriend...?"

"Are you a policeman checking my identity?"

"Take a look. Right here. See?"

But she did not bother. Holding up a thermos she said, "Give me your mug. Don't complain that I didn't serve water."

Beck never carried a mug with him. "Do you have coke for sale?"

"Coke?"

"Coke. Coca Cola."

"What are you talking about? You have a stammer?"

"Co–ca–Co–la. You've never heard of that?"

"Do you have a mug or not? No? Then I'm leaving."

"Wait a sec. You don't know Coca Cola? What about Nongfu Spring, Wahaha yogurt or Blue Ribbon fruit beer? You've never heard of them either?"

"What are you talking about?"

"Hey, where are you from? Are you a caveman or terracotta?"

"Shut up! Comrade, this is a Red Flag Compartment. Have some respect, please!"

Beck could not help rocking with laughter. He rose and took a look gasping, and then pulled out his cell phone to call a friend, "Hello, Shrimp. Wake up. You know what I just saw? Hey, listen. I'm in a train and this compartment is full of bumpkins. They've never heard of Coca Cola. Can you believe it? You'd better take a look yourself. They're in Chinese tunic suits and call me comrade. I'm not kidding you ... Are you listening to me?"

It was likely that Shrimp thought Beck was drunk. He was not willing to listen anymore and told Beck he needed to get back to work immediately for his boss was already pissed off at him.

When Beck turned off his phone he discovered two men suddenly towering over him, one was the captain and the other a tall railway police officer, both alert and serious. Xiaoting was hiding behind the captain and blinking her eyes very nervously, saying, "...That thing in his hand, it's really horrid. Do you know what it is?"

Beck saw more and more people swarming around him and staring at his phone. What was wrong with his cell phone? A scene suddenly flashed through his brain. When he had pulled out the phone just before, the attendant, as if bitten by a snake, had dropped the thermos and run away, screaming.

"Your ID, please," the captain said.

"Why?"

"Where are you from? Abroad?"

"No, no, no. I'm an alien from Neptune or Pluto."

"What's in your hand?"

"A cell phone."

"Cell phone? Or actually, a telegraph?"

"Why would I need a telegraph?"

"Ask yourself."

"So, I'm sending messages to the United States? Why, to tell General White of the CIA that there's no coke here, and that the compartment smells of pigs?" Beck almost broke into laughter.

"Save your breath. Your target is Project 563 ... You think we have no idea?"

He had no idea what "563" could be at all, let alone the terms that followed, like war preparations, guidelines of the Party, strike–downs against two counter–revolutionary activities (sabotages by class enemies and attacks from capitalist forces), and campaigns against the three evils (corruption, waste and bureaucracy), and revolutionary committees, but these gave him a hint that he was definitely in trouble. It did not seem like any kind of joke or fun. His cell phone was grabbed away, his bag was searched. Luckily there were no drugs inside. They found an IC card for the public transport system which they passed from one to another but still could not figure out what it was, and several soccer magazines which they had probably never seen before either, and which they checked very carefully by holding each up to the light to look in vain for suspicious fingerprints. And compared to his dirty laundry and slippers, the MP3 player, of course, seemed way more suspicious. No matter how Beck tried to explain about music and digital chips, it was all taken as evidence together with his cell phone, and all checked and stuffed into a briefcase. It then seemed that they were about to leave him.

"Hey, who the hell are you? Do you have a search warrant? Are you nuts? How come you don't know about cell phones?" Beck howled angrily.

He grasped at the captain suddenly and roared, "I will sue you! I'll report you to the media. You think you can abuse me like this? I have many friends in the media. You'll be fired as soon as the next morning if you dare harass me."

Maybe he was being too wild, for the railway policeman gave him a heavy slap on the face, and in no time he saw stars and felt quite ethereal. The sharp pain on his face overwhelmed his brain as he fumbled around for the edge of the counter and adjusted the position of his head, and then a wave of slogans burst out in the compartment: "Down with the vicious spy! Down with all devils! Down with US imperialists and reactionaries!" All the passengers around him raised a forest of fists toward him.

It was really turning out to be no fun at all. Thanks only to the attendant, an old man missed throwing an umbrella at his head, and a child missed spitting on him. An indignant discussion was in progress as he was taken away.

"I could see from the start he's a bad egg. Did you notice his shabby pants?"

"Such a poor spy! He can't even afford a haircut."

"Imperialism creates hybrids. He looks neither like a man nor like a woman."

"No, not a hybrid. He's just being obscene. Dressed like a woman to peep in the ladies' room."

"Yes. You're absolutely right."

"He deserves to be drowned in a cesspool!"

"He's too repulsive."

...

He was thrown into a staff cubicle.

In the isolated room he felt like a real idiot. How had he gotten onto such a strange train? Why had he been dragged here after being slapped and arrested? And, given there had been so many businesses he could have put his hand to, why had Shrimp encouraged a big star like him to go and purchase antiques? He simply had no idea how all this trouble would end, or whether he would retain his job if he did not get back to work soon.

It was deadly dark outside, and occasionally trains heading in the opposite direction whistled by, almost touching his face. The trains came so close that he could almost see the passengers inside. How comfortable, how warm and how safe they all were! Perhaps they were enjoying some beer and chewing chicken wings. They most definitely carried cell phones and knew what a cell phone was and could verify his innocence, but they all seemed so indifferent to an entrapped man, whooshing by as quick as lightning.

He pounded and kicked on the door, and then kicked the aluminum bucket like it was a soccer ball.

But nobody responded.

A little tired, he then sat down, rubbed his face and fell into a dazed stupor. On the ceiling a mouse sprang out from an opening and then went back inside with its tail erect. Not afraid of people at all, it squeaked happily.

Luckily the strange magazine *New Times*, still in his pocket, could help him explore the train.

What comes and goes should come and go,
A century–old stone is still a stone.
What comes and goes should come and go,
The millennial moon is still the moon.
What comes and goes should come and go,
And the ancient sky is still sky...

This was a song, according to page forty–two of the magazine, sung by a blind old man, but there was no such old man on the train, which was another difference, indicating that perhaps the story could not tell the future. Beck was very much clinging to this idea at that moment, but his relief did not last long. As the story went on in the magazine, he trembled, and his body went cold and his heart began to beat hard again. Yes, there were differences, but what about the mouse in the story (which he had just seen)? What about the downpour (the rainwater outside the window painting slashes)? What about the thunderstorm (the lightning outside which had turned the dark night into bright day, illuminating mountains and rivers)? And, then there came a most appalling accident. Page forty–three was about Zilong Gorge, where this train encountered a mud-rock slide causing the train to derail, with compartments overturned, with sparks flying and metal clanging. Two compartments were squashed up into the sky and scattered wheels rolled down the grassy slopes. Everything turned truly catastrophic.

"Hey. It's dry." The attendant entered and threw his warm jacket at him. Noticing his pale face, she asked, "Are you sick?"

He gasped, "Is Zilong Gorge ahead?"

"I'm not telling you anything."

"You really think I'm a spy? Do I look like one? Have you ever seen any spy as impressive as me?"

"Anyway, you have to wait for the security division's assessment."

"But there isn't enough time left for us."

"What do you mean?"

"Tell me. Is there a Zilong Gorge ahead?"

"So what if there is?"

"Goodness! We're in danger! We are through."

"I don't understand."

"Of course you don't. You know nothing." Beck leaped up in a fury and cried out, "You even have no idea what Coca Cola is. What's the use of revolutionary committees? Are you guys horribly insane or something? If I were a spy, do you think I would transmit messages in public? Would I call out for your suspicions?"

She seemed somewhat moved, and said awkwardly, "I apologize if we have wronged you."

"Apologize? How? Did you get a look at my swollen cheek?"

"So you can slap me back. Not a big deal for you to fuss over like this."

"You don't mind? Interesting. How would you like me to slap you?"

"You mean it? Could you do it gently? Could you divide it into small ones? Could you slap my boyfriend instead? He's a commando. He is trained to be beaten in the army."

Beck had no interest in commandos. He turned the *New Times* to page forty–three and showed it to her.

She shifted her eyes from him, to the magazine, then back to him again, before she flashed a final doubtful gawk at page forty–three. Her ability to read was being affected by the bulb blinking from the drastic jolting of the train. She was not highly literate, so she occasionally turned to the railway police officer for help, and when the policeman could not help she would ask Beck, only making it more difficult for her to read. Growing impatient with the two dummies, Beck wished he could knock every word from page thirty–eight to page forty–three into their brains, but before he had time to, a new crowd of passengers thronged aboard, turning the whole compartment into total chaos. Subsequently Beck would learn that the dummies had lost the magazine midst the chaos. When he found out, he almost went mad.

Then there was an emergency. As the train crossed the bridge, the driver saw in the headlights, on the roadbed many people waving their hands to try to stop the train. These people had just survived a flood. They figured the roadbed was not high enough, so they were requesting that the train take them away in case the flood rose further. Their request was approved in no time by the captain. He gave them free pass onboard with a wave of his hand. As a result, weeping and crying families crowded onto the train, along with dripping water and mud, bags, bamboo baskets, shoulder poles and even cackling hens and barking dogs, and all at once the compartment nearly turned into a pastureland. The door was too narrow for so many people, so some crawled in through the windows. The compartment became a can of flesh. Some people transformed into excellent acrobats resting themselves on the backs of chairs and up on the racks, with their feet stepping onto other people's shoulders and occasionally even their heads. The sleeper cars, which the captain ordered open to these people, also suffered great chaos.

That dumb young woman Mo Xiaoting was sweating in no time, with her hair a complete mess. Right after helping an infant carrying a rooster to find his mom, and settling and seating down several old men, she rushed to get down several men high up on the baggage racks, in case the racks collapsed. Suddenly a wave of people bowled her over and she fell into Beck's arms, screaming.

Beck felt as if they were two meat pies squished together, and he also could feel the curves of a woman's body. He said sorry twice, and blushed a little.

She gave him an accusatory glare, "Don't you have hands? Why don't you help me?"

He took two thermoses and a rag from her.

She threw one arm around his neck in order not to fall over.

Beck had just hugged an obese woman peasant, and now he was being forced to kiss the attendant's eyebrows and forehead. The strange smell of her hair made him blush even more, so he tried to turn his body aside, and pushed backwards abruptly and violently with his butt, which was a dirty trick used in soccer games, as the people standing behind him began to moan.

"Don't push so hard!"

"Save me!"

"My bucket!"

"Watch where you put your dirty paws!"

Amidst the disorder, Beck pushed with his hips again and again, until those people falling like dominos cried out one after another, the last domino being a stout man who was pushed off the back of a seat rather violently to fall on Beck's head. Thanks to this fall, a fight between Beck and another man was interrupted before it started. They could not fight now given the tight space, but they were already pointing their noses at each other, spluttering at each other, and there was fierce conflict between their shoulders and chests, though perhaps all they could do next would have been to bite off each other's noses.

"Quiet! Quiet, please! Let's sing a song together," the attendant shouted while waving her hands, "From the four lakes and the five seas, we all come together...Ready? Go!"

Eerily, almost all of them could sing the song. They began to sing together, "From the four lakes and the five seas, we all come together for a common revolutionary dream ..." It was so subtle that once the song commenced, their frustration decreased dramatically. People's movements became gentle and their bodies seemed to shrink. "Every soldier deserves our care and we should care for and help each other ..."

The train was dashing forward through this song. The compartment appeared a little bigger. Maybe it was because some refugees had moved to the sleeper cars. Not until that moment did the attendant find the time to tidy up her clothes and hair and walk Beck back to the staff cubicle with a thermos and other stuff.

"Fight, huh? You don't know it's chaos in here? We're a Red Flag train. We work in the very frontlines and we try to make each passenger feel at home. Understand?"

"I was fighting to give you space."

"You didn't have to. It was special circumstances."

"If I didn't do that, you might think I was so close to you for a dirty reason."

"What are you talking about? You're disgusting."

"No, I..." He did not know what exactly to say.

"Ha-ha, you're blushing."

"I'm not."

"Yes, you are! You have a dirty mind."

"It was muggy in there."

She nodded with jauntiness, as if she had uncovered a big secret, approaching each of her ensuing movements like a cheerful dancer. Very happily she wiped the mud off Beck's head and shoulders, so happily that she ordered him to sit straight, turn around and stretch his hands out, and very happily she was binding a streak of blood, appearing from nowhere, on his wrist with her own handkerchief. Beck felt a little nervous. The room was too small. He could feel her legs pressing against his knees and her hair brushing over his face. He could not help breathing rapidly and sweating all over.

Not until someone outside called her did she go out with a bucket. The door was locked with a click.

Beck, afterwards, only recalled the click of the door. That was all she left behind her.

No matter how hard Beck later tried to recall, all he could remember was the click. There was not even a word or a cough. Should this offer him a reason to feel relieved?

The storm was still raging. The rain was still slashing the windows, and the dark forests were still coming and fading away. The train chugged swiftly ahead. It slipped into another tunnel, producing a series of echoes at that moment, and the next it jumped up onto a bridge exposed to the wilds. Beck felt the mysterious page forty-three approaching. Should he believe that ending? How could he avert it? Should he reveal this to the attendant?

The locomotive emitted two squeals, and the whole train jolted violently again as it sharply slowed down. Maybe it was a curve or a ramp, or maybe they had encountered something dangerous. He grew alert all at once, looked out and without thinking pulled up the squeaking window. Right before jumping out, he pulled a pair of pants out of his bag and tightly bound them around his waist with timely courage and resolve.

He stuck his legs out first and felt his pants being blown about by the strong wind, but since half his body was already out, there was no return. He summoned up his courage and jumped into the darkness.

When he came to, bright sunlight was almost killing his eyes. A while later, his eyes gradually got used to light, and he found himself lying in a field of cabbage, exposed to fresh and pastoral sunshine, with mud all over his body and bugs crawling over his face.

It was just an ordinary morning with chirping birds, green trees and a blue sky adorned with clouds. The world was so quiet. Was he still alive? He tried moving his limbs and blinking his eyes, then he spat out a mixture of spit and dust, and found all his limbs working well except for a sharply painful right knee and right ankle. Of course he also saw a motorcycle at the side of the field. A man came over and stared at him very curiously.

"Help me... Save me..."

The man looked up and down at him, searched the contents of his bag scattered around, and then showed him two fingers.

"Don't worry... When you take me to the hospital, I..."

The man shook his head and showed him two fingers once again.

Beck thought about it again, took off his muddy watch and threw it at the man.

The man wiped the watch clean and put it into his pocket, seemingly very satisfied. He turned around and walked to the motorcycle. Soon he appeared again with a tractor and two young men who carried Beck onto the vehicle with great effort. The most interesting fact to Beck was that the two young men were each holding a coke can. Right, there they were, those most familiar and exciting red and white cans which he had not seen for such a long time.

"What are you drinking?"

The two young men flashed a glance at each other and smiled.

"Don't get me wrong. I just want to know what you're drinking. No, no, I know what it is. I just want to know what you call it. No, no, no, I know what you call it. I just..."

Beck realized his speech sounded rather illogical, but he just wanted someone to confirm his findings and that he had escaped a nightmare. "Liquid medication." One young man then laughed and said, "Too bad. I like Pock Zeng's fermented corn."

What was Pock Zeng's fermented corn? Was that a beverage, too? Beck had no idea.

He was put into a hospital. His right ankle and two wounds healed a few days later. His cousin visited him, gave him a credit card, bought him fruit and canned meat, did his laundry, and gave his boss a lengthy call to talk about an extension on his leave. Luckily, in this place permeating with a slight hint of perfume, he could drink as much cola as he wanted, he was able to find his way to a TV set with the help of a crutch and watch a soccer game, and he could lead his alma mater's team to defeat any team in the English Premier League or the Italian Lega Serie A with at least an eight-goal difference in the videogame. The heavy rain outside threw him into a momentary confusion. Before his eyes he could still see the water slashing the window and the languishing autumn scenery he had seen everywhere — but how could life have changed so suddenly?

A nurse came with a bill and urged him to pay. Seeing the bill he almost fell off the bed, and wanted to escape through the window again. Oh dear! Sixty–five thousand! Are you kidding? What had all that money been spent on? He had no idea whether he was an in–patient or a hostage. No wonder the doctors were so kind to him, checking his blood pressure and heart rate, X–raying him and giving him those CDFI ultrasounds and CT–scans so frequently. They claimed they had done all that for his own good and those services were absolutely necessary. The blood–pressure checks alone cost him more than three thousand. Why would his blood pressure not rise?

His loud complaints about blood pressure caused a rumpus. Several men and women in white swarmed into the ward, but they did not get angry or impatient. Instead, they explained to him why his stay had cost so much money, trying to make him understand there is no reason to raise his blood pressure even further by complaining about it.

Luckily at that point some blood–pressure medication arrived. An old lady in white came over, seemingly a director. She frowned at the bill and made marks everywhere on it: "Give the non–resident guest a discount. This is free, a fifty percent discount on this, and this is discounted too." Then she gave the bill back to Beck. Seeing Beck was still not satisfied, she picked up her ballpoint pen again, while very thoughtfully saying, "Well, let's make some donations." She pointed to her subordinates, "This is on you. This is on you, and this is on me." She patted her own chest.

On being discounted again and again, sixty–five thousand became sixteen thousand. What could Beck say, since all the people in white around him had already put on tragic expressions? Besides, the old lady said he would not have to pay for all this if he was really broke. But how could a famous soccer star do such a thing?

He had no choice but to hand over his credit card and say, "Thanks."

But there was not much money remaining in the credit card, so he had to call his cousin to add more to the card. When his hand reached into his empty pockets, he recalled his cell phone. He thought back with regret for a while, and went to an internet bar to search for information about Zilong Gorge, but found nothing. He went to a news stall to check for any related news, yet nothing was to be found. During the process, for spitting on the ground, he was fined ten yuan according to the latest regulations and taught a lesson by a chengguan officer, which only added to his restlessness.

The missing cell phone still preoccupied his brain, so he took a taxi to the information desk of the railway station. A young woman in a uniform had a look at his ticket and asked, "What's this? I've never seen a ticket like this before..."

"I bought it six days ago at the railway station two stops away."

"Maybe it's fake."

"What? I got on the train with it," he exclaimed.

The young woman glanced at him before summoning over several colleagues. They checked the ticket over and over and whispered to each other. A gray-haired old worker said, "Sir, this was in use over twenty years ago. You know that, right? Money may be good, but we should make it in proper ways."

Of course, this man had heard about such things as cell phones and MP3 players, and was taking him to be a swindler.

"You mean that leap brought me to today from twenty years ago?"

"No, you have no such power, but anyone might have some illogical encounters. Did you ever read that news item? About a man who lost his memory after slipping at the door of his own house, and then could not even remember his own parents."

"How could that be possible?" Beck rolled up his trousers a little to show the white bandage on his leg. "You mean these wounds were inflicted twenty years ago? I was too young to jump off a train then. I was still suckling at mom's breast. Why would I dare to risk my life?"

Some sneered, a few shook their heads, and others winked at him. Perhaps his story was too outlandish. He also saw someone's gloating eyes as if they were saying, "You liar. There's no way you can fool us. You deserve it." For the moment the old man was the only kind and patient one. He put on his reading glasses and checked over the ticket very intensely for another while. Then he walked Beck to an office and made two calls. "Sorry," he said at last, having no choice but to return the ticket to Beck, "It did exist. There was such a train, which met with an accident over twenty years ago. Now I remember. It was terrible. In our division alone there were several coworkers who lost their lives."

"You're lying."

"I'm not. There's a monument in the Zilong Gorge, and I took part in the construction."

"What the hell are you talking about, you old dog?"

"Young man, why would you talk to me like this? I took the time to do you a favor."

"You guys are trying to fool me! Save your sweet talk. You know what? I've got evidence and witnesses, and I won't just call things off."

Beck rushed out of the railway station with his face twisted angrily.

He was determined to get to the bottom of the matter, and with this determination he took a taxi to Zilong Gorge. The driver was listening to a CD and the song sounded a little familiar. "From the four lakes and the five seas, we all come together for a common revolutionary dream. Every soldier deserves our care and we should care for and help each other..." Beck suddenly felt a bit paralyzed, and asked the driver about the song. "I don't know the name, but it's an old song." Just as another song was about to play, Beck asked the driver to replay the song on the repeat mode. Maybe finding his passenger a bit weird, the driver stared at him through the rearview mirror. "Sure you don't want to just listen to Jay Chou?" he asked.

The Zilong Gorge was not very far, and they arrived there quite quickly. After the tests of time, the monument had become too indistinguishable to find, and nobody knew where it was. Beck walked through a school, a cattle farm, a thick bamboo grove, climbed over a mountain, stepped over cowdung and through thorny grass, and finally found a badly damaged cement platform. In front of him appeared the monument covered with thick moss. Indeed, it had been built to commemorate a terrible accident. The carved characters covered with peeling red paint revealed that, one night twenty years ago, a train had hit a mud-rock slide here. To save passengers trapped in the compartments, the crew had refused to leave. Several of them had then been buried by a second landslide. Their names were carved on the monument: Chen XX, Zhang XX, Xi XX, Shan XX...Then on the monument Beck found the name:

Mo Xiaoting.

It was the name in the magazine, and also the name of that attendant.

Could there be such coincidences in this world? He rubbed his head, starting to feel very perplexed about all these things. He pinched the moss. It was wet and smooth, very real. He bent the branches. They were hard and crisp, also very real. Suddenly he heard great crying. It was a flock of crows flying out of the woods, bringing in its wake a gust of chilly wind.

He sat absentminded before the monument for some time, and felt helpless about the terrible carved characters. Then, he took two pieces of white gauze out of his pocket, tied them on the branches covering the monument, removed the moss on the monument with a wedge of stone, and placed some pine branches and wildflowers onto it, to let them keep guard and keep company.

Afterwards, he could only be sure that at that very moment his brain was a total blank.

Afterwards, no matter how hard he tried to recall, he had to admit that he could not even remember what the attendant looked like. It was really like a blank period from twenty years ago.

Nobody knew when he went back down the hill. It was a wordless journey, after which he had a great deal to drink, before staggering onto another train which faded away towards the horizon of this page. In this train there were air-conditioners, high-definition televisions and reclining sofas, which both assured and worried him. He bought a small bottle of Erguotou liquor, and stumbled dizzily from the front to the back of the locomotive as if he was looking for an acquaintance, and several times he asked to look at passengers' magazines to check the covers as if he was very interested. For quite a long time he kept gazing all around.

"I got to page forty-three." The girl sitting beside him closed her book and yawned, before she fell into her boyfriend's arms.

Beck screamed and almost jumped up in terror. Then he realized a cold sweat had been frightened out of him.

He merely shot a quick glance down at the open page, to discover it was a foreign fairytale with a colorful cover.

Thank the heavens, thank the earth!

The train was going faster and faster. Its wheels below were striking the rails and making irregular noises. The train at times slipped into darkness and endless tunnels, while at other times exposed itself on high and open bridges or brushed past trains dashing in the opposite direction. Our hero, who had already escaped out of the story, looked at the transparent windows whizzing by and the passengers be hind them — the multifarious passengers must have been quite untroubled and carefree. But in fact, the only things he could see were compartments compressed by speed, and windows thin as paper, other than which he could see nothing else clearly.

Postscript I

Something worth mentioning is that, while bending the pine branches, Beck had injured his hands. Crinkling his face on the manuscript page, he couldn't help turning around and screaming at me (this author), "Hey, you, what crap are you writing? The girl didn't die in the story. Why did you fabricate the monument and send me looking all over for it?"

"Really?" I turned the pages of what I had written.

"Of course. It was not on page forty-three. I remember it perfectly."

I sighed, "You're right. She didn't die in the story, but you know, fiction is not real life and it can't control life. Sometimes even a writer can do nothing for people like her."

"Even if she died, she died a martyr or in the line of duty. She should enjoy special treatment. But you make her death too ridiculous. Where is her younger brother? Where is her soldier boyfriend? Where are those stupid passengers? Why didn't they save her? Where the hell did they go? You better tell them not to come near me because I'd kick their asses if I ever catch them. And that brick kiln..." With an irritated expression on his face, he pointed to the brick kiln, along with the heavy smoke under the monument, the dense felt of forest around it and the deforestation in that area.

I smile down at the page, "It didn't hurt you so badly. You don't have to get this mad."

"Not so badly? I suffered so much in your story. I almost lost my life."

"You could've picked up fewer branches and flowers and you didn't need to retrace the steps. I had meant to say you..."

"You think I wanted to be here? There is a Lega Serie A game, AC Milan versus Florence. I'll miss it."

"But you came here, with white gauze. Why did you think of that?"

"Think of what? You made me."

"I told you. Sometimes a writer can't control the characters in his or her story."

"You mean it's my own fault?"

"Look at you. You're blushing again. In fact, I didn't say you'd done anything bad."

"Come on. You know what? I hate you most when you make me blush. That's the only stuff you guys are good at. Why didn't you write me into a love triangle? Why didn't write of my one-night stands? Write scenes about my dormientum spermatorrhea and masturbation? Come on, couldn't you have tried something new along more fun paths? You all think you're so smart?"

"I certainly didn't mean you..."

"Stop there, stop!" He gave me a signal to hush, saying, "You guys take yourselves too seriously. Flowers? And white gauze? Sickening, too sickening. Why not delete it all. If you're using a pencil, erase the words, and if you're using a computer, hit the DELETE key at the top right corner. You see where it is? Honestly, I tell you, I really don't want to come here to suffer so much."

"But I am still interested in how you've come, more emotional than in my imagination. I am curious about this."

"Don't talk like this to me. I'm not a cultured man. I'm an idiot. Okay?"

"In fact, you wanted more than your cell phone and MP3 player. I could tell."

"Oh my God! I'm leaving! Why are you so talkative? Looking for more royalties?"

"Okay. It'll be over soon. What you should know is that neither you nor I can decide on literature, since what decides it is the market or something invisible. Indeed, I know little about you and I really didn't want to make it so long, but Editor Wu of *New Times* asked me to write an eight-page-long story and create a gorgeous woman attendant to be your partner..."

He waved at me and limped away saying, "That's it, I can't do this. I'm starving. And you and your pig piss trains can go to hell!" He took a seat in the cab again and let the driver drive back down. That same night, he took a bottle of liquor onto another train, where he is sleeping now, without my permission.

Postscript II

On the same train, an old lady took off her black-rimmed glasses and sneered at me (this author), "You think this is the end of the matter? You've defamed our court more than once. Listen, our lawyer will be coming to negotiate with you." After these words, she angrily snapped, opened a newspaper and rested her eyes on the stocks and shares section.

(*Translated by Zhang Ruiqing*)

第四十三页

韩少功

小说写到这里，我发现主人公想家了，便让他上了一列火车。这一刻夜已深，天很冷，整个站台上人影零落，车站补水管在哗啦啦响着。

我的这位主人公外号阿贝——球友们夸他球场威猛，称他为小贝哥，小贝克汉姆，他也乐意以欧洲球星自居，包括走路时垂肩屈背，像个内敛的猩猩。他稍感奇怪的是，他刚才入座时不但内敛而且礼貌，但对面一个妇人睁大眼睛，张大嘴巴，显然受到了惊吓。身旁一个歪头昏睡的胖子，被火车启动声惊醒，一旦发现他也神色惊慌，急忙撅起肥圆屁股抢出坐椅上的旅行袋，转移到斜对面的卡座去了。不一刻，他的周围空荡荡，只有几个乘客在远处伸长脖子，对他浅一眼深一眼地打量。

他们看什么呢？

他刚想问，那些长脖子立刻沉没在椅背后面。

他的长头发有什么稀奇吗？他是不是身上有血迹，一看就像个杀人犯？

神经病啊。他脱下秋雨淋湿了的外衣，继续挂着线听MP3。但这一刻他倒是看出了车上的某种异样。中山装。他发现这里的男人大多穿中山装。辫子和辫子。他发现好几个女人的耳边都齐刷刷挂着短毛刷。都什么年月了，有人还套着肥囊囊的大筒裤，散发出红薯的气息。一个包着白头巾和怀揣毛主席著作的老村长该出现了吧？只是他眨眨眼，老村长不翼而飞，有点虚幻不实。

他觉出鼻子里不爽，有一种猪屎臭。大概是他脱口而出，正在扫地的女乘务白他一眼：“你才猪屎臭哩。”

“怎么这么冷啊？也不放点暖气？”

“怕冷就别出门，钻你老妈的被窝去。”

“你这是人话吗？”

他冒火了。

对方像没听见，用扫帚敲打他的脚，意思是要他挪脚，只差没把扫帚直接捅向他的耐克鞋，其动作之粗鲁气得他晕。

不过，她把一堆果皮纸屑扫走以后，给他拉上厚布窗帘，还摔来一条棉毯，意思是：冷就披上吧。

披上棉毯，身上暖和些了。球星没法跟小女子斗，只好随手抄捡起一本杂志消磨时光。这是一本《新时代》，破旧得卷了角，大概是哪位旅客扔下的。有意思的是，阿贝的目光一扎进去就拔不出来，女乘务取他的湿衣去锅炉间烘烤，车长来给一位旅客测体温，询问有哪位旅客掉了钱包，他都充耳不闻。

事情是这样，杂志上居然有个奇怪的故事：深夜，下雨，站台，火车，等等。车上有中山装和小短辫，然后一个新上车的年轻人感到鼻子不爽，然后女乘务用扫帚敲敲他的脚，差点把扫帚捅向他的耐克鞋……唯一的出入，是主人公不像阿贝：他不是江湖艺人，而是个球星，正在业余收购文物的归途。

他咬住指尖，忍不住大叫一声。

女乘务赶过来，揉着自己的胸口：“没看见好多人在睡觉？你叫什么？把我都吓着了。”

阿贝这才细看对方一眼。没错，她眼眸大黑大白地分明，就是杂志上写的那种。戴着两个布套袖，与杂志上写的也相同。至于她穿着刻板的制服但翻出了个小花领，挂着短辫但辫尾巴烫成卷毛，算是小说家遗漏了的细节。

吃错药了，我不是在做梦吧？他狠掐自己的胳膊。

“我看你是有点不正常。”对方盯住他的眼睛。

“你叫莫小婷？”

“你怎么知道？”

“这书上写的。”

“鬼才信。”

“不信？你今年是不是十九岁？是不是有个当兵的对象？……”

“你是派出所查户口的？”

“你自己看啊，就在这里，你看你看。”

对方懒得看杂志。她手提一个带布套的开水壶：“杯子呢，把杯子拿出来，等一下不要说我没送水。”

阿贝没有带杯子的习惯。“车上卖可乐吗？”

“你说什么？”

“可乐。可口可乐。”

“什么可可可？你结巴啊？”

“你连可、口、可、乐都不知道？”

“你到底有没有杯子？没有？我走啦。”

“慢点，你怎么不知道可口可乐？那么农夫山泉、娃哈哈、优酸乳、蓝带果啤……你也没听说过？”

“你说什么呢？”

“嘿，你山顶洞人，你兵马桶啊？”阿贝照例把“俑”说成“桶”。

“你才兵马桶呢。同志，这里是红旗车厢，请你嘴里干净点！”

阿贝忍不住笑，忍不住大笑。他站起来环顾四周，呼呼喘着粗气，终于掏出手机给朋友打电话：喂喂，你醒来，快醒来。宋虾子，你知道，知道我碰见什么怪事了吗？宋虾子，你听我说，我在火车上，这趟车啊居然一车土鳖，连可口可乐也没听说过。你说怪不怪？你来看看，他们还穿中山装，还开口叫同志，我骗你不是人……你在不在听？

估计宋虾子把他说的当酒话，不愿听下去，只是要他快回去上班，说老板已经为此拍过桌子了。

他合上手机，发现两个男人不知何时堵在他面前。一位是刚才那位车长，另一位是大个子乘警，都满脸警觉和严肃。小婷躲在车长身后怯怯地眨巴眼睛："……就是那个东西，你看你看，就是他手里那个什么……吓死我了。"

阿贝发现更多的人围过来，都盯着他的手机。他手机怎么了？他依稀想起了什么：对了，他刚才摸出手机时，女乘务像被咬了一口，扔下水壶大叫一声跑开去。

车长说："证件。"

"凭什么查我的证件？"

"你哪里来的？从国外来？"

"不不，我天外来客吧，来自冥王星或者海王星。"

"你手里拿的是什么？"

"手机啊。"

"手机？发报机吧？"

"我为什么要发报机？"

"那要问你自己。"

"我给美国发报是吧？我告诉中央情报局的怀特将军，这里连可口可乐也没有，这里还有猪屎气味……"阿贝差点要笑出声。

"装什么蒜？你就是冲着563号项目来的，以为我们不知道？"

他不知道车长说的563是什么，更不知道车长接下来说的"备战"、"路线"、"两打三反"、"革命委员会"是什么意思。他只知道情况有点不妙了，一切都不像是开玩笑，也根本不好玩。他的手机被一把夺走，背包也被拧过来检查。幸好那里没有毒品。一张坐公共汽车的IC卡，他们似乎不懂，将其一一传看，没看出个所以然。几本足球杂志，他们似乎也不懂，将其仔细查阅，还对着灯光找什么纸纹暗影，还是没找出所以然。比起几件酸臭衣服和一双拖鞋，MP3当然是最大疑点。无论阿贝如何辩解，如何解释音乐和芯片，但它还是连同手机一起成了扣押品，眼看着被乘警略加清点，装入一个公文包，就要离他而去。

"哎哎哎，你们是哪盘菜？有搜查证没有？你们土鳖啊？脑残啊？二啊？你们怎么连手机都没见过？"他愤怒地大喊。

他一把抓住车长，"我要到法院控告你们！要在媒体上给你们曝光……你们不要以为我好欺侮，我报社、电台里的哥们儿有的是！惹毛了我，叫你上午下岗，你不会等到下午的！"

大概是乘警嫌他猖狂，飞来一巴掌，打得他眼冒金花，有点飘飘然不知上下左右。等他抓稳了桌沿，校正了脑袋位置，找到了脸上热辣辣的痛感，他依稀听到车厢里发出一片口号声：打倒狗特务！打倒一切害人虫！打倒美帝国主义和反动派！……周围旅客都冲着他举起了森林般的手臂。

确实一点也不好玩。要不是女乘务拦着，一个老汉就要把雨伞抡到他头上，一个小孩还差点朝他吐痰。直到他被押走，人们还在气愤地议论：

"早就看出他不是什么好鸟。你看他那裤子像裤子吗？"

"当特务也穷成这样？怎么连理发钱都没有？"

"帝国主义是乱了种吧？怎么这家伙不男不女？"

"不是乱种，是耍流氓。男扮女装，就好钻女厕所。"

"对，肯定是这么回事。"

"应该把这个流氓塞到粪坑里去！"

"让我恶心死了！"

……

他被关入了一间窄小的乘务室。

他叫天天不应，叫地地不灵，完全成了个傻子。他怎么上了这么一趟奇怪的火车？怎么鬼使神差来到这里挨巴掌和蹲监房？更重要的是，他阿贝，小贝哥，贝克汉姆，什么事不好干，什么钱不能赚，怎么偏偏听宋虾子的瞎鼓动来收购什么文物？……他不知道眼下的麻烦如何了结，更不知道一旦行程再耽搁，自己还能不能保住公司里的饭碗。

窗外一片寂黑，偶有一辆对开的列车呼啸而过，咣当当差点撞在他的脸上。他看见了一闪而过的明亮车窗，甚至看清了车窗里的男女。他们多幸福啊，多温暖啊，多安全啊，说不定在那里喝啤酒、啃鸡腿。他们肯定有手机，知道手机是怎么回事，能轻而易举证明阿贝的无辜。但他们无动于衷见死不救，刷刷刷消失得太快，像一道闪电。

他打门和踢门，把一铝皮桶当足球踢了好几脚。

没人理他。

他有点累，只好坐下来揉揉脸，发呆。他看见天花板上，一只小老鼠从夹板缝里探出头来，一点也不怕人，欢乐地吱吱两声，支着小尾巴又缩了回去。

好在一本奇怪的《新时代》还插在衣袋里，可供他继续研究这列火车。

来的该来去的该去，
百年石头还是石头；
来的该来去的该去，
千年月亮还是月亮；
来的该来去的该去，
万年天空还是天空……

这是第42页上一位盲老人唱的，可车上并没有这样一位老头。这就是说，又有一处出入，可见小说并非预言——阿贝眼下很愿意相信这一点。但他宽心的时间不够长。随着后续情节在小说中展开，他读得禁不住两手发抖，全身发凉，一颗心再次提起来堵在喉头。没错，小说与他的遭遇确有出入，但小说中的老鼠是怎么回事呢（刚才他已经看见了）？暴雨是怎么回事呢（车窗外的水流已经拉出斜线）？打雷是怎么回事呢（车窗外已有闪光，刹那间黑夜如同白昼，千山万水突然涌现）？……而且差点令他晕过去的是：小说在第43页处说到子龙峡，叙说这列火车在那里与一片泥石流相遇，于是车轮出轨，车厢翻倒，电光迸溅，钢铁声大作，有两节车厢在挤压中升起来冲向高空，散落的车轮在草坡上飞跑……这也太恶毒了吧？

“喂，干了。”女乘务开门进来，把热乎乎的夹克扔给他，同时发现了他的惨白脸色，“你哪里不舒服吗？”

他喘着粗气：“前面，是不是经过子龙峡？”

“我什么也不告诉你。”

“你真以为我是特务？你看我像特务吗？有这样仪表堂堂的特务吗？”

“难说，反正要等保卫处的核查。”

“我们没时间啦！”

“你什么意思？”

“你说，你告诉我，前面是不是要经过一个叫子龙峡的地方？”

“就算……那又怎么样？”

“天啊，我们真要出事了，已经玩完了。”

“不懂你说什么。”

“你当然不懂。你懂个屁啊！”阿贝怒不可遏从椅子里弹起来，“你们连可口可乐都不知道，还革委会呢，一个个脑子里进水，浑身的潮气没晒干。我问你，就算我是个特务，我会当着你们的面来发报？我要千方百计来让你们发现我？”

对方看来被这句话触动，有点不好意思：“要是冤枉你了，我们给你赔不是。”

“赔？怎么赔？你看看我这半边脸。”

“大不了让你还我一巴掌，有什么了不起？”

“你受得了？好笑，你是想成扁的还是圆的？”

“你就那么毒啊？你就不能轻点打？就不能分几次打？再不，我叫我对象来顶替。他是特种兵，在部队里天天练挨打的。”

阿贝懒得对付特种兵，把《新时代》翻到第43页，要她自己去看去看去看。

对方看他一眼，又看杂志一眼，又看他一眼，疑疑惑惑把目光投向第43页。列车发生了剧烈晃动，灯光一暗一暗，当然干扰了阅读。对方有些字不认识，有时要问身旁的乘警，碰到大个子不认识的，还要回头来请教阿贝，更增加了阅读的周折。阿贝不耐烦这两个呆货，恨不能把从第38页到43页的字句一把抠出来，狠狠拍进他们的脑袋。但还没来得及这样做，一大群乘客突然登车了，顿时挤得车厢里秩序大乱。阿贝事后才知道，呆货们在手忙脚乱中还丢失了杂志——他知道这事时，真是欲哭无泪。

事情来得有点突然：当时列车驶过一座桥，司机借着车灯的光柱，发现前面路基上有很多人摇手拦车，后来才知道那是一批从洪水中逃出来的灾民。他们担心路基不够高，央求铁路工人兄弟带走他们，以防更大的洪峰到来。车长当即同意这一请求，大手一挥说全都免票。于是又哭又闹携家带口的灾民们一拥而上，带来了行包、竹筐、水滴、泥浆、扁担甚至鸡鸣狗吠，使车内顿时充满田园气息。很多人没法挤进门，只好从窗口爬。所有车厢内都挤成了人肉罐头，椅背上或行李架上都有杂技高手，脚丫子不时踩到他人的肩膀或脑袋。卧铺车厢也不能幸免，在车长命令下一律开放，装了人再说。

莫小婷那呆子顷刻间已忙得满头冒汗和头发散乱，刚让一个抱着大公鸡的娃娃找到妈了，刚把几个老人扶稳了和坐下了，又得驱赶攀高的几个汉子，以防他们压垮行李架。一声尖叫，她被新的人浪推过来，倒在阿贝的怀里。

阿贝觉得两张肉饼要搓揉成一块。他感到了女人身体的凸凹，有些脸红，忙说了声对不起对不起。

她瞪了一眼。“你没手啊？还不帮帮我？”

他从对方手里接过了两个热水瓶和一块抹布。

这样，对方就腾出一只手，攀住他的脖子，不至于倒下去。

阿贝刚拥抱了一个肥胖农妇，眼下又被迫吻了女乘务的眉毛和前额，嗅到了陌生的头发气味，脸更红了，只好让身体尽量偏转，又拿出球场上的阴招，屁股使劲一撅，撅出身后“哎哟”的叫声。

挤死人啦！救命啊！我的桶子！你的爪子往哪里伸？……各种狂呼乱叫中，阿贝的腰部发力连环传递，一个人叫了，另一个人跟着叫，又一个人再跟着叫，多米诺骨牌一样，最后导致一个坐在椅背上的汉子大摇双臂，仰面倒了下来，正好盖在阿贝的头上。幸好这一盖，阿贝与另一男人的架才没打成。当时他们不便施展拳脚，但鼻尖对鼻尖，唾沫星子互射，肩膀和胸脯已开始过招，接下来就可能要动用嘴巴了，看如何一举咬下对方的部件。

“不要闹！大家安静！我们来唱一首歌吧——”女乘务摇着双手大喊，“我们都是来自五湖四海——预备——起！”

说也奇怪，这首歌大家都会唱，也真唱起来了：“我们都是来自五湖四海，为了一个共同的革命目标走到一起来了……”奇妙的是，一唱这歌就泄了不少火气，很多人的动作开始变得柔和，体积似乎也悄悄收缩。“我们的干部要关心每一个战士，一切革命队伍的人都要互相关心，互相爱护，互相帮助……”

列车在歌声中开动。车厢里更松动一些，大概是一些灾民匀到了卧铺车厢。女乘务这才得以整理自己的衣服和头发，提着热水瓶什么的，把阿贝押回乘务室。

“你打什么架？还嫌车厢里不乱？我们是红旗车组，战斗在最前线的车组，要让每一个旅客都感到温暖如家。你知不知道？”

“我不打，就没法让你。”

“谁要你让？特殊情况嘛。”

“你会以为我故意挤你，耍流氓。”

“你想什么呢？讨不讨厌？”

“我没想……”他说得有些含糊。

“哈哈，你脸红了？”

“我没脸红。”

“就是红了！就是红了！你就是乱想了！”

“那是我热得……”

对方像发现了大秘密，下巴一点一点，有点兴高采烈和得意洋洋。接下来，她的动作也就有了欢快舞蹈的味道。她欣欣然用毛巾擦去阿贝头上和肩上的泥巴，欣欣然又要对方坐正，要对方转身，要对方伸出手来，用自己的手帕包扎手腕上一道血痕——不知阿贝刚才在哪里剐伤的。阿贝倒有些紧张。这间房实在太小啦，他感到对方的腿抵住他的膝，对方的发丝擦过他的脸，自己难免呼吸急促，全身开始冒汗。

直到门外有人叫她，她才提着水桶离去，“咔嗒”一声锁了门。

事后阿贝想起来，当时确实只有“咔嗒”一声。

事后阿贝无论怎样回忆也只得承认，当时只有“咔嗒”一声，连半句话都没有，连咳嗽之类也没有。

他是否应该大松一口气？

风雨还未停歇，车窗上还有斜斜的水流，黑森森的树影在车窗外起伏。列车一下钻入车轮声紧密的隧洞，一下又飘上车轮声柔远而稀薄的桥梁，正头也不回地向前狂奔。阿贝感到前方神秘莫测的第43页正在步步逼近——他相不相信那个结局？他怎样才能摆脱那个结局？或者他是否应该让女乘务也知道那个结局？

车头尖叫了两声，车身再一次剧烈晃动，然后明显放慢速度，大概是进入了弯道或坡道，再不就是又遇到什么险情。他神色一振，全身通了电一般，立刻朝车窗外看了看，几乎想也没怎么想就拉起了吱吱嘎嘎的车窗。在出窗前的那一刻，他扯出背包里的一条裤子，束紧了自己的腰，束出了及时的勇敢和果断。

他把两条腿从窗口先放出去，感到各种布片被疾风鼓荡，但既然半个身子已豁出去了，就是箭已离弦，他一咬牙，终于跃入黑暗。

醒来的时候，他觉得光线太刺眼。又过了好一阵，待瞳孔渐渐适应光明，才发现自己躺在一片白菜地里，完全暴露在清鲜的乡村阳光下，全身都是泥，小虫子在脸上爬。

这不过是一个普通的早晨。有鸟叫，有绿树，有浮云中露出的蓝天。世界太安静了。他还活着吗？他试着挪挪脚，伸伸手，眨眨眼皮，吐一口带着泥沙的唾沫，发现除了右膝和右踝剧痛，其他部件还能听使唤。他当然还发现地边有一辆摩托车，一个男人走过来，好奇地看着他。

"帮帮我……救救我……"

对方上下打量他，把他散落在地边的背包翻了翻，向他伸出两个指头。

"我不会……亏待你……等到了医院……"

对方摇摇头，再一次伸出两个指头。

阿贝想了想，只好把泥糊糊的手表摘下，扔了过去。

对方擦擦手表，把它放入口袋，似乎满意了，起身走向摩托车。不一会儿，他不知从哪里带来一辆农用汽车和两个青年，把哼哼哟哟的阿贝抬上车去。有意思的是，在汽车开动之际，阿贝发现身边两个青年都手握一罐可乐。不错，确实是那种眼熟的红白两色易拉罐，他感到无限亲切和无比激动的久违之物。

"你们……喝什么？"

两后生看看他，对视一眼，笑了笑。

"我不是要喝，我只是想知道你们喝什么。不不，其实我也知道这是什么，只是想知道你们怎么叫。不不不，我其实也知道你们的叫法，我只是……”

阿贝自觉说得太乱，但他就是想让旁人确证一下他的发现，确证一下他逃出噩梦的真实性。“中药水！”一个青年大笑以后又补充，“喝中药水，呸呸，还是曾麻子的包谷烧味道足些。”

什么是曾麻子的包谷烧？也是一种饮料吧？阿贝不明白。

他住进了医院。几天下来，右踝骨节已经复位，两处创伤也已愈合。大表姐已经来过这个县城医院了，给了他一张信用卡，买了水果和肉罐头，洗净了全部衣物，还就续假事宜同他的公司老板打了长长的电话。还好，在这个有香水味隐隐弥漫的地方，他可以大喝特喝可口可乐了，还可以扶着拐杖找电视看足球，去网吧找到足球游戏软件，让自己带领母校代表队把英超、意甲等各大牛队统统狂胜一轮，每一场至少赢下八粒球。他看着窗外的大雨曾略有一刻的恍惚。奇怪，不还是这玻璃窗上的水流吗？不还是这一片到哪里都差不多的萧瑟秋景吗？这生活怎么说变就变了？

护士拿来账单要他去缴款。他一翻账单就差点滚下床，差一点要再次跳窗逃逸。亲爱的！六万五！没搞错吧？不开玩笑吧？什么钱啊？他不知道自己是进了病房还是被绑了票。难怪这些天医生对他笑容可掬，不厌其烦地来量血压、测心律、做X光、做彩超、做CT……口口声声这些绝不多余，完全是为了对他的身体高度负责。这下好，光量血压就量去了三千多，不是明摆着是要逼高他的血压？

他自觉血压升高的叫骂引起了骚乱。三四个白衣男女拥入病室，倒也不生气，倒也很耐心，只是向他详细讲解每种收费的依据，让他明白血压高无理。

降压药总算出现。一个穿白大褂的老太婆走来，有点领导模样的，对账单皱起了眉头，抽出圆珠笔在这里一勾在那里一划：“哎呀呀，对外地客人要优惠一点嘛。这笔免了，这笔减半，这笔也打折……”然后将账单递给阿贝。见他还黑着一张脸嘟嘟哝哝，又再次善解人意地操起圆珠笔，“这样吧，大家都献点爱心。这笔归你出——”她指着一个部下；“这笔归你出——”她指着另一个部下；“这笔归我——”她拍拍自己的胸口。

六万五已一减再减，最后成了一万六，周围的白衣人士已有悲壮表情，阿贝还能说什么？况且老太婆最后还发话，称确实困难的话就不必缴啦——但这种没面子的事，一个“伟大”球星肯定做不出来。

他只能交出信用卡，还傻傻地说了声“谢谢”。

他卡里没多少钱了，得打电话求大表姐再往卡里打一点，往空空衣袋里一摸，才记起了自己的手机。他悲愤地想了想，去网吧上机搜索关于子龙峡的消息，发现毫无线索。又去附近的报摊，看报上是否有类似的报道，还是一无所获。让人心烦的是，一个大盖帽见他随地吐痰，按最新规定罚了他十块钱，把他好好数落了一番。

他觉得手机一事还是戳心，便雇一辆出租车直奔火车站，找到了问讯台。一位穿制服的小姑娘看了看他的车票：“这是什么票啊？我怎么从没见过？”

“我六天前买的，就在你们前两站买的。”

“假票吧？”

“我上了车啊！怎么可能有假？”他大叫起来。

小姑娘看了他一眼，叫来了几个同事，大家也把票看来看去，交头接耳。一个头发半白的老铁路最后对阿贝说：“先生，你这种票二十几年前才用，你不知道？年轻人，生财得有道，你不能乱来啊。”

对方显然听说了他的手机和MP3，把他当成了一个上门取闹的讹诈者。

“你的意思，我一跳就从二十多年前跳到了今天？”

“不能这么说，你没这么大的本事。不过人都有犯糊涂的时候。报上不是说了吗？有一个人，在自家门口摔了一跤，就摔得没记忆了，不认识爹妈了……”

“这怎么可能？”阿贝急急地拉起裤脚，亮出里面的白色纱布。“你的意思，我这些伤口是二十多年前留下的？二十多年前我才多大？敢跳车吗？我奶毛还没脱，牙齿还没长齐，敢拿自己的命开玩笑？”

有人冷笑，有人摇头，有人对他挤眉弄眼，大概听完他的故事，都以为他病得不轻。还有些目光明显透出快意：骗谁呢？黑吃黑，这下活该了吧？只有老铁路还算厚道和耐心，戴上老花镜将车票再细看片刻，引他来到一间办公室，打出了两个电话。“对不起，”他最后无奈地退还车票，“找是找到了。二十多年前是有过这趟车，是有过这么一场车祸。我也想起来了，那次伤亡不小，光我们局就有五六位员工……光荣了。”

“你骗人！”

“我怎么骗人？子龙峡那里还有块纪念碑，我都参与过建设的。”

“你这家伙胡说八道！”

“年轻人，你怎么出口伤人呢？我好心帮你查查……”

“你们休想串通一气！你们休想花言巧语！告诉你，我手上有证据，还有人可以作旁证，我同你们——没完！”

阿贝歪着一张脸冲出了车站。

他决心追查到底，一不做二不休，带上出租车再奔子龙峡。司机正好在播放一盘音乐磁带，听起来有点耳熟。“我们都是来自五湖四海，为了一个共同的革命目标走到一起来了。我们的干部要关心每一个战士，一切革命队伍的人都要互相关心……”阿贝一怔，问这是什么歌。司机说不知道，反正是老歌。当这一曲要转到下一曲时，阿贝请司机将前面的再放一遍，就这么锁定放下去。司机从后视镜看了他两眼，似乎觉得这个人有点怪。“你不要听周杰伦？”他问了一句。

子龙峡不算远，汽车很快到了。只是时过境迁，纪念碑似有似无，很多人对阿贝的问话都只是摇头。这样，这位阿贝颇费周折，先找到一个学校，再找到一个牛场，最后才一拐一拐钻过竹林，爬上山坡，跨过牛粪，分开割脸割手的茅草，找到一块破损不堪的水泥平台。在他前面，一座爬满青苔的石碑果然出现了。这确实是对一场大事故的纪念。从那些红漆剥落的刻字可以看出，二十多年前的一个夜晚，某列车在此地遭遇泥石流。铁路员工们为了搜救车厢里被困旅客，坚持最后撤离现场，不料其中几位被新的泥石流无情吞没。他们的名字是陈某某、张某某、席某某、单某某……阿贝果然在碑面还找到了一个名字：

莫小婷。

就是杂志上出现过的那个名字，也是那位女乘务应答过的名字。

世界上不会有这样巧合的同名人吧？他拍拍自己的脑袋，开始有点怀疑这东东了。捏一捏青苔，发现它是潮的、滑的，应该说真实无欺。他折一折树枝，发现它是硬的、脆的，应该说也货真价实。一声大哭，原来是一声鸟叫，是树林里一大群黑鸦扑棱棱惊飞而去，似乎搅起一阵侵骨的寒风。

他呆呆地在碑前坐了一阵，面对着粗糙的刻字无可奈何。他终于从衣袋里掏出两条白纱布，系在石碑前的小树枝上；又操着石片刮去碑面的青苔，就近摘来一些松枝和野花，让它们守护和陪伴石碑。

事后他想起来，当时脑子里什么也没有。

事后他无论怎样回忆也只得承认，他甚至已记不清那个女乘务的面容，如同真是一片二十多年前的空白。

他不知何时下了山，一路上不再说话，只是喝了不少酒，摇摇晃晃上了另一列火车，在稿纸上朝地平线那边飞逝而去。这列车上有暖气，有高清电视屏，还有可旋转的沙发座，显然让他十分放心，似乎又让他有所不安。他又要了一瓶小件的二锅头，飘飘然从车头游到车尾，像寻觅什么熟人，又几次求看乘客手上的杂志，检查杂志封面，似乎对封面很有兴趣。在很长的时间里，他还伸长脖子东张西望。

“我看到第43页了。”邻座一位姑娘合上手里的书，放出一个哈欠，倒在身边男朋友的怀里。

阿贝“哇”的一声差点跳起来，事后发现自己竟一身冷汗。

他瞥了一眼，发现那是本封皮花哨的外国童话。

谢天谢地。

车速越来越快了。钢铁车轮声时厚时薄时急时缓在脚下响着。列车一下钻入黑暗无边的隧洞，一下又晾在无依无靠的高桥，与迎面而来的列车擦肩而过。这位逃出小说的主人公看见了哗哗而过的明亮车窗，甚至看清了车窗里的男女——那些五光十色的人，想必是无忧无虑的人吧？但他只看到了一节节被速度压瘪了的车厢，看到了一沓薄如纸片的窗口，其实什么也没看清。

附记一

值得补记一笔的是，主人公阿贝摘松枝时划伤了手，在稿纸上五官收缩成一团，曾忍不住回头冲着我（即本文作者）大叫："你乱写些什么？小说里那傻丫头不是没死吗？怎么又冒出这块碑让我找找找？"

"是吗？"我赶紧翻前面的稿纸。

"怎么不是？第43页里可没有这一条，我记得很清楚。"

我叹了口气。"是的，她在小说里是没死，但你得知道，小说毕竟不是生活，更管不住生活。有时候，作者拿她这样的人也没办法。"

"就算死，那也是革命烈士，至少是因公殉职，是有待遇的。你把这里也写得太荒芜了吧？她不是有个弟弟吗？不是有个未婚夫的兵哥哥吗？不是还有他们救下来的那些王八蛋乘客吗？怎么也不来打理一下？他们死到哪里去了？你告诉他们，最好不要让我碰着，不然我见一个修理一个，打得他妈不认得他！还有那个砖窑——"他指着纪念碑下方的砖窑和浓烟，还有逼近纪念碑的林木砍伐，气出了怒发冲冠的模样。

我面对稿纸笑了笑，"也就是给树刺划一下，你如何这样窝火？"

"划一下？我在你这里挨打挨骂，只差没搭上一条命。"

"你本可以少摘些松枝和鲜花，也没必要修整台阶。我是说你刚才……"

"你以为我想来这里？今天有一场意甲赛，AC米兰对佛罗伦萨。亏大了我。”

“可是你还是来了，还带来了白纱布。你怎么想到这一点?”

“什么意思? 不都是你写的?”

“我刚说了，有时候作者并不能指挥笔下的人物。”

“这事赖上我了?”

“看看，你又脸红了，其实我没说你做错什么。”

“得了吧。告诉你，我最讨厌你写我脸红。你们这些家伙，也只有这点味精来吊胃口。你怎么没写我三角恋? 怎么没写我一夜情? 怎么没写我遗精和自慰? 拜托了，你们能不能玩点别的套路? 你们以为自己真那么聪明?”

“当然，我并不说你有什么别的心思……”

“打住，打住!”他朝我做了个叫停的手势，“你们这些人总把自己当根葱。包括刚才你那些摘花什么的，白纱布什么的，酸，太酸，删了吧。如果你现在用笔，就把那些涂掉。如果你现在用电脑，就用DELETE键，就在你键盘右上方。找到没有? 告诉你，我根本不想来这里大汗横流!”

“我感兴趣的是，你还是来了，比我想象的还激动。我对此有些奇怪。”

“不要同我说这些! 我没文化，我猪脑子。”

“其实你不光是想找回手机和MP3，我看出来了。”

“活祖宗，你还让不让我走? 你话痨呵? 骗稿费啊?”

“好吧，就快了，就快完了。你要知道，文学不是由你主宰，也不是由我主宰。也许是市场或者什么在暗中指挥我们。我承认对你的了解有限，本来也不想这么写而且写这么多，但《新时代》的吴编辑一定要我填满八个P的版面，还定要我添上一个漂亮的女乘务与你搭档……”

他摇摇手，一拐一拐地下坡，“不行不行，我饿了。你写的这些狗屁列车统统见鬼去吧!”

他重新钻进出租车，要司机开车下山。当天晚上，他甚至不经我的同意就拎着酒瓶上了另一列火车，就是他眼下正酣睡其中的那一列。

附记二

就在这同一列车上，一位老妇人摘下黑眼镜，对我（即本文作者）冷笑了一声。“你以为事情就这么完了？你已经不是第一次对本院的名誉造成损害了。告诉你，律师会来与你交涉的。”说完气呼呼打开一张报纸，目光落在股票版上。

FAN Xiaoqing is the current president of the Jiangsu Writers Association, and a member of the National Committee of the ChinaWriters Association National Committee. Her works, mainly fiction, were first published in the 1980s. Her major works include the novels *A Young Monk's Story, Urban Look, Female Colleague, Wan Quanhe, the Barefoot Doctor*, over two hundred novellas and short stories such as *Ruiyun, Our Poetic Struggle, A Story of the City and the Countryside*, and screenplays such as *The Fei Family's Girl and Cadre*. *A History of the City and the Countryside* won the National Excellent Short Story Award for the 4th Lu Xun Literary Prize (2004-6).

范小青，作家，现为江苏省作家协会主席，中国作协全委会委员。20世纪80年代起发表文学作品，以小说创作为主，代表作有《香火》《城市表情》《女同志》《赤脚医生万泉和》等，中短篇小说二百余篇，代表作有《瑞云》《我们的战斗生活象诗篇》《城乡简史》等，电视剧代表作有《费家有女》《干部》等。小说《城乡简史》获第四届鲁迅文学奖（2004—2006年）全国优秀短篇小说奖。

We're All on Call

FAN Xiaoqing

The cell phone's alarm began to chirp like a bird before the break of dawn, just as Gui Ping was about to fall asleep. He rolled over, sat up, turned off the annoying tone, and turned on his cell phone. After a few moments, the message indicator began to beep and beep, as always. Gui Ping thought there would be at least five or six messages, but in fact there were more, most having come in after he had pressed the power-off button yesterday, including one from five o'clock in the morning. That last one was no big deal; the caller was always an early bird and often got up before his family when the world outside was still empty. He had sent the message probably because he felt unbearably bored. Of all these messages, only one needed timely reply.

But before he had time to reply to any of them, Gui Ping found himself in the meeting room, setting his cell phone on vibrate mode. He did not realize there was so much business to deal with, like his messages, until the meeting ended at noon. Before attending another meeting in the afternoon, he had a reception to attend. Thanks to a snap lunch he managed to squeeze out twenty minutes for himself, slipping into his office and falling into the sofa for a nap, but unexpectedly two messages and three calls came in even during that short duration. After answering the last call, Gui Ping grew extremely listless. He suddenly realized he had only five minutes left, so he turned off the phone and forced his eyes to close, but his eyelids refused to kiss each other, blinking constantly.

Then he heard Li knocking at his door, "Director Gui! Why can't I get through to your phone? Are you there?"

Gui Ping sat up rather dejected, and said, "Yes. I know there's a meeting scheduled for me."

He picked his cell phone up from the desk, but felt a wave of exasperation rise, forcing him to throw the device back down. But he flung it a little too hard, and the phone slid over the desk and fell onto the floor. Until he picked it up, Gui Ping had not remembered turning it off. He opened it immediately and felt relief that it was intact. As he was walking out with the phone, it rang. It was an old friend. He was hoping Gui Ping could pull some strings with the education bureau for his child's educational prospects. This issue would be a hard nut to crack, because re-fusal would offend his friend, while agreement could cause trouble. Gui Ping was busy hunting for an appropriate reply, when Li knocked at the door and cried out a-gain: "Director Gui, Director Gui!"

Gui Ping became so irritable that he replied his friend rudely, "I've got a meeting to attend. I'll call you soon."

The friend asked uneasily, "How soon? When can I call you again?"

Gui Ping did hear him but pretended not to, and hung up. To vent his spleen, he turned the phone off again, though it was a difficult decision to make, then flung it onto the desk, and walked empty-handed into the meeting room.

Following him, Li asked in a voice full of curiosity, "Director Gui, where's your cell phone? Why was it off when I called you just now? Has it been stolen?"

"I wish," Gui Ping answered angrily.

"Recharging?"

"Save your breath."

Li stuck his tongue out and said no more, but could not help still peering at Gui Ping's hand which usually was playing with a cell phone. Now that the hand had suddenly turned up bare, Li felt quite strange.

Once during a rather confidential meeting allowing no cell phones inside, Gui Ping had left his cell phone at the office. For a full half-day he could never have felt more relaxed. From then on, Gui Ping kept it turned off from time to time whenever he got sick of it, pretending he was once again attending a confidential meeting. But his actions invited many complaints and criticisms from superiors as well as subordinates. His superiors queried, "Gui Ping, have you been going abroad again? Are you on a plane all the time? Why are you always power-off?" His subordinates whined, "Director Gui, you're always power-off, so we can't report to you. How can we continue with our work?" All in all, Gui Ping quickly surrendered. He could not pronounce the final verdict on his cell phone, and ultimately chose to keep it on.

Following Gui Ping into the meeting room, Li started talking again: "Director Gui, is your phone being recharged or did you forget to bring it? Need me to get it for you?" Gui Ping did not know whether to laugh or cry at these surprising words, but Li would not shut up until Gui Ping muttered, "No thanks. Just sit down."

Gui Ping did not have to play a leading role at the meeting, which was different from the morning's meeting, so he could concentrate on his own affairs. On such occasions in the past he would respond to text messages, whisper to callers "I'm in a meeting," or answer a call by sneaking out to the corridor.

He was, however, empty–handed today, so he sat quite relaxed and content in the meeting room, such that he could release a big sigh and feel so free that it was as if all things annoying about his cell phone had vanished.

Not long after this boring meeting began, Gui Ping observed that some of his colleagues around him were hiding their phones under the table, occasionally taking them out for a peek, while others put their phones directly on the table, allowing them occasional glances in order not to miss calls or messages, because vibration mode was not as noticeable as a ring tone. Whenever a message came in, some sentiment, happiness or anxiety would crawl up on the owner's face, then the movement of fingers would follow, and the devoted contact between fingers and phone.

At first Gui Ping bestowed sympathetic stares upon those cell–phone slaves who were under such a tight leash, but gradually he came to feel hints of disquiet growing from his hands to his heart. And then he turned from feeling relaxed to empty, from indifference to anxiety, until he became even rather distracted and uneasy. His mind had already been stolen by the cell phone.

This scenario was observed by a woman colleague sitting by him, who asked, "Director Gui, are you on your period?"

"No. Just menopausal," he replied.

They laughed together, which did not ease Gui Ping's discomfort. He wondered whether this was an important day, with potentially important calls or messages, whether he had anything important to do or had forgotten something, and moreover, could anything special and unexpected be waiting for him to act? The more he thought, the more issues jumped to mind, until he decided to slip out to the restroom. When he came out of the restroom, he stopped at the door, hesitating briefly. Finally he went directly to the office, instead of back to the meeting room.

Though his office did not appear any different, Gui Ping felt like a century had passed, and not until he spied the cell phone on his desk did he came back down to earth. Unconsciously he turned it on, and messages swarmed in one after another in quick succession, and then a call came in before he even had time to read one message. It was his wife. She cried out worriedly on the phone, "What's wrong? You weren't in your office and you were power-off. Are you in hiding?"

He had no answer, so he replied, "Recharging."

"Don't you have a reserve battery?" his wife inquired.

"Forgot to recharge it," Gui Ping answered.

"Oh? Pigs are flying! Everybody knows you're never power-off. How could you forget?"

Gui Ping curled his lips in self-disdain, and his wife began to chatter on about what she needed him to do. To halt her drawn-out monologue, Gui Ping made an affirmative promise. One more promise would anyway not kill him. Gui Ping always owed a lot of favors, and whenever he paid one back, a new one followed through, so he would never be able to pay them all off anyway.

Returning to the meeting room with his cell phone, Gui Ping began to scan the messages.

"Done recharging?" the same woman colleague asked.

"How do you know I was recharging?"

"You always have your cell phone with you, so you must have been recharging. It's inconceivable that you forgot to bring it."

"No, I left it in the office deliberately. It's been annoying me."

"Annoying? But you've brought it back. You can't be without it."

"You really think I dare not turn it off?"

"It's no big deal, but you're likely to turn it on soon enough."

They talked on until their increasingly loud voices even drew the attention of some superiors on the dais. Able to read and reply messages again, Gui Ping found his mental calm returning. He felt at ease once more.

But before he could finish replying, a call came in. Gui Ping took a look, only to see an unfamiliar number. Gui Ping set the phone down on the meeting's pile of paper to cushion the vibrating and left it there, and only after the vibrating stopped did he feel relief. Anyway, nobody could hear the vibrating in the meeting room. However, another wave of vibrations began before long, more durable and patient, and apparently needing an answer. Finally, when a third vibrating storm arrived Gui Ping had no choice but to answer. He lowered himself into his chair a little, covered the receiver, and whispered, "I'm in a meeting."

The caller responded in a deafening voice, "Ha ha! Gui Ping, I knew you'd answer my call. I was just thinking I'd have to turn to others if you refused to answer, when you came on. Ha ha!"

Her shrill voice tortured Gui Ping's ear, and was even heard by his woman colleague, who said, "Wow, a soprano!"

Though he had said he was in a meeting, the soprano started on her long story as if Gui Ping was always ready to listen, which forced him to sneak out again with the phone. In the corridor Gui Ping raised his voice to say, "I'm in a meeting. Superiors are present, and I'm not supposed to leave so frequently."

"What do you mean, frequently? You didn't answer until I called a third time, so you've left just once at most."

You selfish wretch, I wouldn't survive if I answered every call, he thought to himself, but dared not utter it out loud, knowing the soprano to be so unbearably talkative. "Get on with your business," he urged her. The soprano continued, and went on and on so much so that Gui Ping could no longer bear it and interrupted: "Enough. I'm in a meeting. I'll do it after the meeting is over."

On hearing his words the soprano was satisfied, and before hanging up, added, "Call me when you get it done." Gui Ping gave an affirmative.

Though she had hung up, Gui Ping felt full of regret, for if he had not insisted on answering her call, she could have been skipped. Why could he not have desisted from taking her third call? She was not on his contact list because he did not like the soprano, yet she had got hold of him by chance, which now forced him to do her this favor. Gui Ping was about to return with the phone to the meeting room, when Li sneaked out. Seeing Gui looking so remorseful, Li asked, "What happened, Director Gui?"

Gui Ping waved the phone to him and said, "It's so tedious." Li thought Gui Ping was about to throw the phone so he reached out for it but caught nothing.

"On or off, neither is viable..." Gui Ping sighed.

Li looked at him carefully, and then offered a suggestion, "Director Gui, there's another option."

Gui Ping threw a skeptical glare at him and asked, "Either on or off, how could there be another choice?"

Li smiled furtively, "A good clever move invented by some deadbeat."

"What's that?"

"Out of service range."

"How's that possible? We're not in a forest or a desert."

"You can still try it. Pull the card out of the phone when it rings, put the battery back and turn it on again, and you'll be out of range: 'Sorry! The subscriber you dialed cannot be reached at the moment, please try again later.'"

Gui Ping could not have been any happier, for he could now choose any moment to be "on call" or out of range.

The next day, one of Gui Ping's superiors caught hold of him and censured him severely: "I have numerous problems, but you've been avoiding me. Were you in a remote mountain village?"

"No, I wasn't in the hills, I was here at work."

"But why did calls to you say 'no service'?"

"I'm in range. I'm on call."

"What the devil? Is your cell phone an antique or something? Why do calls to you always say, 'no service'? If you're always going to be out of service, then just stay out forever."

Gui Ping grew fearful and never dared go out of service range from then on.

Of course Li could not divert Gui Ping's curses, but he still tried to seek solutions to Gui Ping's problem. He advised, "Director Gui, why don't you try this? You add all the phone numbers you could possibly receive onto your contact list, and then you know who's calling and can decide whether to answer it or not."

Li's advice was accepted again. At the next meeting, Gui Ping took the time to add all the numbers he could get onto his contact list: important ones, unimportant ones, ones not worth answering, and undesirables. When he had almost done it, the meeting was called to an end. The phone rang just as he was walking out. Seeing it was a number he did not need to answer, he put the phone into his pocket.

What Li had suggested was truly a good and practical method. He classed his contacts into several groups, so he could easily decide whether he should answer a call. If the incoming call was a strange number not on his contact list, he would skip it, for the caller was certainly not directly related to him.

He saved himself a lot of trouble over the ensuing days. Most people calling for his help knew him as a yes man, so they rang whenever they needed him. Now that he was not available, they turned to others for help. In the future he would avert blame by saying "Sorry, I didn't know it was you," or "I was in a meeting" saving a whole heap of trouble.

However, this period of leisure did not last long. One day right before a meeting, somebody patted him on the shoulder. It was the executive vice-director of the Organization Department, which gave him quite a start.

"Director Gui, how are you doing?" The vice-director said with a smile.

Gui Ping felt greatly flattered for one second, but in the next he grew suspicious, as the vice-director was not that familiar. So he probed deeper by saying, "Great, thank you so much."

"Well, I know you're busy, but you've ignored my calls, several times."

Gui Ping was astonished, and replied, his blood pressure rising rapidly, "Sorry, but... but sir, I don't remember you calling."

"It just means I'm not a VIP to you, so I've not made it on your contact list." Knowing Gui Ping was worried, he patted Gui Ping's shoulder again to make him relax, and said, "Calm down. It's not a promotion, or I wouldn't be calling you directly."

Gui Ping smiled, embarrassed.

"Don't worry. You didn't miss anything. I called for your help. An acquaintance of mine just started out at the Development and Reform Commission so I wondered whether you could help him. You're the director of the office, very powerful, and someone fresh would show promise if you could give him a leg up."

"Please, which department is he in?" Gui Ping asked.

"Forget it. He left days ago, so nothing more to do with you. That's so typical of young men, so let it be."

The vice-director walked into the meeting room, side by side with Gui Ping, talking to him, and this scene was witnessed by many. Later, somebody told Gui Ping, "You two are so close. Good for you."

Gui Ping felt much regret at having missed out on such a good opportunity, but how could he predict the vice–director would call him directly? To admit that he never answered strange numbers would also be quite wrong, and of course he had to rectify matters, so consequently he opened the directory listing the numbers of all government cadres, and added all those numbers onto his cell phone's contact list. Luckily the phone's memory was big enough to accommodate far more numbers.

Gui Ping felt great relief now, for on the one hand he had escaped many a needless hitch, and on the other hand he would not miss any opportunities. Though he did not receive any more calls from his superiors for quite a long while, he did not think it a waste of time, because he believed in adequate and timely preparation.

Days later, a university reunion was convened. For so many years some of the classmates had come and gone, and now only one solitary table was enough for those left in the city who could be present that day. Most took their cell phones out while sitting down, and put it in a noticeable place between the cups and plates. Gui Ping didn't. He hid his cell phone in his pants' hip pocket and set it to ring tone and vibrating mode, so that in the noisy ambience his butt would feel the vibration if the rings were not loud enough. This was really a sound act. Like him, several circumspect young women did not place their phones on the table, but they kept them close to their bodies or left their handbags open so that any ringing could be heard clearly, and they could enjoy the reunion, totally at peace.

This was an exciting day for everybody, and there was a common topic of open and secret university love affairs. Though sometimes leaving painful and even torturous memories, love affairs could turn sweet after the test of time. Both groups, participants and bystanders, were immersing themselves in the subtle sorrows and joys brought about by time.

Then they moved from the past to the present. Charlie is having an affair, John's wife is so beautiful, and who is Richard's mistress now, or who is whoever's whatever? Suddenly one pointed to another and said, "I saw you the other day. You were walking arm in arm with another woman instead of your wife, so I didn't say hello." They began to kick up a fuss to force him to tell the truth, but the defendant argued earnestly but inarticulately, trying to explain himself amidst swearing, even as he blushed. Seeing nobody believed him, he grew desperately angry and looked everywhere searching for evidence.

Finally he took out his phone and threw it on the table, saying, "Take out your phones."

In fact, most of their phones were already on the table.

Hearing his words, some moved their phones a little forward and some a little backward, but nobody knew what he was going to do.

He said, "A phone is a secret witness. If you have secrets, you'd be afraid to let others look at your phone. Are you? I'm not!"

Right after his speech, several people blanched and tried to take their phones back.

Someone said, "A phone is private, and of course we can't trade it just for others to look. Are you a peeping Tom or something?"

Yet there certainly were some who were calm and unperturbed, while others appeared just a little excited about the idea of swapping, and said, "That's a good one. Let's go for it."

Gui Ping did not mind, but he thought his classmate had gone too far, and said, "Nobody saves such messages. Why keep them? Show them off to a wife? To a husband?"

But that classmate was very serious, saying, "If it's true love, there'd be no deletions."

They all laughed, and said he must have experience.

Failing to convince so many people, he grew angrier. With a blush he squashed his phone into the hand of another and said, "You, take a look."

The group split into two. One group held their phones tightly, while the other group who did not mind, or were trying to save face, put their phones on the table. After that particular classmate closed his eyes and mixed the phones together, the others closed their eyes and picked one. Gui Ping got the phone of a female classmate. He glanced at her and saw her embarrassment before he opened her phone. He was taken aback and said, "Well, I don't read women's messages."

He returned it to her, and she all of a sudden became unfriendly: "Why not take a look? You're wasting your chance."

Gui Ping did not argue, but his tolerant attitude did not bring him any luck.

A most meddlesome guy had taken his phone, but after reading his messages, got very disappointed, saying, "Ha ha, you must have known we'd be swapping phones."

"Of course, otherwise why would I let you take it?" Gui Ping retorted.

The man did not want to give up, so he began to browse the contact list to check whether there were any suspicious numbers.

The browse turned out to be a surprise. He blushed with excitement and cried out, "Wow. Good for you, Gui Ping. You have your top boss' number!" Then he read the numbers on Gui Ping's contact list one by one.

Hearing such eminent names, they all exclaimed with their eyes wide open: "Wow! You're so sly. You never told us about your network."

"He keeps a low profile. You know that? It's in fashion now," somebody added.

Gui Ping knew it was a waste of breath to explain, so he tried to give it closure with a laugh.

But it did not end. The next day, a classmate came to his office with expensive gifts with the hope that Gui Ping would connect him with the vice-mayor in charge of cultural work. The man was preparing to capture the videogame market which in their city was the largest and of highest standards. So far he had obtained the approval of the cultural bureau, but the process could not be completed without the signature of the vice-mayor. He had earlier tried very hard to meet the vice-mayor, but his plan had not gone far. Now he put his entire hopes onto Gui Ping.

Realizing his cell phone had become a source of trouble, Gui Ping told him the truth, "In fact, I don't know the vice-mayor."

"How could you not know him? You have his number."

After Gui Ping told him the whole story, the classmate replied with a derisive laugh: "Gui Ping, you've become a better liar after finding your way into the government. So why didn't you add the number of the President?"

"I would if I knew it," Gui Ping joked, which only made the other man angrier.

"You're an official, and I'm a regular civilian. Seriously, after so many years this is the first time I've ever needed something from you. How could you do this to me?"

Gui Ping realized the classmate would not believe him no matter what he said, but he would not agree to his request. Ultimately, he put on a cold look and said, "It doesn't matter what you think of me. I just cannot do this."

The classmate sulked away angrily, but without taking back those gifts. Gui Ping wanted to call after him to take them, but deemed it rather inappropriate.

Gui Ping felt uncomfortable whenever he saw the gifts. He even put them in a corner, but they still lured his attention. He emptied out his locker in the office, put the gifts inside and closed it, finally achieving some tranquility. He had been getting along with his classmates, but now all those nice feelings were being destroyed just because he had added in some phone numbers. Thinking it over, he came up with the notion that it had not been right to add all his superiors' numbers. He picked up his phone to delete those numbers, but could not decide which ones should be deleted. All the numbers could not be removed, so he gave up.

Then he settled on his let-it-be plan and decided to compensate the classmate over the coming days. The classmate, though offended, had not lost hope. He came back again days later and parked himself on the sofa in Gui Ping's office, claiming, "I won't leave without a promise."

"This is my office. You should not be here," Gui Ping said.

"I'm comfortable."

"It's not comfortable for me."

"Why? Just consider me as something you put on the sofa and go ahead with your work. This is not a security agency, and I won't tell anyone about your work, and anyway, nobody would be interested in it." For a long period, the classmate nearly lived in the office.

But Gui Ping still could not make the call for him, for there was really no common ground between him and the vice-mayor. The mayor was not responsible for Gui Ping's department, and the only time Gui Ping ever saw him would be at meetings or local news conferences. That was the extent of the relationship between them, like two parallel lines. How could he turn to the mayor for help? Moreover, this was not even regarding his own affairs, but on a rather sensitive subject-the videogame market.

The classmate thus plunked himself on the sofa, just like that. Whenever someone came in to make a report or discuss some matter with Gui Ping, the classmate would turn around to show his indifference. But people coming would feel odd and constricted, even if Gui Ping did not, so they dared not say what they wanted, making things complicated. After several hours of this during that day, Gui Ping was too tired to stand anymore, so he said to his classmate, "You sit here. I will go to the restroom."

"You can't escape me," the classmate replied.

In fact, Gui Ping went out just to calm down, and work out some countermeasures, but the corridor was not a good place, so he retreated to the restroom. However, no good ideas came to him, despite a long stay in the restroom, so he summoned up his courage and went back to the office. But to his surprise, when he got to the office his classmate was already waiting at the door, very excited.

"Why are you smiling?" Gui Ping asked.

"You know what? I called the mayor on your phone and he told me he would get back to me."

"How... how could you?" Gui Ping jumped, asking anxiously, "What? What did you say?"

"I didn't say anything inappropriate and things went well."

"What did you say to the mayor?"

"Of course, I didn't say it was I. I said it was you."

Gui Ping still did not get it, and asked, "What do you mean? It was you?"

"I told him, 'Mr. Mayor, I'm Gui Ping from the Development and Reform Commission.'"

"But the mayor doesn't know me! What did he say?" Gui Ping cried out loudly.

"You're lying. He knows you quite well, and said, 'Oh, yes. Gui Ping.' And then I told him I had a relative who wanted to report on something big to him, face to face."

"Why did you lie? You're not a relative."

"Classmate, relative, no big difference. Don't fuss over it. You feel ashamed at having a relative like me?"

Gui Ping was tongue-tied.

The classmate continued, excited, "And the mayor said his secretary would schedule the appointment and give me, no, give you, a reply."

Before he even finished the account, a call came in, and it was the secretary of the mayor. On the other end of the wire, the voice said, "Director Gui? The mayor is available at four p.m. tomorrow, but only for half an hour. At five he has to go to a reception." Gui Ping felt quite desperate, but there was no pulling back. Anyway, he could not tell the secretary it was not he who had made the call. While he was answering this call, the classmate kept winking as if to remind him not to screw it up. Gui Ping threw an accusatory glance, but still he had no control over the whole affair, so he promised the secretary to come to the mayor's office for a thirty-minute talk.

Gui Ping hung up. The classmate could not have been more excited, while Gui Ping felt very confused, saying, "How come? How come?"

The classmate was not angry anymore, and said, "That's it. You come with me tomorrow. And don't worry, I'll bring some gifts."

"You're being ridiculous," Gui Ping said with anger.

After he left, Gui Ping summoned Li and asked, "Do I know the vice-mayor?"

Li was confused, "What do you mean, Director Gui?"

"I don't remember ever dealing with him. He only became vice-mayor recently."

Li replied in the affirmative: "Yes. He was elected at the People's Congress early this year. It's only been two or three months."

"And, we're not under his direct administration. Sometimes he sits on the rostrum while I sit in the audience, but there is no direct link."

"You're right. I sit in the audience sometimes too, but nobody on the rostrum knows me." Seeing Gui Ping's disconsolate expression, Li played the role of problem solver again: "Director Gui, is it possible that you had contacted him before he became vice-mayor, but you forgot because it was long ago, while he didn't?"

"Where did he work before?"

"Let me see," Li said, before coming up with an answer a minute later, "Bureau of Aquatic Products. He was a technician there and a member of the democratic parties, so he met the government's requirement for a mayoral role and was chosen. They say he once said he'd never ever dreamed of becoming a mayor."

"Bureau of Aquatic Products? It's impossible that I ever knew him, for I had no connection with that division."

After thinking for another while, Li said, "There might be another possibility. Maybe he has a muddled brain so he mistook you for another person."

"He can't be that stupid."

"Maybe too many people contact him, so he thinks he's familiar with all callers. Who'd dare call him if the caller didn't know him?" Li was giving him quite a few answers, but Gui Ping's confusion persisted.

Right after Li left, Gui Ping picked up his phone and saw the number of the mayor's secretary who had just called. It was probably the number of the secretary's office, which reminded him that he did not even know the secretary's surname, and all he knew was that the secretary had not worked for long for the mayor. Gui Ping rushed to nose around and finally found out the surname of the secretary. By picking up the phone and moving his fingers a little, he called the secretary back.

In no time the secretary answered the call, "Who's speaking, please?"

"It's Gui Ping, director of the Coordination Division of the Development and Reform Commission. Just now you ... you ..."

"Yes, Director Gui," the secretary remembered him, "The mayor arranged a meeting with you at four tomorrow afternoon. Any problem?"

Having no idea how to answer, Gui Ping hemmed and hawed. Only after a long while did he open his mouth: "Are you available tonight?"

The secretary overreacted at once, saying, "No, thank you so much." In fact, Gui Ping had just wanted to explain, while the secretary thought Gui Ping was trying to offer a bribe, so he was declining, "Director, you don't have to be this way. I know you're close to the mayor. Since the mayor gave his order, we'll go all out to do it for you."

Gui Ping asked tentatively, "How do you know that?"

"He never answers a call in person. I deal with all incoming calls for him. Usually I answer a call first and then ask him whether he would like to take it. But today he skipped me just to answer your call. Doesn't that mean something?" Gui Ping was tongue-tied in response, and gave up any attempt to explain.

Gui Ping went home from work, quite flustered and uncertain. His wife detected his abnormal manner, and asked what had happened. Gui Ping just could not explain, and sighed over and over again, stirring his wife's curiosity. Right at that moment, Gui Ping's phone rang. It was his classmate. He was so irritated that he refused to take the call, letting the phone ring on and on.

"Why don't you answer it?" his wife asked, "Is my being around inconvenient?"

"I just don't want to," Gui Ping answered impatiently.

Her curiosity burst, and she snatched the phone and screamed into it with a strange voice, "Who the hell are you? You're keeping a close eye on him!" But on hearing a man's voice at the other end, her curiosity vanished, as she left the phone to Gui Ping and walked away.

Left holding the phone, Gui Ping was still reluctant to answer it, but hearing the babbling voice, he answered it impatiently, "Stop!"

He was about to be ruder, when the classmate pushed back his words: "You don't need to see the mayor tomorrow." Gui Ping was first shocked and then pleased, but before he had time to say anything, the classmate added, "But tomorrow is not forever." He told Gui Ping that according to a new policy, videogame markets and shops had already been prohibited, and the related supervision had been withdrawn from the mayor's office by the provincial government.

After remaining speechless for a while, Gui Ping laughed bitterly, "It's funny. The mayor had already made a special arrangement. You want me to inform the mayor that we cannot see him tomorrow?"

The classmate laughed too, "You know so many municipal cadres, and of course you know some provincial ones too. The time is not right now, because everything is up in the air. I'll get more information. If there's hope, I'll need you to pull provincial strings."

This news almost killed Gui Ping. He said, "I'm changing my number."

"You really think that'll help?" the classmate laughed again.

The next day Gui Ping went to the mayor's office with a new excuse. Seeing him sitting there solemnly, Gui Ping grew very nervous. It was as if the mayor could read his mind, so he suddenly felt his new excuse would be too stupid to use. He was busy thinking how to bluff it out, when the mayor laughed, "Gui Ping? Director of the Development and Reform Commission? To be honest, I don't know you at all."

Gui Ping grew pale with fear, stuttering, "Why ... why ..."

"Well, it's a long story." The mayor looked at his watch and continued, "We have half an hour, anyway. Let me tell you everything. As you know, mayors' phones are controlled by their secretaries, so I never know anything about my phone calls, and my secretary arranges everything for me. He's my boss and I'm almost a prisoner. This is a tradition in government, and I can't change that." After a pause he added, "I used to be a technician, so I am not used to the new position. I endured and endured till yesterday, when I felt I couldn't endure anymore. I decided to take back control over my phone. Then your call came in, after my secretary had just given my power back to me. My secretary was around looking at me, so I let him work out a schedule. I just wanted him to know that I could do my work without him. That's all."

Gui Ping was speechless for a while. He thought the mayor was kidding but the mayor seemed very serious, consequently Gui Ping got a little tongue-tied. Luckily the mayor did not expect him to say anything. He sighed and waved at him, "Forget it. This will never happen again, and you'll never get in touch with me again, for I've returned my phone to my secretary. I've given up. Following your call, dozens of other phone calls came in yesterday afternoon. They were all requesting me to do favors for them. Goodness me! I give up." And after a slight pause he added, "Alas! Now I know work must be tough for a secretary, let alone a director like you."

"Yes, you're absolutely right. It's annoying," Giu Ping replied.

The mayor took a long look at him and said, "Oh, I have a question. I don't know you, but how could you call me directly?" Gui Ping told him the whole story, and the mayor chuckled, though Gui Ping could not tell whether he was happy or not.

Right after this false alarm Gui Ping changed his phone and revealed the new number to nobody but a few friends, relatives and work companions, which resulted in many problems for others and himself, and drew many complaints. Whatever happened, Gui Ping went all out to hold on. He was determined to remove all problems arising from the cell phone, to say goodbye to the past, to live his life, to take hold himself and escape the control of the cell phone.

At last the phone lay on the desk peacefully, but Gui Ping was not at peace, and felt butterflies fluttering in his stomach. The phone had stopped harassing him, but he began to harass the phone by picking it up every now and then in case of missing calls. No calls or messages came in, however. He wondered whether something was wrong with the ring tone on the new phone and set it to vibrating mode, but it still did not vibrate. He dialed the number of his office, and got through, and he dialed his new phone number with his office phone and also got through, but when there was still nothing after another while, he sent a message to his wife asking, "How are you?" The message flew out, and he soon saw his wife's reply, "What do you mean?" Judging from the message, she was very irritated.

Sure enough, her call soon followed, "What's wrong with you?"

"It's weird. No calls or messages have come in all day," Gui Ping replied.

"You're weird. You always complain about the huge number of calls and problems, but now you've grown anxious on your vacation." After saying this she hung up.

Gui Ping was aware there was no problem with his phone but he still felt uneasy, so he called a colleague asking, "Did you call me this morning?" The colleague said no.

He called a friend, asking, "Did you send me a message this morning?" No, the friend answered.

Accompanied by the deathly silence of his new phone, Gui Ping could not help but miss the old one. He dialed the old number with the new phone just to hear: "Sorry, the number you dialed is out of service."

He called Li over very anxiously, and questioned him, "You put my old number out of service?"

"Director Gui, you had me get you a new number."

"Yes, but I never said I don't need the old one anymore. It had been with me for so many years, like a friend, how could you drop it?"

"Stay cool, Director Gui. I didn't throw it away. I got you a suspension and retention service, five yuan every month, and you can hold on to the number and revive it again anytime."

After a short speechless moment, Gui Ping asked, "What made you think of this service for me?"

"Foresight. I predicted you would want it back."

Gui Ping wanted to ask how Li could tell he would want it back but forced the question back before it slipped out of his mouth, because it was very embarrassing that the young man could see through him. A little angry, he said with great resolve, "I don't need it anymore. Go ahead and cut it now!"

"Okay, okay, Director Gui. Let's save on the five yuan service fee," Li replied.

Things changed dramatically that afternoon. More and more calls and messages started coming in. Gui Ping was sure he had not told all these people about his new number, yet they were calling. "That's strange. How do you know my number?" Gui Ping asked them again and again. Some said, "Who do you think you are? Know your number? No big deal." And others said, "You're the strange one. Why shouldn't I have your number?" While a few touchy ones said angrily, "Why? Do you regret being in touch with me?"

The old life came back. Gui Ping's phone rang time and again from dawn until night, being the normal life he had gotten used to for such a long time now. And as always he kept complaining to others about the maddening phone, yet always kept it with him. But he was still a little curious, how did so many people know his new number?

It was only several days later that he learned Li had quietly and slyly put the old SIM card back in for him.

(*Translated by Zhang Ruiqing*)

我们都在服务区

范小青

天快亮时，桂平才朦朦胧胧要睡去了，结果手机设的闹钟却响了，喳喳喳地叫个不停，桂平翻身坐起来，和往常一样，先取消噪耳的铃声，再打开手机，又和往常一样，片刻之后，手机里的信息就接二连三地响了起来，桂平感觉至少有五六条，结果数了一下，还不止，有七条，都是昨晚他关机后发来的，还有一条竟是凌晨五点发的，也没什么了不起的大事，那个人天生醒得早，一个人起来，全家人还睡着，窗外、路上也没有什么人气人声，大概觉得寂寞了，就给他发个信，消解一下早起的孤独。这些来自半夜和凌晨的短信，只有一封是急等答复的，其他都没有什么太重要的事情，桂平也来不及一一回复了，赶紧就到会场，将手机放到振动上，开了一上午的会，会议结束时，才发现事情也像短信和未接来电一样，越开越多，密密麻麻。中午又是陪客，下午接着还有会。总算午饭抓得紧一点，饭后有二十分钟时间，赶紧躲进办公室，身体往沙发上一横，想闭一闭眼睛，放松一下，结果在这短短的时间里，手机上又来了两条短信和三次电话，桂平接了最后一个电话，心里厌烦透了，一看只剩五分钟了，“嘀”的一下关了手机，强迫自己闭上眼睛，可那眼皮却怎么也合不拢，突突突地跳跃着。就听到办公室的小李敲他的门了，桂主任，桂主任，你手机怎么不通？你在里边吗？桂平垂头丧气地坐起来，说，我在，我知道，要开会了。

他抓起桌上的手机，忽然气就不打一处来，又朝桌上扔回去，劲使大了一点，手机“嗖”地滑过桌面，“啪”地摔到地上，桂平一急，赶紧去捡起来，这才想起手机刚才被他关了，急忙又打开，检查一下，确定没有被摔坏，才放了心。抓着手机就要往外走，就在这片刻间，手机响了，一接，是一老熟人打来的，孩子入学要托他找教育局领导，这是为难的事情，推托吧，对方会不高兴，不推托吧，又给自己找麻烦，正不知怎么回答，小李又敲门喊，桂主任，桂主任！桂平心里毛躁得要命，对那老熟人没好气地说，我要开会，回头再说吧。老熟人在电话里急巴巴说，你开多长时间会？我什么时候再打你手机？桂平明明听见了，却假作没听见，挂断了电话，还不解气，重又下狠心关了机，将手机朝桌上一扔，空着手就开门出来，往会议室去。

小李跟在他后面，奇怪道，咦，桂主任，你的手机呢，我刚才打你手机，怎么关机了？不是被偷了吧？桂平气道，偷了才好。小李说，充电吧？桂平说，充个屁电。小李吐了一下舌头，没敢再多嘴，但是总忍不住要看桂平的手，因为那只手，永远是捏着手机的，现在忽然手里空空的了，连小李也不习惯了。

曾经有一次会议，保密级别比较高，不允许与会者带手机，桂平将手机留在办公室，只觉得那半天，心里好轻松，了无牵挂，自打开了这个会以后，桂平心烦的时候，也曾关过手机，就当自己又在开保密会议吧。结果立刻反馈来诸多的不满和批评，上级下级都有意见，上级说，桂平，你又出国啦，你老在坐飞机吗？怎么老是关机啊？下级说，桂主任，你老是关机，请示不到你，你还要不要我们做事啦？总之，很快桂平就败下阵来，他玩不过手机，还是老老实实恢复原样吧。

跟在桂平背后的小李进了会议室还在唠唠叨叨，说，桂主任，手机不是充电，是你忘了拿？我替你去拿来吧。桂平哭笑不得地说，小李，坐下来开会吧。小李这才住了嘴。

下午的会，和上午的会不一样，桂平不是主角，可以躲在下面开开小差，往常这时候，他定准是在回复短信或压低声音告诉来电者，我正在开会，再或者，如果是重要的非接不可的电话，就要蹑手蹑脚鬼鬼祟祟地溜出会场，到外面走廊上去说话。

但是今天他把手机扔了，两手空空一身轻松地坐到会场上，心里好痛快，好舒坦，忍不住仰天长舒一口气，好像把手机烦人的恶气都吐出来了，真有一种要飞起来的自由奔放的感受。

乏味的会议开始后不久，桂平就看到坐在前后左右的同事，有的将手机藏在桌肚子里，但又不停地取出来看看，也有的干脆搁在桌面上，但即使是搁在眼前的，也会时不时地拿起来瞄一眼，因为振动的感觉毕竟不如铃声那样让人警醒，怕疏忽了来电来信。但凡有信了，那人脸色就会为之一动，或者喜色，或者着急，或者平静，但无不立刻活动拇指，沉浸在与手机相交融的感受中。

一开始，桂平还是怀着同情的心情看着他们，看他们被手机掌控，逃脱不了，但是渐渐地，桂平有点坐不住了，先是手痒，接着心里也痒起来了，再渐渐地，轻松变成了空洞，潇洒变成了焦虑，甚至有点神魂不定、坐立不安起来，他的心思，被留在办公室的手机抓去了。

坐在他旁边的一个女同事，都感觉出他身上长了刺似的难受，说，桂主任，你今天来例假了？桂平说，不是例假，我更了。大家一笑，但仍然笑不掉桂平的不安。他先想了一想今天是什么日子，会不会有什么重要的电话或信息找他，会不会有什么重要的事情要他去做，有没有什么重要的工作忘记了，除了这些，还会不会有一些特殊的额外的事情会找到他，这么一路想下去，事情越想越多，越想越紧迫，椅子上长了钉似的，桂平终于坐不住了，溜出会场，上了一趟洗手间，出来后，站在洗手间门口还犹豫了一下，终究没有直接回会场，却回了办公室。

办公室一切如常，桂平却有一种恍若隔世的奇怪感觉，看到了桌上的手机，他才回到了现世，忍不住打开手机，片刻之后，短信来了，哗哗哗的，一条，两条，三条，还没来得及看，电话就进来了，是老婆打的，口气急切地说，你怎么啦，人又不在办公室，手机又关机，你想躲起来啊？桂平无法解释，只得说，充电。老婆说，你不是有两块电池吗？桂平说，前一块忘记充了。老婆"咦"了一声，说，太阳从西边出来了，你是出了名的"桂不关"，竟然会忘记充电？桂平自嘲地歪了歪嘴，老婆就开始说要他办的事情，桂平为了不听老婆啰嗦个没完，只得先应承了，反正虱多不痒债多不愁，桂平永远是拖了一身的人情债，还了一个又来一个，永远也还不清。

带着手机回到会场，桂平开始看信，回信，旁边的女同事说，充好电了？桂平说，你怎么知道我充电？女同事说，你是机不离手、手不离机的，刚才进来开会没拿手机，不是充电是什么？难道是忘了？谁会忘带手机你也不会忘呀。桂平说，不是忘了，我有意不带的，烦。女同事又笑了一下，说，烦，还是又拿来了，到底还是不能不用手机。桂平说，你真的以为我不敢关手机？女同事说，关手机又不是杀人，有什么敢不敢的，只怕你关了又要开噢。两人说话声音不知不觉大起来，发现主席台上有领导朝他们看了，才赶紧停止了说话。桂平安心看短信、回短信，一下子找回了精神寄托，心也不慌慌的了，屁股上也不长钉了。

该复的信还没复完，就有电话进来了，桂平看了看来电号码，不熟悉，反正手机是振动的，会场上听不到，桂平将手机搁在厚厚的会议材料上。减小振动幅度，便任由它振去，一直等到振动停止，桂平才松一口气，但紧接着第二次振动又来了，来得更长更有耐心，看起来是非接不可，桂平一直坚持到第三次，不得不接了，身子往下矬一矬，手捂着手机，压低声音说，我在开会。那边的声音却大得吓人，啊哈哈哈，桂平，我就知道你会接我电话的，其实我都想好了，你要是第三次再不接，我就找别人了，正这么想呢，你就接了，啊哈哈哈。不仅把桂平的耳朵震着了，连旁边的女同事都能听见，说，哎哟喂，女高音啊。虽然桂平说了在开会，可那女高音却不依不饶，旁若无“会”地开始说她要说的说来话长的话，桂平只得抓着手机再次出了会场，到走廊上才稍稍放开声音说，我在开会，不能老是跑出来，领导在台上盯着呢。女高音说，怎么老是跑出来呢？我打了你三次，你只接了一次，你最多只跑出来一次啊。桂平想，人都是只想自己的，每个人的电话我都得接一次，我还活不活了。但他只是想想，没有说，因为女高音的脾气他了解，她的一发不可收的作风他向来是甘拜下风的，赶紧说，你说吧你说吧。女高音终于开始说事，说了又说，说了又说，桂平忍不住打断说，我知道了，我现在在开会，走不掉，会一结束我就去帮你办。女高音这才甘心，准备挂电话了，最后又补一句，你办好了马上打我手机啊。桂平应声，这才算应付过去。心里却是后悔不迭，要是硬着心肠不接那第三次电话，这事情她不就找别人了吗，明明前两次都已经挺过去了，怎么偏偏第三次就挺不过去呢，这女高音是他比较烦的人，所以也没有储存她的号码，可偏偏又让她抓住了，既然抓住了，她所托的事情，也就不好意思不办。桂平又悔自己怎么就不能坚持到底，抓着手机欲再回到会场，正遇上小李也出来溜号，见桂主任一脸懊恼，关心道，桂主任，怎么啦？桂平将手机一举，说，烦死个人。小李以为他要扔手机，吓得赶紧伸出双手去捧，结果捧了个空。桂平说，关机吧，不行，开机吧，也不行，难死个人。小李察言观色地说，桂主任，其实也并非只有两条路，还有第三种可能性的。桂平白了他一眼，说，要么开，要么关，哪来的第三种可能性？小李诡秘一笑，说，那是人家逃债的人想出来的高招。桂平说，那是什么？小李说，不在服务区。桂平“嘁”了一声，说，怎么会不在服务区，我们又不是深山老林，又不是大沙漠，怎么会不在服务区？小李说，桂主任，你要不要试试，手机开着的时候把那卡芯直接取下来，再放上电板重新开机，那就是不在服务区。桂平照小李说的一试，果然说：“对不起，您拨的电话不在服务区，请稍后再拨。”桂平大喜，从此可以自由出入“服务区”了。

如此这般的第二天，桂平就被领导逮到当面臭骂一顿，说，我这里忙得要出人命，你躲哪里去了？在哪个山区偷闲？桂平慌忙说，我没去山区，我一直都在单位。领导说，人在单位手机怎么会不在服务区？桂平说，我在服务区，我在服务区。领导恼道，在你个鬼，你个什么烂手机，打进去都是不在服务区，既然你老不在服务区，你干脆就别服务了吧。桂平受了惊吓，赶紧恢复原状，不敢再离开服务区了。

小李当然也没逃了桂平的一顿臭骂，但小李挨了骂也仍然不屈不挠地为桂平分忧解难，又建议说，桂主任，你干脆别怕麻烦，把所有有关手机都储存下来，来电时一看就知道是谁，可接可不接，主动权就在你手里了。

桂平接受了小李的建议，专门挑了一个会议时间，坐在会场上，把必须接的、可接可不接的、完全可以不接的、实在不想接的电话一一储存进手机，储得差不多了，会议也散了，走出会场时，手机响了，一看，是一个可以不接的电话，干脆将手机往口袋里一塞，任它叫唤去。

桂平找到了一个切实可行的好办法，他已经把和他有关系的大多数人物都分成几个等次储存了，爱接不接，爱理不理，主动权终于掌握在他自己手里了，如果来电不是储存的姓名，而是陌生的号码，那肯定是与他没有什么直接关联的人，那就不去搭理它了。

如此这般过了一段日子，果然减少了许多麻烦，托他办事的人，大多和那女高音差不多，知道他好说话，大事小事都找他，现在既然找不上他，他们就另辟蹊径找别人的麻烦去了。即使以后见到了有所怪罪，最多嘴上说一句对不起，没听到手机响，或者正在开会不方便接，也就混过去了，真的省了不少心。

省心的日子并不长，有一天开会时，刚要入会场，有人拍他的肩，回头一看，吓了一跳，竟是组织部的常务副部长，笑眯眯地说，桂主任，忙啊？桂平起先心里一热，但随即心里就犯嘀咕，部长跟他的关系，并没有熟悉亲切到会打日常哈哈的地步，桂平赶紧反过来试探说，还好，还好，瞎忙，部长才忙呢。部长又笑，说，不管你是瞎忙还是白忙，反正知道你很忙，要不然，怎么连我的电话都不接呢？桂平吓了一大跳，心里怦怦的，都语无伦次了，说，部、部长，你打过我电话？部长道，打你办公室你不在，打你手机你不接，我就知道找不到你了。桂平更慌了，就露出了真话，说，部长，我不知道你给我打电话。部长仍然笑道，说明你的手机里没有储存我的电话，我不是你的重要关系哦。他知道桂平紧张，又拍拍他的肩，让他轻松些，说，你别慌，不是要提拔你哦，要提拔你，我不会直接给你打电话哦。桂平尴尬一笑。部长又说，所以你不要担心错过了什么，我本来只是想请你关照一个人而已，他在你改革委工作，想请你多关心一下，开个玩笑，办公室主任，你们都喜欢称大内总管嘛，是不是，年轻人刚进一个单位，有大内总管罩一罩，可不一样哦。桂平赶紧问，是谁？在哪个部门？部长说，现在也不用你关照了，他已经不在你们单位了，前两天调走了，放心，跟你没关系，现在的年轻人，跳槽是正常的事，不跳槽才怪呢，由他们去吧。说着话，部长就和桂平一起走进会场，很亲热的样子，会场上许多人看着，后来有人还跟桂平说，没想到你和部长那么近乎。

桂平却懊恼极了，送上门来的机会，被自己给关在了门外，可他怎么想得到部长会直接给自己打电话呢。现在看起来，他所严格执行的陌生号码一概不接的大政是错误的，大错特错了。知错就改，桂平把领导干部名册找出来，把有关领导的电话，只要是名册上有的，全部都输进手机，好在现在的手机内存很大，存再多号码它也不会爆炸。

现在桂平总算可以安心了，既能够避免许多无谓的麻烦，又不会错过任何不应该错过的机会，只不过，过了很长很长的时间，也没有等到一个领导打他的手机。桂平并不着急，也没觉得工夫白费了，他是有备无患，凡事预则立。

过了些日子，桂平大学同学聚会，在同一座城市的同班同学，许多年来，来了的，走了的，走了又来的，来了又走的，到现在，搜搜刮刮正好一桌人，这一天兴致好，全到了。坐下来的第一件事，大家都把手机从包里或者从口袋里掏出，搁在桌上，搁在眼睛看得见的地方，夹在一堆餐具酒杯中。桂平倒是没拿出来，但他的手机就放在裤子后袋里，而且是设置了铃声加振动，如果聚会热闹，说话声音大，听不到铃声，屁股可以感受到振动，几乎是万无一失的。也有一两个比较含蓄的女生并没有把手机拿出来搁在桌上，但是她们的包包都靠身体很近，包包的拉链都敞开着，可以让手机的声音不受阻挡地传递出来，这才可以安心地喝酒叙旧。

这一天大家谈得很兴奋，而且话题集中，把在校期间许多同学的公开的或秘密的恋情都谈出来了，有的爱情，在当时是一种痛苦，甚至痛得死去活来，时隔多年再谈，却已经变成一种享受，无论是当事人，或是旁观者，都在享受时间带来的淡淡的忧伤和幸福。

谈完了当年还没谈够，又开始说现在，现在的张三有外遇吧，现在的李四艳福不浅啊，谁是谁的小三啦，谁是谁的什么什么，怎么怎么，接着就有一个同学指着另一个同学，说那天我看到你了，你挽着一个女的在逛街，不是你老婆，所以我没敢喊你。大家哄起来，要叫他坦白，偏偏这个同学是个老实巴交不怎么会说话的人，急赤白脸赌咒发誓，但谁也不信，他急了，东看看，西看看，好像要找什么证据来证明，结果就见他把手机一掏，往桌上一拍，说，把你们手机都拿出来。大家的手机本来就搁在桌面上，有人就把手机往前推一推，也有人把手机往后挪一挪，但都不知他要干什么。这同学说，如果有事情，手机里肯定有秘密，你们敢不敢，大家互相交换手机看内容，如果有事情的，肯定不敢——我就敢！话一出口，立刻就有一两个人脸色煞白，急急忙忙要抓回手机，另一个人说，手机是个人的隐私，怎么可以交换着看，你有窥视欲啊？当然也有人不慌张，很坦然，甚至有人对这个点子很兴奋，很激动，说，看就看，看就看，大家摊开来看。桂平也是无所谓，但他觉得这同学老实得有点过分，说，哪个傻×会保留这样的信？带回去给老婆老公看？那同学偏又顶真，说，如果真有感情，信是舍不得马上删掉的。

大家又笑他，说他有体验，感受真切等等。这同学一张嘴实在说不过大家，恼了，涨红了脸硬把自己的手机塞到一个同学手里，你看，你看。

结果，同学中分成了两拨，一拨不愿意或不敢把自己的秘密让别人知道，不肯参加这个游戏，赶紧把手机紧紧抓在手心里，就怕别人来抢；另一拨是桂平他们几个，自觉不怕的，或者是硬着头皮撑面子的，都把手机放在桌上，由那同学闭上眼睛先弄混乱了，大家再闭上眼睛各摸一部。桂平摸到了一个女同学的手机，正想打开来看，眼睛朝那女同学一瞄，发现那女同学脸色很尴尬，桂平心一动，说，算了算了，女生的我不看。把手机还给了那女同学，女同学收回手机，嘴巴却又凶起来，说，你看好了，你不看白不看。桂平也没和她计较，但他自己运气就没那么好了，他的手机被一个最好事的男生拿到了，先翻看他的短信，失望了，说，哈，早有准备啊。桂平说，那当然，不然怎么肯拿出来让你看。那男生不甘心，又翻看他的储存电话，想看看有没有可疑人物。

真是不看不知道，一看吓一跳，那男生脸都涨红了，脱口说，哇，桂平，你厉害，连大老板的手机你都有？接着就将桂平手机里的储存名单给大家一一念了起来，这可全是有头有脸有来头的大人物啊，惊得一帮同学一个个朝着桂平瞪眼，说，嗬，好狡猾，这么厉害的背景，从来不告诉我们。也有的人说，这是低调，你们懂吗？低调，现在流行这个。桂平想解释也解释不清，只好一笑了之。

却不知他这一笑，是笑不了之的。第二天，就有一个同学找到他办公室去了，提了贵重的礼物，请桂平帮忙联系分管文化的副市长，他正在筹办一个全市最大也最规范的超霸电玩城，文化局那头已经攻下关来，但没有分管市长的签字，就办不成，他已经几经周折几次找过那副市长，都碰了钉子被弹回来了，现在就看桂平的力度了。

桂平知道自己的手机引鬼上门了，只得老老实实说，我其实并不认得该副市长。同学说，不可能，你手机里都有他的电话，怎么会不认识？桂平只得老实交代，从头道来。那同学听后，“哈”了一声，说，桂平，你当了官以后，越来越会编啊，你怎么不把胡锦涛、温家宝的电话也输进去？桂平开玩笑说，我知道的话一定输进去。那同学却恼了，说，桂平，凭良心说，这许多年，你在政府工作，我在社会上混，可我从来没找过你麻烦是不是？这是第一次，第一次求你你就这么对付我，你说得过去吗？桂平知道怎么说这同学也不会相信他了，但他也无论如何不可能去替他找那副市长的，只得冷下脸来，说，反正你怎么理解、怎么想都无所谓，这事情我不能做。同学一气之下，走了，礼物却没有带走，桂平想喊他回来拿，但又觉得那样做太过分，就没有喊。

那堆礼物一直搁在那里，桂平看到它们，心里就不爽，搬到墙角放着，眼睛还是忍不住拐了弯要去看，再把办公室的柜子清理一下，放进去，关上柜门，总算眼不见为净。本来他们同学间都很和睦融洽，现在美好的感觉都被手机里的一个错误的储存电话破坏了，左想右想，也觉得自己将认得不认得的领导都输入手机确实不妥，拿起手机想将这些电话删除，但右看左看，又不知道哪些是该删的哪些是不该删的，全部删了肯定也是不妥，最后还是下不了手。

原来以为得罪了同学，就横下一条心了，得罪就得罪了，以后有机会再弥补吧。哪知那同学虽然被得罪了，却不甘心，过了两天，又来了，换了一招，往桂平办公室的沙发上一坐，说，你不答应我，我就不走了。桂平说，我要办公的，你坐在这里不方便。同学说，我方便的。桂平说，我不方便呀。同学说，有什么不方便，你就当是自己在沙发上搁了一件东西就行，你办你的公，你又不是保密局、安全局，你的工作我听到了也不会传播出去的，即使传播出去别人也不感兴趣的。就这样死死地钉在桂平的办公室里。

即便如此，桂平还是不能打这个电话，因为他实在跟这位副市长没有任何交往，没有任何接触，这副市长并不分管他们这一块工作，即使开什么大会，副市长坐主席台，桂平也只能在台下朝台上远远地看一眼，主席台上有许多领导，这副市长只是其中一位，除此之外，就是在本地电视新闻里看他几眼，他和副市长，就这么一个台上台下屏里屏外的关系，怎么可能去找他帮忙办事呢，何况还不是他自己的事，何况还是办超霸电玩城这样的敏感事情。

同学就这样坐在他的沙发上，有人进来汇报工作，谈事情，他便侧过脸去，表示自己并不关心桂平的工作，就算桂平能够不当回事，别人也会觉得奇怪，觉得拘束，该直说的话就不好直说了，该简单处理的事情就变复杂了，半天班上下来，桂平心力交瘁，吃不消了，跟同学说，你先坐着，我上个厕所。同学说，你溜不掉的。

桂平只是想溜出去镇定一下，想一想对策，但又不能站在走廊上想，就去了一趟厕所，待了半天，没理出个头绪来，也不能老在厕所待着，只得再硬起头皮回办公室。哪曾想到，等他回到办公室，那同学已经喜笑颜开地站在门口迎候他了。桂平说，你笑什么？同学说，行了，我拿你的手机打过市长了，市长叫我等通知。桂平急得跳了起来，你、你、你怎么——同学说，我没怎么呀，挺顺利。桂平说，你跟市长怎么说的？同学说，我当然不说我是我，我当然说我是你啦。桂平竟然没听懂，说，什么意思，什么我是你？同学说，我说，市长啊，我是改革委的桂平啊。桂平急道，市长不认得我呀，市长怎么说？同学笑道，市长怎么不认得你，市长太认得你了，市长热情地说，啊，啊，是桂平啊。后来我就说，我有个亲戚，有重要工作想当面向您汇报。桂平说，你怎么瞎说，你是我的亲戚吗？同学说，同学和亲戚，也差不多嘛，干吗这么计较。我当你的亲戚，给你丢脸了吗？桂平被噎得不轻，顿住了。那同学眉飞色舞又说，市长说了，他让秘书安排一下时间，尽快给我，啊不，不是给我，是给你答复。话音未落，桂平的手机响了，竟然真是那位副市长的秘书打来的，说，改革委办公室桂主任吧？市长明天下午四点有时间，但最多只能谈半小时，五点市长有接待任务。桂平愣住了，但也知道没有回头路了，总不能告诉人家，刚才的电话不是他打的，是别人偷他的手机打的。同学怕他坏事，拼命朝他挤眉弄眼，桂平狠狠地瞪他，却拿整个事情无奈，赶紧答应了市长秘书，明天下午四点到市长办公室，谈半小时。

挂了电话，那同学大喜过望，桂平却百思不得其解，说，怎么可能？怎么可能？同学也不生气了，说，反正事情就是这样，你明天得陪我去，你放心，我不会空手的。桂平气得说，没见过你这样的。同学却高兴而去了。

同学走后，桂平把小李叫来，说，小李，我认得某副市长吗？小李被问得一头雾水，说，桂主任，什么意思？桂平说，我不记得我和他打过什么交道呀，他才当副市长不久呀。小李说是，年初人大开会时才上的，不过两三个月。桂平说，何况他又不分管我们这一块，最多有时候他坐在主席台上，我坐在台下，这是八竿子也打不着的呀。小李说，那倒是的，我也在台下看见领导坐在台上，但是哪个领导会知道台下的我呢。小李见桂平愁眉不展，又积极主动为主任分忧解难，说，桂主任，会不会从前他没当市长的时候，你们接触过，时间长了，你忘记了，但是市长记性好，没忘记？桂平说，他没当市长前，是在哪里工作的？小李说，我想想。想了一会儿，想起来了，说，是在水产局，他是专家，又是民主党派，正好政府换届时需要这样一个人，就选中了他，后来听说他还跟人开玩笑说，我做梦也没有想到我会当副市长哎。桂平说，水产局？那我更不可能认得了，我从来没有跟水产局打过交道。小李又想了想，说，要不然，就是另一种可能，市长不是记性好，而是记性不好，是个糊涂人，把你和别的什么人搞混了。以为你是那个人？桂平说，不可能糊涂到这样吧？小李说，也可能市长事情太多，他以为找他的人，打他手机的人，肯定是熟悉的，你想想，不熟悉不认得的人，怎么会贸然去打领导的手机呢？无论小李怎么分析，也不能让桂平解开心头之谜，等小李走了，桂平把手机拿起来看看，看到刚才市长秘书的来电号码，这是一个座机号码，估计是市长秘书的办公室电话，就忽然想到，自己连这位副市长的这位秘书姓什么也没搞清楚，只知道他是刚刚跟上市长不久的，桂平赶紧四处打听，最后才搞清了这位秘书姓什么，于是又拿起手机，手指一动，就把那秘书的电话拨了回去，那边接得也快，说，哪位？桂平说，我是改革委办公室的桂平，刚才、刚才——那秘书记性好，马上说，是桂主任啊，明天下午市长接见已经安排了，四点，还有什么问题吗？桂平支吾了一下，一时不知道该怎么说，停顿片刻后，才说，我想问一问，你今天晚上有没有时间——那秘书立刻有习惯性的过度反应，说，桂主任，不用客气。桂平想解释一下，但那秘书认定桂平是要给他请客送礼，又拒绝说，桂主任，你真的不必费心，我知道你跟市长关系不一般，市长吩咐的事，我们一定会用心办的。桂平赶紧试探说，你怎么知道我跟市长关系不一般？那秘书一笑，说，市长平时从来不接手机的，他的手机都是交给我处理的，一般都是我先接了，再请示市长接不接电话，但是今天你打来的电话，却是市长亲自接的，这还不能说明问题？桂平被问得哑口无言，只得作罢。

桂平下班回家，心里仍然慌慌的、虚虚的，老婆感觉出来了，问有什么事，桂平也说不出到底是个什么事，只能长叹几声，老婆心里就起疑，正在这时候，桂平的手机响了，桂平一看，正是那同学打来的，人都被他气疯了，哪里还肯接，就任它响去，它也就不屈不挠地响个不停。老婆说，怎么不接手机，是不是我在旁边不方便接？桂平没好气说，我就不接。老婆疑心大发，伸手一抓，冲着那一头怪声道，谁呀？盯这么紧干吗呀？一听是个男声，就没了兴致，把手机往桂平手里一塞，无趣地走开了。桂平捏着手机，虽然心里一千一万个不情愿，但听得手机那头喂喂喂地叫喊，也只得重重地“嗯”了一声，说，喊个鬼。正想再冲他两句，那同学却抢先道，桂平啊，明天不用麻烦你了。桂平心里一惊，一喜，还没来得及说话，那同学却又说了，明天不麻烦，不等于永远不麻烦噢。就告诉桂平，刚接到文化局的通知，上级文件刚刚到达，电玩城电玩店一律暂停，市长也没权了，审批权被省里收去了。桂平愣了半天，竟笑了起来，说，笑话笑话，这算什么事，人家市长那边已经安排了时间，难道要我通知市长，我们不去见市长了？那同学笑道，那你另外找个事情去一下吧。桂平气得说，你以后别再来找我。那同学仍然笑，说，那可不行，以后还要靠你的。桂平说，你不是说审批权被省里收去了吗，我又不认得省领导。同学说，得了吧，你能认得这么多的市领导，肯定就是一个四通八达的人，省领导必定也能联系上几个的。不过现在还不到时候，情况还不明确，我马上会了解清楚的，如果省里可以松动，到时候要麻烦你帮我一起跑省厅省政府呢。桂平差点喷出一口血来，说，我要换手机了。同学笑道，你以为穿上马甲别人就认不出你了。

第二天桂平硬找了个借口去了市长办公室。见到正襟危坐的市长，心里一慌，好像那市长早已经看穿了他的五脏六腑，忽然就觉得自己找的那借口实在说不出口来，正不知怎么才能蒙混过关，市长却笑了起来，说，你是桂平吧？改革委的办公室主任？桂主任，其实我根本就不认得你噢。桂平大惊失色，说，市长，那你怎么……市长说，嘿，说来话长……市长看了看表，说，反正我们被规定有半小时谈话时间，我就给你说说怎么回事吧——你们都知道的，我们的手机，一直是秘书代接的，一直在他手里，我自己从来都看不到，听不到，什么也不知道，个个电话由他接，样样事情由他安排布置，听他摆布，我一点主动权也没有，一点自由也没有，因为机关一直就是这样的，前任是这样，前任的前任也是这样，我也不好改变。停顿一下又说，你也知道，我原来是干业务的，忽然到了这个岗位，真的不怎么适应，开始一直忍耐着，一直到昨天下午，我忽然觉得自己忍不下去了，就下了一个决心，试着收回自己用手机的权利，结果，我刚让秘书把手机交给我，第一个电话就进来了，就是你的。当时秘书正站在我面前，看着我，我就让他给安排时间，我要让他知道，没有他我也一样会布置工作，事情就是这样。桂平愣了半天，以为市长在说笑话，但看上去又不像，支吾了一会儿，实在不知道说什么才好，好在那市长并不要听他说话，只是叹息一声，朝他摆了摆手说，不说了，不说了，今后没有这样的事情了，你也打不着我的手机了——我又把手机还给秘书了，我认输了，我玩不过它，就昨天一个下午，从你的第一个电话开始，我一共接了二十三个电话，都是求市长办事的，我的妈，我认输了。停顿了一下，末了又补一句说，唉，我也才知道，当个秘书也不容易啊，更别说你办公室主任了。桂平说，是呀，是呀，烦人呢。市长又朝他看了看，说，对了，我还没问你呢，桂主任，我并不认得你，你怎么会直接打我的手机呢？桂平也便老老实实地把事情的来龙去脉说了出来，市长听了，哈哈地笑了几声，桂平也听不出市长的笑是高兴还是不高兴。

桂平经历了这次虚惊，立刻就换了手机号码，只告知了少数亲戚朋友和工作上有来往的人，其他人一概不说，结果给自己给大家都带来很多麻烦，引来了很多埋怨。但无论出现什么情况，桂平都咬牙坚持住，他要把老手机和手机带来的烦恼彻底丢开，他要和从前的日子彻底告别，他要活回自己，他要自己掌握自己，再不要被手机所掌控。

现在手机终于安安静静地躺在办公桌上，但桂平心里却一点也不安静，百爪挠心，浑身不自在，手机不干扰他，他却去干扰手机了，过一会儿，就拿起来看看，怕错过了什么，但是什么也没有，桂平怀疑是不是手机的铃声出了问题，就调到振动，手机又死活不振动，他拿手机拨自己办公室的座机，通的，又拿办公室的座机打手机，也通的，再等，还是没有动静，就发一条短信给老婆，说，你好吗？信正常发出去了，很快老婆回信说，什么意思？也正常收到了。老婆的信似乎有点火药味。果然，回信刚到片刻，老婆的电话就追来了，说，你干什么？桂平说，奇怪了，今天大半天，居然没有一个电话和一封短信。老婆说，你才奇怪呢，老是抱怨电话多、事情多，今天难得让你歇歇，你又火烧屁股。老婆搁了电话，桂平明明知道自己的手机没问题，仍然坐不住，给一个同事打个电话说，你今天上午打过我手机吗？同事说，没有呀。又给另一朋友打个电话问，你今天上午发过短信给我吗？那人说，没有呀。

桂平守着这个死一般沉寂的新号码，不由得怀念起老号码来了，他用自己的新号码去拨老号码，听到“对不起，您拨打的电话已停机”，桂平心里一急，把小李喊了过来，责问说，你把我手机停机了？小李说，咦，桂主任，是你叫我帮你换号的呀。桂平说，我说要换号，也没有说那个号码就不要了呀，那个号码跟了我多少年了，都有感情了，你说扔就扔了？小李说，桂主任，你别急，没有扔，我帮你办的是停机留号，每月支付五元钱，这个号码还是你的，你随时可以恢复的。桂平愣了片刻，说，你怎么会想到帮我办停机留号？小李说，桂主任，我还是有预见的嘛，我就怕你想恢复嘛。桂平还想问，你凭什么觉得我想恢复。但话到嘴边，却没有问出来，连小李一个毛头小子，都把自己给看透了，真正气不过，发狠道，我还偏不要它了，你马上给我丢掉它！小李应声说，好好好，好好好，桂主任，我就替你省了这五块钱吧。

到这天下午，情况忽然发生了很大的变化，打到他手机上的电话多起来，发来的短信也多起来，其中有许多人，桂平明明没有告诉他们换手机的事情，他们也都打来了。桂平说，咦，奇怪了，你怎么知道我的电话？对方说，哟，你以为你是谁，知道你的电话有什么了不起的。也有人说，咦，你才奇怪呢，我凭什么不能知道你的电话？也有心眼小的，生气说，唏，怎么，后悔了？不想跟我联系了？

桂平又恢复了从前的生活，手机从早到晚忙个不停，那才是桂平的正常生活，桂平早已经适应了这样的生活，他照例不停地抱怨手机烦人，但也照例人不离机，机不离人，他只是有点奇怪，这许多人是怎么知道他的新手机号码的。

一直到许多天以后，他才知道，原来那一天小李悄悄地替他换回了老卡。

PAN Xiangli, owns a master degree in literature. She studied for two years in Japan and served as editor of a literary magazine, and then of a newspaper supplement. She is known for works such as *Hopeless Love, Tender Touch, I Love Maruko,* and essay collections including *Purity in the Secular World, The Age of Innocence, Age Sacrificed for Love*. She has won the Shanghai Best Works Award and has hit the bestseller list for Chinese Fiction consecutively from 2002 to 2005. She has won the Shanghai Youth Cultural Talent Award, the 1st Youth Literary Prize and the 10th Zhuang Chongwen Prize for Literature. Her novella *Clear Soup of Greens* won the National Excellent Short Story Award for the 4th Lu Xun Literary Prize (2004-6).

潘向黎，作家，文学硕士。曾留学日本两年，先后在文学杂志和报社副刊任编辑。著有小说集《无梦相随》《轻触微温》《我爱小丸子》《白水青菜》和散文集《红尘白羽》《纯真年代》《相信爱的年纪》等多部。作品曾获上海文学优秀作品奖等，2002－2005年连续四年登上中国小说排行榜。曾获上海文化新人称号、首届青年文学创作奖、第十届庄重文文学奖。小说《白水青菜》获第四届鲁迅文学奖（2004—2006年）全国优秀短篇小说奖。

Clear Soup of Greens

PAN Xiangli

When he returned, there was no hint of her presence in the livingroom. An imperceptible smile came over his face as he walked towards the kitchen. As he had expected, she was there, using a ladle to stir the rice in the rice cooker. She al ways did that. Just before ladling the rice into the bowls, she would scrupulously turn the rice over once in the rice cooker. When he had once asked her, what for, she replied, "That's to get rid of the extra moisture in the cooked rice, to improve the taste of the rice."

She had obviously heard the sound of the door when he came in. Steam was rising from the rice. For a moment her face was hidden behind the steam. He could smell the rice. The aroma was quite strong.

The strange thing being that he seldom smelled such a strong fragrance any-where else. Only the very best rice that has such aroma. He knows she only cooks with one brand of rice. It is grown in the northeast, and very pricey, since it is organic.

The very best rice holds its aroma within. You need to add just the right amount of water, soak it for the right amount of time, and then cook it in the best rice cooker. Once the rice cooker has done its job, keep the rice warm at the right temperature for just the right moment. Not until then would the aroma fully burst out, like breaking open a small vial of balsam.

When it comes to rice, she is the best cook of all the women he has met. He mentioned this once. "I respect the rice," was her reply. Before he broke out into laughter, she added, "But only rice of the best quality."

After washing his hands he sat down at the table, where two bowls of rice were already set. On his side there was an extra empty bowl. The chopsticks were in their usual position on the fish-shaped chopstick holder. She brought in two small plates of china with a blue floral pattern. In one plate, a dozen or so freshwater snails, not very large sized but very clean, appeared like translucent jade with a touch of dark inside. On the other small plate was asparagus lettuce, reddish brown yet translucent. Dinner at home would always be this simple, because he would most likely have already eaten before coming home. The late meal at home would usually be a second dinner.

Then she carried in a small clay pot. This is the highlight of his yearning for dinner at home. He removed the lid right away to look inside the pot. Something green, something white, and something red — very pleasing to the eye. She said, "Have some soup first." She then sat down and began to eat. She ate some rice and then a little bit of the asparagus lettuce. It seemed she only ate rice, and could do without the other dishes.

He served himself about half a bowl of soup. It was a very clear soup with not even a trace of oil. Green the color of the vegetable, white the bean-curd, and red the few specks of goji wolfberries. That was all that was in the soup. But, the flavor, ah, was so good. It was a very clean and simple taste, yet so mellow, so rich, with a touch of sweet, free of any flavor enhancer like monosodium glutamate, and as natural as a fresh hibiscus in the clearest of water.

With just one sip like this, his whole stomach felt so soothed. All the senses in his whole being, numbed all day long, came back to life. Even his facial expressions started to revive, like the thin shell covering him being cracked open. All his muscles, every strip and string of them, became alive again. What a good soup!

He finished two bowls of soup before he started eating the rice, with the snails and the asparagus lettuce. The snails were smooth and the asparagus lettuce crisp. Both were excellent dishes to go with the rice. Before he realized it he had finished a whole bowl of rice. He did not reach for more rice. Instead, he finished another bowl of soup, without a pause. At last he put down the bowl, and smiled at her.

She smiled too, "It's as if you never get to eat rice when you dine outside."

"I don't. Nowadays nobody eats rice anymore."

And this was true. He went to a lot of business dinners and banquets, where rice was not served. It was always too much oily food prepared in a complicated manner with very strong flavors that bombarded the taste buds into numbness. Not until her soothing soup did his taste buds slowly come back to life.

"How do you make your soup?"

She beamed with the warmth and sweetness of sunshine. "Is it good?"

"Very good."

"Then have another bowl."

"I did already. But, how do you make it? Everyone says the soups at Wang's Soup House are good. But I don't think we could get any soup there this good. Tell me how you make it."

"Actually, it's very simple. It just takes patience."

Later on in life, on more than one occasion he would come to miss terribly the peaceful life he was leading then. Such serenity, the way he felt when he was waiting at the dinner table for the small clay pot to be brought out by his wife ... the pleasure he enjoyed when he took the lid off and the pretty colors greeted his eyes, and the blossoming tastes when he took his first sip of the soup...slightly hot, simple, aromatic, tasty, and so soothing. The softened fibers of the vegetables lingered on his teeth gently in a pleasing way, and the tofu, ever so smooth and soothing, caressed his tongue, as the soup slipped through his esophagus merrily to his stomach and consoled it.

Their family was a "platinum family," or white gold family, envied by everyone. White gold meant they were white collar, and wealthy. White collar in its wider context means well educated, cultured, refined, and respecting social ethics. They made their wealth through their education and their intellectual ability. Not the type of new money makers who showed off by wearing several gemstone rings on their fingers.

He had first worked as a government official. Then he decided he did not want to take the sure but painfully slow way of climbing to any position of seniority by being obedient and pleasing to his superiors. So he took the jump into the "sea of business" and went out on his own. After having tried many things and having made many changes, he finally made his fortune in real estate. Then he went on to websites. Then he went into operating exclusive and expensive private schools.

His business had been galloping at an unstoppable speed, like a startled wild horse.

He had risen to become the man of the hour in this city, with television and radio stations always interviewing him. He was a major donor to a great many philanthropic activities and charities. It is precisely due to his highly educated background, that his poise and demeanor, his speech and eloquence had won him a lot of attention and a good reputation. In a poll of white-collar women conducted by a certain television station, he was chosen as one of ten men in the country who would make an ideal husband. He actually made it in ahead of a few famous movie stars and singers. Today's white–collar women were far from naive. Many of those men with names, who were good at hopping around, might be good to look at from a distance, but they would not be so good in a close relationship. If only these women knew that he went twice a week, in his BMW, to that top–notch university to attend classes for a Master of Philosophy, they would probably start shrieking — what power in a man would produce such effort and persistence, and all with such gracious ease? Yet he had never let anyone know this. Such a thing was best for other people to find out accidently. The more casual he was about such a thing, the more he would come across as a cultured man with class. At his age and in his position this was a no–brainer type of choice.

Of course he was a married man, married for about seventeen or eighteen years now. His wife was his university classmate. They were each other's first loves. Moreover, that first love turned out to be a perfect combination of the initiation of the romantic rush of youthful hormones, love, sex and marriage, all cooked together in one pot.

Neither one of them had ever considered looking around for other possibilities. Neither had even thought of needing more time to make their choices. They were married the year after graduation. Soon after, they had a child, a son. This son was now a student in that elite bilingual boarding school. Their son was their pride, not only a very bright boy who excelled in schoolwork, but also a very handsome boy. He knew he could not take all the credit. It was very obvious their son was a combination of all the best things from both parents. The mother in her university days was known for her fine looks. Even without any makeup she had always been a beautiful woman, with the refreshing look of a tender new green leaf.

With such an outstanding wife, it was not easy for this man to lay eyes on another woman. Not to mention he knew too well that these days the outward beauty of a woman might be more chemical than he would like.

Dudu had dashed into his life as a total surprise. At the beginning he thought she was merely an innocent, still a rather childish young woman, like a fine crystal vase, good-looking and see-through, yet without much practical use. By the time he knew of her ambitions regarding him, he actually thought the whole thing was comical—was it not a ridiculous farce? If not for the fact that she was his employee, by Chinese custom she should be addressing him as "Uncle." Needless to say, he secretly felt good about it. Secretly but quite unmistakably. This was a woman twenty years his junior, pretty and from a very well-to-do family. Her father was a big-name lawyer, and her mother a well-known doctor. She was supposed to go to Cambridge University to study. She would have no monetary intentions for going after a man .

At first it was true that he really did not care so much about her. He thought it was just an infatuation on Dudu's part. What's more, he would never do anything to harm his own family. All these years his wife, sacrificing a very good position as a high-school teacher, had given her all being a most dutiful wife and nurturing mother. He had never ever thought of betraying her. If he betrayed her, she would have nothing to live for. A woman just reaching forty, with no job, no career, and no friends. How would she live? Not to mention, of course, he did not want to fall into this all too typical pattern, like a great many ordinary men, who after success searched for new romance and abandoned their wives. These kinds of lapses in a man's character were so common — well, he did not want to be a common sort of man. This was a standard he had set for himself.

At first he did not waver. He was just trying to minimize the hurt that Dudu would suffer after it all ended. But today's young women were so self-indulgent. If they want something badly enough they would not hold back. They would shout and scream, cry and weep. They would even threaten to die. And he could not bring himself to dismiss her. Dudu was like a crystal vase. Desperate for his love and hopeless at getting it, she became a crystal vase poised on the edge of a cliff. She could fall any time and break into pieces. Finally, he had to reach out his hand to catch her.

He started not to return home for dinner. Eventually he stopped going home for the night. He said he was really too busy and could not come home. Then he said he just wanted to be by himself to have some quiet time.

She remained silent. So every time he called to tell her he was not coming home for dinner, the long heavy silence pressed on him. But he would not have the courage to hang up. Finally, she said, "Then, from now on, if you want dinner you can call me."

He thought, what she meant was, if he did not call, she would not make his dinner. Nor would she make that soup for him and wait up for him. This was his home. But from now on there would be no dinner for him, no one awaiting his return. He began to feel a little lost. Yet then he felt a great relief. This was very good. She would no doubt have her interpretation of the situation. She would be angry. She would be hurt. However, given her personality she would not take on any active role to rupture the cover. All these years he always knew he had chosen the right woman for marriage. He became very convinced now. Of course, after having fallen in love with someone else, it seemed a little absurd to feel that way. But that was exactly how he felt.

He did not like the idea of renting. He said, even if it were just for three months he would still want to own his place rather than live in another person's apartment. Dudu, looking at him adoringly, said, "Me neither. Me neither." He told her he wanted to buy an apartment suite, all decorated, with furniture and all the electrical appliances. "I want to move in just bringing my toothbrush," he said gleefully. Dudu objected. She said that kind of apartment suite had no character. In the end she convinced him to move into her place.

Dudu was living alone in a two-bedroom suite with a livingroom. Her parents had bought it for her. She had picked the decor. The style was modern minimalist, yet even more costly than more luxurious-looking decor. Complete sets of Scandinavian furniture, and imported bathroom fixtures. Everything was in white, even the carpets in the bedrooms. Such superiority was not affordable for someone of her age. It was obvious her parents spoiled her.

To welcome him Dudu purchased designer bathrobes and slippers for him. He had never heard of the brand. He just remembered she had said that was a brand made for some royal family. She liked the brand, and said the feeling of luxury on the skin was a lot more tangible than any visual sense. But there were no pajamas. She said it would be unnecessary. True enough. Once in bed they had no need of any clothes.

New passions, new excitements and indulgences, a new place to live in, and a new ambience to breathe in; he even felt himself like a new being. Several months thus flew by.

It was not to say they had no problems. The problem was an unexpected trivial one: they still needed to feed themselves.

He was a public figure and could not be seen eating dinner with her in public. So Dudu would go out alone to get some chicken at the KFC. He felt this was acceptable, but somewhat funny. He said, "This is what my son likes most." Dudu's face changed, and she refused to buy any more fried chicken after that.

Then they had to order takeout: food from cafes, soya drinks from Yon Ho outlets, Japanese bento, dishes from the Bi Feng Tang restaurant, or even pizza and Italian pasta... They tried almost anything they could order. But there were no soups with the takeout. So sometimes they drank canned oolong tea. More often they drank colas.

Gradually, eating became a burden. He had to hide the fact that he found the food hard to swallow. Such sloppily prepared food, some hard as rock, others as dry as paper, or as woody as tree bark. He terribly missed the bowl of steaming rice, the grains soft yet chewy enough to play on his teeth. He missed even more the bowl of piping hot yet soothing soup that awakened his taste buds. How could a cold drink replace a soup? Compared with the dinners he had always been served at home before, these meals were, to put it simply, junk food.

But he did not dare say any of this. The minute he displayed any dissatisfaction, Dudu would get angry, "Well then, let's go out to eat. We can eat anything we want. I don't like eating like this either! This is all because of you! Perhaps...I know, you must be missing the good old days. You are feeling sorry for yourself now? If you have regrets, just say so!"

Every time this happened he had to take the risk of taking her out to dinner in order to calm the storm.

Dinner thus turned into a minefield buried in their minds. It became such a dilemma that on his way to their little love nest, he would be already worrying about dinner. He would debate whether he should go somewhere to eat something by himself first. Otherwise, after he stepped into the room, they would express their passion and fool around for a while, then snack on whatever they could find, and he would be hungry all over again in the middle of the night.

According to popular classification, Dudu would be a genuine "petit-bourgeois" by any accounting. The word "genuine" is proper to describe her because she took her lifestyle for granted. She did not pretend to live like this just to impress. She did not do anything just for show. She actually took much more care in private details. He never knew a woman could spend money to enjoy life the way she did, no self-restraint or second thoughts on expenditures. Her undergarments were even more expensive than her outfits. She basically wore little makeup. Yet the skincare or healthcare products she used could cost her one month's salary. And if she tried something and felt it was not good, she would just shelve it.

She said, "Name brands, so what? Chucking expired brand-name cosmetics is a very luxurious feeling. I like it!"

She also explained, "What my ears hear and what my eyes see and what my skin feels, I want all of these things to be nothing but the best. That way I exude the best demeanor."

Dudu had two hobbies. One was body-building. The other was reading books by Haruki Murakami. She not only had every single book by Murakami, but also had collected various editions of them. He wondered if she had bought all the editions available in the country of all of Murakami's books. She even owned some original editions in Japanese–even though she did not know any Japanese. "But I can learn!" she would say in a singsong voice. Whenever she had some spare time, she would pick up a novel by Murakami and flip it casually to just any page and read. After reading for a while she would appear to frown, her smooth-skinned face seeming to age several years. On the shelves, on the couch, on the pillow, and even on the counter in the bathroom besides her toiletries were to be found Haruki Murakami's books, some closed, some opened, some put upside down with the cover facing up.

He tried a few times to read the books but just could not get into it. They seemed to be all writings on mysterious episodes in life, like strange dreams and fantasies. He could not understand what was being said and what was in the writer's mind. All so messy. Strange, what could Dudu possibly see in Murakami? What drew her so? He never asked. He was afraid that she would not bother to explain anything to him. Moreover, she might actually laugh at him and tease him about being behind the times. Dudu was so young. Her youth made her assume she was entitled to her confidence and legitimacy in everything she did. This was one of the things that made her so lovable. But it also made him feel a little intimidated.

One day, he walked into the apartment to be surprised by Dudu's face rosy with excitement. "Today we are going to have some delicious food. I'm making dinner for you!" He looked at her, puzzled, as if she were speaking in English. He could understand what she was saying, yet he needed time to find the right way to react. She said the same thing one more time, before he could believe his own ears. This was such good news. The best news he could expect to hear from her.

He followed Dudu into the kitchen. He saw that the kitchen was completely different from its usual tidy and quiet state. It had been turned into a busy, fully-packed miniature supermarket. On the counter were two large chopping boards, brand new, with two knives on them, one a dark color chopper, and the other a shiny long knife with serrated teeth for slicing. Beside the chopping boards were a pink ham, green cucumbers, yellow cheeses, a huge bag of greens, and a long baguette. There were also cans with colorful labels and bottles and bags of spices. It resembled a mini supermarket in a post-quake zone. Everything appeared mislaid. On Dudu's hair there was a small smear of a yellowish cream. All this went to show enthusiasm, wholehearted and relentless enthusiasm.

He was rather touched and wanted to help. Dudu determinedly refused his offers, and sent him to relax in the livingroom and read the newspapers. She pushed him to sit down on the couch, handing him the newspapers. She even made tea for him. He took a look at the tea, and it actually was the highest-reputed Dragon Well green tea. She said with a smile, "I just bought it today. The people at the tea store said it's new tea." Then she went back into the kitchen, just like a dutiful, clever, good wife.

Finally Dudu had finished, and invited him to sit down at the dining table. He went over eagerly, and then saw what was on the table.

They each had a plate of sandwiches, cut into small pieces and stacked up in decks. On the side were baby corn and French fries. In the middle of the table sat a big platter of a mishmash of something red. On careful examination he could see there were some sausages. The only thing familiar to him on the table was the beer, a famous brand imported from Japan.

Dudu asked, "What do you think?"

"It looks very pretty," he said. He decided to start with what appeared to be the most tolerable. So he poured himself some beer and started drinking. Taking off her apron, Dudu spoke with animation and anticipation, "This is not just an ordinary meal. This is a Murakami dinner."

"What?" He swallowed his beer hurriedly.

"There are lots of gourmet dishes described in Murakami's books. So in Japan they formed 'The Society of Gourmet Food for Murakami Fans.' They created a cookbook of recipes for the dishes Murakami had written about, to share among his fans. So I made today's dinner using some recipes in the cookbook. Isn't it great fun! You never expected this, right?"

So that was what this was all about. He took up a sandwich and asked, "What kind of sandwich is this?"

"Sandwiches with cucumber, ham and cheese. This was what the biologist's granddaughter made, in the book Hard-boiled Wonderland and the End of the World. This one takes a lot of work. I had to soak the lettuce leaves in cold water to make them crisp. I had to first put a thick layer of butter on the bread, or else the moisture from the greens would make the bread soggy. And I sliced the bread myself. For that I bought a new knife. I cut the bread nicely, right?"

He took a bite of the sandwich. To avoid making a comment on it, he pointed at the tray of red mush and asked, "What's that?"

"Strasburg sausages stewed in tomato sauce. But I couldn't find any Strasburg sausages. Luckily, the cookbook says you can also use original Vienna sausages. So I used Vienna sausages. The main ingredients are tomatoes and Vienna sausages. To make the sauce you need garlic, onion, carrot, celery, olive oil, bay leaf, thyme, mint, basil, tomato paste, salt, pepper, and sugar. I counted, a total of thirteen ingredients. At first I wanted to make mushroom omelets. But that is from Norwegian Wood, which is an earlier work, and the style is not the same. So I made this stew instead. This is from Hard-boiled Wonderland and the End of the World. This is the dish that, on the day the world ends, after spending the night with the girl from the library, he makes breakfast in her house."

A feeling of tenderness overtook him. Yet he did not make any movement. But Dudu took up her knife and cut a sausage into a few pieces. She picked up a piece and put it into her mouth, crying out, "Oh! This is so good. It's so different! So sumptuous! So rich! So pure Murakami!" She kept on chewing, while drinking her beer too. Her eyes took on a misty look. She went on to babble some more, "This is a taste of a melancholy world." "Not bad for the day to say farewell to life." He knew she had entered the world of Murakami. She was playing a role in that world and uttering her parts in the drama.

He, too, went on to act like he was eating with abandon. Foods that looked so unappealing actually did not taste so bad. But to think that it took so long, and needed all that complicated setting up, and so many ingredients, it was rather laughable. And this was the most Murakami way to enjoy life? Then there must be some problem with this person's taste and class. Yet, this was a world-famous author and it would seem unthinkable for him to be so crude. Could it be this writer named Murakami was just making a fool of his fans? Yet to think that would be too unfair to Dudu, so he ended up trying his best to gulp down a clump of sandwich squares. He chewed in a hurry and then washed them down with the beer. He felt like he was in the economy seats of some domestic airline.

"So what is the big deal about a mere sandwich? No matter how you look at it, it is basically something to stuff yourself with if you are hungry. Delicious? Mere rubbish. Even if one dropped Yasunari Kawabata's name it would not change a thing about this dinner. Instead, one should read the Chinese classic A Dream of Red Mansions—all that description of fine food and good taste. That is gourmet, that is class." He decried this in his heart but did not utter a word. Dudu had spent a long time laboring on this dinner. He could not hurt her feelings. Not to mention, she simply would not understand.

After this unforgettable Murakami dinner, he finally announced, "From now on, don't go to all this trouble. For eating at home, it's more comforting to eat simply."

"This is not comfortable?" Dudu asked, puzzled.

He took Dudu's hand into his. Caressing her hand gently, he said, "This is not the case. For someone who really knows how to cook—a clear soup of greens is enough to make you feel good." The moment he said this, he saw clouds moving over the bright moon that was her face. He knew right away he had said something he should not have said.

There was someone, a woman, who the both of them had always avoided recalling. Yet she managed to pop up at the most inconvenient and unexpected moments. Just like a cunning creditor, she never tried to stop you in the middle of an open road. She let you drive all the way home to your doorstep. And you still would not see her standing there in her anger. Then you felt relieved and walked into your house. You turned the lights on, and then were rudely surprised to see someone standing quietly there in a corner. And that someone was none other than the person you had been trying to hide from.

When she heard the doorbell, for a second she thought it was him. But right away she knew it could not be him. She looked through the peephole and knew she was right. It was a woman.

She opened the door. In front of her was a young woman, with firm youthful skin and a fresh complexion. She looked at her with a smile to cover the question in her mind. The young woman said, "You can call me Dudu. I'm a friend of your husband's."

She understood immediately. She knew who the young woman must be. She opened the door wide and asked her to come in. She behaved like a very polite lady welcoming her husband's friend. Dudu tried to look for any signs of emotion and could find none.

She allowed Dudu to tour their residence, but did not show her the bedroom. Then they sat down for tea. For a few moments they could not find any topic of conversation. Then Dudu said, "Thank you for receiving me. Actually I came to visit for a couple of reasons. I wanted to find out what you look like. I also wanted to eat a dinner cooked by you." Seeing her puzzled look, Dudu added hurriedly, "I heard from him what a good cook you are and that you can make very tasty dishes out of simple ingredients. It made me extremely curious."

She seemed to be having a hard time deciding. Finally she said, "Alright then. You can stay for dinner."

Dudu acted like she was her guest. She sat by the dining table and waited. She watched her hostess bring in a bowl of rice, two small plates, and a clay pot. She was wide eyed with surprise, "That's it?" The hostess served soup into a bowl and said, "Normally this is what we eat for dinner. He ladles the soup into his bowl himself. He's usually quite keen about his food and gets impatient while waiting."

Dudu was listening, watching how she served the food and looking into the soup to see what was in it. She was completely taken with all of this. But she did notice the hostess did not plan to eat because she had no place setting for herself. So Dudu asked, "Aren't you eating?" It sounded as if she were the hostess.

The hostess shook her head. Dudu did not know whether that meant she did not want to eat, or did not want to eat any dinner with her. She felt a little chastened and said nothing more.

She took a sip of the soup. Without thinking she cried out, "Whoa!" And she looked incredulously at her hostess and asked, "Is this the clear soup of greens?"

The hostess said, "Well, this is what he calls it."

"Can you tell me how you make it?" asked Dudu, an earnest look on her face, as if she were sitting in a cooking class, and looking at her cooking teacher.

The hostess paused for a while. She seemed to sigh, however imperceptibly, before replying, "You have to first do a great deal of preparation. The best pork ribs you can find, that specialty ham from Jinhua, meadow fowl from northern Jiangsu, live shrimp from Lake Tai, bamboo shoots from Mount Mogan, clams, mushrooms, and if you can find it, a freshwater crab from Lake Yangcheng cut into two halves. Put all these ingredients into a clay pot and simmer at low heat for three to four hours. You must put in the right amount of water right from the start. Don't add any salt or spices."

Dudu looked into the pot, and felt astonished. Pork ribs? Ham? Shrimp? And so many other things? Where were these ingredients in the soup?

The hostess continued, paying no attention to her, but saying slowly, "After that, you take everything out. So no residue is left in the soup. When it's time to serve the soup, you add the tofu and the greens. These will also soak up whatever oil or grease remaining in the plain soup."

Dudu sucked in a mouthful of air. "This is the clear soup of greens? Plain soup? How deep is this woman's mind? And what nonsense had that man uttered? He had enjoyed such refined and sophisticated cooking every day and thought all such things were prepared in the simplest ways? He really does not know his wife at all." Right at that moment Dudu experienced her epiphany. She acquired a profound understanding of this woman sitting in front of her. She understood, in this world the difference between one kind of love and the other kind could be this huge.

"You make a big pot of soup like this every day?"

"Oh, yes. I go to the market to buy the ingredients after I get up in the morning and make all the preparations. I do the simmering in the afternoon. I have enough time. He anyway comes home very late."

"How come you had the soup ready today? Isn't it true that he doesn't come any..."

"You mean he isn't coming home to eat today? It's true that he hasn't come home for dinner for half a year. But I still make the soup every day. Who knows maybe one day, suddenly he'll come home for dinner? In any case, I am used to it. Making the soup gives me something to do."

Dudu sat there stunned. After a long, long pause, she said, "You're really great."

The hostess was a bit taken aback. Then distracted and gently she said, "He works so hard the whole day long. Some clear soup is good for him." She seemed to be talking to herself, oblivious of the other person sitting in front of her.

Dudu said without thinking, "Now that you have told me everything, aren't you worried that after I have learned everything he might never come back to you?"

The hostess seemed to have come back from her spiritual wanderings. She took a look at Dudu and smiled. The smile seemed to ask, "Is it not true that he is already not coming back?" or "How can he not come back to me?" or seemed to impugn, "Aren't you being presumptuous?" Yet the smile also appeared to be a forgiving smile, given the ridiculousness of the question itself.

After smiling like that for a while, the hostess asked in a quiet voice, "Could you do this for him?"

Dudu held her head in a slightly tilted way, and thought deeply for a while, before saying, "I could also do this. But it will not be necessary." After saying that, she stood up and took her leave. Reaching the door she stood there, and turned to smile at her, "I am not you."

She left the way she came, suddenly, without warning.

Another month passed. One evening like on any other day, this wife was in the kitchen. The soup pot was sitting on the gas stove, exuding its customary warmth. Her eyes were wandering over the back porch, gazing out. It seemed she was looking down at the lawn or looking in a nonspecific direction.

The doorbell rang. She answered, "Coming," as she went to open the door. Earlier realizing that she had run out of rice, she had gone out to the usual rice store to order a bag of rice. The same kind of rice from the northeast, the rice she had always used. This rice was a green product free of toxins, costing five to six times more than any ordinary new rice on the market. So now she thought the doorbell must be the rice being delivered.

She opened the door to see him standing there. She paused for a moment, and blurted out, "What happened? You don't have your key?"

He replies, "No."

She immediately went back into the kitchen, leaving him standing there by himself. He did not know why she had done that. Part of him wanted to follow her into the kitchen, but another part felt it would not be the right thing. He felt as if something thorny was under his skin. After a while she called out from the kitchen, "When the rice comes, could you answer the door?"

He said, "Alright."

"It's still the same rice."

"I know," he said.

Then the man from the rice store arrived. He took the bag of rice from him and casually asked, "It's paid for?"

The young man replied, "Oh yes. Madam always pays in advance."

With both hands, he carried the bag by its two corners into the kitchen. She said, "Set it down here." He set it down, as if putting down a huge load.

By now he felt quite sure it would be alright for him to sit down at the table to wait for his dinner. So he sat down.

As if from the kitchen, she could see him sitting down, she said, "Go wash your hands."

He washed his hands. By the time he was sitting down at the table again she came in carrying a large tray. He thought there had actually been certain changes at home. She no longer went in and out several times to bring in the dishes separately anymore. She put the tray down on the table. There were two bowls of rice and two dishes, tofu with shrimp, and scrambled eggs with tomatoes. And a small pot. This was what he had missed so much. He could not hold himself back any longer. He lifted the lid, took a look and said, "I'll have the soup first."

He ladled soup from the pot until he had half a bowl. It still had the green, the white and the red ingredients. And it was still a very clear soup. Not a trace of any oil or grease. He quickly took a sip. With just that one sip his face changed. It was as if he had suddenly been pulled out of his warm bed, frightened and angry, still hoping to dive right back under the warm quilt.

"What soup is this?" He did not dare to spit out the soup, but struggled to swallow it all down, before his question came out in a rush.

"It's the clear soup of greens."

"Why does it taste so bad? It's not like the soup before," he protested like one who had been shortchanged.

She took a sip to taste it, and said, "Clear soup of greens. That's what it is. What were you expecting?"

He put down his spoon, and looked at her. She did not look at him. There was no emotion on her face. She still liked her rice, but no longer as much as before, when she would eat her rice without any dishes to go with it. She now spooned some tofu with shrimp and some egg with tomato. She mixed these things with her rice. She ate and seemed to enjoy the meal thoroughly. He gave up eating, and lit a cigarette. He normally did not smoke in front of her. But now, it seemed it would no longer matter. She did not even look at him.

After she finished eating, she put everything on the tray and finally looked at him directly in the eyes, and said, "We are going to need to hire a domestic helper paid by the hour. I've found a job. And there's too much to take care of at home."

He is stunned, "A job? What kind of job?"

"Teaching in a cooking school."

"You? A cooking teacher?"

"You've forgotten. I was a teacher before. And I passed the exams for the chef's certificate."

That soup he swallowed now seemed to be acting up in his stomach. He blurted out without thinking, "This is something so important and you didn't even consult me. Why are you behaving like this now?" The minute he finished saying this he was sorry. He was clearly the one in the wrong. He had betrayed her. No matter what she had decided to do, he no longer had any right to question her. And he had almost never come home all these days. Where could she find him to consult with? What he just said now would only give her ammunition to hit back at him, to truly cut him down.

And yet, she did not hit back. She actually did not say anything. She merely gave him a glance. With this glance, he began to feel his own folly. Her eyes were clear yet so deep and so unfathomable. It was like on a dark night in a long-abandoned garden without a soul in sight, a cold mist from a long-deserted well had come rushing at him. He could not help feeling the chill.

(*Translated by Yuvonne Yee*)

白水青菜

潘向黎

他进门的时候，客厅里没有她的身影。他微微一笑，向厨房走去。她果然在，正在用饭勺搅电饭锅里的饭。她总是这样做，盛饭之前要把电饭锅里的饭彻底搅翻一下。他曾经问为什么，她说："好把多余的水分去掉，口感才好啊。"显然她是听见了开门的声音。

饭冒着蒸汽，她的脸有一瞬隐在水汽里。他闻到了饭香。

饭很香。奇怪的是，他在别的地方几乎闻不到这种香。这是好米才有的香味。他知道她只用一个牌子的米，东北产的，很贵，因为是有机栽培。

好米只是密闭着的香味，要加适量的水，浸适度的时间，然后用好的电饭煲煮，跳到保温之后，焖合适的时间，香味才会爆发出来，毫无保留，就像一个个储满香膏的小瓶子打破了一样。

她是他遇到的最会煮饭的女人。他这样说过，她回答：我尊重米。

在他笑起来之前，她又加了一句：不过只尊重好的米。

他洗了手，坐在餐桌边时，两碗饭已经在桌上了，他的这边多一个空碗，筷子照例搁在搁筷上，是一条鱼的形状。她端上来两个青花小碟，一个碟里是十几粒黄泥螺，并不大，但很干净，一粒粒像半透明的岫玉，里面有淡淡的墨色。一个碟里是香菜心，嫩嫩的酱色，也是半透明。家里的菜一向这么简单，因为他都是在外面吃过了，回来再吃一遍。

最后她端来一个小瓦罐。这才是他盼望的重点。马上打开盖子看了一眼，里面有绿有白有红，悦目得很。她说："你先喝汤。"自己坐下来，开始吃饭，拨几口饭，就一点儿菜心，看她吃饭的样子，好像不吃一口菜也可以似的。

他就自己从瓦罐里舀了小半碗汤。清清的汤色，不见油花，绿的是青菜，白的是豆腐，还有三五粒红的枸杞，除了这些再也不见其他东西。但是味道真好。说素净，又很醇厚；说厚，又完全清淡；说淡，又透着清甜；而且完全没有一点儿味精、鸡精的修饰，清水芙蓉般的天然。

就那么一口，整个胃都舒服了，麻木了一整天的感官复苏，脸上的表情都变了，好像一个薄薄的壳被敲碎了，所有的肌肉、每一条纹理都活了起来。真是好汤！

他一连喝了两碗，然后吃饭，就着黄泥螺和菜心，一个滑，一个脆，都是压饭榔头。不知不觉就把一碗饭都吃完了。他也不添，而是又酽酽地喝了一碗汤。然后把碗放下，对她笑。

她也笑："好像在外面没饭吃似的。"

"是没饭吃。现在谁吃饭？"

他说的是真话。他的工作宴会应酬多，那种宴会不会有饭。总是太多的油腻、浓烈的味道轰炸口腔，味蕾都半昏迷了，直到喝了她的汤，才缓缓醒过来。

"你的汤怎么做的？"

她莞尔一笑，笑容里有阳光的味道："好吗？"

"好。"

"那就多喝一点儿。"

"喝了。到底怎么做的？人家都说老王家汤馆好，我看就是那里都喝不到这么好的。说给我听听。"

“说起来——其实也简单，就是要有耐心。”她说。

后来，他不止一次怀念那时的生活。那种安宁，那种坐在餐桌前等着妻子把瓦罐端上来的感觉，掀开瓦罐的盖子时看到的好看的颜色，第一口汤进口，微烫之后，清、香、甘、滑……依次在舌上绽放，青菜残存的筋脉对牙齿一点儿温柔的、让人愉快的抵抗，豆腐的细嫩滑爽对口腔的爱抚，以及汤顺着食道下去，一路潺潺，一直熨帖到胃里的舒坦。

他们的家是让人羡慕的白金家庭。白金的意思是，既有钱又白领，这个白领的意思是泛指，指的是读过书，有修养讲规则，凭知识和智力挣钱，不是手上戴好几个宝石戒指的暴发户。

他先是吃皇粮的机关干部，后来不愿意看人脸色慢慢从孙子熬成爷爷，早早下了海，折腾了许多行当，最后在房地产上发了。然后是网站，然后是贵族学校，他的事业像匹受惊的野马一样势不可当。

他成了本市的风云人物，电视台人物访谈的明星，各种捐款、善事的大户。毕竟是受过高等教育的，他的风度、谈吐，赢得了瞩目和好评。有一次电视台让女白领评选全国范围的十佳丈夫人选，他就上了榜，而且击败了几个电影明星、歌星。现在的女白领真是不傻。那些又蹦又跳的男人，只能远处看看，怎么能近距离相处？要是她们知道他还每星期两次开着宝马到那所著名的大学读哲学硕士，她们可能会发出尖叫——要多少实力才能有时间和闲心做这样的事情啊。但是他从来没有对外面透露过，这种事，要等人家自己无意中发现才好。越不经意越有风度，像他这样的年纪和身份，这种选择已经不需要经过考虑了。

他当然结了婚，都十七八年了。妻子是他的大学同学，是初恋，而且是那种把情窦初开和爱和性和婚姻一锅煮的关系。他们从来没有想过两个人还会有其他选择，那时候也不知道要给自己多留一点儿时间，毕业后第二年就结了婚，然后很快就有了孩子，就是现在进了寄宿制双语教育的培鹰学园的儿子。儿子是他们的骄傲，他不但聪明、成绩优异，而且长得非常漂亮。这不能完全归功于他，因为儿子明显地集中了他们两人的优点，而妻子当年也是学校里的美女，不化妆也青枝嫩叶一样清新可人。

因为有这样的妻子，他对女人是不容易惊艳的。而且他知道现在的女人的漂亮已经充满了化学的味道。

嘟嘟的出现完全是一个意外。起初他觉得这是个稚气未脱的女孩子，像个水晶花瓶一样好看又透明，但是不实用。等到看出她的企图还觉得有些好笑——这不是胡闹吗？要不是她是他的下属，本来可以叫他叔叔的。当然心里还是有点儿高兴的，很隐蔽但是很真切，这可是一个比自己小二十岁的女孩子啊，又漂亮，而且出身很好，父亲是大律师，母亲是名医，家里本来要送她去剑桥留学的。这样的女孩，没有任何为了钱而接近男人的嫌疑。

起初他真的没有什么。因为觉得嘟嘟是一时冲动，再说他不可能破坏自己的家庭，这么些年，妻子辞掉干得好好的中学教师工作，专心在家相夫教子，他没想过要辜负她。他若是辜负她，她真是什么都没有了，一个四十出头的女人，没有工作没有事业没有朋友，她怎么活？况且，许多男人成功了就另觅新欢抛弃发妻，他不想也掉进这种俗套，犯这种通俗的常见病——他不是一般的男人，这是他对自己的要求。

起初真的没有动心，他只是考虑怎么让嘟嘟少受一点儿伤害就退出去。但是现在的女孩子真是任性，她们想要什么就敢大喊大叫、又哭又闹、要死要活，他又下不了狠心把她开除掉。嘟嘟真是一个水晶花瓶，而且因为对他无望的爱，这个水晶花瓶就站到了悬崖边上，随时可能掉下来粉身碎骨。最后，他只好伸手把她接住。

他不回家吃晚饭了。后来，他连晚上都不回来了。他说，实在太忙，不赶回来了。后来又说，想一个人静静。

她沉默，就像他每次说不回家吃饭时一样，绵长而细密的沉默，那重量使他感到压迫，但是不敢挂电话。最后，她说："这样吧，你要回来吃饭就打电话。”

他想，这等于说，如果不打电话，她就不会做好他的饭，还有那罐汤，等他回去了。那是他的家，但是从现在起，没有他的饭了，没有人等他了。他有点儿失落，但是马上感到了巨大的轻松。这太好了。她当然会有看法，也会生气，会伤心，但是以她的性格，不可能会主动挑破、发作出来。这些年来，他一直觉得自己选对了人结婚，现在又一次这样觉得。在爱上别人之后这样想，也许有点儿荒谬，但是他就是这样觉得。

他不喜欢租房子，他说哪怕只住三个月，我也要住在自己的房子里。嘟嘟欣赏地看他，说：“我也是，我也是。”他就说要买一套房子，全装修的，带全套家具和电器的。“只要带上牙刷就可以住进去。”他愉快地说。嘟嘟却不要，她说那种房子没有风格，她不喜欢。最后她让他住到她那里去。

嘟嘟住着两房一厅，是父母给她买的，装修是她自己来的，是很现代的简约风格，但是却比华丽更费钱的那种。全套北欧风情家具加全进口洁具，一色的白，卧室里连地毯都是白的，这不是这个年龄应该有的气派。看来她父母确实把她宠坏了。

嘟嘟为了欢迎他，给他买了名牌的浴袍和拖鞋，他没有听说过，只记得她说那是某个国家皇室用的牌子。她喜欢这个牌子，她说皮肤感觉到的奢华比眼睛看到的更真实。但是没有睡衣，她说他不需要。真的，一旦上床，他们都不再需要衣服。

新鲜的爱情，新鲜的疯狂，新鲜的住处，新鲜的气氛，好像连他自己都成了新的。几个月的时间过得像飞一样。

也有问题。问题是出乎意料的小问题：他们还是会肚子饿。

他是半个公众人物，不能到外面吃饭。嘟嘟一个人出去买肯德基，他倒是可以接受，只是觉得好笑，说：“我儿子最喜欢吃。”嘟嘟就变了脸，拒绝再买了。

只好叫外卖，从茶餐厅的简餐到豆浆坊，从日式套餐到避风塘，从比萨到意大利通心粉，他们都叫了个遍。外卖没有汤，他们有时喝罐装的乌龙茶，更多的时候喝可乐。

慢慢地，吃饭成了个苦差事。因为难吃，而且他必须掩饰他对这些食物的难以下咽。真潦草啊，有的硬邦邦的，有的干巴巴的，有的木渣渣的。他思念一碗香香柔柔有弹性的米饭，更思念一碗热热润润让味觉苏醒的汤，冰凉的饮料怎么能代替汤？和他以前吃的晚餐相比，这些简直是垃圾。

但是他不敢说。只要他一流露出不满，嘟嘟就会生气："那我们出去吃啊，什么好吃的都有！我也不喜欢吃这些！还不是因为你！或者说……我知道，你又在怀念你过去的生活了！你是不是后悔了？后悔了就明说嘛！"

每次他都要冒险出去请她吃一顿饭才能平息。

吃饭成了他们的一个心病。甚至下了班在往那个甜蜜的小巢走的时候，他就在犯愁，要不要自己先到哪里吃一点儿东西？不然等一下进了门就是一通昏天黑地的亲热，然后吃点儿吃不饱的东西，半夜又要饿醒。

按照现在流行的划分，嘟嘟在这个城市里应该算个真正的"小资"了。说她真正，是因为她小资得天经地义，而且不是为了在人前装样，她不欺暗室，在别人看不见的地方更下工夫。他从来不知道一个女人可以为了享受，这样认真把钱不当钱，这样一丝不苟。她的内衣比外衣更贵，她基本上不化妆，但是她的保养品一套就是她一个月的工资，而且用了觉得不好就被丢在一边。

她说："用名牌有什么？把过期的名牌化妆品丢掉，那种感觉才算奢侈，我喜欢！"

她也解释为什么这样："我要让自己眼睛看的、耳朵听的、皮肤接触的都是好东西，这样气质才会好。"

嘟嘟有两个爱好，一是健身，一是读村上春树。她不但有村上春树的所有作品，而且每种都不止一本，有各种版本，他怀疑只要国内有的她都买齐了。甚至还有日文原版的，虽然她不懂日语。“我可以学啊！”她唱歌般地说。只要有空，她就会随手拿起一本村上春树，随便翻到哪一页，开始看。看着看着，她的眉头就会微微蹙起来，光洁的脸似乎突然长了几岁。书架上、沙发上、床头甚至洗手间的梳妆台上，都放着村上春树，有的合着，有的打开封面封底朝上趴着。

他看过几次，但是都看不下去，好像是一些莫名其妙的生活片段、稀奇古怪的梦和幻境，不知道在说什么，也不知道想说什么。这么乱哄哄的，真奇怪，嘟嘟在里面看到了什么呢？是什么吸引了她？他没有问，怕她根本不解释，反而笑他落伍。嘟嘟太年轻了，她的年轻使她的一切都有一种理直气壮，这一点让他感到可爱，也有点儿怯意。

没想到有一天，他一走进门，就看到嘟嘟因为兴奋而泛着粉红的脸。“今天有好东西吃！我给你做！”他望着她，好像她突然在说英语，虽然他能听懂，但是一时反应不过来。她又说了一遍，他才相信自己的耳朵。

他跟着嘟嘟走进厨房。眼前的厨房热闹得像个小型超市，工作台上放着两块硕大的案板，崭新的，上面搁着两把刀，一把黑黝黝的切菜刀和一把雪亮而窄长的、带着锯齿的刀，旁边还有红的火腿、绿的黄瓜、嫩黄的奶酪，一大袋蔬菜，还有一个长面包，还有五颜六色的罐头，瓶里袋里的各种调料。这是个地震后的小型超市，一切都显得有点儿凌乱，嘟嘟的头发上也沾了一抹可疑的黄色膏体物质。但是也显出了热诚，心无城府、掏心掏肺的那一种。

他感动地表示要帮忙，嘟嘟坚决拒绝了，要他到厅里休息、看看报纸。她把他推到沙发上，把报纸递到他手里，甚至给他泡了一杯茶。他看了一下，居然是龙井，她笑着说：“刚买的。茶庄的人说是新茶。”然后她就像一个贤惠的妻子那样进了厨房。

嘟嘟终于忙完了，让他坐到餐桌边。他急切地过去，看到了餐桌上的东西。每人一碟三明治，切成小块的，一摞一摞的几摞，旁边点缀了嫩玉米芯和炸薯条。中间是一大盘红红的、一片混沌的东西，仔细看可以辨认出里面有腊肠一样的东西。唯一熟悉的东西是啤酒，麒麟一番榨。

嘟嘟说："怎么样？"他说："看上去很漂亮。"他决定先从容易接受的开始，就自己倒上啤酒，开始喝。嘟嘟一边解着身上的围裙，一边兴致勃勃地说："这不是一般的东西，这可是村上春树餐啊。"

"什么？"他赶快把一口啤酒咽下去。

"村上春树的小说里写的美食很多，日本就成立了一个村上春树美食书友会，根据他书里的描写，编了一本村上春树食谱，让大家分享。我今天就是按照这本食谱做的。好玩吧？没想到吧？"

原来是这样。他拿起一摞三明治："这是什么三明治？"

"黄瓜火腿奶酪三明治。《世界末日与冷酷仙境》里生物学家的孙女做的。这个做起来很麻烦，生菜叶子要用凉水泡，吃起来才脆。面包片上要先涂上厚厚的黄油，不然蔬菜里的水分容易把面包泡软，最后也是我自己切的，特地买了一把刀，切得很整齐吧？"

他吃了一口，为了躲避作出评价，就指着那盘红乎乎的东西说："这是什么？"

"番茄泥炖斯特拉斯堡香肠。我买不到斯特拉斯堡香肠，还好书里注明原味维也纳香肠也可以，就用了维也纳香肠。主料是西红柿丁和维也纳香肠，调料是大蒜、洋葱、胡萝卜、芹菜、橄榄油、月桂油、百里香、花薄荷、罗勒、番茄酱、盐、胡椒、糖，我数过了，一共十三种，本来想做蘑菇煎蛋卷，但是那是《挪威的森林》里的，早期作品，风格不一样，所以做了这个，这也是《世界末日与冷酷仙境》里的，就是世界末日当天，他和图书馆女孩过了一夜，在她家做的早餐。"

他心里涌起了爱怜，但是仍然没有动，倒是嘟嘟，把一条香肠用餐刀切成几段，用叉子叉起一段，送进嘴里。"哎呀，太棒了！另类！浓烈！丰富！绝对村上春树！"她吃着，又喝啤酒，渐渐地眼里泛起了迷蒙，又说了一些"真是忧郁世界的美味情怀"、"对于挥别人生而言似乎是个不错的一天"之类的话。他知道，她已经进入了村上春树的世界，正在里面扮演一个角色，这些都是台词了。

他也做出毫不迟疑的样子吃了起来，这么难看的东西，居然不是非常难吃。但是想到居然要花上那么长的时间，动用那么夸张的阵势、那么多的调料，他还是觉得有点儿可笑。这就叫用最村上的方式享受生活？那么这个人的品位真成问题。不过这么出名的作家，应该不会这么粗糙。慢着，这个叫村上春树的人，会不会故意戏弄这些崇拜他的人呢？这样想，又马上觉得有点儿对不起嘟嘟，于是努力往嘴里塞进一摞三明治，马马虎虎地嚼几下，急忙用啤酒把它冲下去，感觉好像自己正坐在某架国内航班的经济舱里。

什么玩意儿呀，就是夹馅面包片，怎么看都是简单对付肚子的东西，好吃？见鬼吧。搬出川端康成来也没用。看看中国的小说家，看看《红楼梦》，里面写的好吃好喝的，那才叫美食，那才叫见识！可是这些他都没有说，因为嘟嘟忙了半天，他不能让她伤心。何况说了她多半也不懂。

吃完这顿难忘的村上春树餐，他最后说了一句："以后不要这么麻烦了。在家里吃越简单越舒服。"

"今天这样不是很舒服吗？"嘟嘟奇怪地反问。

他把嘟嘟的手抓起来，轻轻爱抚着说："不是这样的。真的会做的人，就是一碗白水青菜汤，吃起来就够好了。"他说完这句话，看到嘟嘟脸上的月亮被云遮住了，他立即知道，自己说了一句不该说的话。

他们都不愿意想起一个人，一个女人。但她总是在最不经意的时候出现。就像一个狡猾的债主，从来不会拦在大路中间，让你可以放心地开车回家，回到家门口，也不会看到有人气势汹汹地站在那里。于是你松了一口气，走进房间，打开灯，却猛然一惊，角落里赫然站着一个人，正是躲也躲不掉的那一个。

她听见门铃响的时候，有一秒钟以为是他回来了。但是她马上知道不是。先从猫眼上往外看了看，果然不是。是一个女人。

她打开了门，一个年轻女孩出现在她面前，有着紧绷的脸颊和鲜嫩的皮肤的女孩。她用微笑的眼神发问，这个女孩子说："叫我嘟嘟吧，我是你丈夫的朋友。"

她立即明白了，明白了这个女孩是谁。她打开门，请她进来。像一个有礼貌的女人对待丈夫的朋友那样。嘟嘟从她脸上寻找一点儿情绪的流露，没有找到。

她让嘟嘟参观了他们的家，但是没有让她看卧室。然后她们坐了下来，喝着茶，一时都找不到话题。嘟嘟说："谢谢你接待我。其实我今天来，一是想看看你是什么样子的，另外就是想吃你做的饭。"看到她脸上的惊讶，嘟嘟急忙解释，"我总听他夸你是个高手，最简单的菜都能做得最好吃，真的很好奇。"

她似乎有点儿为难，想了一下，说："那，你就在这里吃一点儿便饭好了。"

嘟嘟像一个真正的客人那样，坐在餐桌边等。看着女主人端上来一碗饭，两个小碟，然后是一个瓦罐。她惊讶地睁大眼睛：就这些？女主人给她盛了一碗汤，一边说："平时我们吃饭，也就是这样。他总是自己盛汤，脾气急。"

嘟嘟一边听，一边看她的手势表情，又注意汤的内容，简直忙不过来。但是她还是发现女主人没有碗筷，就问："你不吃吗？"她的语气，好像她是主人。

女主人摇了摇头。嘟嘟不知道是她不想吃，还是不愿意和她一起吃，就不敢再说什么了。

她喝了一口汤。她不假思索地"哇——"了一声。然后她难以置信地看看女主人，"这就是白水青菜汤？"

女主人说："他这么叫。"

"你能告诉我怎么做的吗？"嘟嘟一脸恳切，好像她正在上烹调课，面对着给她上课的老师那样。

女主人停了一下，好像微微地叹了一口气。然后说："要准备很多东西。上好的排骨、金华火腿、苏北草鸡、太湖活虾、莫干山的笋、蛤蜊、蘑菇，有螃蟹的时候加上一只阳澄湖的螃蟹，一切二，这些东西统统放进瓦罐，用慢火炖三四个钟头，水一次加足，不要放盐，不要放任何调料。"

嘟嘟难以置信地看看面前的瓦罐，排骨？火腿？虾？还有那么多东西，哪里有它们的影子啊。

女主人自顾自慢慢地说："好了以后，把那些东西都捞出去，一点儿碎屑都不要留。等到要吃了，再把豆腐和青菜放下去。这些东西顺便能把油吸掉。"

嘟嘟倒吸了一口冷气。这就是所谓的白水青菜汤？白水？这个女人的心有多深啊。那个男人说的是什么胡话？他每天享用着这样的东西，却认为是非常容易非常简单就可以做出来的。他真是完全不懂自己的妻子。就在这一瞬间，嘟嘟深深地明白了眼前的这个女人，也明白了世界上，爱情和爱情之间有多大的不同。

"你每天都要弄这样一罐汤吗？"

"是啊。早上起来就去买菜，然后上午慢慢准备，下午慢慢炖，反正他总是回来得晚，来得及的。"

"那今天你怎么也准备了呢？他不是……"

"你是说他没有回来吃晚饭吧？是啊，都半年了，不过我还是每天这样准备，说不定哪天他突然回来吃呢？再说我都习惯了，守着一罐汤，也有点儿事情做。"

嘟嘟整个人呆在那里。半天，才说："你真了不起。"

女主人愣了一下，然后失神地、轻轻地说："他整天那么辛苦，能让他多喝一口汤也好啊。"她好像在自言自语，完全忘记了眼前还有一个人。

嘟嘟突然说："你今天都告诉了我，你不怕我学会了，他永远不回来吗？"

女主人回过神来，看了嘟嘟一眼，笑了。那笑容，好像在说，他不是已经不回来了吗？又好像在说，他怎么会不回来呢？好像在责备：你这样说是不是有点儿过分啊？又好像在宽容，因为这问题本身很可笑。

这样笑完了以后，女主人轻轻地问："你能这样为他做吗？"

嘟嘟偏着头，认真地想了想，说："我也可以的，但是不必了。"她说完，就站起来走了，走到门口，她站住，回头一笑，说："我不是你。"

她走得就像她来时那样突然，毫无征兆。

又过去了一个月。傍晚，女人照例在厨房里，汤罐在煤气灶上，微微冒着热气。女人的目光穿过后阳台，往外看，好像看着楼下的草坪，又好像看着一个不确定的地方。

门铃响。她应着"来了"，过去开门。她刚刚发现家里的米快没有了，就到那家固定的米行买了一袋米，还是那个牌子的东北大米，完全绿色无公害的，价钱比普通的新米贵了五六倍。这是米行的伙计给她送米来了。

她打开门，却发现是他。她愣了一下，一句话脱口而出："怎么？忘了带钥匙？"

他回答："是啊。"

她马上回到了厨房，丢下他一个人。他不知道她这样算是什么意思，有点儿想跟进去，又觉得不妥，一时有些浑身长刺的感觉。过了一会儿，她在厨房里说："等一下米行的人会送米来，你接一下。"

他说："哦。"

"还是那种米。"

"我知道。"他说。

米行的人来了，他接下来人手里的米袋，随口问道："钱付了吗？"伙计说："付了付了，太太每次都先付的！"

他用双手握住米袋的两角，把它提进厨房。她说："放这里。"他就放下了，同时感到如释重负。

这时他确定自己可以坐到餐桌边等了。他就坐到了餐桌边。

她好像看见他坐下来了，就说："洗手去。"

他洗了手，坐在餐桌边时，她端着一个大托盘过来了。他想，家里还是有改进，她不再分几次跑了。托盘放到桌上，里面有两碗饭，两碟菜：一个是虾仁豆腐，一个是番茄炒蛋。一个小瓦罐。这是他思念的，忍不住马上打开盖子看了一眼，说："我先喝汤。"

他从瓦罐里把汤舀了小半碗。还是有绿有白有红，还是清清的汤色，不见油花。他急忙喝了一口，就那么一口，他脸色就变了。像被人从温暖的被窝里一下子揪出来，又惊又气，又希望一下子挣醒，发现是梦，好难回到温暖的被子里。

"这是什么汤？"他不敢吐出来，挣扎着把嘴里的一口汤咽下去，急急地问。

"白水青菜汤啊。"

"怎么这么难喝？以前的汤不是这样的！"他委屈地抗议。

她尝了一口，然后说："白水青菜，就是这样的。你要它什么味道？"

他放下调羹，审视她。她不看他，脸上没有任何波动。她还是那么喜欢吃饭，但是现在不像过去，好像没有菜也吃得下去的样子，她把虾仁豆腐和番茄炒蛋都舀了一些，和饭拌在一起，自顾自吃起来，吃得很香。他干脆不吃了，点起了一支烟。过去在她面前他是不抽烟的。但是现在，这些好像无所谓了。她连看都没有看一眼。

吃完最后一口，她把所有的碗碟都收回托盘里，然后正视着他，说："我们家以后可能要雇一个钟点工，我找到工作了，家里这么多事。"

他吃了一惊："工作？什么工作？"

"到烹饪学校上课。"

"你？当烹饪老师？"

"你忘了，我本来就是老师。烹饪考级我也通过了。"她说。

刚才那口难喝的汤好像又翻腾起来，他脱口而出："这么大的事，也不跟我商量。你现在怎么这样了?"话一出口，他就后悔了。他不该这样说。理亏的人是他自己，是他对不起她，不管她做什么他都失去了质问的权利。而且这些日子，他几乎不回家，让她到哪里找他商量呢？他现在这样说，只会给她一个狠狠反击的机会，反击得他体无完肤。

但是，她没有反击，她甚至没有说什么。她只是看了他一眼。这一眼，让他真正开始感到自己的愚蠢。那目光很清澈，但又幽深迷离，好像漆黑的夜里，四下无人的废园子中井口蹿出来的白汽，让人感到寒意。

ZHANG Ling, born in Zhejiang province, graduated in 1983 from the College of Foreign Languages and Literature at Fudan University. In 1986 she went to study in Canada, where she received a Master's degree in English Literature from the University of Calgary, and later also a Master's degree in Aural Rehabilitation from the University of Cincinnati, US. She now lives in Toronto and works as the chief audiologist in an aural clinic. Her major works include novels such as *Sleep, Flo, Sleep*, *Gold Mountain Blues*, *Mail Order Wife* (published in Taiwan as *The Woman from Wenzhou*), *Beyond the Ocean* and *Sisters from Shanghai*, as well as collections of novellas and short stories such as *Yan's Journey Home*, *Blind Date* and *The World of Flesh*. She has won the 7th and 8th October Literary Prize, the 2nd Excellent Prose Award for World Chinese Literature Prize (2003), the 1st Yuan Huisong Literature Prize in Canada (2005), the 4th People's Literature Award in China, and the biennial prize for Selected Novellas (2008).

张翎，1983年毕业于复旦大学外文系。1986年赴加拿大留学，分别在加拿大的卡尔加利大学及美国的辛辛那提大学获得英国文学硕士和听力康复学硕士。现定居于多伦多市，在一家医院的听力诊所任主管听力康复师。主要作品有长篇小说《睡吧，芙洛，睡吧》《金山》《邮购新娘》（台湾版名《温州女人》）《交错的彼岸》《望月》（海外版名《上海小姐》）中短篇小说集《雁过藻溪》《盲约》《尘世》等。曾获第七届、第八届十月文学奖，第二届世界华文文学优秀散文奖（2003），首届加拿大袁惠松文学奖（2005），第四届人民文学奖（2006），《中篇小说选刊》双年度优秀小说奖（2008）等。

Empty Nest

ZHANG Ling

I dedicate this story to all the "empty-nesters" and their children who have traveled far from home.

Over the last two years He Tiantian had come back to China three times, and each of those trips was for her father, He Chun'an.

Her first trip back had been to find a housemaid for her father. This was somewhat the same with the second trip. The third trip, though not for a housemaid, had something to do with a housemaid.

He Chun'an was a retired teacher, who used to teach English and American Literature at a university in Beijing. His wife Li Yan'an had worked in the library of the same university. The couple had a son and a daughter. Their son He Yuanyuan lived far away in Guangzhou, as a sales manager of a famous joint venture. The daughter He Tiantian had moved even farther. Five years before, she had migrated to Toronto. She was now working in the commercial credit department of the TD Bank in Canada. The two children of the He family had an age difference of only sixteen months between them, and shared many similar experiences. Yuanyuan and Tiantian both majored in business at college, and the jobs they got later on were somewhat related to business. They were both very busy. Both of them had married, and eventually both got divorced. Neither of them had any children. They were now both living in that gray area between single and not single.

It was after her divorce that Tiantian had decided to go abroad—of course she meant to start a new life. The course of Tiantian's divorce had been like a drawn-out drama that reached one climax after another. It was played out over three whole years. Over those three years, Tiantian lived at her parents' place. Her parents' home became a nest where Tiantian had a chance to rest, a pillow on which to sleep, a handkerchief with which to wipe her tears, and a bamboo basket into which she placed her ill-considered words. While she was going through her round of divorce, her parents grew old.

Her parents grew old before Tiantian's very eyes, yet she seemed totally oblivious to it. Much like someone who permanently lives by the riverside and is used to seeing the river flow, and may not see that today's water is different from yesterday's water. By the time Tiantian finally became aware of her parents' aging, matters had already entered the dead end of an irreversible cycle.

In retrospect, in fact, there had long been signs of her mother's quirks. Mother liked going through Father's pockets, Mother liked looking through Father's manuscripts and opening Father's letters, and Mother liked eavesdropping on Father's phone calls. Mother, though quite courageous and forthright when young, had gradually grown prickly and loved to grow suspicious about everything on no grounds at all. Tiantian had always thought it was Mother's sense of crisis brought about by Father's increasingly rising social status, and it was only later, after she accidentally came across a medical journal at the home of a Canadian colleague, that she suddenly realized this was actually an early symptom of Alzheimer's disease. Mother simply had had to worry about too many people before, yet Mother had left such clues scattered throughout the too varied and numerous contents of living, like gravel buried shallowly along a beach, missed by others ignorant in their muddled rushing through life. When Yuanyuan went to Guangzhou and Tiantian went abroad, Mother's backdrop of living suddenly turned into a huge blank, and only then did her abnormal behavior float to the surface, becoming increasingly unmistakable.

Father did not know Mother was ill either. He thought Mother was just too lonely, so after his sixty-fifth birthday he went through his retirement process without delay. At that time Father had been a supervisor of several graduate students, and there were many incomplete papers in his hand. A senior professor like Father, who had made somewhat of a contribution, could in fact wait to retire after extensions of a few years, but he wanted to spend more time with Mother at home. Having no senior title, Mother had already retired earlier.

But it was to be of no use.

Father's staying with her every day, Tiantian's overseas calls every other day and Yuanyuan's home leave once every three months did not pull Mother back from that dark road which only became narrower and narrower. Mother still insisted on going to extremes.

Only after about a month did Tiantian get to know about Mother's mishap–it was Yuanyuan who had deliberately held it back from her. Yuanyuan, no longer able to hide the truth, then had no other way out but to make a call to Toronto to ask for help. The very next day after Tiantian had received the phone call from Yuanyuan, she got on a plane and flew back to Beijing.

On walking in, Tiantian's first glance fell on the enlarged photograph of

Mother on the main wall of the living room. The photo had been taken when Mother was a little younger, with her hairstyle and clothes looking somewhat outdated. It looked as if, as soon as Mother's smile had begun to spread, it was suddenly cut off by the shutter. So there was a slight hint of surprise at the corners of her eyes and at the edges of her eyebrows. Like a yawning mouth, the black frame of the photo sucked Tiantian up in one bite. Tiantian could not modulate her breathing. Her body sagged and slumped onto the sofa. A mass of salt and acerbity gushing in her throat, she could neither spit it out, nor swallow it back. Choking with sobs, her tears surged out.

Seeing his daughter crying her heart out, He Chun'an could only rub his two hands on his knees, his chapped palms pulling out with a hissing sound one thread after another from his pants.

"Who would have thought? Who would have thought?" He Chun'an said over and over again. Each time he said it his breath got a bit shorter. Later, his voice resembled a fly on a hot summer afternoon, flying and hitting Tiantian's eardrums with a faint and weak buzzing.

The day Li Yan'an had the mishap had really not been that much different from any other day. Rising as usual in the morning He Chun'an had gone to the park where he practiced Tai Chi, while Li Yan'an had gone to buy vegetables at the food market nearby. When He Chun'an had finished practicing Tai Chi and returned home, Li Yan'an happened to have finished heating up breakfast. They sat face to face at the small kitchen table, drinking soymilk while reading the newspapers. He Chun'an was reading *Morning Post*, and Li Yan'an was reading *Health News*. By the time the bottom of the bowl of soymilk came into view, the newspapers were almost finished. He Chun'an wiped his mouth, stood up and said he would go to the university to fetch a few letters. Reaching the door, he heard an exceptionally loud laugh from Li Yan'an in the kitchen. She said, "If your Yan Hua'er doesn't show up, you'll get worried, right?"

"Yan Hua'er" from Li Yan'an's mouth, when used in a general sense, referred to all of He Chun'an's female colleagues and female students; while in particular sense, it meant Yan Hua, He Chun'an's favorite student. After graduating as a doctorate student, Yan Hua had been hired by the university and worked in the same staffroom as He Chun'an. They had been teacher and student earlier and then colleagues, so they were relatively close. On ordinary days at home Li Yan'an would from time to time chatter about or even make a big deal out of "Yan Hua'er," sometimes generically, sometimes specifically, words which merely went through He Chun'an's one ear and out the other. He never made too much of it. But on that day, who knows what came over him, an inexplicable anger seemed to flare up in his heart, and he could not help retorting, "I'm worried, so what?" He then made for the door and rushed out.

Arriving at the university, He Chun'an met several colleagues whom he had not seen for quite a few days. They brought up some embellished stories and malicious gossip about the department. Caught up in the high spirit of the banter, several of them had lunch at the university restaurant and downed several cups of liquor, so he got home late. Blushing and hot-eared he walked in, shouting repeatedly for Li Yan'an, "We must have dinner early this evening. Professor Zhou gave me two tickets. It's *The Jade Hairpin* by the Xiaobaihua Yue Opera Troupe." He had long completely forgotten their earlier altercation.

Walking through the door of the bedroom, He Chun'an felt something sticky under his feet. Looking down it seemed as if his feet had stepped into a pool of tomato sauce. Rushing into the room, he saw a whole floor of scarlet, thick and semi-dry, flowing into big posies of flowers in the corners and behind the door. Yet the bed looked smooth, not seeming to have anybody in it. Trembling, He Chun'an lifted the quilt, only to see a body as flat as a sheet of paper–it was Li Yan'an, whose blood had drained and whose body had deflated. Li Yan'an had used a blunt knife, so the injury to her wrist was as jagged as the teeth of a saw. This woman, who had been born in a cave house in Yan'an and spent her early childhood on horseback, had taken the logic of her inherent strong soldier–like character and integrity to an extreme.

He Chun'an ran out of the room, stumbling along and rushing downstairs. Squatting under the large acacia tree outside the doorway, he vomited all over the ground. The fermentation of the liquor and meat flew very far with the wind down the street, and a blurred mass of flies encircled the muck. After vomiting as if wrenching his guts out, he got back on his feet by leaning against the tree trunk. Looking up at the sky, he saw a bloody sun dropping precisely over himself. Wanting to hide, he could not escape and was knocked to the ground with a thud.

When he awoke fully again it was three days later. Over these three days a lot of things had happened in his life. While his consciousness had still been floating in that gray area between sleep and wake, his wife Li Yan'an had been cremated and buried. He Yuanyuan, his son, had hurried back from Guangzhou, hired someone to clean his apartment thoroughly, and rearranged the furniture. All traces of Li Yan'an had been carefully concealed.

After being discharged from hospital and returning home, He Chun'an was profoundly distressed and at a loss as to what to do, as though he had walked into someone else's home. He repeatedly walked in and out of the apartment, and would not stop opening drawers and cupboards, as if looking for something, even as nothing was to be found. He Yuanyuan's concern was entirely unnecessary, for He Chun'an did not ask about Li Yan'an, not breathing even one word about her.

It continued like this for several days running.

Yuanyuan had originally prepared for a variety of possibilities, which were all to be used against Father's memory. The only thing that he had not prepared for was Father's loss of memory. To remember was a pain, and to forget was also a pain, but these two could not be offset or replaced. They both had to be endured one after the other.

Yuanyuan went quietly to the hospital for consultation with a psychiatrist, who said that, after experiencing such a huge shock, a temporary loss of memory was a means of self-preservation, and restoration of memory would be a sign of recovery.

Two weeks later, while having dinner one day, Yuanyuan put the food on the table. While fiddling with his chopsticks he said, seemingly unintentionally, "The dishes cooked by Ma are much more delicious than those bought on the street."

He Chun'an did not speak for a long moment. Turning around, Yuanyuan saw a drop of clear mucus flowing down from Father's nose. His eyes were tightly fixed on the wall, as if to drill a hole in the wall.

"The employee ID," He Chun'an muttered after awhile.

"What employee ID?" Yuanyuan was puzzled.

"The photo in the employee ID card, take it out, enlarge it, and hang it on the wall."

Only then did he realize that Father had been looking for Mother's photograph for several days. Yuanyuan then set his mind slightly at rest.

After Mother's funeral, Yuanyuan had wanted to take Father to Guangzhou to stay with him for a while, for a change in the environment to relieve Father's boredom. He Chun'an persisted in his refusal, saying that Mother would not be able to find him when she came back. Yuanyuan said Mother was now ashes and smoke, she could follow him wherever he went. Yuanyuan meant to persuade He Chun'an with these words, but upon hearing them the old man seemed horrified, sitting motionlessly for a long time like a clay or wooden sculpture, even refusing to have his meals. Yuanyuan had no alternative but to say that Father might as well go to Canada to stay with Tiantian for a few months, at least he understood English. Shaking his head again and again, the old man said that if she dragged such an old oil bottle around with her, no one would dare marry her.

This was how the matter of looking for a housemaid was put on the agenda.

As far as housework was concerned, He Chun'an could basically be counted as a softhead. In the past, from grocery shopping and cooking to washing clothes and sweeping floors, matters big and small at home had all been taken on by Li Yan'an. He Chun'an was too lethargic to even remember the PIN number for their bank account. Since Li Yan'an had suddenly gone west, He Chun'an did not even know how to use the washing machine, and he also had to learn how to make tea and boil water from scratch.

However, He Chun'an strongly disagreed about getting a housemaid, saying he would feel uncomfortable and insecure if a stranger came into his home. In fact, He Chun'an could not tell his son the real reason: his wife had died over a group of fictitious women. Although he was innocent, the innocence, however large, after grappling with his wife's strong character and integrity, would more or less be left blotched like a sheet of paper that had been crumpled. The retention of that blotch may be just a momentary slip, but he might spend the rest of his life trying to wash the stain away. Walking on the street, he felt as if covered with thorn-like eyes on both his chest and back. Under such eyes, anyway, he could not peacefully enjoy the comfort that another woman who was not his wife might bring him. He Chun'an, a sixty-six-year-old retired professor, had been frightened out of his wits through that sudden turn of events in his life.

Yuanyuan's month by his father's side had gone by in the blink of an eye. His company in Guangzhou sent him an ultimatum, saying if he did not come back to work, they would have to employ someone else to replace him. He Chun'an urged his son to leave, and said, "You can take care of me temporarily, but could you do so for the rest of my life? After all, I have to learn to live my own life." Before leaving, Yuanyuan went to the supermarket and bought a refrigerator full of bread, dumplings and instant noodles, taking the trouble to teach Father how to boil water and cook these things. He also called colleagues and students in the department of the university who were on good terms with Father and asked them to look in on his father now and again. However, only three days after returning to Guangzhou he received a call from a neighbor, saying Father had knocked over a pot of boiling water to the floor, scalding his feet, and had been admitted to the hospital. Yuanyuan could take no more time off, so he had to make a phone call that very night to his younger sister Tiantian, who was far away in Toronto, asking her to immediately catch a flight back.

Domestic Help Wanted: to take care of an educated elderly man, must be skilled in housework and patient, junior high school level or above. Offering a monthly salary definitely higher than market rates, other benefits negotiable.

As soon as Tiantian arrived home, she drafted a classified ad. Drawing a lesson from what Yuanyuan had done previously, this time Tiantian played hardball. Even before He Chun'an had a chance to interrupt, the ad appeared in the *Morning Post* and *Evening News* in black and white.

In the few days that followed, quite a few phone calls were received one after another. Several applicants who did not sound on the phone to have the makings of a housemaid were refused by Tiantian, without bothering to call them in for an interview. None of the remaining ones who had sounded fairly pleasant actually looked anymore more pleasing to the eye upon interviewing. All had dolled themselves up. They would finally agree to sit down and talk only after they had, on walking in, inspected all the appliances, kitchen and toilet facilities. Each time Tiantian saw one off, one more knot appeared over her eyebrows. Later, extremely depressed, she could not help but sigh while wondering where all the good honest working women in China had gone. The applicants were nothing much more than those who might have been recruited by nightclubs.

Sitting on the sofa, He Chun'an sneered with his eyes closed, "Mrs. Xiang Lin has gone abroad, Sifeng is in business, leaving only Bailu Chen, but would your Papa dare hire her?"

Hearing this, Tiantian could only smile uneasily.

Later, the telephone calls gradually grew scarcer.

Tiantian was planning on amending her strategic objectives in the direction of an hourly employee, when she suddenly received a phone call one morning, someone asking for "Professor He." He Chun'an happened to have gone to the hospital to have his bandages changed. Tiantian thought it was a student of Father's, so she asked her for name and phone number. The woman paused, and then said her name was Zhao Chunzhi, and that she had no telephone. She was calling on a public phone, and wanted to ask if Professor He's family had found a domestic aide yet. Only then did Tiantian understand it was another woman looking for the job. Among the many applicants, only this woman had referred to her father as "Professor He," so Tiantian's heart had an inkling of a good opinion of this person.

When she asked the woman where she was from, she said she was from Zaoxi

Township in Wenzhou. Tiantian felt surprised, because Father's hometown was in that region in southern Zhejiang Province. Although his father had left his birth-place fifty years ago, and it had been a long time since he had heard from any relatives left there, as Father had been growing old over the last few years, in his own words, there was often some lingering homesickness. Thinking this might be good luck, Tiantian then laughed and said, "I only hear of Wenzhou people looking for housemaids everywhere. How come you are a Wenzhou person wanting to come and work as a housemaid?" The woman also laughed, and said that even in the richest places there were poor people, and everybody has their own fate. The woman's laughter was hoarse, as if laden with a helpless acceptance of her fate, along with a sturdy bluntness not submitting to fate. Tiantian's heart was naturally moved, and she instantly decided to arrange a meeting with the woman. By this time she had grown smarter, and did not ask the woman to come to their home.

Tiantian arranged to meet this woman named Zhao Chunzhi that afternoon at a teashop close to the house. Arriving on time, the woman ordered a cup of chrysanthemum tea, and sipped it. The tea gradually got low, but she simply refused to add more water. Surprisingly thin and slender, the woman wore neat short hair, a light blue blouse that had seen many washes, and a pair of dark blue pants also of similar vintage. Though old, the clothes were incredibly clean and neat. She looked like a girl student in a black and white photograph from the 1950s or the 1960s. There was sweat all over the woman's face and neck, and her hair was dripping wet into small curls on her forehead — Tiantian guessed that the woman had perhaps been reluctant to take a bus and had walked all the way here instead.

She then asked the woman about her general situation.

The woman was thirty-eight years old. She had a high-school education. She was divorced, and had a fourteen-year-old daughter who lived with her grandmother at home. The woman had worked as a housemaid in Beijing for four years. Her previous employer had just died, and she was now looking for a new one.

"Why did you get divorced?"

Tiantian knew this was not a question she should ask, yet she knew also it was impossible for the woman to refuse the wages offered, so fixing her eyes on the woman's face, she asked this question in a calm and collected tone.

"He had picked up some bad habits," the woman said.

"What habits?"

The woman lowered her head, took out a handkerchief, and wiped the sweat from her face over and over again. A long while passed before she said gently, "Elder Sister, there are many things for you to worry about. These small details of mine are not worth worrying about."

Since the woman's answer was neither haughty nor humble, Tiantian could not continue, but had to change the subject, asking the woman what her needs were. She said she had no needs, and she could handle any kind of old person.

So Tiantian took the woman home to see Father. In fact, by this time Tiantian had already made up her mind to hire this woman. Father's approval, like the stamp of the Queen of England on national documents, would be just a basic formality.

Tiantian led the woman into the apartment and said to Father, "This is Zhao Chunzhi. The household for whom Chunzhi previously worked was also a teacher's."

Father was cutting his fingernails. The strength of Father's reading glasses was not adequate enough, so it was a bit difficult for him to cut his fingernails. Father had to stretch his hand way out. His eyes were squinting. His nose had shrunk into a meatball with deep wrinkles under his glasses. Father took a look at the woman, then bowed his head and continued to trim his fingernails, the nail clipper clicking in the silence, making a perturbing sound.

"Give me the clipper," the woman said.

The noise of the nail clipper suddenly became quiet. Chewing over and over again the words of the woman, Father gradually came to understand it was an accent from his hometown. Father looked up and stared blankly at the woman. Father's eyes penetrated the wall behind the woman, before shifting to the distant air. Then there appeared to be some wetness in Father's eyes.

During the pause, the woman took the nail clipper from Father's hand and began to help him cut his fingernails. At first Father was a little shy, but the woman looked so stern, in a flash Father's coy reluctance was snipped at the bud. The woman clipped from the upside and trimmed on the downside, left hand first and then right. Father's ten fingernails, after going through the coarse palms of the woman, became smooth, bright and clean, almost as if polished. Sitting to one side and looking on, Tiantian's eyelids gradually stuck together. The drowsiness that had been lost for a number of days suddenly returned on this unromantic afternoon. Only then did she understand that some of her own burden could perhaps be lifted.

"Chunzhi, if you could stay here today, I'll find someone to help you fetch the rest of your baggage," Tiantian told the woman.

"Who's promising this? I said strangers could not stay at our place." He Chun'an suddenly stood up and gave a strong flick of his hand at the woman. With a clatter, the nail clipper fell onto the iron corner of the tea table, tinkling with a high-pitched hum.

Startled, the woman said nothing, but she bent down to pick up the nail clipper.

"An acquaintance is at first a stranger. Chunzhi is from your hometown. She is better than someone we do not know well at all," Tiantian patiently reasoned with Father in a soft voice.

"She can come to help during the day, and find her own place to live at night. This is my requirement. If she accepts, she can come. If not, she can leave." Though He Chun'an was facing Tiantian, his words were for Chunzhi.

Picking up the backpack resting in the corner, Chunzhi walked out the door without looking back. "If you pay my rent, I'll live outside. This is my requirement. If you agree, I'll come. If not, I can't."

Tiantian ran hurriedly outside after her, but the woman had already gone quite far. While walking, the woman's feet stayed fairly close to the curb. The cotton blouse on her body swelled and quivered in the wind, like a sparrow hawk (or kite) that could not fly upwards. Tiantian had to run half up the street before catching her. She gasped to the woman, "I'll find... a dorm at the university, that two or three share. You could start tomorrow, alright?"

The woman stopped and sighed, "Elder Sister, where else could a daughter like you be found today?"

Tiantian also let out a sigh, saying, "You're older than me. Don't call me Elder Sister. Just call me by my name, Tiantian. When people are old they become like children. They can only be coaxed. This temper of yours, will it do?"

The woman said, "We country people call it this way. It's hard for me to change. Elder Sister, you're better educated than me and also know more things about the outside world than me, but I've seen more old people than you and I know when they should be coaxed, and when they should not be."

Tiantian saw some truth in the words of the woman, so she said nothing more and accompanied her all the way to the bus station. The previous bus had just left, and the next bus had not come yet. They were both a little tired, so they leaned against a pillar on the platform and waited. All the red clouds had set as it gradually grew dark. Street lamps turned on one after another, from this end of the street to the other, like an old string of beads which had been collected over the years, drooping yellowish on the chest of the downtown street. Pigeons flew low homeward, with their wings scratching a path across the dusk sky.

"Elder Sister, how old is your child?" the woman asked.

Tiantian shook her head, saying that she had neither any children nor a husband—but had divorced.

"Why did you get divorced?"

Looking at the woman, and stressing each syllable, Tiantian said, "He picked up bad habits."

The eyes of the two met, and they could not help laughing heartily. When the woman laughed, two shallow dimples loomed on her cheek. The shallow dimples quivered until they showed themselves entirely, for a moment transforming the woman's expression as clear, bright and vibrant.

Finally the bus arrived. The woman got on, chose a window seat and sat down, then popped her head out from the window and said, "I'll take care of Professor He, Elder Sister. Feel rest assured when you go back. Find yourself another suitable man."

Her eyes brimming with tears, Tiantian fished for the right words to say something warm to the woman. But before she could say anything, the bus had started to move. The woman gradually changed into a small blue dot and disappeared in the light dust that covered the whole street.

At this very moment, the cell phone in Tiantian's handbag tinkled.

It was Qin Yang.

"So have you found a suitable person?"

Separated by a great expanse of ocean, Qin Yang's voice sounded a little tired. Tiantian calculated the time difference. At that moment it was early morning in Toronto. Working until midnight, Qin Yang would have slept only three or four hours. Tiantian asked him why he was calling at such a time. Qin Yang smiled and said, "Miss, I've not gone to bed at all, and I've been dialing your phone for several hours. The line's been busy." Tiantian said, "Can't you call again tomorrow?" Qin Yang said, "Do you want me to be sleepless for one night or two?" Tiantian tittered — the things Qin Yang said could always strike a chord in her heart of hearts.

"I've found one, who seems pretty honest. Only this one was given the nod by my pa."

"The old man... is he in good spirits?"

"How can he be in good spirits? Facing that photograph all day long..." Tiantian had only said half of what she meant to say, before, unexpectedly, tears were streaming down her face. She had been busy with Father's affairs all these days and had not had time to think carefully about Mother. In a flash, mixed memories about Mother suddenly welled and piled up, unrestrained, in the narrow space between throat and nasal cavity. In another flash, her tears were blown dry by the night wind, but the traces of the tears along her face itched for a long time.

"Qin Yang, I don't... don't have a mom anymore."

There was a brief silence at the other end. Later, Qin Yang gently coughed and said, "Anyway, Tiantian, you still have me."

Among Tiantian's circle of friends in Toronto, many people did not know Qin Yang by name. But if you talked of Tiantian's "reservist," almost everyone knew who this was. Even Tiantian herself did not avoid it very much. To be precise, the term "reservist," in fact, was first coined by Tiantian herself. One day, for the first time, Tiantian had taken Qin Yang to attend a friend's birthday party. Many people secretly pulled her aside and asked who the man was. On no account would Tiantian admit that this was her boyfriend. Only when pressed hard for an answer did she say that he was her "reservist" —if by age forty, she had still not settled down, she would then consider marrying him. At that time, the U.S. was about to wage war on Iraq, and there were military terms all over the newspapers, television and radio, and Tiantian casually picked one up for her use. She had not expected it to be quite so apt, or that it would later spread so widely. But when the tag circulated among her circle of friends several times and again flew back to the edges of Tiantian's ears, she felt it had become a little strange and stale. It seemed as if, what she had originally poured out was a glass of water, yet what flew back over some time had turned into a cup of tea. The tea was originally from the water, but the tea was not entirely water.

Qin Yang was a waiter at a café next to Tiantian's office building. Once when Tiantian was there to grab a coffee on her lunch break, she had heard Qin Yang speak two or three sentences of poor English to the customers and recognized he was a fellow countryman. Diving straight in, reckless and unbridled, she began to speak Chinese with Qin Yang. Tiantian lived alone, as did Qin Yang. Of course, people being alone would have a lot of free time, especially in a city such as Toronto which has an extremely long and cold winter. So naturally they got together to plan and fill up their spare time. Qin Yang went in at noon and worked until midnight, working for two days and resting one, while Tiantian was a well-disciplined nine-to-fiver. On the days Qin Yang was working, the two would meet in the café during the lunch break. Tiantian deliberately arranged her lunch break to start at two o'clock, when business at the café was slowing down. On days when Qin Yang did not work, he would buy some vegetables in Chinatown, waiting for Tiantian to get home, so they could cook and eat together—the two seldom ate out. Tiantian was a white-collar beauty with an annual salary of seventy thousand Canadian dollars, while Qin Yang's income was close to the minimum wage line. At first, Tiantian proposed cooking at home to prevent Qin Yang from feeling hard-pressed. Later it became a habit, and they found that eating at home had many advantages, so they were unwilling to eat out any longer.

The greatest advantage was that they could drink without regard to becoming drunk and having to drive.

Qin Yang was nimble of limb, and he was also a good cook. When the dishes had all been served on the table and a glass had been put down before each, they would begin to pour gently and drink slowly. Qin Yang kept away from beer and wine, and only drank the cheapest imported *Erguotou* liquor from Beijing found in Chinatown. Slowly getting used to this strong traditional Chinese liquor, without thinking, Tiantian found she had also become a hard drinker. They drank slowly, so a glass of liquor could be nursed through most of the night. The liquor flowed down their guts in drops. In this way, it was only enough to splash one or two thrilling flushes on their cheeks, but it still could not lift the storms in their hearts. When they drank to the extent that their bodies felt as if being dismantled into numerous fragments while their brains were still one integrated mass, they would stop drinking. Lying on the sofa and throwing a few glances at the TV, they would then drift off to sleep. When they woke again, it would probably be the middle of the night. At home, Tiantian wore the most casual everyday clothing. After being soaked in liquor and dreams, and with a smelly mouth, disheveled hair and dirty face, she rather resembled a female ghost—yet she did not display the slightest state of coyness in front of Qin Yang. Halfway between drunkenness and waking, desire would grow.

They also did the thing that all urban men and women wanted to do when staying together, and they did it violently.

Tiantian, who had already gone through the mud of marriage, naturally did it as easily as traveling along familiar roads in a light carriage, though Qin Yang was neither her previous road nor her previous carriage, something that she had known from the outset. Qin Yang was a zigzagging route, and each bend of it hid a number of unpredictable surprises, skill and tenderness, as if from unremitting practice in his lifetime.

When the days were warmer, the two would go downstairs and sit in the street—side park next to the apartment building, listening to some dreary tunes played by street musicians far away, and tearing off a few bits of bread to feed the pigeons strutting all over the ground. Then they would walk to Chinatown's Chinese Theater to watch a late movie. They were mostly Cantonese films with Mandarin subtitles—Qin Yang's English was so poor that he could not follow English films. Then Qin Yang would walk Tiantian home, before driving back to his own residence.

One day, after Qin Yang had seen Tiantian to the door of her apartment building, he got into the car and stuck his head out to say, "Tiantian, I'd better move here to live, or I'll get tired out from coming and going in a rush." As Qin Yang uttered this, he had a slight stutter, yet Tiantian said nothing. Looking at Qin Yang's secondhand car spluttering in bursts into the thick darkness of the whole street, Tiantian's mood suddenly turned complicated.

Before that night, Tiantian's feelings toward Qin Yang had been unusually simple—a sort of expediency, a level of convenience and a period of transition. Qin Yang was four years younger than Tiantian. Qin Yang had not formally gone to any university. Qin Yang had no official immigration status. Using someone else's social insurance number, he was working illegally. One month of his income, beyond his expenses on rent, food and the car, was perhaps enough to buy only a few bottles of *Erguotou*. Qin Yang's wretchedness not only lay in the fact that he had nothing to his name, but also in that he had no potential to make any sudden transformation. Qin Yang's existence seemed only to resemble a footnote for people like Tiantian. In those stories about successful immigrants, which filled Chinatown's newspapers, Tiantian was the headline printed in red, while Qin Yang was the referred object which set off the title. Other than age, there was no comparability between Qin Yang and Tiantian. Moreover, the age contrast made Tiantian's thoughts about Qin Yang even simpler—Tiantian had never had a second thought about him.

On that night after Qin Yang uttered that sentence, what came to Tiantian's mind from chatting on ordinary days was Qin Yang mentioning he wanted to run a coffee shop. Over the past few years, Qing Yang had worked in that café. Though it was hard work, he still learned a few tricks about making money. Then he wanted to open a café of his own—like one below a large office building, offering breakfast and lunch, a large flow of customers, and short business hours. Qin Yang had very specific and detailed ideas about the café. He had thought of the types of food, decor and staff. He had even thought up a name, "Dragon Tower" (or "Long Ta" in Chinese). *Long Ta* sounded like "long time" in English, implying "everlasting." Qin Yang had taken into account every detail of his tower and its pinnacle, but the only thing that he had not mentioned was the foundation of the tower—capital and immigration papers. Without these two things, Qin Yang's tower could amount merely to flowers in the mirror or the moon in the water—an illusion, however carefully and specifically he had imagined it through.

Qin Yang, however, did not have these two things.

But Tiantian had them.

Tiantian had already obtained her Canadian citizenship a long time before. Though there might not be much cash on hand that could be spent, Tiantian would be able to take full advantage of her job to apply for a commercial bank loan.

If what Tiantian had could also become Qin Yang's, then Qin Yang's Dragon Tower could be erected solidly and beautifully.

Tiantian was surprised by these connections. In retrospect, it seemed that each look and deed of Qin Yang had been paved with a layer of eagerness. From that day onwards, Tiantian deliberately alienated Qin Yang. Using excuses of meetings, business trips or guests at home, Tiantian gradually had fewer chances to meet Qin Yang. Of course, she no longer went to the café where Qin Yang was working to have her lunch.

During those days without Qin Yang, time suddenly stretched longer, without any order. Arriving home from work and walking into that empty apartment, Tiantian's head would be wrapped again by the loneliness of the previous night like a soft but all-pervading net. No matter how Tiantian knocked and kicked at it, she could not chisel even a small hole through it. Then she thought of the various merits Qin Yang possessed—his gentle disposition and carefulness, his humor, his enthusiasm for life and vitality, and his just-right flattery. Throughout her contact with Qin Yang, the distance he gave her was always apt. If it had been a bit closer, it would have been possible to feel suffocated, and if a bit farther, to lose her sense of security. Close or far, he was seldom thrown into confusion. So Tiantian began to cherish memories of Qin Yang, and several times she even picked up the phone to dial the string of numbers she had by now learned by heart. However, each of Qin Yang's merits also made her anxious—all such merits seemed to be possessed by all the gigolos in modern or ancient times, in China or elsewhere. Woman's favor was their rice bowl and their heaven. Tiantian, though willing to be coaxed and flattered by a man, had never thought of being a man's rice bowl and his heaven.

So she would in the end put down the phone in a panic.

Tiantian later found other ways to kill those endless nights. She began chatting online with strangers one night after another, and she also began to participate in a variety of friend clubs. She had thus associated with a number of men. Her heart had become hot for a while, and then cooled off for a while. Her expectations would fly high among the clouds, but then fall low into the mud or earth. The hot and cold spells and ups and downs simply exhausted her vigor. Gradually, Tiantian discovered that thoughts about Qin Yang in her heart had worn thin.

The story between Tiantian and Qin Yang would actually have drawn to a crisp full stop, but something unexpectedly happened to Tiantian at this point. The incident made this full stop slip and acquire a small tail, changing into a comma. So the story, like a tree that had almost dried up, accidentally grew a new branch.

One day Tiantian had come home from work, and driven her car into the underground parking lot. Just as she was getting out, she felt a sudden burst of a roaring in both her ears, as if thousands of autumn cicadas were colliding in flight. The lights on the ceiling turned into a meteor shower, spilling and wheeling down at her one burst after another. Her both legs became soft, and she fell down.

Waking up, she dimly saw a wreath before her eyes and on the wreath some flowers hung. The flowers were very big, and their stamens and pistils kept wriggling, giving out a variety of sounds. After a while, her eyesight gradually cooled and brightened. Only then did she see that those flowers were people's heads. Later, the flowers gradually dispersed, leaving only one, which stuck close to the side of her face.

"You're really lucky. You had driven home before having the mishap."

The flower was Qin Yang.

Tiantian had been truly shocked and asked, "What did you come here for?"

Qin Yang took a look at her, and stressing each syllable said, "I'm on call at every hour." Only at this moment did Tiantian vaguely remember that she seemed to have dialed a phone number before she fainted. That number had probably been buried shallowly in her subconscious, and just a gentle sweep could make it float to the surface. When she thought of her deliberate estrangement of late from Qin Yang, some motley traces of shyness could not help but float on to her face.

"You thought of me in the end. Haven't you heard people say, 'Faithful or not, you should see who you think of when you fall ill.'"

Qin Yang had just said it without thinking, yet Tiantian fell into a trance on hearing this, and for a moment she had no words.

Tiantian had Meniere's disease. Since she had had severe symptoms when it attacked, the doctor ordered a temporary suspension of her driving license for six months. Tiantian's residence was some distance away from the bus line. She would have to hurry to catch a bus, so Qin Yang picked her up to go to work. After a few days, Tiantian said, "You might as well live here, so as to avoid getting up so early every day."

Qin Yang in fact moved in the next day. From then on he had never moved back to his own place.

Before Tiantian went back to Canada, she found a room at Father's university for Zhao Chunzhi to live temporarily in a women's residence. It was a dormitory the university had prepared for visiting students taking foreign-language training classes. Chunzhi lived together with three visiting female students. The Department of Housing's administrative office knew that something had happened at Professor

He Chun'an's home, so they took pity on the old man and just closed one eye to the infraction, letting it go. Tiantian also went and bought a women's bicycle for Chunzhi to commute between the campus and home. After taking the keys of the room and the bicycle, housemaid Zhao Chunzhi formally took up her post.

In the morning, Chunzhi would bicycle to Professor He Chun'an's home. She went to the small food market and bought the vegetables for the day, prepared three meals, cleaned up the rooms and washed the bedding and clothing. Professor He was basically in good physical health. He had no difficulty getting about, and he was seldom choosy about food. The modest simple housework of the He family, like playing a piano before having enough time to mobilize all of her fingers, would be completed by Chunzhi in small steps. After this, a lot of time was left on Chunzhi's hands. There was only one way in which Chunzhi used her spare time. It was embroidery.

Chunzhi did not embroider the usual flowers and plants and mandarin ducks, she reproduced European oil paintings instead. Chunzhi's embroidery hoop was very large, as large as a painting. She stuck the print of an oil painting onto some fabric, and according to the colors of the painting, she would directly embroider with the needle, dark thread for the dark part and light thread for the light. But sometimes Chunzhi would not entirely follow the printed painting. For example, when embroidering a roof, she used a lot of golden thread. While doing a treetop, she should clearly have used green, but she deliberately used powder-like white instead. At first glance that yellow and white looked like bird droppings falling from midair, sticking between the roof and the branches, protruding and awkward. Only after the embroidery of a painting had been finished and hung far away on the wall, if one squinted the eyes and savored it carefully, one would find the yellow and white made patches of waterfall-like sunlight suddenly emerge out of the original dark scene.

He Chun'an looked at it stunned for a long while, and then uttered softly, "I never imagined..."

Chunzhi threw the scissors and the spools of thread back into the sewing kit with a bang, and smiled, saying, "What couldn't you imagine? You never imagined us country folk could have some creative gray matter, could you?" Over the few days Tiantian had been in Beijing, Chunzhi had had to think twice before speaking. As soon as Tiantian left, Chunzhi showed her true self, saying whatever she thought of, shooting from the lip. Finding no way to respond to her, He Chun'an could only chuckle.

In fact, He Chun'an also had a lot of free time. He rarely went to the university anymore. He could not handle people's evasive, half sympathetic, half speculative eyes. Those eyes, like webs of fine silk that hung from the treetops on spring days, could be broken with a gentle pull of the finger. Broken on the fingers, though invisible, it still stuck, and always made one feel not that clean and pure.

He Chun'an loved reading in his spare time. While reading, he did not at all adopt the methods chosen by ordinary readers. His preparations and positions for reading were truly finicky. First of all, tea was a must. It had to be the best-quality *mao jian* (a high-quality Chinese green tea, poured the second time—the first having to be filtered and drained). Second, his reading glasses had to be wiped carefully after breathing on them; they could not retain a shred of mist. Furthermore, the tilted angle of the reclining chair had to be at an exact position. It had to be adjusted to the position where his head and neck would form an almost forty-five-degree angle with his body. Only after all these preparations in grand style had been set up would He Chun'an try to immerse himself in his reading. His heart would calm down, but he still could not read his book. Like slabs of shadowy rock, the characters in the book in a seething throng would block out He Chun'an's thoughts. He could understand each slab of rock, but he failed to comprehend the mountain. After his eyes had made several anxious and confused strides between the rocks, he became very tired. Sleepiness came tripping down, as the book fell on to the floor with a thump.

Picking up the book, Chunzhi lifted up the front of her dress and wiped off He Chun'an's saliva which had fallen on the book. She saw a photograph on the cover of a European woman with a steeply bridged nose, black brows and sunken eyes. The woman's smile was faint, her lips tightly closed, and she looked somewhat forlorn. Flipping through the pages of the book, she could not locate a single Chinese character throughout the text. Taken aback, she suddenly remembered the old man had a background in teaching English. She could not help but chuckle loudly.

The laughter woke up He Chun'an. Sitting up, he could not figure out where he was for a moment. Being drowsy, he suddenly called out, "Yan'an!" After this yell, he became completely awake. Sitting there distracted for a while, he then got up slowly and went to the toilet.

With a click, the door was locked from the inside. After a while, there was some tinkling water sounds, followed by the swish of rushing water. Still later, there was a long period of solid silence. Chunzhi had heard about how Li Yan'an had died. During this hush, she suddenly got a bit scared. She could not help but quietly walk over, put her ear to the door, listening with bated breath. Startling her, before she could stand upright again, the door suddenly opened. With her body leaning over, she almost fell. He Chun'an held her up, and with a sigh said, "She was a fool. How could I be as foolish as she was?"

Chunzhi's heart calmed down from its roaring. With a sigh, she added, "People say she was a fool, but they did not understand her. Even you are following behind them. She was not silly at all. She'd clearly fallen ill. She endured such suffering, since you couldn't take on her suffering for her or free her from the pain, why not let her go free? You were reluctant to let go of her, because you're selfish, yet she freed herself. Suppose you tried this illness, with its endless and incurable suffering inflicted on you, how would your body stand it?"

He Chun'an had never heard others try to influence him this way. Suddenly, a narrow ray of light flew into a heart that had turned dark and thick as a tunnel. In the light, a fine dust rose slightly. A heart, downcast and tight for many a day, began its first tiny bit of loosening up.

They both returned to the living room—the one who had been embroidering was still embroidering; the one who had been reading was still reading. Chunzhi held the end of a thread in her mouth for a long time before spitting it out. Pouting her lips at the book in He Chun'an's hands, she asked, "Professor He, that Woolf, are her writings good?"

He Chun'an was surprised, and he asked, "Can you read English?" Flushed, Chunzhi said she knew just a few words. That family whom she used to work for had liked to watch videos. One film was about this Woolf. It said she was a famous English writer, and had drowned herself in a river.

"The film you mention is called *The Hours*. It describes the period before Woolf's death. In fact, she was already very famous when she had been alive, but her death brought little. The year I visited London, I propped up a broken umbrella under heavy rain to look for Virginia Woolf's residence in Gordon Square. I found it. There was not even a sign. Yet on the house beside it was a big sign, saying it was such and such a person, who had sponsored Woolf. Even in England, it's the same—hey only remember the rich patrons, but not the talented scholars."

Giving out a snort of laughter, Chunzhi said, "Why don't they remember?

Professor He, you're reading whose book now? Do the rich leave behind any books? Haven't you heard that anyone can buy a degree after getting rich? It is clear that scholars are somewhat more peculiar than the rich."

He Chun'an was amused by Chunzhi, and he laughed, saying, "Yes, right enough, that Woolf, everyone studying foreign literature has to read her books. She really spoke for you women. It is she who said that if a woman wanted to write books, she had to first have her own room, and then she had to have an annual income of five hundred pounds. What she said was that a woman should be self-supporting—all these things were the initial flickers of feminism."

Pursing her lips, Chunzhi said, "Feminism or whatever, I don't understand it. I only know that woman may look pretty and bright, but her heart was cold, all the way dark and cold to the end. Even the nicest man would not be able to warm her up."

He Chun'an did not speak. After a long while, Chunzhi looked up and saw the mottled stains of tears on his cheeks.

In Li Yan'an's heart, it was perhaps dark and cold all the way to the end as well, and no one could warm her up, so she had decided to go to a kind of extreme, right?

However, when Li Yan'an was young, she had been a torch, or a lamp. Even when standing at the darkest intersection, she could easily light herself and light others up as well.

When He Chun'an had first met Li Yan'an, he had already graduated from university several years before. He had stayed at the university to teach European and American literature in the foreign language department, while she had just been assigned to the library of the university to become a librarian. He occasionally heard from other people that her father had been a well-known general, and so he began to grow a tiny bit curious about her. At that stage of his life, it was just about right to describe his curiosity over her as being "a tiny bit."

By that time he had already long stopped resembling a sheet of white paper.

He Chun'an had begun to learn English at a missionary school when he was young. His accent had a trace of Oxford, and his writing in English rang authentic and elegant. From childhood, he had read all the classics and knew them thoroughly by heart. He would often have great facility speaking about whatever came to mind — he was naturally a topnotch professional in the foreign language department — yet he did not have the usual superficiality and frivolity of other foreign language professors. He was honest and down-to-earth when conducting himself, so naturally he won female favor. Before getting to know Li Yan'an, he had already had two love affairs. One was a college classmate, and the other was the younger sister of a friend. However, when it came to the extent of considering marriage, both women had stepped back. He was from a locale inhabited by returned overseas Chinese and relatives of overseas Chinese. His life experience was full of stories, and he had many close and distant relatives overseas, but in the department this meant, whether it was concerning rank or pay raise, he always fell behind all the others. Both his girlfriends had also left him because of this.

The two women were not of the empty-headed and vulgar kind at all. They were from the elite among people, the flowers of flowers. They both knew very well his strengths. But his strengths were like an umbrella, while his life experience was the rain. No matter how good the umbrella was, it could only withstand the rain for a season, but would not withstand a whole life of downpours. So later each of them chose a sunny day that did not need an umbrella.

Through those two love affairs, he had been half dead and half alive. When they had ended, he felt as if his heart and spirit were worn out. In an era when people paid attention to purity and simplicity with regard to everything, his experience of feelings could be counted on to be complicated even to the point of suspiciousness. After that, whenever he met young women of marriageable age, he would grow quite anxious, fearing loss before gain. The anxiety had been initially hidden vaguely in the depths of that corner of his heart. Later it was stirred by the passage of time and emerged in fragments, accumulating at the corners of his eyes, the tips of his eyebrows, sideburns and on the edges of his lips. Until one day while wiping his hair in front of a mirror in a bathhouse, he suddenly discovered he had acquired his first gray hairs of abjection and vicissitude.

That day had been He Chun'an's twenty-fifth birthday. He had come out of the bathhouse of the university after having a shower. Carrying a string bag holding the dirty clothes he had changed from, and walking in the warm April spring across the campus, his wet hair was being raised by the wind freely, so his head resembled a blooming dandelion. His state of mind that day had been in precise line with the metaphor of the dandelion — from blossom to death, only a gust of wind seemed to be needed. The age of twenty-five was like a threshold, before which he had ap peared unconscious, and after which he suddenly felt the rising winds.

But, unlike him, the Li Yan'an of that day had still been a stack of white paper. Just nineteen pages, she was as white as snow, without any marks or creases.

At that time Li Yan'an's parents had come to the end of their military years, and were gradually adapting to the stability of city life. When the parents had finally realized the presence of their child, Li Yan'an had already grown into a robust young tree of her own, like a tuft of grass in a crevice. Despite having had the best schools or the most competent teachers, Li Yan'an had by then lost all interest in reading books. Being a repeater, Li Yan'an had barely graduated from junior high, but in any case she could not pass the entrance exam into high school, so she worked in a factory as a lathe operator for a few years. Although Li Yan'an had long known that she did not have the makings of a student, she had still been looking forward to working in an environment of scholars. Feeling guilty about his daughter, Li Yan'an's father did the one personal thing in his life with his authority — and arranged for her to work at a university library. However, Li Yan'an's father's privilege could only be exercised outside the doors of the library. Everything inside the doors was to be decided by fate. After Li Yan'an came into the library, she became a librarian, though actually all she did for a long period of time were things that an unskilled worker would do — moving the books, cleaning the shelves, and doing general maintenance. A few years later, when there were younger recruits to the library, she was transferred to work in the cataloging section.

On that fateful day, after having a bath, He Chun'an had gone to the cafeteria and had his dinner, and then returned to his dormitory to leaf through a few pages of Hardy's novel. Not being in the mood for his book, he eventually decided to go to the library to locate a collection of poems of the English Lake Poets. In the aisle he found himself knocked over by a cart full of books. A tapered iron protrusion on the wheel cut straight into his ankle, and though at that moment it only felt weak and numb — the pain was later to be an issue. His body sank, and he collapsed onto the floor like a cloth bag, his hands nursing his ankle tightly. The woman, who had been pushing, quickly stopped the cart to help him, but he was not willing to let go of his hands. After a while, liquid seeped slowly through his fingers, dyeing his socks into a purple and red picture. Onlookers began to exclaim. The woman pushed his hands aside, whipped his socks off, tied a firm knot around his ankle, and helped him to the clinic of the university. The woman was not very tall, so he had to hunch his body to lean on her shoulder, but that day he felt as if he were leaning against a short yet strong brick wall, on which he actually propped his own weight at peace.

Only after his wound was treated did he get a chance to look at the woman. This first glance brought many surprises — he had not at all expected that she was actually that young, so young that she almost could not be called a woman. Her clothing, hairstyle, the expression in the eyes and her stature, everything impeccably displayed her non-flirtatious bewilderment. He asked her what her name was, and why he had not seen her in the library before. She said her name was Li Yan'an, and she was new, being there only three days. When answering questions, she was very honest in her manner, and even a bit nervous, almost completely lacking any further explanations, which formed a striking contrast to the bold sophistication shown when she was dealing with the incident. Her face was a little smudged — probably from hauling books, her sweat streamed mottled splotches resembling the shadows of trees midst the smudging, and her damp hair at the temples curled into small circles. She was different from all the women he had ever met, and she also made those women seem pale, morbid, arid and overdone.

Suddenly he began to have a good feeling about her.

He asked her why she was not afraid of blood, and how she could have so much strength. This time she only smiled, but did not answer.

The real answers were gathered after he gradually became familiar with her childhood.

Li Yan'an was born in Yan'an, the old revolutionary base. Like most Yan'an children at that time, she had been sent to local villagers to be brought up. After she was weaned, she had entered nursery school. Her parents might have gone to the nursery school to see her, or they might not have. Before the age of six, other than knowing her father was surnamed Li, Li Yan'an had almost no inkling of who her parents were at all.

Since the nursery school was often moved, Li Yan'an quickly adapted herself to a life of sleeping on horseback and awaking on horseback. Once she had been so fast asleep that she fell off the horse, which no one actually noticed. Only that very next morning, when she was awakened by the cold dew, did she realize the horse team had already vanished far away. She walked for three whole days along the residue traces of horse hoofs and horse manure, until she finally caught up with the great cavalcade. That day when an "Auntie" from the nursery school had gone to the well to fetch water, she thought she saw a dirty dog lying by the well. Kicking out casually with her foot, she heard a sound, only to then discover this was a human being. She used an oil lamp to shed some light, and realized it was Li Yan'an. Li Yan'an had lost a shoe, and her bare foot was blurred by pus and blood. Her ankle had been lacerated by a rock, and the wound was so deep that the bone could almost be seen. The Auntie washed her wounds, picking out the thorns in the foot one by one. What she picked out looked not so much like thorns, but rather blood pins, dropping with pinging sounds onto and almost filling a plate. As she was picking out the thorns this Auntie was on the verge of tears, yet Li Yan'an did not cry through it all. She just repeatedly told the Auntie to pinch her next time if she fell asleep.

At that point Li Yan'an would have been about five and a half years old—like most of the children in the nursery school, she did not know her own exact date of birth.

Not long after that, like the other children at the nursery, Li Yan'an was reunited with her parents. The children had little knowledge of the changes in the world, only knowing they had to leave the nursery school and go to the city. The next day when she entered the city, Li Yan'an was led into a big courtyard with gray bricks, in which sat two adults — a man and a woman — and three children who were younger than she was. Holding her hand, the person who accompanied her inside asked her to call the two adults, "Papa and Mama," and then asked those children to call her "Elder Sister." She neither called out nor replied. The wind was blowing hard that day. Dirty-snow-like catkins covered the sky. The sun looked like a big bowl molded from loess turned upside down listlessly on a roof thick with dust. A family separated by war and four children who did not know each other were thus hastily joined together that afternoon, an afternoon that was very gloomy both in colors and emotions. Yet at that moment, no one could have had the foresight to know that the process of adaptation would still be continuing for the rest of their lives.

Only after a few years did Li Yan'an learn from other children in the compound that the woman she called Mama was, in fact, not her mother. Her own mother had marched out of the snowcapped mountains and then out of the grasslands, but had died of some disease on the way to the city. The one who had later walked into the city with Father was a female soldier in an art troupe.

But this was no longer important to Li Yan'an.

Li Yan'an's father and stepmother, upon climbing down from their horses, both had walked straight into an office building. There were so many new things in town, and what they were to learn was so rich that they had no time at all to attend to their children. It was a nanny who was over fifty years old who took care of the children's daily needs. In Li Yan'an's view, she had merely moved from one nursery school to another. Carrying on as before, in the style where the older children took care of the younger in the nursery school, she naturally assumed the tasks of caring for the younger siblings. Soon, under her training, this troop, which had only three soldiers, was in good order. In this new order, the adults merely loomed inessential in the background. Li Yan'an never had a childhood. After her first cry as a baby, she seemed to have assumed the responsibilities of an adult, taking care of herself, and taking care of others as well.

This feeling, like a tendon, ran through her relationship with He Chun'an, all the time.

After getting to know him, almost with no ritual of handover, transformation or transition, she had immediately reverted to her usual role. Like a large and healthy hen, she plumped her wings open and covered him completely. Although he was six years older than she was, she became his elder sister and mother as well. She took care of all his needs. Instantly his world became smaller, so small that there was only a space one wing wide. In that one–wing space, only one season out of the four remained, and it was perpetual spring. In the perpetual spring, he could stretch his limbs and soul freely. But, unconsciously, all those functions that he once used to deal with other seasons gradually shrank and decomposed.

In the third year after their marriage, that storm, which later became research topics for modern Chinese history, devastatingly raged across the campus. In the foreign language department, He Chun'an was neither a person in power nor a favorite with the people in power. He was essentially a carefree personality, and did not make many enemies. With his old father–in–law the general as a shield, he went through the initial stages in relative safety.

Later, the prominent personalities in the department came a cropper in succession and became dead tigers. The workers' propaganda team moved in, and a new leading group gradually formed. When the sound of fierce hand–to–hand fighting grew quiet, everyone suddenly realized they had lost the new targets of struggle. Using a buzzword in today's political arena to explain the circumstances of that time, we might say that the foreign language department was situated in a stagnating phase where it lacked achievements. The attention of members of the new leading group therefore gradually turned to He Chun'an.

The workers' propaganda team located He Chun'an and had a discussion with him.

That evening Li Yan'an had arrived home a little later than usual. The situation at the library was very tense as well — someone had "confessed" about the business of Li Yan'an's father planting his daughter in the library, and Li Yan'an thus found herself kicked onto center stage with no preparation. Fortunately, in the library Li Yan'an was merely one of the support personnel, not included in the authorized allotment of cadre. In that environment where there were loads of intellectuals, Li Yan'an's junior-high-school diploma and simple life experience, written on less than one page in her file flap, made the ones criticizing and denouncing her almost fail to find any suitable words, so after being reprimanded hastily with a few words, Li Yan'an was sent home.

Li Yan'an walked into a room that was completely dark. She thought her husband had not come home, and she turned on the light, preparing to make a fire and cook. On bending down to measure the rice, she suddenly found He Chun'an sitting on the floor, holding his head like a clay or wooden sculpture. Greatly surprised, she asked him why, but he did not speak. She asked again, and he then said he had a headache.

Li Yan'an helped her husband to bed, let him lie down, and began to wash the rice and vegetables to make the meal. As soon as the fire was hot, she was overcome by the fumes of hot oil, and a mass of acid gushed up to her throat. Hardly had she had a chance to find a washbasin, when she had to squat on the threshold, where she vomited all over the ground. At noon, she had not eaten anything, so what she spat out was no more than bile. By then, Li Yan'an had been pregnant for seven and a half months, yet her morning sickness had not disappeared. Hearing his wife vomiting violently, while in bed He Chun'an just sighed over and over again, saying, "What time have you chosen to come, you?" Li Yan'an knew that her husband was referring to the baby in her belly, so she could not help but retort, "Was this chosen by me alone? Can you tell what time is a good time?"

The two had a quiet meal, only taking a few gentle stabs at the rice and dishes before putting everything back into the cupboard. When Li Yan'an was clearing the table, she heard her husband sigh quietly behind her, saying, "Yuanyuan, just call it Yuanyuan, that means the 'one.'" Hearing this, Li Yan'an felt a thump in her chest, and after a long while smiled and said, "Don't give me a set number. If I'm happy, I could give birth to a dozen. I'd like a large family. It would be lively." But secretly she grew on guard against He Chun'an, carefully watching every move of his.

That night Li Yan'an lay down but she dare not sleep. Autumn insects were buzzing at an extremely high pitch outside the window, and the baby in her belly was kicking quite ferociously, as if to kick a hole through her belly. Afraid of disturbing He Chun'an, Li Yan'an dared not turn over fully. With her body stiff in one posture, every joint and each pound of flesh became so sore and itchy that she could hardly bear it. Only after midnight, when she felt she could stand it no longer, did she finally fall asleep. Muddled, she had a dream where He Chun'an, wearing a snow-white, front-buttoned, soft plain-weave silk gown, sailed up to her like a willow blown by the wind. She held out her hand to grab him, but each of her attempts came up empty. It was as though he had turned into smoke or gas, slipping here and there through her fingers. Brimming with anxiety, she woke up. When she felt around the bed next to her, she discovered the space was empty, so she flopped herself down onto the floor, to stumble and fumble about making her way to the outer room. Darkness was gathering, the moon hanging outside the window, lighting up the whole room as brightly as water, and the shadows made by the trees on the gray brick floor seemed to wander about like ghosts and goblins. She turned on the light with a tug, and vaguely saw a person standing at the corner, holding a cup and pouring water down his mouth in a hurry. She dashed over like a wolf and slapped the person hard on the face. That person was unprepared, the cup in his hand fell down with a bang, and white pills rolled all over the ground.

This slap was so violent that her body tumbled over and she fell, plopping like a sack to the floor. Her arm felt sprained, and suddenly swelled into a ball of flesh. Her eyes were filled with tears of pain. He came over to hold her up. She held her arm, yet gave out a hard kick towards him. He staggered and struck the washstand. The washbasin turned and fell, rolling with a hum all the way to the foot of the wall before it stopped with a clang. The lights in the corridor of the dormitory building clattered on, and someone opened a window to peek out. He hastily cupped his hand over her mouth, helping her back to bed, half supporting, half shoving her a-long.

She indeed lay down, but her sleepiness had long disappeared. Covered with a quilt, she muttered to him through clenched teeth, "After hiking over snowcapped mountains and grasslands, my papa lost a leg, a wife and two sons. Now what did he get in the end? He did not feel wronged. How could you feel wronged? Have you had a single hard day in your life, you?"

But these curses woke up He Chun'an. Thinking it over, he actually had nothing to respond with. Gradually, he felt some sense of shame in his heart, and then he laughed softly and said, "Wife, you are a light, and once you light up my heart, there are no more dark corners in there any longer."

"Bah," Li Yan'an snorted, then added, "Even if the brightest light was used to light up Louis the whatever, it would have been a waste of time."

He Chun'an, not understanding, asked, "What do you mean by Louis the whatever?"

Li Yan'an gave him a sharp pinch and said, "I mean the one who said, 'When I am dead, let the deluge come for all I care.' He was as repulsive as you are." Only now did He Chun'an realize that Li Yan'an had also read the materials he normally used to prepare his lessons. They hugged each other, no longer talking. Looking at the moon outside the window gradually sinking, faint red on the horizon, all of a sudden they felt as though everything had happened in a remote past.

From then on, He Chun'an slowly became thick-skinned, allowing the world to vigorously stage all sorts of operas, some going onstage and others offstage, while he himself always played the role of a deadpan audience. He was at first taken into custody and under investigation for a while, then sent to perform manual labor in the countryside for a time, before later being transferred back to the foreign language department just like the others. Although there were fluctuations in his moods, he no longer had the will to try to commit suicide.

But when did Li Yan'an's light get extinguished?

In fact, Li Yan'an's light had not gone out in any single instant. From its brilliance to its last breath, it went through a process of dimming. This process was gradual, and the people inside it had not sensed it. All the signs were only to be realized afterwards.

After the Cultural Revolution, He Chun'an was among the first batch of teachers to be promoted to become professors, who were granted qualifications to supervise graduate students, and selected and sent to go abroad for short-term studies. He Chun'an's life, after a long period of hibernation, suddenly revived in middle age. The revival brought about many unanticipated scenes. Li Yan'an gradually realized that He Chun'an no longer needed her light, for he had become his own light. He became more than his own light, he even became her light. And he was more than a light to her alone, for his light came to also shine upon many others, including his colleagues and students. Her worried heart, which had been trembling for many years for him, gradually relaxed. Of course, she did not know at that time that the most suitable state of survival for her was actually tenseness. At the moment of tension, she was a drawn bow. Held in the hand, it had a secret reserve of strength, and when issuing arrows it would clang, making the arrows fly straight to the bull's-eye. Relaxed, she was like a pool of water splashed on the ground, floating casually along the fissures in the ground. As it ran, it no longer ran with purpose and vigor, yet having no alternative, it bowed to the inevitable wherever it went.

As all of the nerves had relaxed, only one nerve suddenly tightened. Li Yan'an's eyes and ears became unusually sensitive to certain scenarios and voices. He Chun'an was acquiring more and more students, and he was also assuming heavier and heavier responsibilities in the department. Li Yan'an's eyes indifferently scanned like radar the busy life of her husband's world. Most of the data was filtered out as irrelevant background, until what was left on the screen were just a few fine points. But those few fine points, like grains of sand, rubbed here and there in Li Yan'an's eyes, making her unable to sleep and eat with any peace.

Those grains of sand were He Chun'an's female students and female colleagues.

Li Yan'an began to monitor He Chun'an's telephone calls, to break into his office and peek through his letters, and she asked everybody about every single one of his actions in the department. Gradually, when meeting He Chun'an, female colleagues in foreign language department dared not joke around with him so easily.

In order to protest his innocence, He Chun'an dared not be seen alone with any female students either, and he was also afraid to invite female students or female colleagues home. God had played a neither big nor small joke on He Chun'an: God had broadened He Chun'an's field of vision and made him see various possibilities under the sun, but in that vast and unlimited world, all he could have was but a window even narrower than before.

Li Yan'an's sight had already become beclouded by grains of sand and her light had gradually dimmed as well. She was lost along a road she had grown used to walking for years. At the beginning, He Chun'an kept helping his wife clean out those grains of sand, but later he learned that the harder he cleaned, the faster the sand would accumulate.

He had no choice but to choose silence.

Li Yan'an finally walked into that darkness beyond redemption. No one could warm her up, and no one could light her way. Even her children, or even her husband, could only watch her walking farther away step by step, alone.

After returning to Toronto, He Tiantian heard some sporadic reports giving different versions about housemaid Zhao Chunzhi's performance by Father's side.

The first report was from Father's student Yan Hua.

Li Yan'an's suicide, like a rock, smashed a big hole in the waters of the bottomless pond of the foreign language department. The hole soon recovered, but the ripples lasted a longer time. Like winds blowing among the treetops, the rumors were neither visible nor tangible, but they slipped in through the cracks of the doors, the crevices in the walls, and the gaps along the window frames, quietly climbing out to hover over kitchen tables and the heads of the beds without leaving any traces, but then with accumulated dust, after climbing into neighboring homes, growing bigger and bigger. He Chun'an's female students more or less knew that they were lengths of lace among the swirling tidbits of news. And Yan Hua also knew that she was that "Yan Hua'er" (flower in the eyes) in the mouth of her teacher's wife, as the lace set in the brightest part among all the tidbits. She also understood the truth that, "Although I did not kill Bo-ren, yet Bo-ren died because of me," so for a while she lowered her voice and held her breath too much. After some time, only when the rumors fell slightly quiet, could Yan Hua inevitably think of the considerable support her supervisor had given her before, so she could not help now but go and pay a visit to Professor He at his home.

It was about ten o'clock on a Saturday morning when Yan Hua arrived. She had picked this time because Professor He should have finished his exercises and be reading books or newspapers. Yan Hua, holding a bouquet of white chrysanthemums, walked up the flights of steps. Along the landing of each floor, there were curious eyes. When she finally knocked at the door of Professor He Chun'an's home, her back was sweating from the pressures of layer upon layer of eyes.

It was Zhao Chunzhi who came to open the door.

Zhao Chunzhi was wearing a peach-red sweater that day, light beige trousers, and a white silk scarf around her neck. Although the clothes were old, they had just been washed and ironed clean and neat. She did not look like a housemaid, but rather a female relative paying a visit to someone else's home. Yan Hua was slightly taken aback, and she asked, "Is Professor He in?"

Zhao Chunzhi nodded and showed Yan Hua into the apartment. Walking through the living room, Yan Hua saw at first glance He Chun'an sitting on a stool, washing clothes with his sleeves rolled up. The stool was very low, while He Chun'an was tall. Sitting down, he covered everything, as if he were sitting on the floor. He Chun'an was rubbing a shirt awkwardly, the washboard sliding back and forth between his knees. At the back of his head was a lock of hair, which had not been combed well, shaking to and fro along the direction of his body movements. Yan Hua's words, "Professor He," rolled back and forth on the tip of her tongue several times. By the time she managed to spit them out, the words had been broken up. He Chun'an looked up and accidentally glimpsed the visitor, his eyes gradually becoming blurred—after the accident of Li Yan'an, Yan Hua was the first and only female student to come to visit him.

He Chun'an wiped his hands dry, walked into the living room and sat down. Yan Hua asked Chunzhi for a tall glass and stuck the chrysanthemums into it. The flowers were a handful of snow-white petals, and only the pistils had hints of light green which glowed faintly. Dipped in water, they immediately acquired some vitality, setting off a clean brilliance in the whole room. Yan Hua placed the flowers below the photo framed in black, and the two sat silently for a long time. After the long while, He Chun'an breathed out a sigh, saying, "In fact, when my wife was clear of mind, she often praised you."

Tears started gushing down Yan Hua's face. It was distress, sickness at heart, and helplessness altogether. The tears were for herself, for her supervisor, and also for the wife of her teacher. The steps taken in a momentary slip actually created such a gap that could never be bridged. Looking from this side of the gap to the other side far away was like looking upon another world in the remote past.

He Chun'an saw Yan Hua crying, yet he did not know how to console her. Rubbing his palms, he went into the kitchen to make some tea. Yan Hua heard the cups clinking in the kitchen for a while, and then Chunzhi chuckling, "Professor He, why so big a teapot, are you watering a donkey? Just one guest, the small pot with red flowers is enough." He Chun'an also laughed and said, "It's alright to abuse me as a donkey. But you are not allowed to curse my guest." He then asked about the kind of tea to use. Chunzhi said that the steel tin on the left side of the second shelf in the cupboard held jasmine tea, which was just right for entertaining female guests. He Chun'an carried a stool, climbed onto it, and opened the cupboard to take out the tea tin. Hearing this exchange, Yan Hua had a slight feeling that this housemaid was somewhat sharp-tongued and lazy. She did not sound like a servant, but more like a master. After about ten minutes, He Chun'an appeared, tottering in holding a pot of tea, but Chunzhi was not following behind him. He Chun'an put down the hot teapot. Yan Hua rushed to get up and pour the tea, for her teacher first and then for herself.

Over tea, the two discussed some university and department business. Yan Hua could not help but ask, "Professor He, why are you washing clothes by yourself?" He Chun'an replied he was not washing them by himself. He just rubbed the dirty rings on the collar and cuffs first, and then put them in the washing machine to wash.

Yan Hua had not meant exactly that in her original question, so pursing her lips toward the kitchen she lowered her voice, "Why not ask her to wash them?"

With a smile, He Chun'an said, "Chunzhi is teaching me to do housework, and I am teaching her some English. We two complement each other, so it's fair to both of us."

After leaving He's place, Yan Hua grew angrier along the way. She thought to herself, "How could Professor He, such an honest and kind person, cope in this world? This housemaid is clearly competent. She takes the money but does not do the work, and she also gets to learn English. Complementing each other as if there should be such a balance?! Professor He will probably be cheated someday by this woman, but still be helping her count the money."

Arriving home, Yan Hua sent Tiantian, far away in Toronto, an email detailing her concerns.

In fact, when Tiantian usually called home, she always asked about Chunzhi. Father only said that she was good and also very intelligent. Perhaps her father was reluctant to worry her, so he was hiding the truth. After reading Yan Hua's email, Tiantian immediately gave Father a call. She called a few times in succession. The calls were all answered by Chunzhi—Father was out. Chunzhi called her "Elder Sister" whenever she started to speak, and her voice was very affectionate. Given Yan Hua's preceding report, Tiantian felt there was a little deception and deliberation in her words. So she coldly gave Chunzhi a few words about taking good care of the elderly and so on, and then hung up.

She also called her brother in Guangzhou. Hearing this, Yuanyuan grew anxious as well, so he immediately asked for leave and flew to Beijing.

Yuanyuan stayed at home for three days. Some of Yuanyuan's feedback to Tiantian echoed Yan Hua's concerns, while other aspects were different. Yuanyuan said that Father had changed. He had taken interest in housework. Chunzhi was actually not the type of housemaid not to do any housework at all. But as long as it was something the old man could do himself, Chunzhi would give him a free hand and let him do it. If it was something that he could not do, Chunzhi indeed did it, yet she would ask him to stand beside her and learn how to do it.

Hearing this, Tiantian could not help but snicker, saying, "It's a bit of surprise but this woman is really not that simple. She's actually taming the old man—had you ever before seen him even wash a pair of chopsticks?"

Yuanyuan tried to mollify her, saying, "As long as papa is happy, let him be. Can't you see the old man is quite keen about teaching her English, even urging her to take some English tests of various levels? Didn't you worry papa would not get along well with the housemaid? Since they get along well, it saves us a lot of worry."

Tiantian thought this was true, so she put this matter aside. At night when she could not fall asleep, she nudged Qin Yang awake and asked, "Why are people so despicable when they grow old? In the past he even needed others to squeeze toothpaste onto toothbrush for him, but it's the opposite now."

Qin Yang knew that Tiantian was still thinking about the old man, so he laughed and said, "Is being troublesome related to whether or not one is old? If one is, he can be like that anytime. It is because your mother did not capture your father's heart. No one else is to blame."

Tiantian said, "Bah! How many years haven't you brushed your teeth? Why does it stink when you open your mouth? Your little speech makes it sound as if my dad were having an affair with the little housemaid."

Qin Yang remained comically cheerful, saying, "If he didn't, would he be so despicable? I have personal knowledge in this respect." Tiantian reached out her hand to poke at Qin Yang's ribs. Qin Yang was so ticklish that his body had long curled up into a ball from laughter. He curled at the end of the bed, and she could not get him to stretch out no matter how she tried, leaving only his tongue still sharp.

"Before your father married your mother, they should have consulted me first. Their names had not been given properly. Each of them has an 'An' (Peace) to their names, and the two 'Ans' do not match in the horoscope, resulting in storms. This little housemaid is named Chun (Spring) whatever. In your father's name, there is a pool of water. When water meets spring, what will ensue? Just imagine! How could he not be despicable?"

Tiantian flew into a rage out of wounded pride. Grabbing a shirt off a chair, she chased after him, swishing at him around the room. Qin Yang could not escape, so he had to flee into the bathroom and lock the door, still trembling from laughter.

"Our names are a match made in heaven. You are a Tian (Field), and I am a Yang (Sun). A field needs a sun, for all things to grow."

After being in a daze for a long while, Tiantian sneered from the other side of the door, "Unfortunately, my field is not the field you seek. Phone your high-school Chinese teacher and ask if the 'Tian' in the name He Tiantian means 'field'."

Three or four months passed at He Chun'an's side without mishap. At the end of the lunar year, Tiantian suddenly received a New Year email greeting card from Yan Hua. The card was just a cover, for the actual contents of the letter did not have much relationship with any New Year's greetings.

Yan Hua was appealing for emergency assistance.

Professor He had had a serious quarrel with the housemaid and had even smashed the casserole dish used to make soup. The housemaid had taken her bags and gone back home. Professor He's gums were terribly inflamed, and he could not even eat porridge. He had been in bed for two days. Spring Festival was around the corner. Yuanyuan was in Germany leading a group from his company for training there. The household had done no Spring Festival shopping. This being the first Chinese New Year after her teacher's wife passed away, Professor He was indeed in a bit of pathetic situation.

After reading the letter, Tiantian's head exploded with a bang. Like broken pieces littering the floor, her thoughts were so confused she was unable to gather them together. Seeing her so panic-stricken, Qin Yang advised her to make a trip back. Hearing this, Tiantian grew angry and said, "Do you think I'm so much of a millionaire that taking a plane to China is like going downstairs?"

With a smile, Qin Yang said, "Anyway, he's your father."

Tiantian repeatedly shook her head and said, "No, no, I won't go back. At worst, I'll ask someone to find a housemaid again. Those wages are enough to hire a robot with artificial intelligence. Who does Zhao Chunzhi think she is? Country people, despite rubbing off a thousand layers of skin in the city, are still rustics in their flesh and bones."

Qin Yang laughed again and said, "You didn't even think to ask them why they quarreled before letting loose a stream of abuse against her. Maybe it's your dad who's being unreasonable."

Tiantian said, "Bah! Bosses are always justified, this is an ageless truth." On saying this, she pulled the sheet up over her head, lying flat on the sofa. Under the sheet, she turned over and over again like a pancake being cooked. After a while, her body gradually grew flat and soft.

Qin Yang thought Tiantian had gone to sleep, so he went into the room. After a while, he just felt an itch on his neck. He stretched his hand out and touched it, it turned out to be Tiantian who was standing very close behind him.

She said, "Perhaps I'd better make the trip back. It's the end of the lunar year though, so I don't know if there'll be any seats left."

Qin Yang held up a piece of paper in his hand, "Missy, I already checked for you. Only Korean Air has a seat for tomorrow night. There'll be a stopover on the west coast and one in Seoul as well. When you arrive home after stopping here and there, it'll be the night before Chinese New Year's eve. As soon as you get to work tomorrow, talk to your boss and ask for leave. Make it sound a bit sensational–just say your dad has had a stroke, and is paralyzed and perhaps dying."

Tiantian did not speak. She put her hands around and hugged Qin Yang from behind.

Tiantian's plane had a slight problem, so it was delayed in Seoul for a day.

When it arrived in Beijing, it was already the night of the third day. Outside the airport, the roads looked very lonely. After more than ten minutes a taxi arrived, a driver wearing a military overcoat got out, and slowly helped lift Tiantian's baggage into the trunk of the car. Cutting open the emptiness of the whole street, the car whizzed through the chilly night wind. The driver did not try to make conversation at all. He just smoked all the way in silence. The smoke was so irritating that Tiantian began to cough a little, but she put up with it and only concentrated on reading the highway billboards on both sides. Although only a few months had passed, all the billboards had clearly been changed, for the subject on them was already a bit rusty for Tiantian. Although she read every word, she did not fully understand the connective tantalizations and suggestions between the words. Despite the familiar street views, Tiantian suddenly felt hints of estrangement as if she were a stranger.

Suddenly, with a whiz, a volley of fireworks leaped up into the sky. The fireworks were lavender color. They started as very high and lonely thin streaks, and then gradually grew fluffy and corpulent, like umbrellas opening in the darkness of night, and then slowly fell like fine rain, vanishing onto the ground with a hiss. The driver uttered a deep curse, "Seeking death, ah, it's not allowed."

Tiantian lifted her neck, waiting for the second volley, and the third, but they did not come along. Although the sky was still dark, due to the brief flashy traces, this darkness was also different from the darkness earlier. Having not spent the lunar New Year at home for five or six years, Tiantian secretly sighed, "Is this New Year's eve in Beijing?"

The taxi stopped near her home. Tiantian paid the driver, who opened the trunk and took out the luggage, but he did not make a move to leave. With both hands inserted in his sleeves, he looked at her with piercing eyes. Tiantian sudden–

ly understood, opened her purse and took out a bill, thrusting it into the driver's sleeve. Holding out two fingers, the driver grasped the bill and pulled it out. Taking a look at it under the street light, he recognized its green coloration. With a chuckle, he put it away and said, "These days, dollars are also weak, worse than before. Elder Sister, enjoy your lucky New Year at ease." He then drove off slowly.

Dragging her suitcase, Tiantian lurched upstairs floor by floor. Flowing down the corridor of each floor was the joyous din brimming through the cracks of the doors—the same melody, and the same correct pronunciation of words in that sweet and mellow voice which had undergone numerable rehearsals. Tiantian recognized right away that it was the Spring Festival Gala being broadcast. But before the door of her home it was very quiet, with no sounds of the TV. After putting her suitcase down, and smoothing out her breathing, she prepared herself to press the doorbell. She only pressed once before the door opened, as if Father had been waiting for her, leaning against the door.

Father, walking weakly from the doorway, was wearing a Chinese-style, front-buttoned, silver-gray silk-padded jacket, its front stained with scattered soup and oil marks. His jacket was new and also so thick that fat bulky wrinkles spread under his armpits and elbows. Despite such a heavy winter jacket, Father still looked very cold, with semi-dry mucus flowing down to his upper lip, and his body shaking, as if holding lots of urgent urine unable to find its right destination. Half his face was swollen, and a set of blisters had erupted around his nostrils. His lips quivered for a long while before uttering the sentence, "Little Tian, you, you came back." Tiantian had not expected this of Father, always neat and nimble, to suddenly fallen down on his luck to such awkward extent. She felt saddened, and her voice grew hoarse.

It was chilly everywhere in the apartment. The only flashes of color midst this vast expanse of murky gray were atop the TV set, two New Year cards, printed in some foreign language—mailed by her from Canada and Yuanyuan from Germany. Tiantian cleared her throat and said, "Pa, let me take you out to dinner. Besides, I'm hungry."

Father shook his head, saying, "You've really become a foreigner. How come you don't know it's New Year's eve, so except for hotels and large restaurants, everything's closed?"

Tiantian said, "Then let's go eat at a hotel. We can handle any price. I'll dig deeper into my pocket."

Father said, "All the tables at hotels were reserved a month ago. Ordinary people like you and me cannot just stand in line." With this, he went and opened the refrigerator, brought out a large bowl, and said, "I simmered pork-rib soup waiting for you yesterday, but you didn't come. We might as well add some Chinese cabbage and have pork-rib noodles now. It'll be steaming hot and delicious as well."

Father then turned on the gas stove, poured water into the wok, and heated the soup. He was still a bit awkward in his movements, but not like before, when he would not know what to do. Tiantian then knew that over the past few months, Father had gained experience in many things. She could not help sneering coldly, saying, "This Zhao Chunzhi, she actually trained you well. We spent money to hire a housemaid, only to find she was a trainer."

A noodle slipped off Father's chopsticks, fell into the metal rim around the fire, lighting a thin blue flame, giving off a hint of char, which lingered a long time. "She has her ideas: she said she came to our home to help cope with an emergency, not to give permanent help—just teaching me to learn to live by myself. Anyway, I can't rely on others for the rest of my life."

"If she really thought so, why would she leave on a whim? For such high wages, I'd like to be hired—even I'd want to be a housemaid."

With a sigh, Father said, "She didn't want to leave. It was I who drove her away. Her daughter is graduating from middle school this year. The school in her town has low standards, so she wants to transfer her daughter to a high school in Beijing. She suggested moving in with her daughter and living here in our home."

"Of course you could not promise her that. If you promised her daughter, a boyfriend could appear next, and you're not running a hotel or an inn. She had plotted against you, an old man with both property and money," Tiantian said irritably.

Father smiled, and after quite a long while, said, "My daughter, of course, is as caustic as I am—I cursed her that day. Later when Yuanyuan called me from Germany, he also scolded her."

The two remained silent, mutely having their dinner against the lively sounds coming from the other families. The noodles were very hot, the steam was enshrouding, and they both had some sweat on their foreheads. Tiantian saw Father's mouth gradually open wide, his eyes half-closed, and she knew it was long past the time he usually went to bed. She said, "Dad, please don't worry. When the holidays are over, we'll advertise in the newspaper right away, or approach the housemaid market directly. I can't believe we won't find a better housemaid than her."

Father washed his face, and went to bed. After clearing up the table, Tiantian sat down on the sofa. There was a whole twelve-hour time difference between Toronto and Beijing, so it was midnight here, when it was noon there. Although Tiantian had lost a full night's sleep during her trip, she was extremely clearheaded. Just as she was about to turn on the TV, she suddenly heard someone throwing wine bottles out on the street, waves of the sounds of breaking glass, mixed with wild shouts and voices belting out blurry lyrics beating upon the window. She then realized she had missed the bell-striking moment.

Just then, the telephone rang shrilly, almost scaring Tiantian. By the time she picked up the handset, she only heard the click of the other side hanging up. After several repeated attempts the caller finally got through again, but the line was extremely noisy. A man's voice came over intermittently, sounding sluggish and vague across the ocean.

Quite a long time passed before Tiantian figured out that the other side was asking, "Have you tried on your New Year's gift?"

Tiantian asked, "What gift?"

The other side said, "Open your handbag."

Tiantian picked up her bag, and looked everywhere both inside and out. But she could find nothing at all. Then the other side said, "It's in the hidden pouch on the left side, which you never use."

Tiantian felt around and found a little golden velvet box there. She opened it. There was a ring inside it. It was of thin silver, in the middle of which was inlaid a sapphire. The silver was of the grayish type, and the blue was a grayish blue too. At first glance it looked very dull and old, as if it had already gone through several lives over the ages. After looking at it a few more times, it slowly evinced some subtle sense of an ancient simplicity, distinct from the glitters of the market. Tiantian decided she liked it very much. She took it out and put it on her finger, before giving it a closer look, and found it was as if her hand also now possessed a profound history, and suddenly gained curves and silkiness and dignity.

"Which hand are you wearing it on?"

"Left..."

"Which finger?"

Tiantian's mouth opened a bit, and she suddenly came to her senses, so she swallowed the answer not given. There was a long while of silence at the other end of the phone, and then, a sigh swept over the line like a breeze. Tiantian's earlobe grew slightly warm.

"Tiantian, I know it's my own wishful thinking. You just choose, and decide slowly. Maybe you will find someone better than me."

Tiantian thought of countless phrases to protest her innocence, but before they could float to the tip of her tongue, she could feel they were insincere. In the end, though there might be a thousand sentences as her last resort, she could not actually find one to use as an answer. She only said in a husky voice, "Qin Yang, have a good New Year, all right?" and hung up.

After putting the phone down, she felt a touch of emptiness. Tiredness from the trip gradually floated up from the soles of her feet onto her eyelids. But she did not want to go to bed, so she sat on the sofa, raised a corner of the curtain and leaned against the windowsill to view the stillness of the night. Up until this moment, the night had been really rather like night. The moonlight had lit up the branches of the trees as if they were bloated and fat, covered with frost and snow. The wind was blowing. Waste paper and plastic bags, like birds whose wings had been broken, hobbled low as if walking along. People who had stayed up were now so tired that the lights in the windows started going out one after another. All the streets appeared deserted, after all the revelry. The most important eve of the year, the turn of the old year into the new, had passed before she could appreciate it.

Over this year, how many things had she encountered? Mother's death, her illness, Father's troubles. She had had to carry everything that had come on her own shoulders. But, in fact, she had not carried it all by herself, since Qin Yang had carried half for her. She had used Qin Yang's shoulders as freely as using her own shoulders. Before this night, she had never considered that he was just temporarily lending his shoulders to her, and that one day he would take away his shoulders and give them to another woman, one willing to wear his ring.

This thought surprised Tiantian. She realized that, in reality, she truly cared about Qin Yang in some way. She just did not know if such a bit of caring was worth her putting her whole life upon it — but she understood it would be impossible for her to use his shoulders infinitely for free. The loss of his shoulders was one type of heaviness, while the possession of his shoulders was another. Which of the two types of heaviness would she carry?

Lost in her own thoughts, she then heard someone chuckling behind her. Tiantian thought it was Father. She looked around. The door of Father's room was tightly closed, and the light was off. With bewilderment in her heart she suddenly shivered with fear, silently crying out, "Ma, as to your sufferings, we had no idea. If we had known of them, how could we have let you take this path? Since you have gone, you should feel at ease. Sooner or later, we will all meet you there. It's just a matter of time..."

Before Tiantian could finish what she was saying, she again heard the sound of laughter inside the room. The laughter this time seemed to be coming from inside her own ears. Tiantian felt the warm and gentle weight of another body getting closer, and her nose picked up a very clear hint of that extremely light scent of blooming lilacs — the only flowers Mother had liked in her lifetime. Tiantian's body seemed to have been cut in half: one half of it wanted to reach out to catch that hint of soft warmth, determinedly adding to its weight to make it stay; yet the other half wanted to close all of its tactile nerves, in an attempt to desperately withstand the invasion of such gentle warmth. Tiantian became the knot in a tug of war, pulled back and forth by two evenly matched forces. Her whole body, as if under a spell, was completely immobile. She became temporarily soaked with sweat, so she opened her eyes wide and fixed them on Mother framed in black on the wall. Mother's dashing spirit was blunted by the half-concealed lighting, traces of the passage of time hidden in the shadows. All of a sudden, slight signs of gentle peace appeared on her face. Tiantian's anxiety, after going through Mother's clear and bright eyes, gradually quieted down, as if a hot iron had fallen into cold water.

At this time Mother's lips faintly quivered and uttered one sentence. This sentence, like a shaft of smoke, gently trembled off Mother's lips, and dissipated before it had enough time to take shape. Mother said, "You go..." Mother's words which had no ending contained almost endless possibilities, like a fork in the road that could access many other roads. Only later, after the dust had settled, and one of the possibilities had gradually become obvious and grown closer to reality, Tiantian would come to understand the trajectory of this sentence. However, at that moment, Tiantian only kept demanding an answer from Mother over and over again, and only when she woke up with a start did she realize it had been all a dream...

On opening her eyes, she found Father standing in front of the sofa with his sweatshirt draped over his shoulders. He asked, "What's wrong, little Tian? You were moaning in such a way it scared me."

Tiantian took out a tissue, wiped the sweat off her forehead and, after a long while, murmured, "Nothing, I just had a weird dream." Father did not ask what the dream was, but sat down beside Tiantian, with a cup of tea moving back and forth between his two hands, clearly having no intention of leaving.

After a while, he said hesitatingly, "Maybe you can take a trip to southern Zhejiang and find Chunzhi after the New Year? That day I was so impatient I was rather extreme in what I said."

"What would you have done if you had not been extreme? You would have promised they could move in here to live?"

"In fact, she's also a reasonable person. She said she could save on the rent outside if she moved in, and with a deduction of half of her wages, the combination of the two could be counted as compensation for her daughter's expenses here."

While listening, Tiantian kept feeling scornful. Finally she had had enough. "Pa, are you truly being honest or just stupid? Don't you see she is using you as her cat's paw?"

Father was not angry, but with his head lowered he just kept pulling again and again at the end of a strand of thread on his sweatshirt, before saying, "Little Tian, I've thought about it. Someone using me would still be better than me becoming completely useless. How many other people would otherwise find an old and useless man like me useful, except for her? When you come to my age, you'll understand this experience of mine."

Father's tone was the calmness and stupor after the mood had been strained and filtered. Distracted for a moment, Tiantian held her temper and said in a gentle, soft voice, "After the New Year, we will go look for another one with a simpler background and fewer nefarious ideas. Don't worry. I won't leave until I find someone."

Father's answer was also patient and soft-spoken, "I got used to Chunzhi. I'm not going to find anybody else except her."

Tiantian had to walk back and forth several times before she found Chunzhi's home.

Tiantian had actually noticed the house earlier, but she did not expect Chunzhi's home would be like this.

Come to speak of it, the house had that design common to those suburban places between cities and rural areas south of the lower reaches of the Yangtze River—a four square, upright two-story building, with outer walls totally decorated with a layer of tiles. The tiles appeared to be gray, being the traces of weather and accumulated dust. The lower part would be snow white just after the cleansing of a heavy rain. The difference between this building and the others around it could be described with just one word — "large." Without a doubt, such a thickset chunk would originally have had some imposing facade. If the building was big, so would be its entrance. It was not a usual iron gate, but a large bivalve thick wooden structure. The wood was black touched with red, after layers of paint. In the middle there were two heavy copper rings. The color, texture and style of the gate would naturally remind people that there were stories hidden behind it. Nailed on the lintel was a cross, and on the gate, there were two lines of a bright red Spring Festival couplet, displaying contentment in fresh ink. The first line said, "God so loved the world, he gave them his only begotten son." The second read, "Whoever believes in him shall not perish but have eternal life." The first and second lines of the couplet had different numbers of words, and were neither antithetical nor rhymed, so it was not like the kind of festive Spring Festival couplet of a usual rural household, but rather one selected from the Bible. Tiantian felt surprised, wondering when Chunzhi had also started believing in a foreign religion. In addition to the large gate, there were also many windows. The windows, which were the eyes of the building, originally deep and dark, seemed to have a graceful hint of a smile due to the many paper-cuts decorating them. Approaching, Tiantian saw the fine skill apparent in the paper-cuts. They were all cut from red paper, and were all of fish, but they posed in different designs — some quiet, others noisy, some simple and honest, and others deceptively cunning. Their expressions were weak, while their details solid. Being very vivid, not a single one was identical with another—simply meaning, the liyu or "the carp has jumped over the dragon's gate," or "every year there will be greater surplus" (also pronounced yu in Chinese). Speaking of this building, it was neither new nor old, yet it had taken on a number of various styles — urban, rural, Chinese and Western — hastily mixed together. Although a bit unnatural, yet some brisk vitality emerged. If vulgarity reaches its extremes, perhaps some kind of entirely new harmony seems to come forth. Tiantian thought to herself, "A woman who owns such a building should have a well-off family. Why should she travel a thousand miles northward to become a housemaid for others?"

Then she decided to knock on the gate.

The gate was not locked, so she opened it with a gentle push. In the vestibule sat an old lady, knitting with wool, with her reading glasses on. The old lady wore her hair short, even and shiny, with imprints of a comb's teeth. She wore a short lilac woolen overcoat, and a pair of black cloth pants underneath. The wide rolled-up edges of a sweater and woolen pants showed beyond her cuffs and trouser legs — Tiantian guessed this was probably Chunzhi's mother. The wool knitting in the old lady's hands had taken shape by and large, appearing to be a pair of man's pants. The waist had been completed, and the old lady was knitting an opening in the crotch. Seeing someone walking in, she raised her head, so her glasses slipped to the tip of her nose, and the ball of wool in her hands rolled down onto the ground.

"What, what's the matter with He ... Professor He?"

Tiantian was surprised, saying, "How do you know I am from Professor He's place?"

The old lady saw she was not bringing bad news, and seemed to gradually sense relief, picking up the ball of wool from the ground. Whisking the dust off it, she said, "Chunzhi showed me a photo of your family. The photography in the capital is not as good as in our small places — you look prettier than in the photo."

Then she asked Tiantian to sit, and hurried into the kitchen to prepare tea. When she came out, there was an additional wooden tray in her hands, on which were placed seven or eight small porcelain bowls containing kumquats, olives, Chinese torreya–nuts, shelled walnut kernels, sweet potato chips, so on and so forth. Although they were all New Year snacks, they appeared slightly more refined than the snacks found in the north.

The old lady selected a small and exquisite kumquat and handed it to Tiantian, while asking, "Is your father also from our hometown?"

Tiantian said, "My grandfather was from Fanshan—Fanshan is very close to Zaoxi, and our accents are the same. Later he went to Southeast Asia, and died there, before he was forty years old. My papa was also born in Fanshan. He was taken by his uncle to Xiamen to go to school at the age of six or seven. Later he went to Beijing. He's not been back home for five or six decades."

The old lady said, "Why didn't you bring your father here this time? He could get to know his hometown again."

Tiantian smiled, but only asked where Chunzhi had gone. The old lady said she had taken her child to offer New Year greetings to the head teacher—they went there on the third day of every lunar New Year. This child's father and mother not being around, the teacher was taking care of her, so she could be considered a parent deserving extended gratitude. Tiantian paused, before asking why her father did not take care of her.

The old lady did not answer. Gazing at Tiantian, she then asked, "Is there anything you want Chunzhi to do?"

Tiantian slowly produced a letter from her pocket, and said, "Chunzhi's admission form for her College English Test, Band Six, which was sent to our home. My pa is advising that Chunzhi should go back and take the test. Having done re–

view lessons for these few months, if she does not take the test it would be a waste."

Taking the letter, and bowing her head, the old lady began muttering. Tiantian vaguely heard the words, "Thank the Lord…" Tiantian laughed, asking, "Does Chunzhi also believe in this religion of yours?"

The old lady sighed and said, "If she had believed in it, how could she have come to such a pass? She's eager to do well in everything, ah, and she has no place for even a grain of sand in her heart, how could she honor the Lord as great?"

She then began to talk about Chunzhi's life.

Chunzhi had been born in troubled times. When she was three months old, her father had to carry a load of some fine rice vermicelli, one of Zaoxi's specialties, to the city of Wenzhou to hawk his wares. It so happened that two factions, the Workers' General Headquarters and the United General Headquarters, were fighting on the street. A stray bullet hit him, killing him instantly on the street. Forced to rely only on her widowed mother's craft in embroidery and bamboo-mat weaving, Chunzhi grew up half starved. When she reached the age of seventeen or eighteen, it was as if a layer of dark skin was suddenly shed, and she became a beautiful woman overnight. Chunzhi was not only good-looking, but she was very good at embroidery as well. Chunzhi's embroidery was not the peonies or phoenixes usually done by her mother, but novel designs people in Zaoxi had never seen. Chunzhi went to the town's Xinhua Bookstore, not to buy books, but to see newly arrived European prints — German village styles, street-side churches in England, French classical portraits, so on and so forth. One month's money for food was all saved by Chunzhi to buy such pictures. After buying them, she did not put them on the wall, but used them as sources for embroidery. When the people of Zaoxi saw the foreign images embroidered by Chunzhi, they would cover their mouths and exclaim. Some people bought them and used them as decorations for their bridal chambers. Still later, they were purchased as festive gifts. It was this skill that Chunzhi relied on to support herself to finish high school.

Chunzhi was not only good at embroidery, but she was also good at school. From primary school to junior high and later to senior high, in such a township with poor teaching staff, Chunzhi's results could be considered the head standing above a flock of chicken. Zaoxi Township was located in the south. In an environment with gentle breezes and light rains, attractive young women were common enough. Yet it was rare for them to have both fine looks and fine skill in needlework. It seemed Chunzhi was the only one who was not only fine-looking, but also fine-fingered, and very good at school as well. So when Chunzhi was young, she enjoyed some repute in the town. At first, Chunzhi's family did not have much in the way of property. No one expected that in such barren soil, such a fine flower could grow, so her mother's bent back was also able to grow somewhat straighter.

When Chunzhi was still in high school, matchmakers began to approach the Zhao family frequently. Chunzhi never looked at those photos left on the dinner table, only telling her mother she wanted to go over her lessons and take the university entrance examination. Of course, it was only later that her mother would know the real reason.

Chunzhi's university entrance exam scores would have been barely enough for her to get into a provincial capital university, but due to the cost of living and a job assignment nearby she chose Pingyang Normal School, a three-year college program. Chunzhi had only stayed there for a year and a half, before leaving school and coming back home. Chunzhi had dropped out, not because she could not keep up with her lessons, but all because of a man.

A man named Liao Jianping.

Liao Jianping was Chunzhi's high school classmate, a grade higher than Chunzhi. Not passing the college entrance exam after graduating from high school, he joined the army and became a soldier. Liao Jianping was quick thinking and very dexterous. Not long after he went to the army, he received a big award, relying on a few small inventions, and joined the Party, to be promoted to a higher position. While enjoying a bright career, an event of vital importance happened—his mother became paralyzed due to a stroke. There was also a father who was perennially sick, and two younger brothers at Jianping's home. His mother had been the principal breadwinner in the family, like the handle in the center of an oil-paper umbrella. If the mother was present, the umbrella could be held up. Once the mother collapsed, the umbrella became a useless piece of thin paper. Jianping, still in the army, grew very worried, so he wrote a letter to Chunzhi.

Both Chunzhi and Jianping had been cadres with the student union in high school, and together had been responsible for the school radio station. After classes, the two used to go into a small studio to edit the news reports. He would start a new piece, to which she added the ending. He would read the previous paragraph, and she the next. Chunzhi's voice was a bit hoarse, like a blade of grass shriveled by morning dew. Jianping's voice was changing, so it was stiff in the sort of way of a flag stretched flat and flapping in the wind. In fact, both of their voices had draw-backs if listened to separately. Yet, together, all imperfections were wiped away. Then, gentleness and charm gradually grew into the hoarseness, while the stiffness also gave birth to a virility, which made all those reading and listening feel a certain charm.

Although the two got along with each other every day, ear to ear and temple to temple, they in reality confirmed their own marriage in their letters from afar, after Jianping had joined the army. The matter had long spread like wildfire among the schoolmates, but on the contrary, the only one in the dark was Chunzhi's mother.

That day Chunzhi received the letter from Jianping, and without a word of discussion with anyone, she dropped out of Pingyang Normal School and returned to Zaoxi, to take care of Jianping's mother and her meals three times a day. She also cleared one of the two old rooms in her own home for a tailor shop, supporting the expenses of both homes by tailoring clothes for others and doing embroidery. At first, Chunzhi's mother had been extremely unhappy, and it was unknown how many cycles of quarrels mother and daughter had over the matter. Later, when the mother saw certificates of merits sent home one after another by Jianping, she figured out the guy probably had a bright future, so she tacitly consented.

Jianping spent several years in the army, and was promoted several ranks. On reaching his highest rank, he could not be promoted any further. After a soldier spends the requisite years in the army and cannot be promoted anymore, he has to be transferred to civilian work. Then Jianping was transferred to the city of Wenzhou as an administrative cadre in a state-owned enterprise. He returned home and married Chunzhi. The next year, they had a daughter, Xiaozao. A small family was divided, living in two places. Jianping lived in Wenzhou, and he went back to Zaoxi on weekends and other holidays of the year. Chunzhi lived perennially in Zaoxi, taking care of the three sides—her mother's, her husband's family, and her daughter. Jianping sat in an office in Wenzhou for a few years, watching people around him making money as if by magic. Refusing to let such brilliance all the world over just flow away so colorfully around him, he resigned and returned to Zaoxi, opening a small factory, specializing in teaching aids—most of them being his own inventions.

At the beginning, there was simply a tiled house and three to five workers. It was known as a township enterprise, but in reality it was a family workshop. Jianping was in charge of product development and distribution, while Chunzhi managed their accounts, and two of Jianping's brothers, plus a brother's wife, made up the staff of the company. Jianping had been very sociable in the army, so there were friends all over the country to help him set up sales outlets. The new products developed were innovative and artful, and at reasonable prices, so they soon began to sell very well. Hardly had Chunzhi found the time to finish her accelerated accounting courses, when Jianping's company accounts became too big for Chunzhi to handle. So Jianping specially hired an accounting team, and sent Chunzhi home to become the young mistress of the house with undivided attention. After several expansions of the workshop, the company's headquarters were set up in Shanghai. Then Jianping embarked on a very busy life, flying between Shanghai and Zaoxi.

Jianping was a man who had seen much of the world, so he was quite different from the other township entrepreneurs in the eyes of ordinary people. First, unlike those people, Jianping was not full of tricks. On ordinary days, Jianping did not like drinking or entertainment, and he rarely went to such places as karaoke clubs, bars or spas. When he was free, he would take his daughter Xiaozao fishing on the Zaoxi stream. It was the fishing method of Jiang Taigong—merely waiting for willing victims. Even if they caught any fish, they would throw it back into the stream so as to free the captive.

Jianping's difference from ordinary folk also lay in his affection for his wife. For much of the year Jianping was away, so he grew afraid that Chunzhi would get bored at home. He bought various CDs of movies and TV series, and sent them home in packages for Chunzhi to watch. What Jianping sent were not pirated copies chosen casually at small stalls along the street, which would get stuck the second time you watched them, with captions blurred and colors indistinct. Jianping would choose CDs recommended by his secretary and they had to be the legal kind with anti-counterfeit trademark stickers. Chunzhi's seasonal clothes had all been selected and bought personally by Jianping, from Guangzhou, Shenzhen, Hong Kong, and other places. If he settled on a style, he would buy a dozen in various colors, so Chunzhi could pick and choose whichever she pleased. Wearing such fashionable clothes and walking on the roads of Zaoxi, Chunzhi always felt as if there were eyes all over her chest and back, so she took these things off and hung them in the closet, only wearing them for Jianping whenever he came home. On days Jianping was home, in addition to visiting the elderly on both sides, he rarely went out. He would stay at home all throughout his visit, keeping company with Chunzhi. Someone had even seen with his own eyes, the tableaux of Jianping sitting on a stool, washing Chunzhi's feet, which would kick wildly at Jianping's chest, splashing water all over on the ground.

Jianping then hired housemaids for the elders on both sides. The burden of taking care of her husband's family and her own family for many years was finally taken off Chunzhi's shoulders. All the people in Zaoxi said that Chunzhi was a woman with late-arrival blessings. She had suffered so many years for the Liao family, and finally her bitter life had come to an end. Of course, these were the things said by Zaoxi people in front of Chunzhi and her mother. When mother and daughter were not present, the Zaoxi folk's words would not have been so pleasing to the ear, but fortunately Chunzhi did not hear them. Chunzhi was very hardworking. When she suddenly became free, she felt as if she had an extra pair of hands and feet, and did not know where to put them, so every day she began to think of ways to pass the time.

During the Dragon Boat Festival one year, Jianping did not return to Zaoxi due to overtime work in Shanghai. The husband of a high-school classmate of Chunzhi's was a long-distance bus driver, so the woman took Chunzhi on her husband's bus and made a trip to Suzhou and Wuxi. On the way home, prompted by a sudden impulse, Chunzhi changed onto a train for Shanghai to see Jianping. Arriving at the Shanghai Railway Station, she called Jianping. He was not at the company office, nor was his cell-phone on. Chunzhi thus proceeded alone to find the hotel room Jianping had rented on long-term lease, and waited for him to come back. She waited and waited until it got quite dark, when she faintly heard Jianping's voice outside. She opened the door, only to find Jianping, with a basket in his hand, turning and going into another room at the end of the corridor.

Jianping had not been alone. There was a woman by his side.

Chunzhi softly followed him, to find the door wide open. Jianping had put the basket in his hand onto the floor, and at first glance Chunzhi saw there was a baby in it. That baby had a wrinkled face, of a dark reddish complexion, as ugly as a field mouse. It looked like a month or two old at most. The woman bent down to lift the child out from the basket. She was very young, with a smooth pale complexion, hair as black as ink, coiled up loosely by a plastic barrette at the back of her head. A few strands had fallen out and drooped all the way from her forehead to the inside of her neck, which was another sort of randomness Chunzhi had never encountered. The woman was very tall, as if her legs grew directly from her waist. She was wearing a tight-fitting, long-sleeved skimpy black sweater with an extremely low neckline. When she bent down, her deep cleavage thrust out. Although the woman had just had a baby, her waist was still tight and thin. However, her breasts seemed rather terribly protruding, seemingly ready to come out at one's call. The movement of the woman in lifting the child was a little awkward, so the child suddenly woke up and began to cry violently. The woman held the child and swung it back and forth rather widely ranging, those paired objects at the front of her chest quivering jumpily, as though ready to fly out at any moment. Jianping went to the bathroom, wringing and bringing out a wet towel to wipe the sweat off the woman's face. As he wiped, his hand moved into the woman's neckline. The woman's body cringed under the man's fingers. Curses flew out of the woman's mouth, "Liao Jianping, you are looking for trouble?" while in her eyes was laughter.

Chunzhi leaned weakly against the door, in a trance, feeling as if Jianping's fingers were stroking her own chest leaving traces of itchiness. How many years had Jianping not acted like this with her? Chunzhi's mind went blank. She only remembered that day when she had started the trip: the sun had been round, the moon round, and the long journey had just started. Only two days had passed, then the ninety–nine suns and ninety–nine moons that had been shining on her suddenly had all fallen together to the ground with a bang, the world becoming as dark, as without distinction between day and night. Her way had suddenly come to an end.

"Jianping, you, how..."

She heard a voice drifting and dancing gently back and forth between the walls. That voice, as if not going through her mind, not even through her lips, was falling through the air, having no connection to her. Suddenly, the towel in Jianping's hand fell to the floor. With a huge bang, the Earth stopped rotating, and silence reigned everywhere.

Jianping's face, after changing between a variety of colors, gradually settled itself in between red and green. On the contrary, the woman remained relatively calm. Tapping Jianping with her arm, she said, "Chunzhi has come a long away to see you, so why don't you both go to your room for a chat?"

Jianping then came to his senses, and pulling Chunzhi, walked toward his own room. In a trance, Chunzhi followed Jianping into the room and sat down. Handing her a glass of water, Jianping asked, "Chunzhi, you, you're thirsty, right?" In that tone, there was a hospitality derived out of being at a loss, and politeness due to guilt, but it sounded only exceptionally strange. By listening to this, Chunzhi knew she had all along been a guest in his life. She had saved up a lot of words to say, but at that moment grief suddenly welled out of her, so she smashed the glass, made for the door and dashed out.

As soon as Chunzhi got back to Zaoxi, she filed for divorce. Her husband's family did not agree. The paralyzed mother-in-law, who was over seventy years old, had to be carried by someone to the Zhao home, where shedding tears she yelled, "Oh my heavens, how did Jianping, this villain, grow a sixth finger?" Holding Chunzhi's hand, she said, "Jianping and that woman each have their own reasoning. One wants money, while the other wants a son. Chunzhi, you have been surgically sterilized, and can no longer have a child. Without a son, who would inherit the huge fortune of Jianping? We country people, no matter how rich we are, will still have our country thinking. Jianping only intended to have a successor. Jianping and you can truly be called husband and wife by first marriage. In these days, plenty of rich men have mistresses. You know best how Jianping treated you. Nobody can change your position as the 'legal wife of the emperor.'"

Hearing this, Chunzhi understood that her husband's family had actually long known the truth, and yet kept her in the dark. Thinking of the scenes where she had waited upon her mother-in-law rain or shine, and where in the end, after all, blood was thicker than water, she became even more grieved in her heart, and her determination to get a divorce grew only firmer.

Chunzhi's own mother naturally only violently cursed that Jianping had no conscience—at first, it had also been Jianping's idea to have a surgical sterilization. Then once he had money, he had changed his mind. But later, after all the cursing and anger, she advised Chunzhi to consider the matter carefully. Mother had said, "As long as Jianping mends his ways by cutting off all contact with that woman, and then takes you to live together in Shanghai, you should not necessarily get a divorce — at this age, if you are divorced and live your life alone, could it be any better? You have been used to a cozy life; can you withstand a hard life starting from scratch again?" Hearing this, Chunzhi just felt her mother had been spoiled by Jianping's money over the years. What she had considered was just daily living, rather than her daughter, so she just did not discuss the matter further with her mother.

Returning from Shanghai to Zaoxi, Jianping had stayed at his parents' home — Chunzhi did not allow him to enter the house. He found someone to take a message to Chunzhi, saying that he did not want a divorce. Though it was his own fault, yet since he had already done it, this page could not be turned back. "In fact, it's merely a hurdle that you could get over with your eyes closed. The point is whether you are willing to do so. If you wish to, we can still lead our life with all our hearts as before. I will stay right here in Zaoxi awaiting your reply. I will not leave until your reply comes."

With a sneer, Chunzhi also got someone to take a message back, asking: "How do we live our life with all our hearts? By living together with that woman?"

Jianping replied, "She has never had any extravagant ideas. It is you who cannot tolerate her."

Hearing this, Chunzhi could only feel deeply disappointed, and she replied immediately, "The hurdle cannot be gotten over."

The divorce was a little hard, mainly due to the issue of custody over Xiaozao. Although Jianping had been unfaithful to Chunzhi, he loved this daughter terribly and simply wanted to take her away with him. Chunzhi resolutely refused. Jianping said, "Chunzhi, give Xiaozao to me, and I will set you and your ma up for life as long as you live." Chunzhi said, "If I give Xiaozao to you, what would I look forward to all my life?" Jianping grew worried, saying, "If you don't give her to me, you'll never get one cent of maintenance from my hand." Chunzhi signed her name to the divorce agreement at once, giving up all claims to Jianping's assets, but making Xiaozao stay.

In this way, coming out of a ten–year marriage, Chunzhi merely took away with her a daughter and the house she was now living in.

One of Chunzhi's high–school friends, who had married a northern husband and lived in Beijing for many years, heard about Chunzhi's predicament. Taking up cudgels for Chunzhi, she bought a train ticket and took Chunzhi to Beijing for a break. Chunzhi had not intended to stay long, but it so happened that her female friend's husband's boss had asked her friend about finding a housemaid from the south, who could cook meals to Zhejiang tastes, to take care of two elderly people at home. The female friend advised Chunzhi to try it out. Chunzhi had unexpectedly ended up staying there for four years after she left home, until she finally arranged for the burial of the two old people. That old couple had some regular savings, and they had also hit it off well with Chunzhi, so in a detailed will left behind after their deaths, there was a share for Chunzhi, which amounted to twenty thousand yuan. Before, when Chunzhi had been extravagant, twenty thousand yuan would have been just pocket money. But even though she had been extravagant, that had been with Jianping's money, which was separated by a layer of skin from her. Today, with the passage of time, twenty thousand yuan had suddenly come to weigh a great deal more, not only because she needed the money, but also because this money had been earned by her cent after cent, with so much toil and sweat.

After obtaining this money, Chunzhi immediately deposited it in the bank in a current account. Although not even one cent of the money had been spent, Chunzhi had extensive plans for it. This money, coupled with accumulation through economizing on daily expenses over four years, now reached thirty–seven thousand yuan.

Chunzhi had long realized that, if Xiaozao was to be transferred to attend school in Beijing, a forty thousand yuan sponsorship fee would be needed. If Chunzhi borrowed two to three thousand yuan from relatives to cover expenses, Xiaozao could come to Beijing for school next term—if a residence could be found.

While telling her all this, Chunzhi's mother had not looked up at Tiantian, her hands, knitting the woolen pants, seeming to tremble slightly. The hole in the crotch had been completed, and the old lady reached a finger into the hole to figure out its size. Tiantian was amused by this reaction but she finally managed to restrain herself before she laughed out loud.

"My pa is a retired teacher. With a fixed salary, he has no savings, nor inheritance," Tiantian said. "Although we have three rooms in our apartment, the both of us, brother and sister often go home, so we use all of them."

Chunzhi's mother could not squeeze in a word. The silence of the entire room, like a mountain of rock, pushed down on Tiantian's shoulders and made them ache, so that her body gradually felt pressed down. After a long while, the old lady gently laughed, breaking open a tiny hole in the rock, and the air began to circulate a bit.

"Up to now, one of the most regrettable things for Chunzhi has been that she did not finish her education at the Pingyang Normal School back then, due to Liao Jianping. So she desperately wanted Xiaozao to study at a good school. If Xiaozao were a boy, Chunzhi would not have worried so much. A woman's destiny cannot be put into a man's palms—this is what your pa told Chunzhi. She believes your pa."

At this moment, the door opened with a bang, and in came an overly skinny girl. Breathing out to warm both her hands in front of her mouth, as she kicked off her shoes, the girl said, "Grandma, this year the teacher gave me gift m..." The girl had uttered half of the words and swallowed the rest when she suddenly noticed the stranger in the room. With her head bowed low, she stood blushing in the hall.

In followed Chunzhi. Seeing Tiantian, she was also stunned. Hardly had she spoken, when Tiantian produced a sheet of paper from her handbag, spread it on the dinner table and said casually, "You've come just in time, Chunzhi. Find me a pen — it had better have black ink, for we are drafting a contract, on our conditions for living in our home."

Chunzhi did not move, but said to the girl, "Xiaozao, you go to Nan's Shop and buy a kilogram of fresh dates. Better if they're a little green in color. Take out the ones with wormholes."

The girl replied with an "Aye," and as she was about to go out, Chunzhi's mother stood up and said, "She won't know anything, so I'd better go along too." The old lady had gone out of door, and then came back saying, "Miss Tiantian, if you leave tomorrow, I'd have finished knitting these woolen pants. You can then take them back for your father. Your pa is a scholar, so he is particular. He said that cotton-padded trousers are too bulky, and look ugly. Chunzhi bought this mohair for him, and they are warm, light and look nice as well."

After grandmother and granddaughter had left, the two in the room said no words for some time. Later, after clearing her throat several times, Chunzhi asked, "Is Professor He, is he all right?"

Taking a good look at Chunzhi, Tiantian said, "What do you think? On the eve of the lunar New Year, he was sitting alone in a dark room, forlorn and helpless. Even his tea was cold."

Chunzhi said nothing. Tiantian thought that she would feel guilty, and was about to take the advantage to reprove her with a few words.

Unexpectedly, Chunzhi cocked her head up, and looked at Tiantian with brightly shining eyes, to say, "Elder Sister, it was you who left Professor He alone, not me."

Rumors about the merger of departments and laying off of employees had been circulating in the bank for several months. At first when such news made the rounds, everyone had felt endangered and panic-stricken. A phone call, an email or a look, could all be readily interpreted as an omen. After this news had been spreading for a few months, its momentum gradually faded. Fear, like sand, slowly sank in, while numbness gradually floated to the top, the way oil blobs do. Then people grew used to the circumstances where they numbly muddled about. Therefore, until the day Tiantian received a phone call from the general manager of the department, she had had no idea at all this would be her last day of work at the bank.

Two members of the bank's security department followed Tiantian into her office, overseeing her clearing up of personal items from what had been her desk. Her belongings, after three or four years there, were gathered into but a small cardboard box. Colleagues gathered around, hugging and shaking hands, with complex emotions. The parting was a reality, so was the rejoicing — with one leaving, the rest of them seemed to gain an additional share of security. The security staff escorted Tiantian all the way out of the doors of the bank, fearing she would take away with her the internal data and computer memory files. Although she had long known this was an old rule when banks laid off employees, Tiantian still could not yet help shedding tears as, clasping that cardboard box, she walked out of the bank.

On the street, she found the day's weather was fine — usually at this time, Tiantian would be at work, so she could rarely see such midday scenes on the street. The sun had rested for a season and was now fully strong. When it shone on her body, she felt its weight, and wondered when the wind had lost its edge and calmed down. Only a bare layer of snow remained on the roads, weakening into lumps of mud as cars passed over. As her boots made steps onto the ground, she indistinctly felt the impulse of spring in the mud. But these faint signs of spring only seemed to hurry Tiantian on her way, since today of all days she could not care about spring.

Walking to the corner where she would take the bus, Tiantian saw someone had set a bucket down to sell flowers. There was a young girl selling them, and her cries held traces of inexperience and shyness, "Fresh for your Valentine, buy a bunch." Tiantian then remembered it was Valentine's Day. She bent down, carefully selected a pink rose, and thrust the change into the girl's hands.

The girl thanked and thanked again, saying, "Wish you and your Valentine a pleasant evening."

Tiantian inserted the flower into the handle of the cardboard box, smiled and said, "This is the first flower, in my life."

Tiantian then got on the streetcar, and passing many stops she did not get off to transfer to the subway, but stayed on until the last stop. This was High Park. The park was very quiet. The trees in February were still bare, and since the wide avenue had lost its cover from branches and leaves, it suddenly looked open and straight. Looking toward the end of the road, she could see only a neatly dressed old couple, tugging at a dog and walking slowly. Tiantian had very light footsteps, heard only by the dog, which began to bark alertly with his ears upright. Instantly the surrounding woods came to life, the tranquility broken and scattered all over the cold ground.

Tiantian had thought to look for a bench to sit down on, but unexpectedly she failed to find one even after walking a long distance, as the cardboard box in her arms gradually grew heavier. So she found a patch of dry ground, put the box down, and sat on top of it.

Tomorrow a CV would have to be written, and copies sent to several employment agencies. The last one was written four years ago, the contents now long out of date. Who would be references? She could not choose the department manager. She had always been a go-getter under him, developing a customer base for him, winning quite a lot of glory and honor for him from headquarters. But as a result, she became the first person under him to be fired. What's that Chinese proverb? After the cunning hare is killed, the hound is boiled. Yet, who is the hare and who the hound? When he had handed her the notice of dismissal, he dared not even look in her eyes—hard to believe there would be no guilt in his heart. So it might be good to see how far this bit of guilt can go. Perhaps, he'd introduce her to another bank—he's been working in the banking sector for a long time, so he'd probably have extensive contacts. If she were to change professions now it would mean having again to start from scratch and adapting. In that case, she might as well give him a call. And it was not all his fault, since the headquarters wanted to lay off employees: when the quota was assigned, it must always fall on someone's head. It is said that Chinese rightists were also selected in this way. Tomorrow, just leave it to tomorrow. The sun was high now, falling on her body like warm snow, soft yet crisp. Her eyelids gradually growing heavy and scrunched up, her thoughts running into a vast desert, with every one of the roads turning into a dead end...

The old couple who were taking their walk had turned around from the end of the avenue, and noticed a petite Chinese woman sitting under a huge cedar tree. With her face leaning against the trunk, the woman had fallen asleep, some brown bits of bark sticking to her hair and cheeks. A rose was laid across the woman's knees, its head drooping listlessly. The dog lowered its head and sniffed at the flower, and then quietly walked away.

When Tiantian woke up, it had already become dark, the avenue appearing shadowy and far-reaching under the streetlights. Tiantian had been awakened by the vibrating of her phone. Tiantian's cell phone had been set up for customers. Usually she had many phone calls, so she had set the ring tone to silent vibrating for fear it might affect other people's work. Tiantian now opened her handbag in a great rush, and rummaging in the tight encirclement between her wallet, cosmetics, tissues, comb, notebook and checkbook, she finally found the cell phone, alive and kicking. Grasping it and accepting the call, she reflexively said in English, "Hello, this is He Tiantian, TD Bank, what can I do for you?" With these words, she suddenly remembered that history had been rewritten, but felt too lazy to correct herself.

On the other end was Qin Yang: "Tiantian, where are you? I called almost all of your acquaintances. The bank said that you had been gone for a long time, and you were not answering your cell phone."

With a loud yawn, Tiantian said, "I fell asleep under a century-old tree and had a grand dream. I thought, as I opened my eyes, the world had spanned another millennium, with dinosaurs resurrected, and aliens strolling the streets. The upshot is still same old people and same old things—your phone call really let me down."

Qin Yang paused, then said, "Tiantian, don't move, tell me where you are, I'll come and pick you up right away. Isn't it only a job? We'll find one again."

Tiantian also paused, and said, "It is just a job, right? If worse comes to worst, you will provide for me. So I have nothing to worry about."

After a long interim of wordless hesitation, Qin Yang replied, "As a matter of fact, it would be good if we really took over that café across the street. When you're your own boss, nobody can give you the heave-ho."

Qin Yang had seen the classified ads in the Toronto Star that the owner of the café was seriously ill, so he was eager to sell it. Qin Yang had gone and seen it several times. He thought business was excellent, and the price was right. When he came back, he would drop this idea into her ear. Qin Yang's purpose was very clear—to borrow money from Tiantian, but he knew Tiantian would pretend ignorance and never commit herself. Today, somehow, she became extremely upset and said, "Qin Yang, stop plotting over my bit of money, it won't be enough for you to show off for a few days? If you want to become a boss, just go ahead. I'll work for you—who does not want to get away from worries?" With this, she turned the phone off. The inexplicable anger welling in her heart, which had been held in for a long time, gradually calmed down.

When the two returned home that day, Qin Yang had already prepared a table of various dishes and wine—originally meant to celebrate Valentine's Day. Since Tiantian had been walking outside for the whole day, she was so hungry and thirsty that she guzzled a few glasses, and fell into drunkenness for a time. Awakening in the middle of the night, she heard Qin Yang snoring, like the noise of running water, finely filling in every corner of the room, leaving her no place to escape to. Then she slipped out of bed down onto the floor, and opened a drawer in the dark, rustling through it until she found a pack of cigarettes. The cigarette was stale and damp, so she had to try several times before she could manage to light it. Tiantian had picked up smoking while going through the process of suing for divorce. Of course, she had to hide the habit from her mother, not because she was afraid, but because she would not have been able to stand the nagging. Later she had developed a bad cold, and suddenly tired of the taste, so quite naturally she had quit smoking. Smoking now again after so many years, she felt the smell was both familiar and unfamiliar. It could not be said that she loved it, nor could it be said that she did not love it. She just felt as if she had been cut off from the outside world for an age. Squatting in a corner of the room, she saw the moonlight, through a gap in the curtains, shining on Qin Yang's face with tints of yellow, as though a layer of fuzz had dimly grown there, making him look as serene as a baby.

It was also a kind of blessing, if one had nothing to one's name in the world. The one who traveled naked through the world would find a harvest whenever desiring to seize on one thing. He had met her, and grasped her tightly. She paid his rent, while he drove her car. She was his eave which sheltered him from the rain, his pot from which he scooped rice, his feet with which he walked along the road, and his bed on which he rested. She was the reason why he could sleep peacefully. But what was he with regard to her? She had just paid a tiny sum on a down-payment for her mortgage; the rest was a massive debt, which needed to be paid monthly. Moreover, there were all the utilities, car insurance, gasoline, property management fees, and of course, there was also all the spending for feminine adornments. Her unemployment insurance would now be a little more than half of what had been her normal income. She had to support herself, him, and her father as well. Father's expenses for a housemaid and part of his medical costs, as the years went by, would be no small amount of expenditure. Waking up in the middle of the night, she suddenly felt as if the whole world were leaning against her shoulders, and this was how she began to resent Qin Yang being so free of worry.

Opening her eyes in the morning, she found Qin Yang already up. Tiantian looked at her watch; it would be time for her to go to work on an ordinary day. She then thought of taking advantage of this free time when the boss had just arrived at work, to give him a call and ask him to help introduce her to a new job. When she picked up the phone, she heard the voice of a strange woman in it, and then understood Qin Yang was in the living room using the telephone.

"How long will you drag this out? You've got to settle it..." She only heard half the woman's words, for Qin Yang then quickly hung up the phone. After a while, the telephone rang. He did not answer it, nor did she. The ringing finally quieted down, but only for a moment, before sounding again extremely loudly. She could not help running out barefoot to answer it, but the one on the other end did not speak.

With a sneer, Tiantian said, "Qin Yang, don't you have anything to tell me?" Qin Yang's face suddenly turned white, but he did not reply.

Tiantian pulled the curtains open abruptly. The sunlight, like white water, poured violently and intensely into the living room. The room suddenly seemed full of flying dust in a state of chaos. Hardly had a young morning had time to experience things in this world than it blazingly matured enough to age. Through this passage of time, Tiantian felt totally disillusioned with life. Raising her hand, she said to Qin Yang, "You, you move out, immediately."

Qin Yang spoke haltingly, "In fact, just now..."

Tiantian grabbed the paper-cutter on the table, pointed its tip to her chest, and exclaimed, "If you say anything more, I will thrust it in for you to witness."

Qin Yang was startled, and then he clammed up and went into the bedroom. The knife fell with a bang from Tiantian's hand, Tiantian's body trembling all over, as if ready to break up into bits all over the floor. Wrapped in the thick sunshine, she still only felt the cold, a kind of gloomy cold that seeped in trickles from the tip of her heart, which could not be wiped dry.

Qin Yang was rustling about the room packing his belongings. All the memories accumulated over a few months, when packed up, came to but two suitcases, one large and the other small. After locking them, he slowly dragged them through the living room to the door, and then returned to the bedroom, took out a thick bathrobe and handed it to Tiantian, saying, "Put it on, and come with me downstairs, will you?" Tiantian wanted to say no, but she involuntarily followed Qin Yang into the elevator.

The two stood in the elevator, he not pushing the button, she not moving either. The doors of the elevator closed automatically, but it did not move. He said, "I've put the key on the bedside table, and I'll use the car, to move the suitcases, and then I'll drive it back." She did not speak. Actually, she was expecting him to say something else, but he did not. The elevator was not very big. With the two of them separated by two suitcases, in fact, it was a little crowded. With just a little stretch of a hand or foot, they could have touched each other at any time. However, they only stood face to face, as if they were one hundred million light years away from each other. Finally, his hand reached out through those light years, and pressed the P1 button which had already been rubbed shiny by the touch of too many hands. The elevator dived down with a loud hum.

"No, there will not be a third beginning between us," Tiantian thought drowsily.

Suddenly the elevator gave a violent shake, and abruptly stopped. Tiantian's vital organs were pulled up high, then fell heavily, with her blood violently beating in her eardrums, her ears overcome by a burst of roaring. The suitcases fell with a muffled noise to press down on her toes. Tiantian wanted to pull her feet out, but she could not see the suitcases—the elevator was in total darkness.

"The elevator has broken," Qin Yang said.

He fumbled over the suitcases to search for the alarm button on the panel. His memory told him it might be on the lower right corner. He tried one button after another, but there was no sound of response.

"Your cell phone, call nine-one-one," he reminded her.

She fumbled around in her pocket, before realizing she was wearing a bathrobe, and her cell phone had been left in the room.

"Just wait..." he said with a sigh, groping to place the suitcases flat for her to sit. He then sat down beside her. She took off her shoes, and touched the wet and sticky stuff on her toes. Knowing it was blood, she suddenly felt the searing pain.

She had never before experienced such darkness with neither a beginning nor an end, not revealing even a thread of any aperture. Darkness crowded toward her from all directions, growing ever heavier and heavier. Every organ in her body seemed to be squeezed tightly into this thin sliver, each falling over the other trying to break through from her chest. Emitting a scream, she punched the wall of the elevator. The level of her strength and madness startled both of them.

He held his arms tightly around her, saying, "Tiantian, if you want to live, you've got to preserve your strength and reduce your oxygen intake–we are stuck between two floors, no one will hear you."

He fumbled to untie the sash of her bathrobe, and instantly felt her gentle warmth, which like water flowed all over his palms. In the water were two small pebbles which he rubbed firmly and erectly between his palms. Groaning softly, she finally quieted down, leaning her head weakly against his shoulder. Her stomach gave a loud rumble, as did his soon afterward, as though a croaking of frogs was echoing in a summer pond. The two could not help but laugh aloud.

"Tiantian, in case we die here, some words, I was always meaning to tell you."

"That woman is my boss' cousin. She's from Hong Kong, a twenty-odd-year immigrant. Her husband is dead, so she's eager to find another."

"I was bored of my life back home. I came abroad to change my way of life. The human smugglers said I would be able to obtain an identity within six months of arriving in Toronto, that any job I found would offer an annual salary of forty or fifty thousand dollars, which then was equivalent to three or four hundred thousand yuan."

"Once here, I realized their words were untrue, but it was too late. I had thought of going back once I earned enough to pay my debts. Then, unexpectedly I met you."

"I know you've wanted me to help you, but if you do not help me first I cannot help you. You know this, but you're also afraid once you invest you will not get it back. You don't trust me."

"In fact, she's as shrewd as you, but she dares to wager the bet which you don't."

Tiantian did not speak throughout this. The desire to urinate gradually gathered in her, forming sharp traces of pain in her lower abdomen. Qin Yang found the zipper of the suitcase, pulled it down, felt around and pulled out the helmet he normally wore riding his bicycle, put it upside down in a corner, and said, "Just make do with this."

The water sounds lasted for a long time, going from shallow to full. When the sounds finally came to an end, he slipped her a piece of cloth, saying, "Here, wipe yourself clean." As she wiped herself, she realized it was his tie. She thought this man might somewhat love her. Her relationship with him, in fact, was nothing more than a form of venture capital. If it made good, maybe she would have someone to rely on. Otherwise, for the rest of her life, she would be drawing water with a bamboo basket—with everything falling through.

But perhaps things were not so serious. If it were a bad investment, at most she would be exploited once again. If she did not lay down the stakes, she would not even have the hope of owning any water. Being exploitable was better than being completely useless. Whose words were these? They seemed to be her father's. When had he said them? She could not remember.

Tiantian fell to sleep in a trance.

Before long, she was awakened by hunger. At first, the hunger was sharp and intense, the way insects, ants or needles might squirm through the stomach, pricking with every step they crawled. Tiantian recalled carefully the contents of the refrigerator, until she saw the detailed and specific plan of every container, each shelf and drawer, and every item. In her imagination she cooked these things in various ways and various combinations into a large number of dishes, each dish making her mouth drool with greed. She could hear her tongue rolling over and over again in her mouth, until the saliva gradually all dried up, and her tongue was too swollen to roll any longer. The hunger growing gradually numb, she once again fell into sleep.

In this way, Tiantian slept and woke up several times, until she completely lost any concept of time. The last time she woke up, she wanted to ask Qin Yang what time it probably was. She moved her lips, but could not get any words out. She knew she had no strength. She suddenly remembered the fish in the dry pond—the slightly open mouth, and white eyes dimmed with corneal opacity.

"I don't want to die. I really, really, really do not want to die."

Tiantian said to herself silently, over and over again. These words supported her for a long time, but before holding out to the end, she once again slipped into a prolonged lethargy.

Later, she was awoken by a dazzling white light, and heard a voice passing over from a distance, "Put the blinders on her." The white light disappeared, but the memory of it, like a knife's edge, was placed upon her retinas longer than seemed possible, sharp and bright, so scars would surface as long as it was touched. She heard the sounds of the street. She could hear the splashing of mud under the rolling of wheels, hear the gentle tinkling of wind chimes in a shop window, then voices arguing, between a little girl and her mother, and she heard the sounds of friction between rubber gloves and of syringes falling on a tray.

"Where's he?" she asked in a hoarse voice, as her hand laid hold of a paramedic's sleeve.

"He is in another ambulance, safe and sound."

"Tell him—ask him to set a date."

"What date?"

"He knows."

With this, Tiantian lost consciousness.

Tiantian and Qin Yang held a wedding ceremony on April the fifth.

They had chosen to get married on this day, because it happened to be a Saturday, and the coffee shop jointly run by them would open in two weeks—and they would not have time to get married after it opened.

The wedding was held in the greenhouse in the backyard of a good friend of Tiantian's. They invited a judge to the scene, who signed the marriage registration, and then they went to a cafeteria and had a meal, which was counted as the completion of the ceremony.

Qin Yang wore a dark blue suit, and an orange tie. The suit fitted him very well, though the color of the tie was a bit garish—but Tiantian had insisted on it. This was the very tie used by Tiantian to meet an urgent need when she had urinated in the elevator that day. Qin Yang had tried to throw it away, but Tiantian had taken it for dry cleaning, saying that they would keep it as a memento. Noticing that somewhat strange-looking accessory while Qin Yang was otherwise neatly dressed, everybody chuckled. They said that when reservists were promoted to become regular soldiers, perhaps they would all look like this.

Tiantian wore a pink dress at the wedding. There was lace inlaid both on her neckline and at the hem of her dress. She resembled more a bridesmaid than a bride. Qin Yang asked Tiantian why she had not chosen a white dress. Tiantian said it did not look good for people with dark complexions to wear white, for there would be too much contrast. Qin Yang would probably never guess at the other half of those words which Tiantian never uttered. One of the colleagues in Tiantian's bank had told her that most women who married again did not wear white — they had, after all, already lost their innocence.

When the dinner party was over and all the guests seen off, on their way home Tiantian suddenly remembered that day was Qingming (Pure Brightness) Festival. Giving Qin Yang a shake, she said, "Why did you pick such a day to get married? This should be a day for paying respects to the dead."

Flushed from drinking, Qin Yang began to laugh, revealing a mouth full of gums, "We two have died once, so what can we be afraid of?"

That day when the two had been trapped in the elevator, they had only thought that their elevator in the building was out of order, but they had not known the entire outside world was experiencing a disaster that had not occurred for decades. From North Carolina to New York all the way to eastern Canada, the power grid had been paralyzed completely for three or four days. Some people said it was due to the obsolete equipment, while some said it was the fault of hackers, yet others said it was done by Osama bin Laden's terrorist organization. As Tiantian and Qin Yang were floating back and forth between the edges of oblivion and consciousness, the so-called city of Toronto, like a roc with broken wings, had suddenly dropped into a cage of its own making. Exhausted, irritable, completely irrational, it could fall into this state of craziness at any moment. Numerous vehicles were left parked along the streets, immobilized due to their inability to get fuel, and the stores became filled with spoiled food, the smells permeating the air. The connectivity networks of cell phones coped barely for a few hours, before they all ultimately collapsed into a full range of busy tones. Patients suffering frostbite filled the corridors outside the e-mergency wards of the hospitals. Candles and lighters went totally out of stock within two hours. Overnight the price of mineral water at the corner grocery stores rose three times. Although the heavens did not collapse entirely, people had already sensed the weight of the clouds pressing overhead. In this war without a trace of gun-smoke, people lost badly. They had not lost to other people; rather they had lost to the power of electricity instead. Creatures turned against their creator, while the tools actually defeated the craftsmen. After the disaster, the city recovered slowly, yet the fear that followed in its wake soared day by day.

Hearing the variety of horror stories during the great blackout, Qin Yang merely smiled in silence. But he would say privately to Tiantian, "If there had not been a major power outage, how could there have been the today of you and me?" Hearing this, Tiantian could not help but hesitate. God had let such a large city walk through such a disaster, a part of the city having collapsed, with people forced to walk through the valley of death, as if only to fulfill a difficult marriage. Thinking of this, she gasped with astonishment in her heart.

Tiantian returned to China twice, but she never spoke of Qin Yang to Father. Compared to her ex-husband, Qin Yang almost did not have any features that would attract Father's interest. A week before the wedding, Tiantian had called home and told Father that she was going to be married. The word "told" here was a relatively accurate usage, because Tiantian did not intend to seek Father's ad-vice. Tiantian had prepared in advance some responses to cope with Father's questions, but at the last moment they did not have to be put to use at all.

Silent for a while, Father then asked, "Is that guy, well, is he good to you?"

Tiantian replied, "Except for being good to me, he has nothing."

Father laughed, the way a steel ball rolled across a glass surface, a resilient yet hearty sound, "If he is not good to you, you will have nothing at all." Father's laughter that day drew deep scratches on Tiantian's eardrums. It was not painful, but an unexpected surprise—for many years Father had not laughed in this way.

"My responsibility is finally finished."

With this, Father gave a sigh, which did not sound like sadness, but more like a sort of coziness which comes from removing an extremely heavy burden. Putting down the phone, Tiantian felt very relaxed—the way of people living perennially in areas lacking water suddenly experiencing a shower in a spa. Tiantian felt her last traces of fear of marriage completely disintegrating with the dirt on her body.

Tiantian spoke to Qin Yang of the call to Father. Tiantian faintly sensed that some changes had happened to Father. When Qin Yang asked her what the changes were, Tiantian thought for a long time, yet she had nothing to say in reply.

Tiantian soon knew what burden Father had removed.

In the early morning of the third day after the wedding, Tiantian's bedside phone rang. The telephone ringing at such a time sounded faintly ominous. Tiantian suddenly woke up. Sitting up, she felt very scared.

It was Yuanyuan.

"Papa has disappeared. For three whole days, I've looked for him everywhere."

At the other end of the telephone line, Yuanyuan's voice sounded like firewood gone dry in the wind, full of cracks. Every crack was filled with panic. Tiantian felt that her elder brother, who was nearly forty years old, had suddenly turned into a helpless child.

"Two days ago he called me and said he was going to get married, with Chunzhi. I said he had to discuss such a big thing with us. He said, 'I hadn't thought to discuss it with you. I just want to tell you about it—did you discuss it with me when you got married?'"

"I was so furious that I scolded him that the woman was actually too shrewd. Treading out the right path, she popped in first one foot, then the whole body, and then pushed her daughter inside too. Hookers would not have her ability. Papa then banged the phone down. When I redialed, I could not get through, however many times I tried. I rushed to Beijing—the door was locked, but nobody was inside—they were both gone."

"Let's hope nothing has happened—after Ma's accident, we have not been able to hold up our heads in front of others. If something happened to him again, we will never be able to explain it clearly."

Putting down the phone, Tiantian held her head in both hands, speechless for a long time. Qin Yang also woke up, and asked several times what had happened. Pointing at his temple, Tiantian then said with her eyes staring angrily,

"Qin Yang, you listen to me, we will never live another day past seventy—heavens, how stupid people can get when they're old."

Tiantian found her father He Chun'an by the stream called Zaoxi.

Zaoxi was a stream, with water flowing like threads between the rocks. The rocks were in a mess, zigzagging from that bank over to this, and thus forming the stepping stones for wading across. The sun was still tender, falling on the surface of the water palely and weakly. The willow leaves had not grown to their full size. Yet observed from a distance, they had already emerged dimly in a semblance of some lushness. Sitting on a rock, Father was fishing, and squatting by him was a girl about fourteen or fifteen of age, who was helping him to put earthworm bait on the hook. Father's movement of casting was very powerful, as if he were acting in an opera with appropriate details, the fishing line scratching a curving arc through the air.

This whole opera of Father's had only one audience, this being Chunzhi.

Tiantian suddenly remembered the words uttered by Qin Yang before her departure, "A thousand pieces of gold cannot buy the happiness of a fool."

(*Translated by Zhou Gang*)

空巢

张翎

谨将此故事献给世上一切空巢的父母和离家远行的儿女

何田田最近两年里连续回了三趟国，趟趟都是为了父亲何淳安。

第一趟回去是为了给父亲请保姆。第二趟多少也是。第三趟虽然不是为了请保姆，却也与保姆有关。

何淳安是个退了休的教书先生，从前在京城一所大学里教授英美文学。妻子李延安也曾在同一所学校的图书馆工作。夫妇俩育有一子一女。儿子何元元远在广州，是一家很出名的合资企业的销售部经理。女儿何田田走得就更远了，五年前移民来到多伦多，现在加拿大道明银行的商业信贷部供职。何家的两个子女岁数上只相差了十六个月，经历上也有诸多相似之处。元元和田田在大学里学的都是商，后来的工作也多少与商有关。都忙。都结了婚，又都离了婚。都没有子女。现在都在单身和不单身的那个灰色地带生活。

田田是离完了婚才决定出国的——当然是从头过起的意思。田田离婚的过程像一场漫长的高潮迭起的戏剧，整整演了三年。这三年里田田就住在父母身边。娘家成了田田歇脚的窝、睡觉的枕头、揩眼泪的帕子、装气话的竹篓。一场婚离下来，父母就老了。

父母是在田田的眼皮底下老的，田田却浑然不知。犹如一个常住河边看惯了河水的人，是看不出今日之水原来不同于昨日之水的，等田田意识到父母的老时，事情已经进入了一个无法挽回的死圈。

现在回想起来，其实母亲是早就有迹象的。母亲爱掏父亲的衣服口袋，母亲爱翻父亲的文稿，母亲爱拆父亲的信，母亲爱偷听父亲的电话。年轻时很有些英武豪爽之气的母亲，五十岁过后却渐渐地变得敏感和爱猜疑起来。田田一直以为这是母亲对父亲日益上升的社会地位的一种危机感，直到后来在一位加拿大同事家里偶然翻到一本医学杂志，才恍然大悟这其实是老年痴呆症的一些症状。只是从前母亲在操着太多人的心，母亲的这些蛛丝马迹，散落在太多太纷繁的生活内容里，如沙滩底下浅浅地埋着的石子，被人在忙乱之中混混沌沌地错过了。待到元元去了广州，田田出了国，母亲的生活天幕突然变成了一片硕大的空白，她那些反常的举止才日渐清晰地浮到了表层。

父亲也不知道母亲有病，父亲以为母亲只是太寂寞了，于是父亲在过了六十五岁生日之后就刻不容缓地办了退休手续。当时父亲还带着几名研究生，手头还有几篇论文尚未完成。像父亲这样多少算有些贡献的资深教授，其实完全可以延续几年才退的，可是父亲想多在家里陪陪母亲——母亲没有高级职称，退休得早。

然而没有用。

父亲的日日相守，田田隔天一个的越洋电话，元元三个月一次的探亲假，都没有把母亲从那条越走越窄的暗路上扯回来。母亲还是执意地走了那样的极端。

母亲的事，田田是过后一个月才知道的——是元元刻意对她隐瞒了的。后来元元再也瞒不下去了，才百般无奈地打电话来多伦多搬救兵。田田接到元元的电话，第二天就坐上飞机飞回了北京。

田田进了门，一眼就看见客厅正墙上母亲的那张放大照片。照片是母亲略微年轻时拍的，衣装发式都有些过时。母亲的笑容似乎刚刚展开，就被快门骤然切断，眼角眉梢便有了微微一丝的惊讶神情。照片上的那个黑框如同一张大嘴，将田田一口嘬了进去。田田没顺过气来，身子一矮，就瘫坐在沙发上，喉咙里涌上一团咸涩，吐也吐不出来，咽也咽不回去，哽噎之中，眼泪便汹涌地流了出来。

何淳安看着女儿倾金山倒玉柱地哭，只将两手在膝盖上磨来磨去，干裂的手掌在裤子上刺啦刺啦地钩出一条条细丝。

“谁想得到呢？谁想得到呢？”何淳安一遍又一遍地说。每说一遍，气就短了一截。说到后来，那声音便如炎夏午后的蝇子，有气无力嘤嘤嗡嗡地飞撞在田田的耳膜上。

李延安出事的那一天，实在和任何其他一天没有太大区别。早上起来，何淳安照例去公园练太极拳，李延安照例去小区的菜市场买小菜。等何淳安练完太极拳回家，李延安也正好热完了早餐。两人面对面地坐在厨房的小餐桌上，一边喝豆浆，一边看报纸。何淳安看的是《晨报》，李延安看的是《健康报》。一碗豆浆喝得见了底的时候，报纸也就翻得差不多了。何淳安擦过了嘴，站起来，说要去学校一趟，取几封信。走到门口，听见李延安在厨房里异常响亮地笑了一声，说：“眼花儿不来，你就急了吧？”

李延安嘴里的“眼花儿”，泛指的时候，说的是何淳安所有的女同事女学生；特指的时候，说的是何淳安的得意门生颜华。颜华博士毕业后留了校，和何淳安在一个教研室里工作，先前是师生，后来是同事，来往算是比较密切的。平日在家里李延安也时不时地拿“眼花儿”说事，时而泛指，时而特指，何淳安一味地这只耳朵进那只耳朵出，并不计较。那天也不知碰着了哪根筋，心里有一股无名火噌地蹿上来，便忍不住回了一句“急了又怎么着”，便夺门而去。

何淳安到了学校，见着了几个多日未见的同事，说了些系里的飞短流长，一时聊得兴起，几个人就在学校的餐厅吃了顿午饭，喝了几盏小酒，回家就晚了。脸红耳热地进了门，一迭声地喊李延安："晚上早点吃饭，周教授给了两张戏票，小百花越剧团的《碧玉簪》。"——早把先前的口角忘了个一干二净。

走到卧室门口，觉得脚底有些黏，低头一看，脚上像踩了一泡西红柿酱。冲进屋里，只见满地的猩红，浓浓稠稠半干未干的，在墙角门后流成大团大团的花。床铺看上去却是平平的，不像是有人的样子。何淳安哆哆嗦嗦地掀开被褥来，才看见了一片扁平如纸的身子——那是流完了血缩了形的李延安。李延安用的一把钝刀，腕上的伤痕如锯齿般参差不齐。这个在延安窑洞里出生、在马背上度过最初童年的女子，就这样将她世袭的军人般的刚烈演绎到了极致。

何淳安从屋里跌跌撞撞地跑出来，冲到楼下，蹲在门口的大槐树下，哇地吐了一地。酒和肉的腐臭随着风在街上飞得很远，蝇子在秽物上黑压压地围了一圈。撕心裂肺地吐完了，扶着树身站起来，抬头看天，只见天上一颗鲜血淋漓的太阳，朝着自己正正地飞坠过来。想躲，却没躲过，就被咚的一声砸倒在地上。

等他完全清醒过来，已是三天以后的事了。三天中他的生活里发生了很多事。当他的意识还在沉睡和苏醒中间的那个灰色地带飘浮时，他的妻子李延安已经火化入葬了。他的儿子何元元从广州赶回来，雇人将他的房子彻底地清理打扫了一番，并将家具都重新摆置过了。所有关于李延安的痕迹，都被小心翼翼地掩藏了起来。

何淳安出院回来，像走进了别人的家，惶惶不安，手足无措。他在屋里频繁地进进出出，不停地打开抽屉柜橱的门，仿佛在寻找什么，却又仿佛什么也没有找到。何元元的担心，几乎完全是多余的，何淳安没有问及李延安，一句也没有。

一连几天都是这样。

元元原先准备了多种可能性，都是用来对付父亲的记忆的。元元唯一没有准备到的，是父亲的失忆。记得是一种痛，不记得也是一种痛，只是这两种痛却是无法抵消取代的，都得一一痛过。

元元悄悄去医院咨询过心理医生，医生说经历过这样巨大的刺激之后，暂时失去记忆是一种自我保护的方式，恢复记忆就是痊愈的一个迹象。

两个星期之后，有一天吃晚饭的时候，元元把饭菜都摆上了桌，一边拔筷子，一边貌似无意地说了一句："妈妈做的菜比街上买的好吃多了。"

何淳安很久没有说话。元元转过身来，发现父亲的人中上流着一条清鼻涕，目光死死地盯在墙上，仿佛要把墙看出一个洞来。

"工作证。"后来何淳安喃喃地说。

"什么工作证？"元元不解。

"上面的那张照片，你拿了，放大，挂墙上。"

元元这才知道父亲这么多天一直在找母亲的照片，一颗心方稍稍地落到了些实处。

办完母亲的丧事，元元要带父亲去广州住一阵子，也算是换个环境、散散心的意思。何淳安执意不肯，说你妈回来找不着人呢。元元说妈现在是灰是烟，你到哪里她就跟你去哪里。那原本是一句劝解的话，老头听了，却像是受了惊骇，竟泥塑木雕般地呆坐了半天，连饭也不肯吃了。元元无奈，只好说要不你跟田田去加拿大住几个月，反正你听得懂英文。老头连连摇头，说她拖了我这么个老油瓶在身边，更没有人敢娶她了。

请保姆的事就这样提到了议事日程上。

何淳安在家务事上基本算是个低能儿。从买菜做饭到洗衣扫地，从前家里的大事小事都是李延安一手包办的，何淳安甚至连银行密码都懒得去记。李延安骤然一撒手，现在何淳安连洗衣机都不知怎么使，烧茶坐水也得从头学起。

可是何淳安坚决不同意请保姆，说家里来个生人不习惯也不安全。其实真正的理由何淳安却没有告诉儿子。妻子是因为一群莫须有的女人而死的。自己虽然是清白的，可是再大的清白在妻子的刚烈里走过了一遭，就像一张搓揉过的纸，多少就有了印记。印记的存留，只在一念之差。而洗刷这个印记的过程，可能就是他的余生了。他行在街上，前胸后背似乎都贴满了芒刺般的眼光。在这样的眼光里，他无论如何也不能安然享受另外一个不是妻子的女人带给他的安逸。六十六岁的退休教授何淳安，已经被这样一个突兀的人生变故吓破了胆子。

元元一转眼就在父亲身边待了一个来月。广州的公司来了最后通牒，说再不回来上班就要另请人顶替他了。何淳安就催儿子走，说你管得了我一时，还能管得了我一世？我终究得学会自己生活的。元元临行前，去超市买了一冰箱的面包饺子速食面，不厌其烦地教父亲如何烧水煮食。又给父亲系里要好的同事学生一一打了电话，让时时关照父亲。谁知刚回广州三天，就接到了邻居的电话，说父亲将一锅开水打翻在地上，烫伤了脚，住进了医院。元元再也抽不出假期了，只好星夜打电话给远在多伦多的妹妹田田，让她火速回来一趟。

诚聘家庭助理，照顾一位知识老人。精通家务，有耐心，初中以上文化水平。月薪绝对高出市价。其他优惠面议。

田田一到家，就起草了一则聘人广告。吸取了元元前次的教训，田田这次采用的是强硬高压手段，何淳安连插嘴的机会都没有，广告就在《晨报》和《晚报》上白纸黑字地登了出来。

后来的几天里，倒是陆陆续续地来了好些电话。有几个在电话上听起来就不是那块料的，田田面也不见就给拒了。剩下的几个听起来还算顺耳的，等约来了一见，竟没有一个看上去略微顺眼些的。个个打扮得花枝招展，进门先把家电厨厕设备都巡视了一遍，才肯坐下来说话。每送走一个，田田的眉心就多了个结子。到后来沮丧至极，忍不住感叹善良淳朴的中国劳动妇女都到哪里去了，夜总会招人，来的也不过如此。

何淳安坐在沙发上，闭了眼睛冷笑："祥林嫂出国了，四凤经商了，陈白露倒还是有，只是你老爸敢要吗?"

田田听了啼笑皆非。

后来电话就渐渐稀少了。

田田正打算调整战略目标，朝钟点工的方向转移，有一天早上，突然接到了一个电话，有人找"何老师"。正逢何淳安到医院换药去了，田田以为是爸爸的学生，就问人家要名字电话号码。那人顿了顿，才说自己叫赵春枝，没有电话，是借了公用电话打的，就想问问何老师家里找着人了吗？田田这才明白又是一个找工作的。这么多个人里头，也只有这个女人管父亲叫何老师，田田心里便有了一丝好感。

就问女人是哪里人，女人说是温州藻溪乡人。田田吃了一惊，因为父亲的老家就在浙南那一带。虽然父亲离家五十多年了，老家也早已没有什么亲属，可父亲这几年老了，话语里常有些怀乡的意思。田田心想这说不定是个好彩头呢，就笑，说只听见你们温州人到处找保姆的，哪还有温州人出来给人做保姆的？女人也笑了，说再富的地方也有穷人，各人有各人的命呗。女人的笑声哑哑的，有几分认命的无奈，也有几分不认命的刚倔，田田的心不由得动了一动，当下就决定约女人见面。这次多长了个心眼，没把女人约到家里来。

当天下午，田田约了这个叫赵春枝的女人在离家不远的一家茶室见面。女人准时到了，点了一杯菊花茶，小口小口地喝着。茶渐渐地浅了下去，却死活不肯再添。女人出乎意料的瘦弱纤细，剪了一头齐齐的短发，穿了一件洗了很多水的浅蓝衬衫，一条同样洗了很多水的深蓝裤子，虽是旧了，却异常地干净平整，整个人看起来像是五六十年代黑白照片里的女学生。女人的脸上、脖子上到处都是汗，头发在额上湿成一个个小卷——田田猜测女人大概没舍得坐车，是一路走过来的。

就大致问了问女人的情况。

女人三十八岁，念过高中，离了婚，有一个十四岁的女儿，在老家跟着外婆生活。女人在京城做了四年的保姆，前一个东家刚去世，正在找新东家。

“为什么离的婚?”

田田知道这不是她该问的问题，可是田田知道她给的工资让女人没法拒绝，所以她把目光定定地放在女人脸上，神情自若地问了这个问题。

“不学好。”女人说。

“怎么个不学好?”

女人低了头，掏出一块手帕，一下一下地擦着脸上的汗。半晌，才轻轻地说：“大姐你该操心的事很多，我那点事，不值得你操心。”

女人回答得不卑不亢，田田却问不下去了，只好换了个话题，问女人有什么要求。女人说没要求，什么样的老人她都伺候得了。

于是田田就领着女人往家去见父亲。其实这时田田已经拿定了主意要留下这个女人，父亲的过目如同英国女王在国家文件上的签名一样，只是一个必要的形式。

田田将女人带进家，对父亲说：“这是赵春枝。春枝先前工作过的那家，也是老师。”

父亲正在剪指甲。父亲的老花镜度数浅了，父亲剪起指甲来就有些吃力。父亲把手伸得远远的，眼睛眯得细细的，鼻子在眼镜底下蹙成一个皱纹深刻的肉团。父亲看了一眼女人，便又低了头，继续修剪指甲，指甲剪在静默中毕毕剥剥地响得闹心。

“把剪子给我。”女人说。

指甲剪的声音突然安静了下来。父亲把女人的话翻来覆去地咀嚼了几次，才渐渐明白过来那是乡音。父亲抬起头来，呆呆地看着女人。父亲的目光穿过女人，穿过女人身后的墙壁，遥遥地散落在半空中。父亲的眼中，就有了些水汽。

女人趁着空当，拿过父亲手中的指甲剪，帮父亲剪起指甲来。父亲起先有些扭捏，可是女人神情凛凛，把父亲的扭捏瞬间碾灭在萌芽状态。女人正着剪，反着修，先左手，再右手。父亲的十根手指在女人粗粝的掌心走过一遭，如同抛了一次光，就有些平整光洁起来。田田坐在边上看着，眼皮渐渐黏夯起来。走失了多日的睡意，在这个平淡无奇的下午骤然回归，方明白自己的担子大约是可以卸下一些了。

"春枝你今天就住下，剩下的行李我明天找人帮你取回来。"田田吩咐女人。

"谁答应的？我说过家里不住生人。"何淳安突然站了起来，一把拂开女人，指甲剪咚地掉在茶儿的铁角上，溅起一片嘤嗡。

女人怔了一怔，不语，却弯下腰来捡剪子。

"熟人也是生人过来的嘛。春枝是同乡，总比完全不知根底的人好。"田田捺着性子，细声细气地劝着父亲。

"她白天可以来帮忙，晚上自己找地方住。这是我开的条件，她接受就来，不接受就走。"何淳安脸朝着田田，话却是对春枝说的。

春枝拿起搁在墙角的背包，头也不回就往门外走去。"你给我付房租，我就住在外边。这是我开的条件，你答应了我就来，你不答应我就走。"

田田追出去，女人已经走远了。女人走路的时候脚紧紧地贴着路面，身上的布衫在风里一鼓一颤的，如同没能飞起来的鹞子。田田跑了半条街才追上，气喘吁吁地对女人说："学校的宿舍，我给你找一间。两三个人一起住，明天就来，行不？"

女人停下来，叹了一口气："大姐，如今上哪儿找你这样的女儿。"

田田也叹了一口气，说："你比我大，别大姐大姐的，叫名字就好。人老了，就是孩子，只能哄着些。你这脾气，能行吗？"

女人说："我们乡下人就这么称呼的，改不过来。大姐你书读得比我多，外边的事也懂得多，可我见过的老人却比你多了。我知道什么时候该哄，什么时候不该哄。”

田田觉得女人的话有些道理，就不吭声了，一路送女人去了汽车站。前一班车刚走，后一班车还没来，两人都有些累了，就斜靠在站台柱子上等。红云沉尽了，天渐渐地暗了下来。路灯一盏一盏地点过去，从街头亮到街尾，像一串藏过了年代的老珠子，黄黄地坠在街市的胸脯上。归家的鸽子低低地飞过，暮色里到处是翅膀的划痕。

“大姐，你孩子多大了?”女人问。

田田摇头，说没孩子也没老公——离了。

“为什么离的?”

田田看着女人，一字一顿地说：

“不学好。”

两人的眼睛对上了，就忍不住哈哈地笑了起来。女人笑的时候，颊上有两个若隐若现的浅坑。那浅坑一路乱颤着，使得女人的表情瞬间里清朗生动起来。

车终于来了。女人上去了，挑了个窗边的位置坐下，从窗缝里钻出头来，说：“何老师我来管，大姐你安心回去，再找一个合适的。”

田田两眼热了一热，搜肠刮肚，想跟女人说一句略微亲近些的话，话没出口，车就启动了。女人渐渐变成了一个小小的蓝点，消失在一街的轻尘里。

这时田田提包里的手机叮叮当当地响了起来。

是秦阳。

“找着合适的人了?”

隔着一汪大洋，秦阳的声音听起来有些疲惫。田田算了算时差，这会儿正是多伦多的凌晨。秦阳午夜才下班，到这时才睡了三四个小时。田田就问怎么这个时候打电话?秦阳笑了笑，说小姐我压根还没上床，拨了几个小时的电话了，线路都不通。田田说你就不会明天再打吗？秦阳说你是想让我一夜不睡呢，还是两夜？田田哧哧地笑了起来——秦阳总是能把话说到人的心尖子上。

“找了一个，看上去还算老实。也只有这一个，是我爸点了头的。”

“老头子情绪还好吗？”

“好得了吗？整天对着那张照片……”田田说了半截，眼泪就毫无防备地流了下来。这几天一直在忙父亲的事，倒没有时间来好好想一想母亲。此刻关于母亲的记忆突然混混杂杂地涌了上来，按捺不住地堆挤在喉咙和鼻腔中间的那个狭窄空间里。眼泪被夜风瞬间吹干了，可是眼泪爬过的痕迹却久久地刺痒着。

“秦阳，我没、没有娘了。”

那头是一片短暂的沉默。后来秦阳轻轻地咳嗽了一声，说田田，你总还是有我的。

在多伦多田田的朋友圈子里，很多人都不知道秦阳这个名字。可是你若说起田田的“后备役”，几乎人人皆知，甚至连田田自己，也不十分忌讳。确切地说，“后备役”这个名词，其实最早还是田田自己发明的。那天田田第一次带了秦阳去参加一个朋友的生日晚会，众人私下里拉了田田问那个男人是谁，田田怎么都不承认是男朋友，后来逼得紧了，才说是后备役——若到了四十岁还没有着落，再考虑嫁给他。当时美国在伊拉克开战，报纸、电视、电台上到处是军事用语。田田随口抓了一句来用，没想到用得如此到位，后来竟流传得如此之广。当这个称呼在朋友圈子里流传过好几圈，又重新流回到田田耳边的时候，田田觉得有些陌生走味了。仿佛她泼出去的原是一杯水，过些时候流回来的，却成了一碗茶。茶原是从水来的，可茶却又不完全是水。

秦阳是田田办公楼旁边一家咖啡馆的侍应生。田田午休时去那里喝咖啡，听秦阳和顾客讲了两三句蹩脚英文，就听出是同胞，便长驱直入肆无忌惮地和秦阳讲起了中文。田田是一个人过日子，秦阳也是一个人过日子。一个人过日子当然会有许多空闲的时间，尤其在多伦多这样冬季无比寒冷漫长的都市里。于是两人就自然而然地凑在一起，来规划填补那些空闲出来的时间。秦阳中午上班，一直工作到午夜，做两天歇一天，而田田是规规矩矩的朝九晚五。遇到秦阳上班的日子，两人就趁午休的时候在咖啡馆里见面，田田特意把午休安排到下午两点咖啡馆生意清闲一些的时候。在秦阳不上班的日子里，秦阳就在唐人街买好了菜，等着田田回家一起做饭吃——两人是极少到外边餐馆吃饭的。田田是个年薪七万的白领丽人，而秦阳的收入却接近于最低工资线。最初田田提出来回家做饭吃，是为了不让秦阳窘迫。到后来成了习惯，却发现在家吃饭有诸多的好处，就再也不愿意出去吃了。

最大的好处是可以喝酒，而不用考虑酒后驾车。

秦阳手脚麻利，做得一手好菜。等菜上了桌，两人跟前各摆了一只酒杯，就开始轻斟浅饮。秦阳从不沾啤酒葡萄酒，只喝白酒，而且是唐人街超市里走私进口的最便宜的北京二锅头。田田渐渐也跟着喝起了白酒，不知不觉间，田田发现自己有了酒量。两人喝得很慢，一杯酒能喝上大半个夜晚。酒是一滴一滴地滚落到肚肠里的，那样的喝法只够溅起颧上一两片惊心动魄的潮红，却是不能掀动心里的大风大浪的。两人喝到身子像卸成无数碎片，脑子还浑然一体的时候，就停了。歪在沙发上看几眼电视，便昏昏地睡了过去。再醒来，大概就是半夜了。田田在家穿的是最随意的便装，人在酒里梦里揉过一遭，满嘴生臭，蓬头垢面，状如女鬼——在秦阳面前却没有丝毫羞涩之态。

酒半醒的时候，欲望就生出来了。所有都市男女单独相处时想做该做的事，他们也都做，而且做得甚是凶猛。在婚姻的烂泥淖里走过一遭的田田，自然是轻车熟路，尽管秦阳不是她先前的车先前的路，这一点田田从一开始就知道了。秦阳的路曲里拐弯，每一道弯里都蕴藏着一些无法预测的惊喜、娴熟和温存仿佛出自毕生不懈的练习。

遇到天气暖和一些的时候，两人就下楼，到公寓边上的街心公园坐一坐，听流浪艺人远远地吹些恓恓惶惶的曲子，撕几片面包来喂满地行走的鸽子。

然后再步行到唐人街的中国剧院看一部晚场电影，大都是粤语片国语字幕的——秦阳英文不好，看不太懂英文片。然后秦阳就送田田回家，然后秦阳再开车回到他自己的住处。有一天秦阳送田田到了公寓门口，自己钻进了车子，却又探出头来，说田田还是我搬过来住吧，天天赶过来赶回去的，多累啊。秦阳说这话的时候微微有些结巴，田田却没吭声。看着秦阳的二手牛车咣当咣当地撞进一街浓密的夜色里，田田的心情突然复杂了起来。

在那个夜晚之前田田对秦阳的感觉是异常简单的——一种权宜，一些方便，一段过渡。秦阳比田田小四岁。秦阳没有上过正式大学。秦阳没有正式移民身份。秦阳在顶着别人的工卡打黑工。秦阳一个月的收入除了房租伙食汽车开销之外，大概只够买几瓶二锅头。秦阳的糟糕不仅在于他的一无所有，而且在于他不具备任何峰回路转的潜质。秦阳的存在，似乎只是为了给田田这类人作注解的。在那些充斥着华埠报章的成功移民故事中，田田是那个套红的标题，而秦阳却是那个衬托标题的参照物。除了年龄以外，秦阳和田田之间没有可比性。而年龄的反差，使得田田对秦阳的想法越发地简单了起来——田田从来没有对秦阳有过第二种想法。

直到那个夜晚，秦阳说出了那句话，田田便想起平日闲聊时，秦阳提起过要开咖啡馆的事情。秦阳这几年在咖啡馆里打工，虽然辛苦，却也学了几个挣钱的绝招。就想自己去开一家——在大办公楼底层，做早餐午餐，客流量大营业时间短的那一种。秦阳对咖啡馆的想法很具体细致。秦阳想到了食品的种类、装修的格调、员工的配置。秦阳甚至把名字都想好了，就叫“龙塔”——龙塔是英文longtime的谐音，取的是天长地久的意思。秦阳考虑到了塔身塔尖的每一个细节，秦阳却唯独没有提到塔的地基——资金和一张移民纸。没有这两样东西，秦阳的塔设想得再仔细再具体也只能是镜中花水中月。

然而秦阳恰恰就是没有这两样东西。

可是田田有。

田田早已拿到了加拿大公民身份。田田手头可以活动的现款虽然不多，却完全可以利用工作之便申请到银行的商用贷款。

如果田田拥有的也能成为秦阳的，那么秦阳的龙塔就可以坚实美丽地竖立起来了。

田田被这样的联想吃了一惊，回过头来看，似乎秦阳的每一道目光每一个举止都铺垫了一层急切。从那天开始，田田就刻意疏远了秦阳。借口开会，借口出差，借口家里有客人，田田和秦阳见面的机会就渐渐少了，田田当然也不再去秦阳工作的那家咖啡馆吃午饭了。

没有秦阳的日子里，时间突然就多得没了章法。下班回家，走进那个空落落的公寓房间，隔宿的寂寞如一张柔软却无所不在的网，将田田兜头罩住。任凭田田拳脚相加，也凿不透一个小小的口子。这时她就想起了秦阳的种种好处。秦阳的温和细致、秦阳的幽默、秦阳对生活的热情和活力、秦阳恰到好处的逢迎。在和秦阳的交往中，他给她的距离始终是适宜的，再近一分就有可能让她感到窒息，再退一分就会让她失去了安全感。无论是进是退，他很少乱过阵脚，失过方寸。于是田田很是怀念起秦阳来，有几次甚至已经拿起了电话，要拨那串熟记在心的数字。然而秦阳的每一个好处也同时让田田惊骇——这些好处似乎是古今中外所有吃软饭的男人都具备的。女人的欢心就是他们的饭碗他们的天。田田虽然愿意被男人哄着捧着，可是田田却从没想过做男人的饭碗男人的天。

于是她最终还是慌乱地放下了电话。

后来田田就找到了别的方法来打发那些过也过不完的长夜。田田开始整宿整宿地在网上和陌生人聊天，田田也开始参加各式各样的交友俱乐部。交过几个男人，心热过一阵，又凉过一阵。期望高高地飞到了云间，却又低低地落到泥里土里。只是热凉起落都是需要耗费心神的，渐渐地，田田发觉自己心里关于秦阳的念想就给磨薄了。

田田和秦阳的故事其实完全可以在此处画上一个干脆利落的句号的，可是偏偏在这个节骨眼上，田田出了一件事。这件事使得这个句号一滑，带出一个小小的尾巴，变成了逗号。于是这个故事像一棵几近枯死的树又意外地长出了一条新枝。

那一天田田下班回家，把车开进了地下停车场，刚要下车，突然间两耳一阵轰鸣，犹如千百只秋蝉在飞舞碰撞，屋顶上的灯变成流星雨，一阵一阵飞旋着向她洒落下来。她两脚一软，便倒了下去。

醒来时，模模糊糊地看见眼前有一个花圈，花圈上挂着一朵朵花。花很大，花蕊蠕动着，发出各种各样的声音。过了一会儿，眼神渐渐清朗起来，才看出那些花原来都是人头。后来花渐渐都散去了，只剩了一朵，近近地贴在她脸畔。

"算你命大，车开到家才出事。"

那朵花是秦阳。

田田吃了一大惊，问你怎么来了。秦阳看了田田一眼，一字一顿地说："召之即来。"田田这才隐隐记起来，自己昏过去之前似乎拨过一个手机号码。那个号码大概一直浅浅地埋在潜意识里，只需轻轻一扫，就随时浮到了表层。想起自己这些日子里对秦阳的刻意疏远，脸上不禁就浮起些斑驳的臊意。

"你到底还是把我想起来了。没听人说吗，铁不铁，就看你生病了想的是谁。"

秦阳依旧是没心没肺的，田田听了却是一怔，一时竟是无话。

田田得的是美尼尔综合征。发病时症状凶猛，医生下令暂时吊销驾驶执照半年。田田的住处离公车线有一段距离，早上赶车太急，秦阳就来接田田上班。接了几天，田田说你不如就在这儿住吧，省得天天起得这么早。

第二天秦阳果真就搬了进来。从此就没有再搬回去。

田田临回加拿大之前，在父亲的学校里给赵春枝找了一间房子暂且住下——是学校办外语培训班时给外地学员准备的宿舍。春枝和三个外地女学员一起住。房管处知道何淳安教授家里出了事。多少有些可怜老头子，便睁只眼闭只眼，由着去了。田田又去买了辆女式自行车，作为春枝在校园和家之间的交通工具。等拿着了房门钥匙和自行车钥匙，保姆赵春枝就正式走马上任了。

春枝早上骑车到何淳安教授家里，去小菜场买好一天的菜，准备早中晚三顿饭食，收拾整理房间，清洗被褥衣物。何教授身体基本健康，行动方便，也极少挑口。何家的这一点简单家务，春枝弹琴似的顺过一遍，还没来得及调动所有的指头，就完成了。于是，春枝手里就剩下了大把大把的时间。春枝使用空闲时间的方式只有一种，就是绣花。

春枝不绣寻常的花草鸳鸯，春枝绣的是西洋油画。春枝的绣花绷子很大，大得像一幅画。春枝把印刷品的油画贴在布上，就直接按照画上的颜色上针，深的上深色，浅的上浅色。不过春枝有时也不完全跟着画谱走，比方说，绣到房顶时，春枝用了很多金黄色的丝线。绣到树梢时明明应该用绿色，春枝却偏偏用了粉白。那黄的和白的乍看起来像是半空落下来的鸟屎，出挑而别扭地粘在屋顶和树枝之间。等到一幅画都绣完了，远远地挂在墙上，眯了眼睛细细地去品味，才发现那黄和那白使得原本幽暗的景致里突然涌现出一片片瀑布似的阳光。

何淳安看了，愣了很久，才轻轻说了一声“没想到”。

春枝把剪子线团咚的一声扔回针线包里，笑了一笑，说没想到什么呢？没想到我们乡下人也有点艺术细胞，是不是？田田在京的那几天，春枝说话还有些顾忌。待田田一走，春枝就露出了真性情，想什么说什么，口无遮拦。何淳安辩解不得，只好呵呵地傻笑。

其实何淳安也有大把大把的空闲时间。何淳安现在极少去学校。何淳安见不得众人那躲躲闪闪半是怜悯半是猜测的目光。那些目光如春日挂在树梢上的一抹飞丝，拿手指头轻轻一挑就断了。断在手上，看是看不见了，却缠缠绕绕总也感觉不甚清爽。

何淳安空闲的时候，就爱看书。何淳安看起书来，全然不是市井闲散之辈的那种看法，何淳安对看书的准备和姿势实在是很挑剔的。首先，茶是必备的。上好的毛尖，二遍茶——第一遍是要过滤倒掉的。其次，老花镜要仔仔细细地呵气擦拭过，不能有一丝一毫的云雾。再者，躺椅的倾斜角度也是一个定数，要调到头颈和身子大致成四十五度角的那个位置。这些姿势排场都做过了，何淳安才能静下心来看书。心是静下来了，书却依旧看不下去。书里的字像是一块块黝黑的岩石，成团结伙地阻拦着何淳安的思绪。何淳安看懂了每一块岩石，何淳安却没有看懂山。何淳安的目光在岩石之间惶乱地走过几遭，就很是疲乏起来，睡意翩然而至，书咚地落到了地上。

春枝捡起书来，撩起衣襟擦了擦何淳安落在书上的口涎，看见封面上有一张照片，照片上是一个眉黑目深的高鼻梁西洋女人。女人的笑意很浅，嘴唇抿得紧紧的，神情有些寂寥。翻了翻书的内容，通篇上下竟没有一个中文字。正惊异间，突然想起老头子是教英文出身的，才忍不住咕的一声笑出声来。

这一笑，就把何淳安惊醒了。坐起来，一时不知身在何处。懵懵懂懂之间，突然叫了一声"延安"。叫完了，人就完全醒了。愣愣地待了一会儿，才慢慢起身去了厕所。

嗒的一声，门从里边锁上了。一阵之后，就有了些叮咚的水声，接着就是哗哗的水声。再后来，就是一片长久的凝固不化的静寂。春枝听说过李延安是怎么死的，这时突然有些心悸，忍不住悄悄地走过去，把耳朵贴在门上，屏着气听。谁知人还没有站稳，门却骤然开了，春枝身子一歪。几乎跌倒。何淳安扶住了春枝，叹了一口气，说："她糊涂，我哪能也跟着她一般糊涂。"

春枝的心方咚地落到了实处，也叹了一口气，说："别人说她糊涂，是不明白她，连你也跟着说。她哪是糊涂呢，她这明明是病。她病得这般苦，你既不能替她受这个苦，还不让她痛快地走。她走了，对你来说是舍不得，那是你的自私，她却是解放了呢。让你试试看，这样的病，苦得没个尽头没个解救的，放在你身上你受得了？"

何淳安却是从没听过别人这样劝解自己的。突然间，黑隧道般阴稠的心里，窄窄地流进了一线光亮，光亮之下，有纤尘细细地扬起。沉实了多日的心，开始有了第一丝的松动。

两人回到客厅，绣花的依旧绣花，看书的依旧看书。春枝将一根线头在嘴里含了半天，才吐出来，朝着何淳安手里的那本书努了努，问："何老师，那个沃尔芙，文章写得好吗？"

何淳安吃了一惊，问你看得懂英文？春枝将脸涨红了，说就认得几个字而已。从前做事的那户人家，爱看录像带。有个电影，就是讲这个沃尔芙的，说是个有名的英国作家，投河死的。

"你说的那个电影叫《时光》，说的是沃尔芙死前的那一段。其实人家活着的时候就出大名了，倒是死了，却没怎么着。那年我去伦敦访问，下着大雨撑着把破伞去戈登广场找沃尔芙故居。找着了，连个牌子都没有。旁边那座房子，倒挂了个大牌子，说是某某某，赞助过沃尔芙的。连英国也这样，只记得阔佬，却不记得秀才。"

春枝扑哧笑了一声，说怎么不记得？何老师你看的是谁的书呢？阔佬有书留下来吗？没听说人阔了就想买学位吗？可见秀才还是比阔佬稀罕些呢。

何淳安被春枝逗乐了，也跟着笑，说是呀是呀，那个沃尔芙，研究外国文学的，人人都得读她的书呀。她倒是很替你们女人说话的。就是她说的，女人想写书，首先得有自己的房间，再得有五百英镑的年收入。她是说女人当自立——那都是女权主义的最初意识呢。

春枝撇了撇嘴，说女不女权的，我是不懂的，我只知道那女人长得倒是挺灵秀的。可是心里冷着呢，一条路黑冷到底，多好的男人都暖她不过来呢。

何淳安没有说话。过了好久，春枝抬起头来，才看见了老头颊上斑驳的泪痕。

李延安心里大约也是那样一条路黑冷到底，再也没有人可以暖她过来，才决定走了那样的极端吧？

可是，李延安年轻的时候，却是一支火把，一盏灯，站在最暗的路口，也能毫不费力地照着自己照着别人。

何淳安认识李延安的时候，已经大学毕业好几年了。他留校在外文系教欧美小说，她才刚刚分配进学校的图书馆做图书管理员。他偶然从别人嘴里听说了她父亲原来是一位赫赫有名的将军，才开始对她有了星点的好奇。在他那个人生阶段里，用“星点”来形容他对她的好奇，实在是恰到好处的。

那时他早已不是一张白纸了。

何淳安从小在教会学校里学的英文，口音里带着一丝牛津校园味，文章更是写得地道典雅。自小就将一应欧美名著看得滚瓜烂熟，倒背如流。时常信手拈来，出口成章——是外文系理所当然的业务尖子，却又没有洋文教授通常有的虚浮轻佻，行事为人很是稳重厚道，自然是讨女孩子欢喜的。在认识李延安之前，他曾有过两次恋爱经历，一次是他的大学同班同学，另一次是他朋友的妹妹。然而到了谈婚论嫁的地步，两个女人都却步了。他是侨乡来的，身世充满了故事，有许多近亲远亲在海外，所以他在系里，无论是提职还是提薪，都是落在最后的。他的两任女朋友都是因为这个原因离他而去的。

那两个女人，也绝非浅薄低俗之类，都是人中的尖子、花中的花。她们都很懂得他的优点。可是他的优点仿佛是伞，而他的身世却是雨。伞再好，也只能抵挡一时一刻的雨，却抵挡不了一生一世的雨。所以她们后来都选择了不需要伞的晴天。

这两次恋爱，他都爱得死去活来。到分手时，他觉得已经耗尽了他的心神。在那个凡事讲究简单纯洁的年代里，他的感情经历就算是复杂得有些可疑了。在那之后他再见到适婚的年轻女子，便有了尚未得到就已经害怕失去的焦虑。这份焦虑最初是隐隐约约、似有似无地藏在心中最深处的那个角落的，后来被年岁搅动着，零零星星地浮现上来，积在眼角眉梢鬓角唇边，直到有一天，他在公共浴室的镜子前擦头发时，突然就发现自己已经有了第一缕的落魄和沧桑。

那天是何淳安二十五岁生日。他从学校的澡堂洗完澡出来，拎了一网兜换下来的脏衣服，行走在校园四月的暖春里，湿润的头发被风随意扬起，像一株盛开的蒲公英。而他那天的心境，也恰恰符合了蒲公英的比喻——从盛开到凋零，似乎只需要一阵风。二十五岁仿佛是一道坎，二十五岁之前，他有些不知不觉。过了二十五岁，他突然就感觉到了风的存在。

可是那天的李延安还是一沓白纸。十九页，页页雪白平整，毫无印记褶皱。

那时李延安的父母已经结束了多年的戎马生涯，渐渐适应了安定的城市生活。当父母终于意识到子女的存在时，李延安已经像一根石头缝里的小草，自说自话地长成了一棵结实的小树。最好的学校最称职的老师都无济于事，李延安已经无可救药地失去了对读书的兴趣。李延安留了一年级，才勉强初中毕业，却无论如何考不上高中，就在一家工厂里做了几年车床操作工。李延安虽然很早就知道自己不是一块读书的材料，却一直憧憬着在读书人的环境里工作。出于对女儿的内疚，李延安的父亲做了一生中唯一一件利用职权的事——把李延安安排进了大学的图书馆工作。然而李延安父亲的特权只行使到了图书馆门外，门内的一切，却是看李延安自己的造化了。李延安进入图书馆之后，名义上是管理员，很长的时间里其实都在做一个小工的事——搬运存书、清理书架、打扫卫生。数年以后，馆里来了更年轻的新人，她才调到了编目室工作。

那天何淳安洗完澡，就去学校的食堂吃了顿晚饭，又回宿舍翻了几页哈代的小说。终是无心无绪，便决定去图书馆找一本英国湖畔诗人的诗集。在过道上，他被一辆装满了书的手推车撞上了。车轮上的铁片直直地割进了他的脚踝，当时他只觉出了酥麻——疼痛是后来的事：他身子一矮，布袋似的软在了地上，手紧紧地捂住了脚踝。推车的女人连忙停下车来扶他，他却不肯松手。过了一会儿，就有液体从他的指缝里慢慢渗出，将他的袜子染成一幅紫红色的图画。旁边围观的人开始惊叫起来。女人拨开了他的手，一把扯下他的袜子，在他的脚踝上扎了个死死的结，就架着他去了学校的医务室。女人身量不高，他得倾斜着身体才能靠在她的肩上，可是那天他感觉仿佛是靠在一堵矮而结实的砖墙上，他竟放心踏实地在上面放上了自己的重量。

一直到处理完了伤口，他才有机会看了女人一眼。这一看，就看出很多意外来了——他完全没有想到她竟是那样年轻，年轻得几乎还不能称之为女人，衣装发式眼神身架没有一处不在昭著地显示着未解风情的木然。他问她叫什么名字，以前怎么没在图书馆见过？她说她叫李延安，是新来的，才上了三天班。她回答他的问题时态度很老实，甚至有些怯场，几乎完全没有做任何延伸和说明，和她刚才处理事故的大胆老辣成了一个鲜明的对比。她的脸上有些脏——大约是搬书的缘故，汗水在灰尘中间流出一道道树影一样斑驳的印记，潮湿的鬓发在额角蜷成一个个小小的圆圈。她和他以往见过的所有女人都不同，她使得那些女人显得苍白病态贫瘠做作。

突然间他对她就有了好感。

他问她怎么一点都不怕血？怎么有这么大的力气？这回她只笑了笑，却没有回答。

真正的答案是他渐渐熟知了她的童年之后才得到的。

李延安出生在延安。和当时的大部分延安子女一样，她一出生就被送到了当地老乡家里抚养。断了奶，就进了保育院。父母也许到保育院看过她，也许没有。六岁以前，除了知道父亲姓李，李延安对自己的双亲几乎毫无印象。

保育院常常迁移，李延安很快就适应了在马背上睡去在马背上醒来的生活。有一次她睡得太死，从马背上掉了下来，竟无人发觉。等到第二天她被晨露冻醒，才知道马队早已走远。她沿着若隐若现的马蹄和马粪痕迹，走了整整三天的路，终于追上了大队人马。那天保育院的阿姨去井边打水，看见井边躺了一条脏狗，随脚一踢，踢出声来，才知是人。提了油灯来照，照见是李延安。李延安走丢了一只鞋，那只光脚磨得脓血模糊，脚踝被石头扎破，伤口深得几乎看见了骨头。阿姨来清洗伤口，一根一根地挑脚板上的刺。挑出来的不像是刺，倒像是血针，叮当有声地落了一盘子。阿姨挑着挑着就红了眼圈，李延安却一直没哭，只是反反复复地对阿姨说下次睡着了你就掐我。

那年李延安大约是五岁半——和保育院大部分孩子一样，李延安并不知道自己确切的出生日期。

那之后没多久，李延安就和保育院的其他孩子一样，和他们各自的父母亲团聚了。孩子们对局势的变化是一知半解的，只知道要离开保育院进城了。进城的第二天，李延安被人领着走进一个灰砖大院，院里坐着一男一女两个大人和三个比她更小的孩子。领她进来的那个人拉着她的手，让她管那两个大人叫爸爸妈妈，又让那几个孩子叫她姐姐。她没叫，也没应。那天刮着大风，满天飞着脏雪似的柳絮，太阳仿佛是一只黄土捏就的大碗，蔫蔫地扣在尘土厚重的屋顶上。一个被战争离散了的家庭和四个互不相识的孩子在那个颜色和情绪都很灰暗的下午草草地会合在一起。当时谁也没有想到，磨合的过程却持续了后来的半生。

几年以后，李延安才从大院其他孩子口中得知，那个她称呼为妈妈的女人，其实并不是她的母亲。她的生母走出了雪山，走出了草地，却病死在进城的路上。后来和父亲一起走进城里的，是一个文工团的女兵。

不过这对李延安来说已经不重要了。

李延安的父亲和继母都是从马背上下来就直接走进了办公楼的。城里有太多新奇的事情，他们要学的内容实在太丰富了，他们根本无暇顾及子女。照顾孩子们日常起居的，是一个五十多岁的保姆。在李延安看来，她不过是从一家保育院搬到了另一家保育院。她沿袭了保育院里大孩子照顾小孩子的作风，自然而然地担负起了照顾弟妹的任务。很快，那支只有三个士兵的部队在她的调教之下秩序井然。在这个新秩序里，大人只是若隐若现无关紧要的背景。李延安从来没有童年的感受。婴孩的第一声啼哭过去了，她仿佛就担负起了作为一个成人的职责，照顾着自己也照顾着别人。

这种感觉，如一根筋脉，始终贯穿在她和何淳安的关系中。

她和他认识以后，几乎没有任何交接转换过渡，她立即进入了她惯常的角色。她像一只硕健的母鸡，张开丰满的翅膀，将他全然覆盖。虽然他比她年长六岁，她却成了他的长姊、他的母亲。她照顾着他的一切需要。他的世界顷刻就小了，小得只有一翼之地。在那一翼之地里，四季只剩了一季，那是恒常的春。在恒常的春里他可以接近于放肆地伸展他的四肢和灵魂，只是，不知不觉中，他对付其他季节的功能却渐渐萎缩退化了。

他们结婚第三年，那场后来成为中国现代史研究专题的风暴铺天盖地刮进了校园。何淳安在外文系里既不是当权派，也不是当权派的红人，个性本来逍遥，树敌也不多，又有老将军岳父这一层遮挡，便相对平安地度过了最初的那个阶段。

后来，系里的头面人物相继下马，成为死老虎。工宣队入驻，新班子逐渐成形。厮杀声安静下来时，众人突然发觉他们已经失去了新的斗争目标。用当今政坛上的时髦用语来解释当时的情形，就是外文系处在了一个缺乏政绩的真空阶段。于是，新班子成员的视线，就渐渐地转向了何淳安。

工宣队找何淳安谈了一次话。

那天晚上李延安回家比平常晚了一些。图书馆的风声也很紧，有人交代了李延安父亲把女儿安插进馆的事，于是李延安毫无准备地被踢到了前台。幸好李延安在馆里只是一名勤杂工人，不占干部的编制。在那个知识分子成堆的环境里，李延安的初中文凭和档案袋里不满一页纸的简单身世，使得批她的人几乎找不到合适的词，草草地训斥了几句之后，李延安就被打发回家了。

李延安进了门，屋里一片漆黑。她以为丈夫还没回家，就开灯准备生火做饭。弯腰量米的时候，突然发现何淳安捧着头泥塑木雕般地坐在地板上，就大吃一惊。问了，却不说话；再问，才说头疼。

李延安将丈夫扶到床上躺下了，就开始淘米洗菜炒菜。火一热，油锅的味道熏过来，喉咙口就涌上一团酸水。还来不及找个脸盆，就蹲在门槛上哇哇地吐了一地。中午没吃饭，吐出来的只是苦胆。那时李延安已经怀孕七个半月，妊娠反应却一直没有消失。何淳安在床上听见妻子吐得死去活来，只翻来覆去地叹气，说你挑了个什么时候来嘛，你。李延安知道丈夫在说腹中的这个孩子，便忍不住回了一句："这是我一个人挑的吗？那你说什么时候是个好时候?"

两人不声不响地吃了一顿饭，饭和菜都只轻轻地挑了几挑，便都放回了碗橱里。李延安收拾碗筷的时候，听见丈夫在身后又幽幽地叹了一口气，说元元，就叫元元吧，就是一个的意思。李延安听了心里咯噔了一下，半晌，才笑着说：你可别给我定数，高兴了我还能生一打呢，我就喜欢家里人多热闹。却暗暗地长了个心眼，仔细地盯着何淳安的一举一动。

夜里李延安躺下了，却不敢睡。窗外秋虫叫得惊天动地，腹中孩子踢得甚是凶猛，仿佛要将肚子踢出一个洞来。怕吵着何淳安，李延安一直不敢翻身。身子在一个姿势上僵着，每一处关节每一块肉都酸痒难熬。到了后半夜，实在扛不住，才迷糊了过去。糊糊涂涂地做了个梦，梦见何淳安穿了一件雪白的纺绸对襟大褂，一路风吹杨柳似的走过来。她伸出手来抓他，抓来抓去都是空的。他仿佛变了烟变了气在她的指缝里溜过来溜过去。她一急，就醒了。一摸身边是空的，就咚地下了地；赤着脚跌跌撞撞地摸到了外屋。夜正浓。月悬在窗口，照得一屋水似的亮，青砖地上树影如鬼魅游走。她一把扯亮了灯，只见墙脚站着个人，正慌慌地端了个水杯往嘴里送水。她狼似的扑上去，狠狠地掴过一掌。那人不备，手里的杯子嚯啷一声掉了下来，白色的药丸滚了一地。

这一掌掴得过于凶猛，她身子一歪，就麻袋似的跌坐在地上。胳膊闪了，顿时肿成一个肉球，疼得满眼是泪。他过来扶，她捂着胳膊，却朝他猛踹了一脚。他一个趔趄，撞到了脸盆架。脸盆翻落下来，一路嘤嗡地滚到墙边，才咣的一声停了下来。宿舍楼道的灯啪啪地亮了起来，有人开窗探看。他急急地捂了她的嘴，半架半搡地扶着她回到了床上。

躺是躺下了，睡意却早没了。蒙着被子，她咬牙切齿地对他说："我爸爸一趟雪山草地走过来，丢了一条腿、一个老婆、两个儿子，如今是个什么下场？他没说委屈，你倒委屈起来了？你过过一天苦日子吗，你？"

这一骂，倒把何淳安给骂醒了。仔细想想，竟无一句可回嘴的。渐渐地，心里有了些愧意，就嘿嘿地笑，说老婆你是一盏灯，你往我心里一照，就再也没有黑角落了。李延安呸了一声，说再亮的灯，照了路易十几，也是白照。何淳安没听懂，问什么路易十几的？李延安狠狠地掐了他一把，说就是那个我死了拉倒，洪水滔天也行的，跟你一个德行。何淳安这才明白过来自己平常备课的材料，李延安原来也看的。两人相拥着，不再说话，看着窗外那一轮月亮渐渐地坠落下去，天边隐隐地有了潮红，恍恍然，仿佛已若隔世。

从那以后，何淳安的脸皮就慢慢地厚了起来，由着世界轰轰烈烈地上演着诸般的曲目，有人上台，有人下台，自己却始终只做一个不动声色的观众。先是隔离审查了一阵，后来下放劳动了一阵，再后来又随着大流调回了外文系。心情虽有涨落的时候，却再也不曾生过寻死的心了。

可是李延安这盏灯，是什么时候熄灭的呢？

其实李延安的灯，并不是瞬间熄灭的。从明亮到陨灭，中间经历了一个暗淡的过程。暗淡的过程是渐进的，身在其中的人并没有觉察，所有的迹象都是事后才醒悟的。

"文革"过后，何淳安是学校里第一批提升为教授、第一批批准带研究生，也是第一批选派国外短期进修的老师。何淳安的生命，经过了一个长长的冬眠期，在中年的时候突然复苏。这一苏醒，就醒出了许多意外的景致。李延安发现何淳安渐渐地不再需要她的照明了，因为他已经成了他自己的灯。他岂止是他自己的灯，他甚至也成了她的灯。他又岂止是她一个人的灯，他的灯还照着许许多多的别人，包括他的同事和他的学生。她多年为他战战兢兢地操持着的心，就渐渐地放松了下来。当然，她当时并不知道，最适合她的一种生存状态，其实就是紧张。在紧张的时刻她是一张满弓，捏在手里是暗暗一把的力气，送出箭来铮然有声，直奔靶心。松弛下来，她就如泼洒在地上的一摊水，随意地顺着地面的缝隙游走。虽然依旧走着，却不再是有目的有劲道地奔走，不过是走到哪里是哪里的认命和无奈了。

在所有的神经都松弛下来的时候，却只有一根神经，突然地绷紧了。李延安的眼睛和耳朵，对一些景物一些声音，异常地敏感了起来。何淳安的学生越来越多，何淳安在系里的职责也越来越重。李延安的目光如雷达漠然地扫过丈夫繁忙的生活天地，大部分的内容都被过滤为无关紧要的背景，荧光屏上剩下的只是几个细点。可是那几个细点却如沙粒，在李延安的眼中磨来磨去，磨得她寝食难安。

那些沙子就是何淳安的女学生女同事。

李延安监听何淳安的电话，闯进何淳安的办公室偷看何淳安的信件，四下打听何淳安在系里的一举一动。渐渐地，外文系的女同事见了何淳安，轻易不敢说笑了。何淳安为了撇清自己，也不敢和女学生单独相处了，更不敢邀请女同事女同学到家里来坐。上帝跟何淳安开了个不大不小的玩笑：上帝打开了何淳安的眼界，让他看到了大千世界的诸般可能性，可是在那个无限广袤的天地里，他可以拥有的，反而是一扇比从前更加狭窄了的窗口。

李延安的视线，已经被沙粒蒙蔽。李延安的灯，也渐渐地昏暗起来，她走失在多年走惯了的路上。开始时，何淳安不停地帮助妻子刷洗着那些沙粒，到后来，何淳安发现他刷洗得越努力，沙粒堆积得越快。

他只好选择了沉默。

李延安终于走进了万劫不复的阴暗之中。没有人可以暖她过来，没有人可以照亮她的路。即使是儿女，即使是丈夫，也只能看着她孤独地一步一步地渐行渐远。

何田田回到多伦多之后，关于保姆赵春枝在父亲身边的表现，她零零星星地听到了一些不同版本的报告。

第一个报告来自父亲的学生颜华。

李延安的自杀事件像一块石头，在外文系这潭深不见底的水里砸了一个大洞。洞很快平复了，涟漪却持续了很久。流言如树梢的风，看不见，摸不着，却顺着门缝、墙缝、窗棂格缝溜进来，悄无痕迹地爬到饭桌床头，又带着积攒的灰尘，越滚越大地爬入邻家。何淳安的女学生们，多多少少都知道自己是那些沸沸扬扬的花边新闻中的一段花边。而颜华，更知道自己是师母口中的那个“眼花儿”，是所有花边传闻中镶在最明处的那段花边。也明白我虽未杀伯仁、伯仁却因我而死的道理，所以很是敛声收气了一阵子。过了些时日，待流言略微安静了些，颜华难免不想起从前导师对自己的种种关照，便忍不住去了何教授家里探望。

颜华去的那天是个星期六，早上十点左右。她挑了这个时候，是因为何教授应该锻炼完了身体，正是读书看报的时候。颜华抱了一束白色的菊花走过层层楼梯，每一层过道上都有好奇的眼睛。当她最终敲响何淳安教授的门时，她的背已经被重重叠叠的目光压出了汗。

来开门的是赵春枝。

那天赵春枝穿了一件桃红色的毛衣、浅米色的西裤，脖子上系了一条白色的丝巾。虽都是旧衣物，却洗熨得极是干净平整，看上去不像是保姆，倒像是在别人家里做客的女眷。颜华微微吃了一惊，就问何教授在吗？赵春枝点点头，引着颜华进了屋。颜华走过客厅，一眼就看见何淳安卷着衣袖，正坐在一张小板凳上洗衣服。板凳很矮，何淳安的个子高，坐下去，就把凳子盖没了，仿佛坐到了地上。何淳安在笨拙地搓着一件衬衫，搓衣板在他的膝盖之间滑来滑去，脑勺上有一绺没有梳理平整的头发，顺着身体的走势来回耸动着。颜华的一句“何教授”在舌尖滚了好几个来回，吐出来时已是支离破碎了。何淳安抬起头来，意外地看见了来客，眼神渐渐地混浊了起来——自李延安出事以后，颜华是第一个也是唯一一个来探望自己的女学生。

何淳安擦干手，来到了客厅坐下。颜华向春枝要了一个大水杯，将菊花插上。花是满满一捧的雪白，只有花蕊是一抹一抹若有若无的浅绿，沾了水，立刻得了些生气，衬得一屋洁净生辉。颜华把花放在那张镶着黑框的照片下面，两人久久无语。半晌，何淳安才叹了一口气，说："其实，你师母脑子清醒的时候，也常夸你。"颜华的眼泪汹涌地流了下来，是委屈，是伤感，也是无奈。为自己，为导师，也为师母。那一念之差中走出去的一步，竟是那样一条永远无法填补的鸿沟。沟这边和沟那边，遥遥相望，已是隔世。

何淳安看着颜华哭，却不知怎么劝，搓了搓手，就进厨房去泡茶。颜华听见厨房里杯盏叮当地响了一阵子，又听见春枝咕咕地笑："何老师，那么大一个壶。饮驴哪？一个客人，用那个红花小壶就够了。"何淳安也笑，说骂我是驴也罢了，可不许骂我的客人。又问用哪种茶叶？春枝说二层柜子左手边那个铁罐里是茉莉花茶，招待女客正好。何淳安就搬了张凳子爬上去，开了柜子取茶叶罐。颜华听着，只觉得这个保姆嘴有些厉害，手有些懒，听上去不像个下人，倒更像个主子。过了十来分钟，只见何淳安一人颤颤地捧了一壶茶出来，春枝并没有跟出来。何淳安把滚烫的茶壶放下了，颜华赶紧起身自己将茶斟了，先给老师，再给自己。

两人喝着茶，闲闲地说了些学校里系里的事，颜华就忍不住问何教授你怎么自己洗衣服呢？何淳安说不是自己洗，是先将领子袖口的脏处搓一搓，再放洗衣机里洗的。颜华原本问的不是这个意思，就朝厨房撇了撇嘴，放低了声音：怎么不让她洗？何淳安笑笑，说春枝在教我做家务呢，我教她学英文，两下相抵，谁也不亏。

从何家出来，颜华一路愤愤然。心想现在这世界，岂是何教授这样厚道之人应付得了的？这个保姆，本事了得，拿了钱不干活，还自学英文。两下相抵，竟有这样的抵法。恐怕何教授哪天被这个女人骗了，还得帮她数钱呢。

回到家，颜华就给远在多伦多的田田发了一封电子邮件，说了她的担忧。

其实田田平常打电话回家，也是时时问起春枝的情况的。父亲只说人不错，有灵气。如此看来，父亲是不愿意自己担心，而将实情隐瞒了。田田看了颜华的信，立刻就给父亲打了电话。连着打了几次，都是春枝接的——父亲出门去了。春枝一口一个大姐地叫着，声气很是亲热。有了颜华的报告在先，田田就觉得那话语里藏了几分虚假和盘算。于是冷冷地交代了几句好好照顾老人之类的话，就挂了。

又给在广州的哥哥打电话。元元一听也急了，就立刻请了假，飞去了北京。

元元在家住了三天。元元给田田的反馈，和颜华的有相同之处，也有不同之处。元元说父亲现在变了，变得对家务有了兴趣。那个春枝倒也不是完全不做家务的，只要是老头子自己能做的事，春枝就放手让老头子做。老头子做不了的事，春枝做是做了，却是要老头子在旁边看着学。田田听了忍不住冷笑，说没想到这个女人真不简单呢，竟把老头子给驯化了——从前你见他洗过一双筷子吗？元元就劝，说只要爸高兴，就由他去吧。你没看见老头子教她学英文那个起劲呢，撺掇着她考什么英文几级几级的。原先你不就担心爸和保姆合不来吗？他俩合得来，省你多少心呢。

田田想想也是，就把这事放下了。夜里睡不着，就捅醒了秦阳，问："人老了怎么就这么贱呢？从前连牙膏都得让人挤妥，现在倒好。"秦阳知道田田还在想老爷子的事，就笑，说贱不贱跟老不老有什么相干呢？人要贱，什么时候都能贱。那是你妈没抓住你爸的心，怨不得别人。田田呸了一口，说你几年没刷牙了，开口怎么这么臭呀？这话说的，好像我爸和小保姆怎么着似的。秦阳依旧嬉皮笑脸的，说要没怎么着，人能这么贱吗？我这可是有亲身体会。田田伸出手来就掏秦阳的肋，秦阳怕痒，身子早笑得缩成一个球，蜷在床尾，怎么也掰不开，只有嘴巴却还是硬。

"你爸你妈结婚的时候该先问问我，两人名字都没起好呢，一人一个安，两安相克，就不安了。这个小保姆，春什么来着？你爸名字里有一汪水，水遇着春，是个什么景象，你想去吧。他能不贱吗？”

田田恼羞成怒，抓起椅子上的衬衫，追着秦阳满屋打。秦阳躲不过，只好逃进了厕所，锁上了门，依旧笑得抖抖的。

“咱俩的名字才是地造天合呢，你是田，我是阳，田得靠着太阳，才能万物生长。”

田田怔了一怔，半晌，才隔着门，冷冷一笑。

“可惜我的田不是你要的那个田。你打个电话给你的中学语文老师，问问他何田田的田是田的意思吗？”

何淳安那边安然无事地过了三四个月。到了旧历年底，田田突然收到了颜华寄来的一张电子贺年卡。贺年卡只是一个包装，信的真正内容却和贺年没有太大的关联。

颜华是来报急的。

何教授和保姆大吵了一架，把熬汤的沙锅都砸碎了，保姆拿了行李就回老家去了。何教授气得牙床暴肿，连稀饭都喝不下去，已经在床上躺了两天了。眼看要过春节了，元元带着公司的一拨人马在德国培训，家里一样年货都没有置办。这是师母去世后的第一个春节，何教授实在是有些可怜。

田田看了信，头轰地一炸，就炸了一地的碎片，思绪乱得无法捡拾。秦阳见她失魂落魄的样子，就劝她回去一趟。田田听了就急眼，说你以为我是百万富翁呢，飞一趟中国就跟下一趟楼似的。秦阳笑了笑，说：“谁让他是你爹呢。”田田连连摇头，说不回去不回去，大不了再托人找个保姆嘛。这个价码，雇个人工智能机器人都够了。赵春枝以为她是谁？乡下人在城里，磨去一千层皮，骨里肉里还是老乡。秦阳又笑，说你连人家为什么吵嘴都没问清楚，就先骂了个狗血喷头的，说不定还是你爹没道理呢。田田呸了一口，说老板永远有理，这是千古不变的道理。说完就扯过一条被单蒙了头，直挺挺地往沙发上一躺。床单底下先是翻来覆去地贴着饼子，过了一会儿，身子才渐渐地平软了下去。

秦阳以为田田睡着了，就自己进了屋。过了一会儿，只觉得脖子上痒痒的，伸手一摸，原来是田田近近地站在身后。田田说要不我还是回去一趟吧，年底了，也不知有没有机票。秦阳扬了扬手里的纸条："大小姐，都给你打听过了，只有大韩航空公司还有一个座位，明天晚上的。要在西海岸停，还要在汉城停。等你转来转去到了家，就是小年夜了。明天一上班，就找老板请假，耸人听闻一点，就说你爸中风，瘫痪，病危。"

田田不说话，却将两手环过去，从背后搂住了秦阳。

田田的飞机出了点小小的故障，在汉城停留了一天。到达北京的时候，已经是第三天的夜晚了。走出机场，街上很是冷清。过了十几分钟，才来了一辆出租车，车上下来一个穿着军大衣的司机，慢吞吞地帮着田田把行李卸进车厢。车剪破一街空旷，驶进清冷的夜风里。司机丝毫没有搭话的意思，一路沉默地抽着烟。烟很呛，田田低低地咳嗽起来，却隐忍了，只专心致志地读着公路两边的广告牌。虽然只隔了几个月的时间，广告牌显而易见已经换过了一茬，上面的内容对田田来说已经有了几分生疏。虽然看懂了每一个字，却没有完全看懂那些字和字中间的连接挑逗和暗示。在熟悉的街景里，田田突然感到了一丝外乡客似的陌生。

突然间，嗖的一声，天上蹿起了一束烟花。烟花是淡紫色的，先是极高极孤独的一根，然后渐渐地蓬松肥胖起来，如一把撑开在夜幕里的伞，然后又如细雨丝似的缓缓落下，带着嗞嗞的声响消陨在地上。司机沉沉地骂了一句"找死呀，不让放的"。田田仰着脖子等待着第二束、第三束，可是它们却始终没有到来。夜空虽然还是黑暗，却因有过了短暂的浮华痕迹，这黑暗便也与先前的黑暗有了些不同。已经五六年不曾在家过年了，田田暗自感叹难道这就是北京的除夕了吗？

出租车在家门口停下，田田付了钱，司机打开后盖取了行李，却没有走的意思，只将两只手笼在袖子里，目光炯炯地看着她。田田突然明白了过来，就打开皮包掏出一张票子，塞进司机的袖笼里。司机伸出两根手指，将票子夹出来，对着路灯看了一眼，认出了那上面的绿颜色，就嘿嘿一笑收了起来，说这年头美元也疲软了，比不得从前了，大姐你新年慢慢地吉祥吧——方慢吞吞地开走了。

田田拖着箱子一层一层地上了楼，每一层楼道里都流淌着从门缝里溢出的喧闹，一式一样的鼓点，一式一样的旋律，一式一样的经过无数次操练的字正腔圆。田田一下子听出了那是春节联欢晚会的节目。到了自己家门口，却是静静的，并无电视的声响。放下箱子，将一口气喘匀了，才去揿门铃。刚揿了一下，门就开了，父亲仿佛是靠在门上等候着她似的。

父亲从门里软软地走出来，穿了一件银灰色的中式对襟丝绵袄，前襟印着星星点点的菜汁油迹。衣是新的，很是厚实，腋下和胳膊拐弯处绽出条条肥粗的皱纹。在这样厚重的冬衣里，父亲依然看上去很冷，人中上流着一条半干未干的鼻涕，身子抖抖的仿佛憋了一泡找不着去处的急尿。脸肿了半边，鼻孔四周烧着一串燎泡，嘴唇颤颤的，半天才扯出一句小田你、你回来了。田田没想到一向整洁利索的父亲一下子就这样落魄了，心里一酸，嗓子就喑哑了。

屋里四下清冷，只有电视机上那两张印了些洋文的贺年卡，才是这一片灰暗里的唯一颜色——那还是自己和元元分别从加拿大和德国邮寄过来的。田田呵呵地清了清嗓子，说爸我带你出去吃饭吧，我也饿了。父亲摇了摇头，说你可真是洋鬼子了，怎么不知道这是大年夜，除了宾馆大饭店，谁都关门了。田田说那我们就去宾馆吃饭，豁出去大出血一次。父亲说宾馆早一个月就订完位置了，轮不着你我这样的百姓。说着就去开了冰箱，端出一个大海碗来，说昨天就煨了排骨汤等你的，你没来。咱们不如吃排骨面，再加一点白菜，热腾腾的，也是好吃的。

父亲就开火，放水，下面，热汤。依旧有些笨拙，却已经不是从前的那种不知所措了。田田便知道这几个月里，父亲已经经过了许多的事。忍不住冷冷一笑，说这个赵春枝，倒是把你给培训出来了。花钱雇的是保姆，没想到来的却是一个教练。

父亲的筷子一滑，一根面条落进了炉圈，嗤的一声，燃起细细一股黄焰，屋里就有了一丝经久不散的焦味。“她有她的想法，她说她到咱家是救急不救穷——她教我学会自己生活，总不能靠人过一辈子。”

“她若真是这么想的，怎么会说走就走？这份工资，你让她来雇我吧，连我都想当保姆了呢。”

父亲叹了一口气，说她没想走，是我把她赶走的。

“她女儿今年初中毕业。当地的学校质量差，她想把女儿转到北京上高中。她提出和女儿一起搬到家里来住。”

“当然不能答应。你答应了她女儿，下次说不定又来个男朋友，你又不开旅馆客栈。她是算计好了你这个有房有钱的老头呢。”田田愤愤地说。

父亲微微一笑，半晌才说：“我的女儿，当然是和我一样刻薄的——那天我就是这么骂她的。后来元元从德国打电话过来，也是这么骂她的。”

两人无言，在别家的热闹声中默默地吃着晚饭。面很烫，热气氤氲，额角上都有了些汗。田田看见父亲渐渐地嘴大眼小起来，便知道早已过了他平素上床的时间了。就说爸您放心，等过完了节，我们马上去登广告，也可以直接去保姆市场，就不信找不到一个比她好的。

父亲洗了把脸，就上了床。田田收拾了碗筷，在沙发上坐了下来。多伦多和北京是整整十二个小时的时差，这边是子夜，那边却是正午。田田虽然在旅途中丢失整整一夜的睡眠，精神却极是清醒。刚想打开电视，突然听见街上有人在扔酒瓶子，玻璃的碎裂声夹杂着狂呼声和字句不明的歌声一浪一浪地扑打着窗户，才明白自己已经错过了那个敲钟的时辰。

这时候电话铃尖锐地响了起来，几乎吓了田田一跳。拿起话筒来，那头就断了。三番五次之后，才接通了，线路却极是嘈杂。一个男声断断续续地传过来，带着隔洋的迟缓和模糊。半天田田才听清那头问的是新年礼物试过了吗？田田说什么礼物？那头说打开你的手提包。田田拿过提包，里里外外地找过了，都没有。那头又说是左侧的那个暗兜，你从来不用的。田田摸过去，果真摸到了一个小小的金丝绒盒子。打开来，里头是一枚戒指。细细的银圈，正中镶了一块宝蓝色的石头。银是暗暗淡淡的那种银，蓝也是暗暗淡淡的那种蓝，乍看甚是灰旧，仿佛已在岁月里走过了几遭。再看几眼，便慢慢显出些古朴含蓄的意思来，与市场上那些闪烁之物就有了区分。田田很是喜欢，拿出来套在指头上，左看右看，手也仿佛有了历史，顿时丰润厚重起来。

戴在哪只手上？

左手。

哪个指头？

田田的嘴巴张了一张，突然醒悟了过来，就把那尚未出口的回答吞咽了回去。电话那头是一阵长长的沉默，然后，一声叹息如轻风抚过，田田的耳垂微微地热了一热。

"田田我知道我在一厢情愿呢。挑吧，挑吧，你再慢慢地挑吧，说不定就挑着个比我好的。"

田田想了一万句撇清辩白的话，那些话还没浮到舌尖，她就觉出了它们的虚假。到末了，纵有了那一万句话垫着底，她竟然找不出一句可回的话，只哑哑地说了句秦阳你好好过年吧，就挂了。

放下电话，心里空落落的，旅途的疲倦渐渐地从脚底浮上来，浮上了眼皮。却又不想上床，就在沙发上坐了，撩起一角窗帘，靠在窗台上看夜景。夜到这一刻，才真正地有些像夜了，月色照得满街的树枝臃肿肥胖，仿佛挂满了霜雪。风刮过，地上的废纸和塑料袋如折了翼的鸟雀，低矮地蹒跚行走。守夜的人都困了，窗口的灯一盏一盏地灭去，满街都是狂欢过后的清冷。这个一年里的夜中夜。她还没来得及守，就糊里糊涂地过去了。

这一年里，她遭遇了多少事呢？母亲的死、自己的病、父亲的麻烦。每一样事情来了，她都得拿出肩膀来扛。其实，她也不都是自己扛的，秦阳替她扛了一半。她使唤起秦阳的肩膀来，如同是自己的肩膀那样的随意。在这个晚上之前，她从来没有想过，他只不过是暂时借了他的肩膀给她而已，有朝一日他会抽走他的肩膀，给另一个愿意戴他戒指的女人使用。

这个想法让田田吃了一惊。她发觉自己其实真是有些在乎秦阳的。只是不知道这样一点的在乎，值不值得她放上一生一世的价码——她明白她不可能无限期地免费使用他的肩膀。失却他的肩膀是一种沉重，拥有他的肩膀是另外一种沉重。两样的沉重，不知道她能扛得动哪一样？

正胡思乱想着，就听见身后有人咕地笑了一声。田田以为是父亲，回头一看，父亲屋的门紧关着，黑着灯。心里一惊，突然有些毛骨悚然起来，就默默地叫了一声妈——你的难处，我们原本是不知晓的。若知晓了，怎么会让你这样走了呢？既走了，你就安心吧，总有一天，我们都会在你那儿聚会的，不过是个迟早的事。

田田的话还没说完，屋里又是咕的一声。这会儿的笑声，似乎就在耳边。田田感到了另一个身子贴近过来的温软分量，鼻子里传来一丝极清极淡若有若无的紫丁香味——紫丁香是母亲一生中唯一喜欢的一样花。田田的身体仿佛被切成了两半：一半想伸出手来抓住那一缕温软，死死地坠上自己的重量：另一半却想关闭所有的触觉神经，来死命抵挡那份温软的侵袭。田田成了拔河比赛中的那个绳结，被旗鼓相当势均力敌的两股势力拉过来，扯过去，浑身如遭了魔法似的完全动弹不得。一时大汗淋漓，就使劲睁大了眼睛，定定地看住了墙上圈在黑框中的母亲。母亲被半明不暗的灯光磨蚀得失去了棱角，岁月的痕迹藏在阴影之下，容颜竟有了几分安然柔恬。田田的焦虑在母亲清明的眸子里走过了一遭，如灼热的烙铁落入凉水之中，渐渐就沉静了下去。

这时母亲的嘴唇微微一颤，说了一句话。这句话如一缕烟云从母亲的唇上轻轻抖落，还没来得及成形，就已消散。母亲说的是“你去……”母亲这句没有终结的话如同一个可以通往许多条道路的岔口，蕴含了几乎无穷无尽的可能性。后来尘埃落定，当其中的一种可能性渐渐明朗清晰向现实贴近时，田田才明白了这句话的指向。然而在当时，田田只是一遍又一遍地向母亲追讨着答案，一直到自己惊醒，方知道是南柯一梦。

睁开眼睛，父亲披衣站在沙发跟前，问小田你怎么了？哼成这个样子，吓我一跳。田田掏出纸巾，擦了擦额角的冷汗，半晌，才喃喃地说，没什么，做了个怪梦。父亲也没问是什么梦，却在田田身边坐下了，一杯茶在两只手里换过来换过去，却没有走的意思。后来，才迟迟疑疑地说：

“要不小田你过完年去一趟浙南找春枝？那天是我太急了，把话说绝了。”

“不绝怎么办？你答应她们搬过来住？”

“其实，她也是讲道理的人。她说搬过来就好省下在外边租房的钱，再减一半的工资，两项加起来，也算是抵女儿在这里的费用。”

田田一路听，一路冷笑，终于忍无可忍：“老爸，你究竟是老实还是愚蠢？你就没看出她在利用你？”父亲没有生气，却只是低着头，一下一下地扯着绒衣上的线头。“小田我想过了，若有人利用我，总好过我完全无用。我这样的老朽，除了她，还能对多少人有用呢？你们到了我这岁数，就有体会了。”

父亲的语气很是平静，是过滤了情绪之后的木然。田田愣了一愣，才按捺下性子，细声细气地说：“过了年，我们再去找一个，背景简单一些，没这么多幺蛾子的。你放心，找不到我就不走。”

父亲的回答也是捺着性子，细声细气的。

“我习惯了春枝，不想找别人了。”

田田转了好几个来回，才找到了春枝的家。

其实田田很早就看见了那幢房子，只是没有想到春枝的家会是这个样子的。

那幢房子说起来也是江南城乡交接的那些地方常见的模式，方方正正的二层楼房，外墙严严实实地贴了一层马赛克。马赛克是灰色的，那不过是风霜积尘的痕迹。只需一场大雨冲洗，底下就应该是雪白的。这幢楼房和周遭楼房的区别，就在一个大字。敦敦实实的一大块，便先有了一些不容置疑的气势。楼一大，门脸也就大了，不是寻常的一扇铁门，却是大大两开的厚木门。木是层层漆水之后的黑里透红，正中有两个沉重的铜环。那门的颜色质地样式，不由得就叫人觉得这门后应该是藏着故事的。门楣上钉了一个十字架，门上贴着两张艳红的春联，流露着墨汁未干的新喜。上联是“上帝爱人，甚至将他的独生子赐给他们”，下联是“叫一切信他的，不致灭亡，反得永生”。这上下联字数不一，既不对仗，也不押韵，不像是寻常农家的那种喜庆春联，倒像是从《圣经》上摘下来的。田田便惊异，春枝何时也信了洋教。门大，窗也多。窗是楼的眼睛，本来深邃幽暗，却因贴了许多的窗花，便有了盈盈一丝的笑意。田田走近来，便看见了窗花的功底。都是红纸剪的，也都是鱼，却是各样的姿势。有的恬静，有的喧闹，有的憨厚，有的狡诈。虚是神态，实是细节，栩栩如生，无一雷同——无非是鲤鱼跳龙门年年有余的意思。这幢楼房说新不算新，说旧也不算旧，却把城市的乡村的中式的西洋的各样风格都取了一些，匆匆地糅在了一处。糅得虽有几分生硬，那生硬之处反透出些活活泼泼的生气，俗到了极致，就俗出些别开生面的和谐来。田田暗想拥有这样一处楼房的女人，家境应该算是殷实的，何至于要千里北上给人做保姆呢？

就去敲门。

门没锁，轻轻一推就开了。门厅里坐着一个老太太，正戴着老花镜织毛活。老太太剪了一头短发，齐崭崭油亮亮地带着梳齿的痕迹。上身穿一件雪青色的呢子短大衣，下身穿一件黑布裤子。袖口和裤管里肥肥地露出些毛衣毛裤的卷边——田田猜想大概是春枝的妈。老太太手里的毛活大致成形了，似乎是一件男裤。腰已经完工，老太太正在织大腿分岔处的那个洞。见人来，抬起头，眼镜滑落到鼻尖，手里的线团就滚到了地上。

“何、何老师，出、出事了?”

田田一惊，说你怎么知道我是从何老师那里来的?老太太见田田并无报急的意思，才渐渐松了一口气，捡了地上的线团，掸着上头的灰土，说春枝给我看过你们全家的照片。你们首都的照相技术还不如我们小地方——人可比照相好看呢。就招呼田田坐了，慌慌地进了厨房烧水煮茶。再出来，手里就多了个沉甸甸的木托盘，上面摆了七八个瓷盏，装了金橘、橄榄、香榧子、核桃肉、番薯片等等等等，虽都是年节的零嘴，却又比北方的零嘴略微精致些。

老太太挑了一个小巧玲珑的金橘递给田田，问你爸也是我们这个地方的人?田田说我爷爷是矾山人——矾山离藻溪极近，口音也是通的。后来下了南洋，四十岁不到就死在了那边。我爸爸也是在矾山出生的，六七岁就被叔叔带到厦门读书，后来又到了北京，五六十年没回过乡了。老太太就说这回怎么不带你爸来，也好认认乡呢。田田笑笑，却问春枝哪儿去了。老太太说带孩子给班主任老师拜年去了——年年都是初三去的。这孩子，爹娘都不在身边，老师管着，也算是半个父母，很该谢谢的。田田顿了一顿，才问孩子她爸怎么不管?老太太不答，盯了田田一眼，问你找春枝有事?田田慢吞吞地从口袋里掏出一封信，说春枝考英文六级的准考证，寄到我们家来了。我爸劝春枝回去参加考试，补习了这几个月，不考就白废了。

老太太接过信，低了头，喃喃自语起来。田田依稀听见了一句“谢救主恩”，就笑，问春枝也信吗，你这个教?老太太叹了一口气，说她若信了，何至于这个命?好强呀，心里一颗沙子都容不下，怎么能尊主为大?

就絮絮叨叨地说起了春枝的事。

春枝生在乱世。春枝三个月大的时候，春枝的父亲挑了一担藻溪名产细米粉丝去温州城里叫卖，正逢工总司联总司两大派在打巷战，吃了一颗流弹，当场死在了街上。春枝是靠着寡母绣花和编篾席的手艺半饥半饱地长大的。春枝长到十七八岁，一层黑皮猝然蜕去，一夜之间就长成了一个细致的女子。

春枝不仅人长得耐看，还绣得一手好花。春枝绣的不是母亲的那些牡丹凤凰，却是藻溪人没有见过的新奇花样。春枝时常去逛镇上的新华书店，不是为了买书，却是为了看书店里新到的西洋印刷画，德意志乡村风情、英格兰教堂街景、法兰西古典肖像等等等等。春枝一个月的饭钱，都省了去买画。买回来，并不贴在墙上，却拿来做了绣花的蓝本。春枝绣的外国画，藻溪人见了掩了嘴惊叹。就有人花钱买了去，做洞房新居的摆设。再后来，就有人买了用作年节送人的大礼。春枝就是靠这个手艺，才维持自己念完了高中。

春枝岂止是花绣得好，书也读得轻省。从小学到初中到高中，在这么一个师资贫瘠的乡镇里，春枝的成绩也算是鸡群里的那个头了。藻溪乡地处江南，和风细雨的环境里，好看的年轻女子也是常有的。可是脸长得好手也生得巧的，就不多见了。脸长得好，手生得巧，书又读得好的女子，恐怕就是春枝一个了。所以春枝年轻的时候，在乡里是很有点名气的。春枝的家底，原是极薄的，没有人指望这样瘠薄的泥土里，竟能长出这样一朵好花来，于是母亲的腰杆，也就直了起来。

春枝还在读高中，提亲的人就开始在赵家频繁走动了。春枝正眼也不看一下那些留在饭桌上的照片，只对母亲说要复习考大学。当然真正的原因，母亲是后来才知道的。

春枝的高考成绩本来也勉强够上省城大学的，却为了生活费和就近分配的原因，选择了平阳师范。平阳师范是三年制的学校，春枝念了一年半，就退学回了家。春枝退学，不是因为功课跟不上，而是为了一个男人。

一个叫廖建平的男人。

廖建平是春枝的中学同学，比春枝高一个年级。高中毕业没有考上大学，就应征入伍当了兵。廖建平脑子活泛，手也灵巧，到了部队没多久，就凭着几样小发明，获得全军范围的嘉奖，入了党，提了干。正当仕途一片光明的时候，家里却出了大事——母亲因脑溢血突然半身不遂了。建平家里有一个常年多病的父亲和两个年幼的弟弟，母亲本是家中主事的那个角色，宛如桐油伞中间的那把伞柄。母亲在，伞就撑得起来。母亲一倒，伞就成了一片无用的软纸。建平在军中焦急万分，就写了一封信给春枝。

春枝和建平念高中时都是学生会的干部，两人一起负责学校的广播站。下了课，两人就钻进小小的一间广播室编通讯稿。你开一截头，我续一个尾。你念上一段，我念下一段。春枝的嗓子有些沙哑，像是清晨被露水打蔫了的草叶。建平的嗓子变着音，有些生硬，犹如被大风扯得猎猎生响的一面旗子。两人的声音分开来听其实都有缺欠，合在一起，便将那缺欠的地方补平了，沙哑里渐渐有了娇柔，生硬里也生出了阳刚，叫那念的和听的，都觉出了些韵味。

虽然日日相处，耳鬓厮磨，两人真正私定终身，却是在建平入伍之后的鸿雁传书中完成的。学校的同学，早就将这一档子事，传得沸沸扬扬，唯一蒙在鼓里的，反只有春枝的母亲。

那日春枝接到了建平的信，没和任何人商量一声，就从平阳师范退了学，回到了藻溪，一日三餐地照顾建平的母亲。又把家里的两间旧房腾出一间来，做了个裁缝铺，靠替人裁剪刺绣，支撑着两边家里的费用。春枝的母亲原是一百个不乐意的，母女俩为这件事也不知吵过了多少个回合，后来看见建平往家里寄来的一张张奖状，猜想这人大概算是有几分出息的，也就默许了。

建平在部队里待了几年，提了几级干，提到一个坎上，就上不去了。年限一到，提不上去的，就要转业。建平就转业来到了温州城里，在一家国有企业做了一名行政干部。回乡和春枝结了婚，第二年便有了女儿晓藻。一个小家庭，分在两处住。建平住温州城里，周末年假回藻溪。春枝常年住在藻溪，照顾娘家婆家女儿三头。建平在温州城里坐了几年办公室，看着周遭的人变戏法似的发着财，不甘心满世界的精彩就这样五色生辉地绕着自己流走了，便辞职回到藻溪，办了个小工厂，专做教学用品——大部分都是他自己的创造发明。

刚开始时，不过一间瓦房，三五个兵丁。说是乡镇企业，其实就是一个家庭作坊。建平管产品研制经销，春枝管账，建平的两个弟弟再加上一个弟媳妇，便是企业的全体员工。建平在部队里就广结人缘，全国各地都有战友帮忙建立代销点。研制出来的产品新巧，价格合理，销路很快畅通起来。春枝还没来得及学完速成会计课程，建平公司的账号，就已经大到春枝无法处理的地步了。于是建平专门雇了一个财会班子，打发春枝回家，一心一意地做起了少奶奶。厂房几经扩建之后，公司的总部定在了上海。建平就在上海藻溪两地，过起了飞来飞去的繁忙生活。

建平是个见过世面的人，所以建平和寻常人眼中的乡镇企业家很有些不同。首先建平不像那些人那样满肚花花肠子，建平平日不爱喝酒应酬，也极少去歌厅、酒吧、桑拿吧之类的地方。得了空闲，就带着女儿晓藻坐在藻溪边上钓鱼。是姜太公的钓法，有一搭无一搭的。即使钓着了，也扔回溪里放生去。

建平的与众不同，还在于对老婆的好。建平一年在外边的时候多，怕春枝在家闷，便购买了各样的电影、电视剧光盘，一包一包地寄回家给春枝看。建平寄的不是街头小摊上随便一挑、看两下就卡壳、字幕模糊颜色含混的冒牌货。建平挑的片子都是经过秘书小姐推荐的，而且是那种贴了防伪商标的正版片。春枝的四季衣装，也都是建平从广州、深圳、香港等地亲自选购的。若看上了款式，就能买上一打不同颜色的，让春枝可着心情挑着穿。春枝穿了这样新潮的衣服走在藻溪的路上，总觉得胸前背后到处是眼，便脱了，依旧挂在衣柜里，只等建平回家时，才穿了给建平看。建平在家的日子，除了探访两头的老人，极少出门，一直待在家里陪春枝。有人甚至亲眼看见了建平坐在板凳上给春枝洗脚，春枝双脚在建平怀里乱踹、蹬得一地是水的情景。

建平给两边的老人都雇了保姆。多年照顾娘家婆家的担子，终于从春枝肩上卸了下来。藻溪人都说春枝是有后福的人，为廖家受了这么些年的苦，总算熬出了头。当然这是藻溪人当着春枝和春枝妈的面说的。春枝母女不在场的时候，藻溪人的话就没有这么顺耳了，幸亏春枝听不见。春枝本是劳碌之人，突然闲了下来，便觉得多出了一副手脚，不知如何安置才好，就日日思想着打发日子的方法。

有一年端午节，建平在上海加班没有回藻溪。春枝的一个中学同学的丈夫是开长途汽车的，那人就拉着春枝坐了丈夫的车去苏州、无锡玩了一趟。回家的路上，春枝突然心血来潮，改坐了火车去上海看建平。到了上海站给建平打电话，建平没在公司，手机也没开。春枝就自己找去了建平长期租用的宾馆房间，等着建平回来。左等右等，等得天大黑了，才隐隐听见门外有建平的声音。开了门，却见建平手里提着一个篮子，拐进了过道尽头的另一个房间。

建平不是一个人，建平的身边有一个女人。

春枝轻手轻脚地跟过去，只见房门大开着。建平已经把手里的篮子放到了地上，春枝一眼就看见了篮子里是一个婴孩。那孩子一脸褶皱，肤色黑红，丑若田鼠，看上去至多一两个月的样子。女人弯下腰把孩子从篮子里抱出来。女人很年轻，面皮白净光滑，一头黑发如泼墨，在脑后用一个塑料卡子松松地绾起，漏了几根发丝，从额上一路垂挂到脖子里，却是春枝没有见过的那种随意。女人个子很高，腿仿佛直接长在了腰上。穿了一件黑色紧身长袖薄毛衣，领口开得极低，女人弯腰下去的时候，就露出了一道深深的乳沟。女人虽然刚刚生产过，腰身却依旧紧瘦，只是胸乳极是饱满，呼之欲出。女人抱孩子的动作稍稍有些笨拙，孩子一下子就醒了，狂哭起来。女人抱着孩子来回晃动着，幅度很大，胸前的那两坨东西心惊肉跳地颤着，仿佛随时要飞出去。建平去洗手间拧了一条湿毛巾出来，给女人擦脸上的汗。擦着擦着，手就探进了女人的领口。女人的身子随着男人的手指扭来扭去，嘴里骂着廖建平你作死呀，眼里却是盈盈的笑意。

春枝软软地靠在门边，恍惚间觉得建平的手指，正丝丝痒痒地抚在自己的胸前。建平多少年没有这副样子了呢？春枝脑子一片空白，只记得那日启程的时候，日是圆的，月是圆的，路程长长的才开了一个头。才过了两天，那照耀她的九十九个太阳和九十九个月亮，突然间一起轰然坠地，世间是一片不分日月的黑暗。她的路，突然就走到了尽头。

“建平，你、你好……”

她听见一个声音轻轻地在墙壁之间飘过来舞过去。那声音仿佛没有经过她的脑子，甚至没有经过她的嘴唇，与她毫无关联地落在空中。突然，建平手里的毛巾落到了地板上。咚的一声巨响，地球停止了转动，万籁俱寂。

建平的脸在变换了多种颜色之后，渐渐固定在红与青之间。倒是那个女人比较镇定，拿手臂撞了撞建平，说人家春枝大老远的来看你，要不，你们去那屋聊聊？建平这才醒悟过来，拉着春枝就往他自己的那个房间走去。春枝恍恍惚惚地跟着建平进了屋，坐下了，建平端了杯水过来，问春枝你、你渴了吧？那口气里有失措的殷勤、负疚的客气，却是无比的陌生。春枝听着，就明白她已是他生活中的客人了。原本存了许多话要问，到了这时，突然悲从中来，便一把摔了杯子，夺门而去。

春枝回到藻溪，就提出离婚。婆家不肯。七十多岁的瘫婆婆让人背着到了赵家，流着眼泪喊皇天，建平这小人咋就生出了六指呢。又拉着春枝的手，说建平和那个女人，都是各有目的的。一个要钱，一个要儿子。春枝你做了绝育手术，不能再生了，建平偌大一份家产，没有儿子，将来传给谁呢？咱们乡下人，再有钱想的也是乡下人的想法。建平不过是想有个后继的意思。建平和你，才叫真正的结发夫妻呢。这个年头，有钱人包二奶的有的是，建平对你怎样，你心里最清楚，谁也动不了你正宫娘娘的地位。

春枝听了这话，方明白婆婆家其实早就知道了实情的，却把自己蒙在了鼓里。想起这些年风里雨里伺候婆婆的情景，到头来终究还是血浓于水，心里越发悲哀起来，离婚的信念反而越发坚定了。

春枝自己的娘，自然大骂建平没有良心——当初要做绝育手术，原本也是建平的意思，有了钱，就变了想法。可是骂完了，气也生过了，回过头来还是劝春枝慎重考虑。娘说只要建平改了，和那个女的断了往来，再把春枝接到上海同住，这个婚就不一定要离了——这个年纪，离了一个人过，又能好到哪里去？过惯了安逸日子，难道还要从头来过苦日子吗？春枝听了，只觉得娘这些年已经被建平的钱宠坏了，想的只是日子，而不是女儿，便干脆不再与母亲商量了。

建平从上海回到藻溪，在自己父母家里住下了——春枝不让进家门。找人捎了话给春枝，说婚他是不想离的。事情虽是自己的错，可是做也做下了，这页纸翻是翻不回去的。其实也就是一道坎，眼睛一闭就过去了，就看你愿不愿意。你若愿意，咱们还是跟从前那样一心一意过日子。我就在藻溪专程听你的回话，啥时回话来了啥时走。

春枝冷冷一笑，也让人捎话回去，问咋"一心一意"过日子？和那个女人一块儿过？建平说人家从来没有非分的想法，是你容不得她。春枝听了这话，彻心彻肺地凉了，当下就给了回话：这个坎过不去。

离婚离得有几分辛苦，主要是因为晓藻的抚养权。建平虽对春枝有了二心，却是极爱这个女儿的，死活要带着走。春枝坚决不肯。建平说春枝你给我晓藻，我让你和你妈一辈子衣食无忧。春枝说我要是给了你晓藻，我一辈子活着还有什么盼头？建平急了，说你若不给晓藻，你休想从我手里得到一分钱的赡养费。春枝当下就在离婚协议书上签了字，放弃建平的所有资产，却留下了晓藻。

就这样，春枝从十年的婚姻里走出来，只带走了女儿和现在住的这幢房子。

春枝中学的一位好友，嫁了个北方丈夫在北京生活了多年，听说了春枝的事，很是替春枝打抱不平，就买了张火车票接春枝到北京散心。春枝原本没打算长住的，却刚巧碰上女友的丈夫的老板托女友给找一个南方保姆，会做江浙口味饭食的，来照顾家里的两个老人。女友就劝春枝去试一试。谁知春枝这一去，一待就是四年，直到送了两个老人的终。那老两口平时有些积蓄，又和春枝投缘，所以身后留下的一份详尽的遗嘱里，竟然也有春枝的一份，是两万元。春枝从前风光的时候，两万元也就是揣在兜里的零花儿。可是再风光，那也是建平的钱，与她隔了一层皮。如今星移斗转，两万元突然就很有了些重量，不仅因为她需要钱，也因为这钱是她自己一分一厘挣来的，有几分撕心扯肉的感觉。

春枝得了钱，就立马在银行开了个活期户头。这笔钱虽然一分也还没花出去，春枝却早已有了打算的。这一笔钱，再加上这四年省吃俭用的积攒，满打满算刚好是三万七千元。春枝早打听好了，如果把晓藻转到北京来上学，需要四万元的赞助费。再问亲戚借个三千两千的周转一下，晓藻下个学期就可以上北京读书了——如果找得到住处的话。

春枝妈说这话的时候没有抬头看田田，织毛裤的手微微地有些颤抖。裤裆的那个洞已经完工，老太太伸进一个手指探了探洞口的大小，田田几乎被这个动作逗得笑出声来，却终于忍住了。

“我爸是退休教师，固定工资，没有积蓄，也不会有遗产。”田田说。

“我们家的住房，虽然有三个房间，我们兄妹两个常常回家，都是要住的。”

春枝妈没有搭话。一屋的沉默如山石，压得田田双肩生疼，身子便渐渐低矮了下去。半晌，老太太才轻轻地笑了一声，将那山石破开细细一个洞，空气方有些流通起来。

“春枝至今最后悔的一件事，就是当年为了廖建平，没把平阳师范念完。所以死活也得让晓藻读上好学校。晓藻若是个男孩，春枝反不用那么操心。女人的命运不能放在男人的手心上——这是你爸给春枝说的。春枝信你爸。”

这时门咚的一声撞开了，进来一个体态瘦弱的女孩子。女孩将两只手放在嘴里哈着暖，一边蹬鞋一边说：“外婆，老师今年给了压岁……”女孩说了一半，突然看见了屋里的生客，就把后半截话咽了回去，低了头站在门厅里，脸儿涨得飞红，后面跟进来的是春枝。春枝看见田田，也是一愣。还没等说话，田田已经从提包里取出一张纸来，铺在饭桌上，慢悠悠地说春枝你来得正好，给我找支笔，最好是黑墨的，我们起草个合同，关于我们家住房的使用条件。

春枝没有动，却对女孩子说晓藻你去南记称两斤鲜枣回来，颜色翠些的，有虫眼的给挑出来。女孩子哎了一声，正要出门，春枝妈站起来，说她哪里知道，还不得我跟着去。老太太出了门，又折回来，说田田小姐你要是明天走，我的毛裤就织完了，正好给你爸带回去。你爸是读书人，讲究着呢，说穿棉裤太肥，不好看。春枝给买了马海毛的，也暖，也薄，也好看。

婆孙两人走了，屋里的两人一时无话。后来春枝呵呵地清了几回嗓子，才问何老师他，还好吗？田田看了春枝一眼，说你觉得呢？大年夜一个人坐在黑屋子里，孤苦伶仃，连茶也是凉的。

春枝不吱声。田田以为春枝有了愧疚，正想趁势再数落几句，谁知春枝却将头抬了，两眼炯炯地看着田田，说："大姐，是你扔下了何老师，不是我。"

关于部门合并裁员的消息，已经在银行传了好几个月了。刚开始传的时候，草木皆兵，人人自危。一通电话、一封电子邮件、一个眼神，都可以随时解释为某种先兆。消息传了几个月之后，势头渐弱，恐惧如沙子慢慢地沉了下去，麻木如油星子渐渐地浮了上来，人们也就习惯了在麻木之中混吃等死的姿势。所以那天当田田接到部门总经理的电话时，她完全没有想到这竟是自己在银行工作的最后一天。

银行保安部的两位工作人员跟着田田去了办公室，监督着田田清理了办公桌上的个人用品。三四年的日子，积累起来，不过小小的一个纸箱子。同事围拢过来，拥抱，握手，情绪复杂。惜别是真实的，庆幸也是真实的——走了一个，留下的人似乎又多了一份保险。保安部的人员一路护送田田出了银行的门——是怕田田带走内部资料和电脑内存文件。虽然早就知道这是银行裁员的老规矩，田田抱着纸箱子走出银行大门的时候，眼泪却忍不住流了下来。

走到街上，才发现今天的天气不错——平常这个时候，田田大多在上班，极少能看到街上的景致。太阳歇息了一个季节，正有力气，晒在身上有几分重量。风不知何时已失却了棱角，变得四平八稳起来。路上的积雪只剩了一层虚空的架子，车驶过，便瘫软成一团泥泞。靴子踩在地上，已经隐约感觉到了泥泞之下蠢蠢欲动的春意。可是今天田田只是借了这隐隐一点的春意赶路，今天田田管不了春意。

走到街角搭公车的地方，田田看见有人摆了水桶在卖花。卖花的是一个年轻的女孩子，吆喝的声气里带着一丝生疏和羞涩。“新鲜的，给你的瓦伦丁，买一束吧。”田田这才想起今天是情人节。便弯下腰，仔细地挑选了一枝粉红色的玫瑰，又把找头塞回到卖花女的手里。女孩谢了又谢，说愿你和你的瓦伦丁有一个愉快的夜晚。田田把花插在纸箱的把手上，笑了笑，说：“这是我平生的，第一枝花。”

田田上了公车，坐了很多站，也没下来转地铁，却一路坐到了末站。

是海德公园站。

公园极是寂静。二月的树林依旧光秃，林荫道失去了枝叶的遮掩，突然就显得开阔笔直起来。一眼望到头，只有一对衣装整洁的老夫妻，牵了一条狗，在慢慢地散步。田田的脚步声很轻，狗却听见了，警醒地竖着耳朵，吠了起来。树林瞬间活了，宁静嘤嗡地散落了一地。

田田原本只是想找一张凳子坐一坐的，却没想到走了很远的路，依旧没有找到凳子，手里的纸箱却渐渐地沉了起来。就找了一块干地，把纸箱搁下，自己坐在了上面。

明天写一份履历，找几家职业介绍所发一发。上一次写履历是四年前的事了，内容，早就过时了。推荐人找谁呢？绝不找部门经理。自己一直是他手下的干将，替他开发了多少客户，在总部争得了多少风光体面。结果她却成为他手下第一个走的人。那句成语是什么来着？狡兔死，走狗烹。可是谁是兔谁是狗呢？他递给她那张解雇通知的时候，眼睛都没敢看她——不信他心里没有愧疚，看这点愧疚能走多远。说不定，他会给她介绍另一家银行——他在银行界做了很久了，熟人大约总有几个的，换一行还得从头适应。要不，还是给他打个电话吧。也不全怨他，总部要裁员，名额派下来，总得落到某个人头上。听说右派也是这么评出来的。

明天，明天再说吧。

太阳正高，照着身子如暖雪般酥软。眼皮渐渐沉涩起来，思绪陷入茫茫荒漠，哪条路都是死路。

散步的老夫妻从林荫道尽头折回来，看见一棵硕大的雪松树下，坐着一个娇小的中国女子。女子仰脸靠在树干上睡着了，头发和脸颊上沾了些褐色的树皮。女子的膝盖上放了一枝玫瑰，蔫蔫地垂着头。狗低头闻了闻花，静静地走开了。

田田醒来的时候，天已经黑了，路灯照得林荫道黝黑深远。田田是被手机振醒的。田田的手机是为客户预备的，平时电话多，怕影响别人办公，所以就把铃声设置成了无声的振动。田田慌慌地打开手提包，在钱夹子、化妆品、手纸、梳子、笔记本、支票本的重围中，找到了活蹦乱跳的手机。抓住了，接起来，习惯性地用英文说：您好，我是道明银行的何田田，有什么事我可以帮助您？说完了，才想起历史已经改写，却懒得更正了。

那头是秦阳。

“田田你在哪里？我快把你熟人都找遍了。银行说你早走了，手机你也不接。”

田田响响地打了一个哈欠，说我在一棵百年老树之下睡着了，做了一场春秋大梦。原以为眼睛一睁，世上已千年，恐龙复活，满街走着外星人。结果还是那么些旧事旧人——你这个电话打得好不扫兴。

秦阳顿了一顿，才说田田你不要动，告诉我你在哪里，我马上过来接。不就是一份工作吗？我们再找就是了。

田田也顿了一顿，说：“可不就是一份工作吗？大不了你把我养起来就是了，着什么急呢。”

秦阳无话。半晌，才迟迟疑疑地说："其实，大街上的那家咖啡馆，要是真的顶下来，也是不错的。自己做自己的老板，谁也炒不了你的鱿鱼。"

秦阳是在《多伦多星报》上看到那家咖啡馆的广告的，业主得了重病，急待出手。秦阳去看了几次，说生意极好，价格也合适。秦阳回来，就在田田耳边刮风。秦阳刮风的目的很明确，是问田田借钱。田田装糊涂，从不表态。今天不知怎的，却极是烦躁起来："秦阳你别盘算我那几个钱，不够你招摇几天的。要做老板你去做就是了，我给你打工好了——谁还不知道省心呢。"说完就将电话吱的一声揿死了，心里那一股无名火压了很久，才渐渐压了下去。

那天两人回到家来，秦阳早已备下一桌的酒菜——原是过情人节的意思。田田在外边走了一天，饿，也渴。便狂饮了几杯，一时烂醉如泥。半夜醒来，听见秦阳的鼾声如流水细细碎碎地灌满了屋里的每一个角落，竟叫她无处可逃遁。便下了地，摸黑开了抽屉，窸窸窣窣地翻着了一盒烟。烟是陈年的旧货，带着些潮气，点了几回才点着。田田是住在娘家打离婚官司的那一阵子学会抽烟的，当然得背着母亲。不是怕，而是忍受不了唠叨。后来得了一场重感冒，突然就厌烦了那味道，就自然戒了。隔了多年重拾起来，气味熟稔而陌生，说不上喜欢，也说不上不喜欢，只是一种恍若隔世的感觉。蹲在房角，看见月光漏过窗帘缝，黄黄地照着秦阳的脸，朦朦胧胧地仿佛长了一层绒毛，眉眼如婴儿般安详。

一无所有也是一种福气。赤裸裸地行在世上的人，随意抓住一样东西，都是收获。他遇到了她，他紧紧抓住了她。她交着他的房租，他开着她的车。她是他遮雨的屋檐、他舀饭的锅、他行路的脚、他歇息的床。她是他可以安然入睡的原因。可是她呢？她的房子只付了小小的一笔首期，剩下的，是一笔巨大的贷款，需要月月还着。还有水电费、车保险汽油费、物业管理费，当然还有女人买花戴的开销。她的失业保险金比她正常的收入少了一大半。她要管自己，要管他，还要管父亲。父亲的保姆、父亲的部分医疗费用，天长日久的，也是一笔不小的开销。她夜半醒来，突然觉得整个世界都靠在了她的肩膀上，便憎恨起秦阳的安然无虑来。

早上一睁眼，发现秦阳已经起床了。田田看了看手表，已经到了平日上班的时候。就想趁老板刚上班的空闲给他打个电话，让他帮着介绍一份工作。拿起电话，却听见里边有个陌生的女人声音，才明白是秦阳在客厅里用电话。“还要拖多久？总得有个了断……”女人的话她只听了半截，因为秦阳很快就把电话掐断了。过了一会儿，电话铃响了。他不接，她也不接。铃声终于静了下去，却只静了一小会儿，便又惊天动地地响起。她忍不住赤脚跑出去接，那头不说话。她就冷冷一笑，说秦阳你是不是要告诉我点什么呢？秦阳的脸一下子白了，却不回答。

田田一把扯开窗帘，阳光如白水，猛烈汹涌地倾入客厅，满屋飞尘，一片混沌。一个年轻的早晨，还未来得及经历世事，就已经炽烈地熟了，熟得可以随时老去。田田一时万念俱灰，扬了扬手，对秦阳说你，你搬出去，马上。

秦阳嗫嚅地说，其实，刚才……田田抓过桌上的裁纸刀，将刀尖指着自己的心口，大喝一声：“秦阳你再说一句，我就扎给你看。”秦阳吓了一跳，便闭嘴进了卧室。刀从田田手里哐啷一声掉了下去，田田的身子抖得仿佛随时要散成一地碎片。裹在一片厚重的阳光里，却只觉得冷，从心尖上丝丝缕缕地渗出来的，擦也擦不干的那种阴冷。

秦阳在屋里窸窸窣窣地收拾着自己的物件。几个月的记忆，收拾起来，也就是一大一小两个箱子。锁好了，慢慢地拖过客厅，拖到门口，又返回卧室，拿了一件厚浴袍，递给田田，说你穿上这个，送我到楼下，可以吗？田田想说不，却不由自主地跟着秦阳走进了电梯。

两人站在电梯里，他没按电钮。她也没有。电梯门自动关闭了，电梯却没有动。他说钥匙我放在床头柜上了，车子我先开走，卸下箱子再给你开回来。她没说话。她其实是期待着他再说些别的，可是他没有。电梯间不大，两人中间隔着两个箱子，其实略微还有些拥挤。只要略微伸展一下手脚，他们可以随时相碰。可是他们彼此对站着，中间仿佛隔了一亿个光年。终于，他的手伸过那些光年，按住了那个已经被人磨得油光锃亮的P1电钮。电梯轰隆轰隆地俯冲了下去。

没有了，他们之间再也不会有第三次的开始了。田田迷迷糊糊地想。

突然电梯猛烈地晃了一晃，骤然停了下来。田田的五脏六腑被高高地揪了起来，又重重地摔了下去，血猛烈地拍打着耳膜，耳朵一阵轰鸣。箱子闷闷地倒了下去，压在脚趾上。田田想抽脚，却看不见箱子——电梯里一片黑暗。

电梯坏了。秦阳说。

他摸索着跨过箱子，去找电钮盘上的警铃。印象中似乎在右下角。他一个一个按钮地试过去，没有任何声响。

手机，打911。他提醒她。

她摸了摸口袋，醒悟过来她穿的是浴袍，手机放在房间里没带出来。

等吧。他叹了一口气，摸索着把箱子放平了让她坐。他在她旁边坐下。她脱了鞋，摸到了脚指头上的湿黏，知道是血，突然感到了一扯一扯的疼。

她从来没有经历过这样一种没有一丝缝隙、没有开始也没有终结的黑暗。黑暗从四面八方朝她拥挤过来，越来越重。她身上的每一样器官，仿佛都被挤压成薄薄的一片，争先恐后地要从胸腔里突围。她嚎叫了一声，用拳头狠狠地砸着电梯的墙。她的力度和疯狂把她和他都吓了一跳。

他用双臂将她死命地箍住了，说田田你要是还想活，就要保持体力，减少氧气消耗——我们停在两层楼之间，没有人会听得见你。

他摸索着解开了她浴袍上的带子，瞬间摸到了她的温软。她的温软如水流了他一掌，水中有两块小小的卵石，坚挺地磨着他的掌心。她低低地呻吟着，终于安静了下来，将头无力地靠在他的肩上。她的肚子响亮地叫了一声。紧接着，他的肚子也响亮地叫了一声，仿佛是夏日池塘里相互呼应的蛙鸣。

两人忍不住笑出了声。

田田，万一我们就死在这里了，有些话，我总是要告诉你的。

那个女人，是我老板的表妹。香港人，二十多年的老移民。老公死了，急着想再找个人。

我在国内日子过得腻味了，是想换种活法才出国的。蛇头说到了多伦多，六个月就可以拿到身份。随便找份工作，都是四五万年薪，折合人民币，就是三四十万。

出来了，才知道蛇头的话不实，却晚了。原本想赚够还债的钱就回去的，谁知遇到了你。

我知道你想我来帮你，可是你若不先帮我，我就帮不了你。你明知道的，却怕投进去了收不回来。你信不过我。

其实她也和你一样精，只不过她敢赌，你不敢。

田田不说话。尿意渐渐聚集起来，在小腹聚成一丝尖锐的刺痛。秦阳找到了箱子的拉锁，拉开来，摸出一个平时骑自行车用的头盔，倒放在墙角，说你将就吧。

水声响了很久，从低浅响到满盈。到最终停下来的时候，他塞给她一块布，说擦擦干净。她擦了，才感觉出是他的领带。心想，这个男人对她，也许是有一两分真心的。她和他的关系，其实也不外乎是种风险投资。投对了，她也许就有了依托。投错了，她的下半辈子可能就是竹篮打水一场空。

也许，事情并没有这么严重。投错了，她至多不过再被人利用一次。若不投这一注，她连拥有水的希望也没有。能被人利用，总好过完全无用。这是谁的话？好像是父亲的话。什么时候说的？不记得了。

田田迷迷糊糊地睡了过去。

没过多久，就饿醒了。最初的饿意是明确而尖锐的，如虫如蚁如针在肠胃里蠕蠕地爬过，每一步都在刺痛。田田仔仔细细地回忆着冰箱里的内容，每一格每一抽屉每一样物品都有了细致而具体的盘算。田田在想象中把它们以各种方式各种组合烹饪成众多的菜肴，每一道菜都让她垂涎欲滴。她听见自己的舌头在嘴里一遍又一遍地翻滚着，直到唾液渐渐干涸，舌头肿大得再也无法滚动。饿意渐渐麻木起来，她便再次睡了过去。

就这样，田田睡睡醒醒了多次，后来就完全失却了时间的概念。最后一次醒过来，她想问秦阳大概是几点钟了。她动了动嘴，却发不出声音。她知道她已经没有力气了。她突然想起了涸泽里的鱼——微微开启的嘴、蒙着翳子的白眼珠。

我不想死。我真的，真的，真的不想死。

田田默默地一遍一遍地对自己说。她靠这句话支撑了很久，却没有支撑到底，就再一次陷入了长久的昏睡。

后来她被一道炫目的白光刺醒，听见一个声音遥遥地传过来。“给她戴上眼罩。”白光消失了，白光的记忆却如刀刃久久地搁在她的视网膜上，锋利，鲜明，一碰就是伤痕。她听见了街音。她听见泥水在车轮的碾轧之下溅落的声音，她听见商店橱窗里的风铃轻轻震颤的声音，她听见了一个小女孩和母亲的争吵声，她听见橡皮手套相互摩擦、针筒跌落在托盘里的声音。

“他呢?”她扯住了护士的衣袖，喑哑地问。

“他在另外一辆救护车上，平安。”

“告诉他，请他定个日子。”

“什么日子?”

“他知道。”

田田说完这句话，就昏迷了过去。

田田和秦阳于四月五日举行了婚礼。

选择在这一天结婚，是因为正好是周六，而且他俩合开的咖啡店要在两个星期之后开张——开张之后他们就不会有时间结婚了。

婚礼是在田田一位好朋友家后院的玻璃暖房里举行的。邀请了一位法官到场，签字证婚，然后一行人去一个自助餐厅吃了一顿饭，就算礼成。

秦阳穿了一套深蓝色的西服，扎了一条橘红色的领带。衣服很合身，领带的颜色却有些跳——是田田坚持的。这条领带是那日田田在电梯间里小解时应急用过的，秦阳原本是要扔了的，田田却拿去干洗了，说是留个纪念。众人见秦阳穿戴齐整的样子有点怪，都暗笑，说后备役转正规军的时候，大约都是这个样子。

田田婚礼上穿的是一件粉红色的连衣裙，领口、裙裾都镶了些花边，不像新娘，倒更像是伴娘。秦阳问田田为什么不选一件白色的衣裙呢？田田说脸黑的人穿白的不好看，反差太厉害。田田没有说出来的那半截话，秦阳大约是猜不到的。田田银行的同事，曾经告诉过她，二婚的女人居多不穿白——毕竟是失过清白了。

晚宴完毕，送走客人，两人走在回家的路上，田田突然想起今天原来是清明。就推了推秦阳，说你怎么挑了这么个日子娶亲？这是奠祭死人的日子。秦阳酒上了脸，笑起来一嘴牙龈："咱俩已经死过一回了，还怕什么？"

那日两人困在电梯里，只以为是楼里的电梯坏了，却不知外边的世界正在经历数十年未遇的灾祸。从北卡州到纽约州再到加拿大东部，电力网全线瘫痪了三四天。有人说是设备陈旧，有人说是黑客破坏，也有人说是本·拉登恐怖组织所为。当田田和秦阳在昏迷和清醒的边缘来回浮游的时候，那个叫多伦多的都市正如一只断失了羽翼的大鹏，骤然跌落在自己筑就的牢笼里。困顿，烦躁，完全失去理性，随时进入疯狂状态。街边停着无数辆因无法加油而瘫痪的汽车，商店里充斥着臭味四溢的变质食品。手机连通网在勉强应付了几个小时之后，终于陷入全线的忙音。医院急诊室的过道里，坐满了重感冒的病人。蜡烛和打火机在两个小时内完全脱销。街角杂货店的矿泉水一夜之间涨了三倍的价格。天虽然还没有整个塌下，人们却已经感到了云层压在头顶的重量。在这一场没有一丝硝烟的战争中，人输得很惨，人不是输给了人，却是输给了电。所造之物翻脸不认那造物的，工具居然打败了工匠。

灾祸过后的城市慢慢地复苏着，后怕却一天天地猛增。

听到大停电期间的种种恐怖故事，秦阳只是微笑不语。私下里却对田田说，没有大停电，哪还会有咱俩的今天？田田听了，不禁一怔。老天爷让这个硕大的都市在这样的灾祸里走过一遭，城塌了一方，人行过了死亡的幽谷，仿佛只是为了成全一段艰难的姻缘。想及此，心中便骇然。

田田两次回国，都没有和父亲说起过秦阳。和前夫相比，秦阳几乎不具备任何引起父亲兴趣的特征。婚礼的前一个星期，田田打电话回家，告诉父亲自己要结婚了。告诉这两个字在这里是一种相对准确的用法，因为田田并没有打算征求父亲的意见。事先田田准备了一些应付父亲问题的答案，可是事到临头却一点也没有派上用场。父亲沉默了一会儿，才问那个人，他对你好吗？田田说他除了对我好，就一无所有了。父亲笑了，是一种钢球在玻璃面上滚过的富有弹性的开怀的大笑："他若对你不好，你才一无所有呢。"父亲那天的笑在田田的耳膜上划出了一道深深的刮痕，不是疼，而是一种出乎意料的惊奇——父亲已经很多年没有这样笑过了。

我的责任总算是完了。

父亲说这话的时候叹了一口气，那叹息听上去不像是伤感，倒更像是卸下了千斤重担之后的那种惬意。放下电话，田田也是一身轻松——如同常年生活在缺水地带的人突然经历了一次温泉沐浴，田田感觉到她对婚姻的最后一丝顾虑已经随着身上的污垢在水中完全瓦解。

田田和秦阳说起和父亲的那次通话。田田隐隐觉得父亲身上有了一些变化。秦阳问变在哪里，田田思索良久，却无以对答。

很快田田就知道父亲卸下的是什么重担。

婚礼之后的第三天凌晨，田田床头的电话响了。这种时候的电话铃声听起来隐隐有些不祥，田田一下子就醒了，坐起来，很是心惊肉跳。

是元元。

爸爸失踪了。整整三天了。哪里都找过了。

隔着电话线，元元的声音仿佛是风里晾过的干柴，裂了许多条缝，每一条缝里都塞满了惊恐。田田觉得年近四十的哥哥一下子变成了一个无措的孩子。

两天前他给我打电话，说他要结婚了，娶春枝。我说这么大的事，你也得和我们商量一下吧。他说没想和你们商量，只想告诉你们一声——你们结婚，和我商量过吗？

我气昏了，就骂那个女人实在是太精了，踩准了点，先探进一只脚，再进来一整个身子，再把女儿塞进来。三陪几陪的小姐，可没有她这个能耐。爸爸把电话摔了。再打，就怎么也打不通了。我赶去北京，门锁着，人却没有了——两个都不见了。

别出什么事才好——妈出了事，咱们在人前已经抬不起头了。他要再出个事，我们就永远也说不清楚了。

田田放下电话，双手捧着头，久久无话。秦阳也醒了，连问几遍怎么了，田田才指着他的太阳穴，怒目圆睁地说：

"秦阳，你给我听着，过了七十咱们绝不多活一天，人老了怎么就这么糊涂呀。"

田田是在那条叫藻溪的水边找到父亲何淳安的。

藻溪是条小溪，线似的在山石中流过。石头很乱，从那岸歪歪扭扭地铺过这岸，就成了涉水的丁步。太阳还嫩，落在水面苍白无力。柳叶还没有长全，远远看过去，却已隐约有些郁郁葱葱的架势了。父亲坐在一块岩石上钓鱼，身边蹲着一个十四五岁的女孩子，正在帮他穿蚯蚓。父亲甩竿的动作很是有力，仿佛在上演一出细节到位的戏文，钓丝在空中留下一个弧形的划痕。

父亲的全出戏文只有一个观众，就是春枝。

田田突然想起临行前秦阳说的一句话：千金难买糊涂人的快乐。